Praise for L. R. Braden

Winner of:

The Eric Hoffer Book Award for Sci-Fi/Fantasy

The Imadjinn for Best Urban Fantasy

First Horizon Award for debut authors

"L.R. Braden's Magicsmith series contains the best of all worlds—murder, mayhem and magic. How can you go wrong?"
—Jeanne Stein, bestselling author of
The Anna Strong Vampire Chronicles

"I devoured the book in a couple of hours—it was just that great!"
—Sarah Graham, The Book Reading Gals on *A Drop of Magic*

"This series just gets better, and I absolutely love it! The action and world building are exciting and keep you engaged from the beginning. Each installment builds on the last, and the character growth is well done!"
—Richelle Rodart, NetGalley Reviewer

"This series manages to get better and better. How impossible it is to leave this world once I sink in."
—Diana (Lucretia) Stanhope, NetGalley Reviewer

Bell Bridge Books Titles
by L. R. Braden

The Magicsmith Series

A Drop of Magic, Book 1

Courting Darkness, Book 2

Faerie Forged, Book 3

Casting Shadows, Book 4

Of Mettle and Magic, Book 5

Of Mettle and Magic

The Magicsmith – Book 5

by

L. R. Braden

Bell Bridge Books

This is a work of fiction. Names, characters, places and incidents are either the products of the author's imagination or are used fictitiously. Any resemblance to actual persons (living or dead), events or locations is entirely coincidental.

Bell Bridge Books
PO BOX 300921
Memphis, TN 38130
Print ISBN: 978-1-61194-997-1

Bell Bridge Books is an Imprint of BelleBooks, Inc.

Copyright © 2021 by L. R. Braden

Published in the United States of America.

We at BelleBooks enjoy hearing from readers.
Visit our websites
BelleBooks.com
BellBridgeBooks.com
ImaJinnBooks.com

10 9 8 7 6 5 4 3 2 1

Cover design: Debra Dixon
Interior design: Hank Smith
Photo/Art credits:
Woman - (manipulated) © faestock | DepositPhoto.com
Graveyard (manipulated) © Rajesh Misra | Dreamstime.com

:Lmom:01:

For my Dad

Thanks for always being there.

Chapter 1

I TOOK A BITE of buttered toast and watched Cari, the youngest of the children we'd rescued from Shedraziel's prison, push scrambled eggs around her plate with a plastic fork. She huffed out a breath that fluttered her sleep-matted, wheat-blond hair. "My tummy feels funny."

"Take a few more bites," prompted Emma, my friend and co-conspirator who'd helped save the kids. She set her hand on the little girl's back and gave her a warm smile. "We've got a long time till lunch. You don't want to get hungry in between."

My heart ached as I watched the four-year-old load her fork and shove it in her mouth. Emma wasn't wrong about the girl needing to eat, but eggs weren't going to solve the funny feeling Cari described. We'd saved a total of eleven children from Shedraziel's realm and erased the memories of their time there, but the physical effects weren't so easily overcome.

Behind Emma and Cari, children ranging from six to sixteen lounged among pillows and blankets in front of the cabin's large, stone fireplace. All were battered, underfed, and hopelessly addicted to goblin fruit—the effects of which were just starting to show. Three had thrown up that morning. Half the kids had fevers. I could only hope my fae grandfather, Bael, sent the medicine he'd promised before their symptoms became more severe.

Long, cool fingers twined with mine under the table. James smiled at me, though the expression failed to crinkle the skin at the corners of his pale-blue eyes.

They'll be all right. His voice echoed through our telepathic link—a side effect of sharing a piece of his vampire soul to save my life that had grown stronger since I'd given James my "true" fae name. His presence in my mind was simultaneously comforting and unsettling.

I hope so.

Cari took three more bites and announced she was done, then

climbed off the bench to join the other children in front of the fire.

Emma pushed a wavy strand of teal-dyed hair back from her eyes and shook her head, causing her many piercings to flash and jingle. "All the kids are complaining about aches and pains. May says her stomach's been cramped all morning."

We all looked at Emma's little sister, curled up in an overstuffed chair with faded floral upholstery. She wore the body of a girl in her mid- to late teens, but she'd been eleven less than a week ago—before being trapped in the altered time of Shedraziel's prison. She had the same Japanese-Hawaiian features as Emma, but where Emma's body was all soft curves, May had a willowy, stretched-out appearance marked by hard angles and protruding bones. She stared into space, her bandaged fingers tapping out a rhythm on the armrest.

"The treatment will be here soon," I said with more confidence than I felt. "In the meantime, just make them as comfortable as you can."

Emma's deep, brown gaze swung back to me. "That makes it sound like you won't be here."

I shifted in my seat. I would have liked nothing better than to hole up in the little cabin with Emma and James until the kids were recovered and could be returned to their families. Even the single morning of near normal interactions as the kids woke up and ate breakfast had been a welcome break from the chaos of my life. But I had other obligations.

My recorded confession about being a fae halfer who could handle iron without the side effect of burning to death had stunned the human community, though not as much as the footage of my friend Sophie shifting into a werewolf and using my leg as a chew toy. Now the world was being torn apart. Lines were being drawn, sides chosen. Law-abiding members of the paranatural community, like Emma's practitioner teacher Luke, were being rounded up and sent to detention centers. As were suspected paranatural sympathizers, like my very human, very pregnant friend Maggie.

Even with the PTF's seeming acceptance that werewolves were a form of local paranatural—unlike the fae who came from different realms—an anti-fae fervor was sweeping the world. And the questions raised by my confession weren't helping.

"I have to clean up the mess my confession caused, especially now that Shedraziel's free. I need to do what I can to avert another war." I hugged myself, my own breakfast suddenly feeling like a nest of insects crawling around my gut. "I'm turning myself in to the Paranatural Task Force."

Emma's jaw dropped. Her eyes went wide.

James stilled. No breath swelled his chest. I wouldn't have been surprised to find his pulse absent for the space of time it took my words to settle over him. A trickle of silver swirled into the blue of his eyes. Then he blinked, and sucked in a long, deep breath.

"You've got to be kidding," Emma blurted.

Several kids looked our way.

She lowered her voice. "You saved these kids from Shedraziel. How can you just abandon them?"

"So long as the PTF is hunting me, you're all safer without me around. These kids have been through enough. The last thing they need is to get scooped up by the PTF and interrogated until they die of an addiction the humans won't understand or be able to treat. We have to keep them hidden until the goblin fruit is out of their systems, but that could take weeks if not months. Meanwhile, the humans and fae are all gearing up for a war both sides seem to think is inevitable, and paranaturals like the practitioners and werewolves are being hunted and caged because no one's sure where their loyalties lie."

Her shoulders slumped. "I'm starting to think war is inevitable, too. And, speaking as a practitioner, *I'm* not sure where my loyalties lie right now. I feel like I belong with humans, but the humans want to lump me with the fae."

"The problem is a lack of communication. We've got three plus groups that don't understand each other. But Director Harris, for all that she's been a serious pain in my ass, seems like a reasonable woman. If I can talk to her, convince her my immunity to iron is just a genetic fluke and not some fae countermeasure in preparation for an upcoming conflict with the humans, maybe I can get the PTF to stand down from this red alert they've been on since that video hit the internet. At the very least, I can shed some light on the werewolves . . . make her realize hunting them like animals will only make matters worse."

Emma opened her mouth, but before she could speak, a shout went up among the kids.

Cari was kneeling on the hardwood floor, whimpering. The eggs we'd insisted she eat were splattered in front of her. The pungent, sickly-sweet smell of vomit wafted through the small cabin . . . again.

I started to rise, but Emma lifted a hand. "I've got this." She cut her eyes to James, then back to me. "You guys finish talking."

She waded through the wall of children standing in a circle around Cari. Emma wasn't much taller than the oldest kids, but even the relatively subdued outfit of her faded jeans and pale-blue T-shirt with a series of yellow emoji faces across her chest stood out like a beacon in the crowd of oversized green tunics and leather pants provided to the kids by Bael's guards. They looked like a troupe of child actors from a Robin Hood play.

Carefully avoiding the mess on the floor, Emma scooped Cari up and carried her into the bathroom. May grabbed a bottle of cleaner and a roll of paper towels from under the sink.

I shifted my attention to James's profile. His long, jet-black hair fell over his shoulders, unbound. I reached out and slid my fingers through the silky strands. "You're being awfully quiet."

He continued to watch the children, his eyes half-lidded, his lips pursed. "I finally have you back by my side, and now you'd have me watch you leave again?"

I closed my eyes, but I couldn't hide from the hurt and frustration coming through our connection.

"It's not as if I *want* to go."

"Then don't."

His words rattled me, but he hadn't drawn on the power of my true name. His plea was just that—something I could heed or ignore as I chose. James had only issued one command since learning my true name, and it had saved my life. He'd given his word not to use the strange power of the fae name I now carried against me, but I couldn't silence the niggling voice that insisted I'd made a mistake, that I'd regret giving anyone, even James, the means to control me.

"The PTF is looking for someone to lynch right now," he said. "Handing yourself over to those fools is almost as bad as throwing yourself on the mercy of Purity."

I flinched. I'd been in the hands of Purity members before—zealots who believed all magic should be eradicated. I'd barely survived. One of my friends hadn't. James really knew how to hit where it hurt.

"The humans, fae, and paranaturals are all at each other's throats because they're afraid of one another," I said. "As someone with a vested interest in all three groups—" I took a deep breath. I'd only just discovered I had practitioner blood mixed with my already confused DNA, and I hadn't had time to fully come to terms with it yet. "—maybe I can act as a . . . a bridge, an intermediary."

"What makes you think you'll even get to speak with Harris?" he continued. "Or that she'll be willing to listen?"

"Harris will want to talk to me, to interrogate me if nothing else.

But I've also got an ace in the hole that ensures she'll want to hear what I have to say."

He quirked an eyebrow.

"Bael." The name dropped like a bomb. "The PTF doesn't have a direct line to any of the fae lords. I do. If Harris wants to avoid a full-out conflict, I'm her best chance at negotiating."

"What if she doesn't want to avoid a war?"

"Then we're already screwed. But I can't believe that's true."

His pale-blue eyes stared into me, through me. He held my name. I had no secrets from him. I let him see my fear and uncertainty, but also my determination. It was my fault the PTF was freaking out about iron-resistant fae. It was my fault Shedraziel, the psychotic fae general, was out of prison and preparing an army. It was my fault the werewolves were targeted, their secret exposed. I'd made a mess. I needed to do what I could to clean it up before any given side reached a breaking point and the conflict we all feared was coming couldn't be stopped. Right now, there was still a chance.

I have to try. I pushed the thought through our link.

Anger and grief mixed with pride and love flowed back.

For one terrifying moment, I worried he might try to compel me despite his promise—to use the power of the true name I'd given him and command me to stay, to keep me safe despite my wishes.

Then he cupped my face in his hands and pressed his lips gently against mine. "My beautiful, brave, reckless love . . . you will be the death of me."

Resignation radiated through our connection. He wasn't happy—not by a long shot—but he wouldn't try to stop me from doing what I felt I must.

The tension binding my muscles slowly released. I reached in my pocket and pulled out the fist-sized glass marble given to me by Rhoana, the captain of Bael's guards. "Keep this with you. Rhoana, or whoever she sends with the kids' medicine, will use it to find you."

He lowered his hands and I dropped the ball on his palm. The lines around his eyes grew tighter. He looked over the table to the gathered children. May was still scrubbing the floor. The others were sitting or lying on the sparse furniture. Many were pale and glassy-eyed. Some hugged themselves as though cold.

James's frown grew more pronounced. "I might prefer facing Purity zealots and PTF troops."

I started to smile, thinking his words a joke, but the sadness in his heart froze me. James had been alive for a long, long time. He'd had lovers . . . and he'd had children. Facing an armed enemy was easy compared to watching a bunch of kids wasting away when you couldn't do a damn thing to stop it.

"Rhoana will send the treatment soon," I said again, though my words came out choked. "In the meantime, Emma seems capable of taking care of them. But she can't protect them if they're discovered. Not alone." I waited until his gaze locked with mine. "Promise me you'll protect them."

Silver danced in his eyes like whitecaps on a pale ocean, showing the depth of his turmoil, but when he spoke, they settled to the color of pure glacial ice. "You have my word."

Part of me felt like a coward for dumping the kids on Emma and James, but I was useless with children anyway. This way, the kids would be taken care of, and maybe I could prevent a war. That was for the good of everybody, right?

I swung my legs over the bench seat and stood up. "Time to arrange my ride."

MORGAN SIPPED black coffee from a chipped green mug in the shade of the cabin's front porch. The rusty chains of the bench swing she sat on creaked as she pushed herself back and forth with one foot, the other tucked beneath her. Her ash-gray complexion, long, dark hair, and Victorian Gothic blouse made her look like the subject of an old photograph, but her tight leather pants, tall boots, and black trench coat ruined the effect.

I pulled the blanket I'd snagged on my way out the door tighter around my shoulders and watched my breath steam in the chill air. We'd all slept well past dawn, but the pale sunlight couldn't dissipate the cold. Beyond the porch, patchy snow covered the ground, broken by muddy trails that led between a half dozen cabins like our own. One housed the property manager from whom James had rented the cabin. The rest were, presumably, full of vacationers looking for a bit of seclusion. Hopefully none of our neighbors were the type to say hello.

"Mind if I join you?" I nodded to the space next to Morgan on the swing.

She lowered her tucked leg and shifted to make room.

"Was our little escapade enough to ease your boredom?" I kept my voice light, my face forward, but I studied her out of the corner of my eye.

"You tell a good story," she said. "I especially liked the part about Bael showing up to rescue you only to find you'd gotten the upper hand on Shedraziel." She took a drink. "I would have liked to see that for myself."

I nodded. Morgan was a high-ranking fae from the Shadow Realm. As such, she couldn't just walk willy-nilly into Enchantment with us. She'd had to remain behind in the mortal realm while I faced off against Shedraziel—just like James, blocked as he was from crossing realms by the demon twined in his soul.

She took another sip of coffee. "What's next?"

I rocked the swing back, eliciting another loud squeak. "James and Emma are going to stay with the kids, hopefully treat their addiction. Then we'll start contacting their families."

"And you?" She quirked an eyebrow. "I realize I may look young to you, but I'm two hundred and fifty years old. An adolescent slumber party is not my idea of a good time."

"You don't want to come where I'm going."

She straightened, lowering her mug. "Do tell."

I smiled. Like many of the court fae I'd met, Morgan seemed desperate for entertainment, and she was willing to trade services to get it. "Will you give me a ride?"

She pursed her lips. "Depends. Do I get to see the action this time?"

I shrugged. "I'll be staying in the mortal realm, if that's what you mean."

"Where do you need to go?"

"Back to Missouri, near the gas station we visited on our way east." With any luck, there'd be a PTF presence, thanks to my previous phone call, and finding me there would stop them looking as far away as Ohio for my friends.

"And what will you be doing there?"

"Will you take me?"

"One trip? There and back?"

"One trip," I agreed. Though I wouldn't need the return.

She lifted her chin. "Deal. What are you going to do in Missouri?"

"Turn myself over to the PTF. I'm going to try to avert the war Bael thinks is inevitable between the humans and fae."

She perked up. "Now *that* sounds like an interesting diversion."

I frowned. "This isn't a game. As an unregistered, full-blooded fae, in the current political climate, you'd probably be executed if the PTF got their hands on you."

7

She snorted. "I'd like to see them try."

"I wouldn't," I said. "The point of this mission is to *avoid* bloodshed."

"And if you can't?"

I sighed. "Then I guess I'll have a front-row seat for the start of the next Faerie War."

She set her mug on the ground, folded her hands behind her neck, and leaned back. "Battles are fun—I love a good skirmish—but all-out wars?" She shook her head. "They're not as exciting as you might think."

I raised an eyebrow. "What's the difference?"

"A bar fight, a riot, a raid, those are fast and passionate. War though . . . war is cold, calculated. When there's a war, everything becomes about that war. I prefer to observe the full spectrum of mortal behavior. Drama, humor, angst, action, romance." She put her arms down and twisted toward me. "Imagine you're in the mood for a light romantic comedy, but the only movies you can find are dramas."

It was weird to think of human behavior in terms of browsing movie selections, but I could kind of see where she was coming from. And any fae against the war, for whatever reason, was a win in my book.

"Will you help me negotiate a new peace treaty? I can get to Bael and the Shifter Lord—I've dealt with them before—but someone with the ear of the Shadow Lord would certainly help. The more factions we can bring to the table, the better our chances."

"Long, boring conversations aren't exactly my bailiwick," she said. "But if you get the mortals and Enchantment to a table, I'll call my brother. He handles most of Shadow's diplomacy."

Morgan's twin brother, Galen, was the Shadow Lord's heir, and we were on decent terms since I'd saved him from a vampire dungeon not long ago. Too bad I'd already called in the marker that had earned me.

"In the meantime, will you stay with James and Emma? They could use a fast escape if the authorities discover them, and nothing's faster than the shadow roads."

"I'm not a babysitter, and I'm not taking a bunch of snot-nosed bedwetters onto the shadow roads. It was bad enough dragging them through one at a time. Together . . ." She shuddered and held up a single finger. "One kid loses focus and the whole lot are ghosts. I don't need that kind of karma."

My heart sank. "Then what will you do after you drop me off? Do you have a number I can call to reach you? A magic hankie I can summon you with?"

"Maybe I'll head down to New Orleans. Carnival season should be in full swing right now." She smiled at me. "I'll keep an eye on the news. If it looks like you've got a shot at peace, I'll call my brother." She shrugged. "Though, more likely, I'll see a thirty-second report on your arrest and you'll be sitting in a PTF cell while your world burns. I intend to get what enjoyment I can from this realm before that happens."

Chapter 2

MY BOOTS WERE soggy from a half-hour slog through the country-side when i strolled past a sign marking the outer edge of Montgomery City, Missouri. I hadn't wanted to risk shadow walking into a populated area in broad daylight and exposing my magical means of travel, so Morgan had dropped me off beside a grain silo just east of town. From there, I'd made my way through frozen corn fields toward the distant highway and civilization, while Morgan was probably knee deep in Mardi Gras beads.

I'd started to think of Morgan as a friend, but she was just another face in the ever-changing cast of my life. I touched the lump under my coat where the locket holding my father's picture rested—a reminder that connections, however deep, were only temporary.

Gloomy gray skies stretched overhead as I followed a long road past farms, warehouses, and a church with a packed parking lot. Beyond an intersection with a larger road sat a squat, brick building with a metal roof and an empty picnic bench out front. The sign read, *Sheila's Burgers and Shakes.*

A bell jingled when I opened the door. The inside had the feel of a classic diner, with black-and-white checkered floor tiles, bench seats, and an eclectic collection of wall art. I'd arrived in the lull between meals—late for lunch, early for dinner—but even so, the cafe seemed oddly empty, with only a single man in coveralls hunched over his plate in the back corner.

I stepped up to an order window cut in the wall.

"Hello?" I leaned over the counter to look into the back area.

A frazzled woman with deep crow's feet and wispy blond hair streaked white around the temples hurried to the register, wiping her hands with a towel.

"Sorry. Short staffed today, what with . . . well, you know." She shook her head. "What'll it be?"

I glanced at the menu above her head. "I'll take a basket of waffle fries and a chocolate shake." I set some cash on the counter. "Keep the change."

The man in the corner glanced up when I moved toward a booth near the window, but his gaze remained unfocused, as though he were reacting more from habit than actual interest. He went back to munching his sandwich when I sat down.

The vinyl seat creaked as I settled against it. I reached into my pocket and pulled out the two pieces of my cell phone—the actual phone, and the battery I'd removed days ago, when I'd first gone on the run, to prevent anyone tracking me.

No more running. It was time to tell Harris where I was. I slipped the battery into the back of the case, took a deep breath, and punched in the number for Maggie Hawthorne.

I'd known Maggie longer than almost anyone in my life. She, David, and Aiden had befriended me in college—at a time when I thought a healthy relationship meant parting on good terms after a couple months of shallow banter and never speaking to that person again. After college, the two of us had opened a business called Magpie Books, where Maggie sold new and used books, I curated local art displays, and Emma ran a café stocked with goods from her mother's bakery. Now, the bookstore was deserted—its windows smashed and its walls graffitied with slurs about faeries and freaks—Emma and I were fugitives, and Maggie, four months pregnant, was sitting in a PTF holding cell because of her connection to me.

The phone rang three times, and for a moment I feared the PTF were no longer monitoring Maggie's line. Then a man's voice I didn't recognize said, "Hello?"

I exhaled. "This is Alex Blackwood. Please transfer me to Director Harris. I'm ready to turn myself in."

There was a moment of heavy breathing, a series of clicks, then a new voice, a woman's, said, "This is Harris."

She sounded tired.

"I'm in Montgomery City, Missouri," I said without preamble.

"Considering our last conversation, I figured you'd be long gone from Missouri by now."

I'd intentionally chosen this stop because of its proximity to the gas station from which I'd called Harris after escaping her in Colorado. I didn't want her anywhere near James, Emma, and the kids.

"Track my phone's GPS if you don't believe me."

She sighed. "I don't have time for another wild goose chase. Not now."

"No chase. I've finished what I had to take care of, and I have information you need to hear. I'm in a diner called Sheila's Burgers and Shakes. I'll stay here until you arrive."

Harris stayed quiet so long I feared the connection had dropped. When she finally responded, her voice was tight. "Were you behind the attack?"

The packed parking lot at the church, the glazed expression of the diner's single patron, and the waitress's implication that I should understand why she was short-staffed suddenly took on new meaning. Cords of tension snaked through my limbs and squeezed my throat. Clearly something had happened while I was in the fae realm freeing the children, or during the single night I'd been back. Something big. "What attack?"

She laughed, a single sharp bark. "Seriously?"

"I've been out of touch."

Another silence. "Did you have *anything* to do with what happened in Italy yesterday?"

I frowned. *Italy?* "I have no idea what you're talking about, but I haven't been to Europe since I was a little kid."

Harris exhaled a deep, noisy breath. "Last time we talked, you refused to come in. Said you had business to take care of, that lives were at stake. Now you call me the day after a massive attack against the Church—claiming ignorance of the event despite worldwide news coverage—saying your work is done. Excuse me if I find your timing just a little suspicious."

I stared blankly at the chipped Formica tabletop. Italy was home to the Unified Human Church and the seat of the Holy Council—a group of leaders from the world's major religions who came together to decide matters of religious policy on a global scale after the existence of para-natural beings was confirmed. While prejudices and conflicts still existed between the sects, the emergence of a universally feared subspecies did wonders to bridge humanity's religious differences. I figured the main reason they agreed to work together was because they all wanted a say in how their sorcerer assets were handled, since the Church was the only place a practitioner could receive training in the more dangerous magics.

My mouth had gone dry, and it took several tries before I managed to croak, "Someone attacked the Church?"

"You really didn't know?"

I shook my head in a pointless gesture. "I haven't seen a TV in days."

She blew out another noisy exhale. "Fine. We'll collect you and sort it out afterward. Sheila's in Montgomery City, right?"

My mind was racing. If the Church had been attacked, was there even any point to turning myself in? What could I do to avert a war if the first blow had already been dealt?

"Do you know who attacked the Church?" I asked. "Was it the fae?"

"You'd know better than me. Casualty reports are still coming in. Rescue crews are sifting through the rubble, trying to piece together what happened. At this point, no one's claimed responsibility, but most people, myself included, are presuming a preemptive strike."

The last time I'd spoken with Bael, he said conflict with the mortal realm was inevitable. *And when that conflict comes, will your allegiance lie with the fae or the humans?*

Had he been planning this attack? Had Shedraziel led the charge at the head of his army?

"When did the attack happen?"

"Midnight last night, GMT."

I breathed a sigh of relief. Greenwich Mean Time was five hours ahead of Ohio, where my team had entered and exited the fae Realm of Enchantment. That meant Bael and Shedraziel had been with me in the prison realm when the attack occurred. Chances were good a fae was still responsible, but Enchantment was the largest of the fae realms. If I could broker peace between Bael and the PTF, we might be able to get the other courts to fall in line.

"I'm sending a car from the St. Louis office to pick you up." Harris's words cut through my thoughts. "They'll escort you to the airport, and from there to PTF headquarters in Virginia."

The drive from St. Louis would take about an hour. This was my last chance to run. It was also my last chance to try to establish a line of communication with the PTF. If I burned Harris now, she'd never listen to me, no matter what new information I might uncover or what deal I was able to broker with Bael. I'd be lumped with the rest of the fae and halfers in the coming conflict.

"I'll be here."

I SUCKED UP THE last dregs of my shake with a slurping noise and pushed the empty glass away. The woman who brought out my food had disappeared into the kitchen. The man who'd been eating when I first walked in had finished his lunch and left. No one else came in.

I pulled up footage on my phone of the devastation in Rome and read news reports until my fries felt like they were going to come back up. Then I switched to keeping watch out the front window for my promised escort.

Each black car and SUV that passed on the highway ratcheted up the tension in my chest and limbs until my fingers tingled and my legs bounced a jig. I had no way of knowing what normal traffic in the town looked like, but the number of cars on the road seemed sparse. The only time I saw more than one or two was when the church across the way ended service and the vehicles from the overfull parking lot spilled onto the motorway, causing a sudden surge that passed just as quickly.

An hour after my call with Agent Harris, two black SUVs pulled up in front of Sheila's. They didn't park in the designated spaces. One blocked the entrance to the lot while the other stopped right in the middle of the paved area. The doors opened. Three men and one woman in PTF uniforms stepped out.

My milkshake was a cold puddle in my stomach, sapping warmth from the surrounding area.

This was a terrible idea. Of the last two PTF agents I'd dealt with, one had been a serial killer and the other had been a Purity zealot. I'd killed them both.

But Harris seemed practical. In all her televised speeches, she'd encouraged patience while her team investigated rather than jumping to conclusions and endorsing all-out war, the way her counterparts would have. I just hoped my instincts about her were right.

Two of the officers stayed by the cars. The woman, who had pale skin and blond hair pulled back in a ponytail, and one of the men, a wide, dark-skinned fellow with a crew cut, pushed through the front door.

The bell jingled.

"What can I . . .?" The woman who ran the place trailed off as she stepped into the order window and caught sight of the new arrivals.

The male agent swung his attention to me. "Alex Blackwood?"

I nodded and slid out of my booth.

Both agents took a step back, hands moving to their waists. The man fingered his stun gun, while the woman went straight for the genuine article.

I took a steadying breath and raised both hands so they could see my empty palms.

The woman behind the counter looked between us with wide eyes, then slunk back behind the dividing wall.

"I turned myself in," I said. "I won't cause you any trouble."

"Turn around." The man's voice was low and gravelly. The words rumbled like a storm on the horizon.

Nodding, I turned to face my empty milkshake.

A metal cuff snapped around one of my wrists. Rough fingers grabbed the other, pulling my raised arms down and behind me. The Formica table dug into my thighs as the agent pushed me forward, pinning me. The second cuff snapped tight.

The man ran his hands over my arms, torso, and legs in a clinical manner, then grabbed my upper arm and pulled me around. "Let's go."

I stumbled along beside the man as he pulled me toward the SUV. The woman remained at my back, ready to put a bullet in my brain if I made any sudden moves. I considered telling them again that I was coming in voluntarily, but it wouldn't make a difference. I was being taken to Harris; that was all that mattered. *She* was the person I'd need to convince of my willingness to cooperate.

One of the waiting agents opened the back door of the nearest SUV. My escort set a hand on top of my head, guiding me in. As soon as my butt hit the seat, the man leaned in, snapped my seat belt in place, and slammed the door.

The agents exchanged a few words. Then the woman and one of the waiting men went to the other vehicle while the man who'd opened my door slid behind the wheel of mine. The man who'd cuffed me took the passenger seat. The engine turned over. There was a *snick* of automatic locks snapping in place. The other vehicle's lights flashed once, then it pulled out of the lot. We followed onto the highway headed for St. Louis.

My hands went numb after the first five minutes. The cuffs were digging into my back. I shifted, trying to find a more comfortable position, but when I moved, the man in the passenger seat glared at me.

I sighed and tried to focus on the scenery blurring past.

Fields, snow, winter trees, more fields.

I sighed again.

The man driving my car was lean and young with gelled, blond hair.

I looked at the profile of the man who'd walked me to the car. His eyes were narrowed, scanning the horizon. His lips were pinched tight, and a small muscle twitched in his jaw.

"Any leads yet on who attacked the Church?" I asked.

The driver's electric-blue gaze snapped to the rearview mirror, then slid sideways toward his partner. The tense man glared over his shoulder, his dark eyes looking almost black. He punched a button on the dash and scratchy country music filtered into the cab. Guess my escorts weren't up for conversation.

I shifted again, finally managing to twist enough that my wrists weren't being crushed, and stared out the window.

Field, snow, trees, lightning—*wait, wha*—

The SUV flipped sideways and all I saw was sky.

The roof slammed into the ground, buckling slightly. My seat belt snapped tight, knocking my breath out and digging into my collarbone. My skin tingled. My ears were ringing.

Ribbons of purple energy danced over the vehicle's walls.

In the front seat, Mr. Grumpy popped his seat belt and crashed to the ceiling. He pressed a finger to the driver's neck, looked back at me, then twisted and kicked out his window. He crawled through the hole, gun drawn.

Pops and bangs sounded outside the SUV.

Who had attacked the convoy? Why? Were the people who'd attacked the Church hitting random PTF patrols now?

I shook my head and instantly regretted it as a wave of dizziness and nausea swept through me. I was having trouble seeing out my left eye.

The door next to me opened with a groan and the screech of metal scraping metal. Scuffed black boots stepped into view, a stark contrast to the snow. Black cargo pants bent at the knees and waist. A face I'd never seen before dropped into view.

The man who reached for me had tan skin and narrow features. Salt-and-pepper stubble covered his angular chin and dark bags of skin sagged under his dull-green eyes. He tugged once at my seat belt, but the latch was stuck. Then he pulled a long knife from a sheath at his waist and cut the straps.

I hit the ground hard, unable to catch myself since my hands were still bound behind me. With gravity righted, blood dribbled down my face from a cut above my left eye.

"Who are you?" I gasped. "What's going on?"

The man grabbed the back of my shirt and dragged me out of the car.

My knees sank in snow. The cold air helped clear my head.

"Stay low," the man beside me said. He sheathed his knife and replaced it with a gun, then inched up to peek over the car. I did likewise.

Across a patch of white field scattered with debris, I spotted the second PTF vehicle. Like mine, it was lying on its roof, windows broken. One wheel was still spinning. The woman and the driver of the second car were crouched behind the mangled wreck, using it as cover. The man who'd dragged me out of Sheila's was lying in the snow about five feet from the front of my SUV. He was breathing heavily, and the snow around him was streaked red, but he continued to fire his gun at a cluster of trees off to the right.

A purplish ball of light zipped out of those trees and hit the man on the ground. His back arched. Three more shots left his gun. Then he dropped face first in the snow and was still.

Whoever was attacking the PTF clearly had magic. Maybe during the hour I'd sat in Sheila's sipping my milkshake the fae had taken credit for the attack in Italy, and now they were clearing out any PTF agents they spotted.

I squinted at the man next to me. He looked human, and he didn't have the glow of a glamour about him, but I'd come across fae strong enough to fool me before. Had Bael sent them to fetch me? To drag me back to Enchantment in some misguided attempt to keep me safe? I wouldn't put it past him.

The man beside me turned his gun toward the two agents hunkered behind the other SUV.

Barely thinking, I slammed my shoulder into his side, sandwiching him against the open door. He grunted. His gun flashed.

I didn't wait to see him fall. I was up and running. Away from the PTF. Away from the fae.

I made it twenty, maybe thirty feet. Puffs of icy powder exploded around me as bullets buried themselves in the frozen ground. Then a ball of pure agony hit me square in the back. Purple lightning arced over my body, short-circuiting my motor control. I toppled to the ground. Once more unable to brace against the impact, I twisted to land on my back rather than my face.

Waves of cramps seized my muscles, and I flopped like a suffocating fish.

Alex? What's happening? James's panic coursed through me, matching my own, but I didn't have the energy to respond.

The pain passed, spreading to numbness. Twitching limply and gasping, I stared up at pale-gray clouds.

Alex? James's voice grew dim as darkness bled across the overcast sky and I succumbed to oblivion.

Chapter 3

FLAME LANCED through my muscles, flaying my nerves, chasing back the smothering darkness that enveloped me. My soul was burning. I knew this sensation. I'd experienced it once before . . . when James invoked my true name.

Wake up!

James's command was a shout in my mind, laced with fear that blared through our connection like a fire alarm.

My eyes snapped open. I took a shuddering breath. The burning pain settled to a dull ache throughout my entire body.

"Alex?"

A man's face loomed above me, but it wasn't James. Worried brown eyes stared out of a suntanned face topped with dark curls. Thin lips frowned in a wide, stubble-covered jaw.

"David?" The word scratched my throat like sandpaper. My college friend-turned-spy was the last person I expected to find standing over me. He looked more tired than I'd ever seen him. His eyes had a dark, sunken quality, and he was leaner, as if he'd missed too many meals. He'd also trimmed his unruly curls to a uniform length of fluffy tufts that made him look like a chia pet.

What's going on? James's demand pounded against my mind.

David set his hand, firm and warm, on my shoulder and gave it a squeeze. "How are you feeling?"

Are you all right?

"Take it easy."

Where are you?

"You're safe."

What happened?

"Be quiet," I shouted. David jerked away, frowning. I rubbed my eyes, cringing at the effort of lifting my arms. "Sorry, I just . . . give me a second."

Closing my eyes to block out David's hurt expression, I traced my connection to James. Concern, anger, frustration, fear. I waded through his emotions as if fighting the current of a river, seeking the source.

Calm down, I pleaded. *I can't deal with your fears as well as my own.*

Abruptly, the negative emotions cut off, replaced by a wave of relief that wrapped me like a warm blanket.

You've been unreachable for nearly a day. You cried out in pain, then you were just . . . gone. Now that James wasn't screaming, his words were a whisper that buzzed just at the edge of my awareness—I had to concentrate to make them out—but fear stuck to his thoughts, spreading like a contagion. *I could still feel you, but barely. You're far away. I . . . I needed to make our connection stronger.* Shame, guilt, defiance. *I used your name.*

Yeah, I felt it. That explained why I could make out his thoughts, quiet though they were, rather than just his emotions or the dull pulse of *I am here* that was the standby for our connection when we were too far apart to communicate.

He hadn't used my name *against* me exactly, so he hadn't quite broken his promise. And I might have done the same if he'd been suddenly unreachable after some unknown conflict. Sitting on the sidelines was never easy. But the sick, twisting feeling that hollowed out my insides wouldn't let me tell him it was okay. No matter the circumstances, despite the fact I'd handed him this power willingly, I wasn't sure I'd ever be okay with him using my name.

Can you tell me what happened?

I appreciated the phrasing—a question, not a command. Perhaps more of my aversion had transferred than I'd intended.

I scrunched my face, trying to remember details of the day before. I'd called Harris, turned myself in. The PTF had come to collect me, but the convoy had been attacked. *I got zapped by some kind of magic lightning. The fae version of a stun gun, I'm guessing.*

There was a beat of silence. *I should never have let you leave.*

My annoyance flared. *I need to focus on where I am now. You just concentrate on keeping the kids safe. And put the battery back in your phone. I'll call you when I know more.*

I could feel our connection growing thinner, stretching over the distance between us. The amplification provided by my name was wearing off. I just hoped he got that last thought clearly. I was not okay with him using my true name like a collect charge for a long distance phone call.

I love you. James's parting line was more feeling than thought, but it curled inside me and soothed the lingering sting of his earlier command like balm on a burn.

When I opened my eyes, David was staring at me. He sat in a wooden chair beside the bed. Again I was struck by the dark circles that shaded his eyes and the worry lines that etched his face. He seemed to have aged years since the last time I'd seen him, though it had only been a month since I'd stormed out of his apartment in a fit of righteous indignation after learning he was spying on me for Uncle Sol—the man who raised me after my mother died in a car crash. Before that, David had been one of my closest friends. One of my only friends. That made his betrayal hurt all the more.

"Where am I?" I asked.

"Oh, am I allowed to speak now?" David's mouth twisted into a rueful smile.

"Sorry for snapping. I was just a little . . . overwhelmed."

His smile dimmed. "Yeah, I get that. Sorry you got jolted, but we couldn't risk you running or getting scooped up by the PTF again."

More details filtered into my memory, filling the gaps. The man who'd cut my seat belt and dragged me out of the overturned car. The PTF agent who'd escorted me out of Sheila's, face down in the snow.

"You attacked the convoy?" Cobwebs clung to the images in my mind, preventing them from fitting together smoothly. "You're working with the fae?"

David snorted. "Hardly."

"Then how—"

"Sol will explain everything." He glanced toward the closed door behind him, and for the first time, I took in the small bedroom I'd woken up in. White wallpaper with tiny blue flowers covered the walls. Pale-blue curtains dimmed the light coming through the single window. A dark dresser sat against the wall opposite the bed, and the floor between was covered with a frayed oval rug the same pale blue as the curtains.

"I take it Sol organized this little kidnapping?"

He winced. "I was hoping you'd see it more as a rescue."

"I turned myself over to the PTF. I was exactly where I wanted to be."

"But not where you *needed* to be."

"So you and Sol are deciding what's best for me . . . again."

He sighed and ran both hands over his head. "Let's not argue, okay? I know things between us aren't . . . the way they were, but I don't want to fight. I hope, someday, we can be friends again." Color crept into his cheeks. He pushed to his feet. The chair's wooden legs scraped across the floor. "I'll go tell Sol you're awake."

He turned away, eyes downcast.

Pressure twisted through my chest. I'd refused his calls after finding out he'd lied to me, but when I thought I might never see him again . . .

"Hey David," I called, just before he closed the door behind him. "I'm glad you're all right."

The tension in his back seemed to ease. Then he pulled the door shut.

I shook my head, gripping the bed when the room seemed to lurch with the motion. I'd all but convinced myself I never wanted to see David or Sol again, until shit hit the fan with the PTF and my friends were being rounded up like criminals. Sol had tried to warn me. So had David. Then they'd both dropped off the map. Angry as I was at the lies they'd told me, I couldn't deny the swell of relief at learning they were both safe. At least, as safe as any of us in these uncertain times.

Tossing back the covers, I sat at the edge of the bed. My whole body ached. My head throbbed. My muscles felt like jelly. I wiggled my bare toes and looked around, wondering what had become of my boots. The ugly orange sweater I'd swiped from the fae way station—what felt like years ago—covered my torso, torn, singed, and bloodstained from my many ordeals. My jeans weren't faring much better. There was no sign of the fur-lined coat I'd borrowed on my last trip through Enchantment.

I scooted off the bed a little at a time, making sure my legs would support me, shaky as they were. Then I grabbed the comforter off the bed and wrapped it around my shoulders. The protection against the cold was worth a little extra weight.

The door creaked when I opened it. I froze. Nervous guilt coursed through me, but I shoved it aside. I wouldn't act like a helpless prisoner just because I was off balance from the day's events.

I stepped into a hallway. There were two doors to my left before the hall dead-ended. To my right, a single door stood open, revealing a bathroom. Beyond that was a landing overlooking a well-furnished living room. I shuffled slowly down the wooden stairs from that landing, cautious of loose boards, and stepped onto the paisley border of the area rug that covered the living room floor. Upper story windows filled the room with natural light. A glint brought my attention to a chess set on the coffee table. An army of darkly patinaed metal forged into organic curves faced geometric, polished bronze across a cherrywood battlefield. I'd made the set as a Christmas present for Sol . . . before I discovered he'd hired David to spy on me.

The clatter of dishes and murmur of conversation drifted out of a partially open door in the back wall. I skirted around the large living room, keeping out of sight of the dining room, or kitchen, or whatever it was where the people were gathered.

The front door swung open with a turn of the knob, and I stepped into the cold. My bare toes curled when they came down on the frosty wood of a large deck that wrapped around the house. Ignoring the chill seeping into my feet, I walked to one corner of the porch and set a hand on the peeling white paint of the rail.

Beyond the drop of the porch, past a stretch of yellowed grass, a forest greeted me. Being winter, the branches of the deciduous trees were bare, but they, along with the scattered pines, would create a solid wall of green come spring. I breathed deep, relishing the scent of nature. The air was more humid than I was used to, as if a rainstorm had just passed, but the pale sky was a uniform, washed-out blue.

A pair of weathered rocking chairs sat beside me. I could picture long summer days spent on this porch, sipping lemonade, enjoying the view.

The screen door banged behind me. I whirled to find a man in a wheelchair rolling across the porch. A layer of black curls covered the top of his head while the sides and back faded to bare, brown skin. His eyes were dark umber. His full lips turned up in a smile, highlighting the coppery undertones in his cheeks.

"I thought I saw someone sneaking through the living room."

I took a step back. The porch rail pressed into my hip. "Am I a prisoner here?"

He shook his head. "Not at all. I just wanted to say hello."

I pulled the pilfered comforter tighter, feeling exposed. "Who are you?"

He pursed his lips and scratched his index finger along one side of his short, black beard. "Once upon a time, my name was Shale. Before that, it was something else. These days I go by Garrett."

I frowned, caught off guard by the odd introduction. "My name is—"

"Alex. I know." He smiled again, showing straight white teeth. "I've been waiting to meet you for quite some time."

I glared. "Why?"

"Best I leave that for Sol to explain. In the meantime, can I get you anything? Food?" He glanced at my bare feet. "Shoes perhaps?"

I looked down, wiggled my toes, looked back up. "You can tell me where I am, and what I'm doing here."

His smile faltered. "I think it would be better if—Ah! Speak of the devil."

I followed his gaze across the grassy field. Uncle Sol was walking toward us. His salt-and-pepper hair was longer than I remembered, and stubble coated his jaw. He was wearing blue jeans, brown work boots, and a green sweater with the sleeves pushed up to his elbows. My jaw sagged. I blinked. I'd never seen Sol in anything less than pressed slacks and polished shoes. The mountain man strolling toward me was like a stranger wearing Sol's face.

He climbed a short ramp at the side of the porch, nodded to Garrett, and stopped an arm's length away from me. "Hello, Alex."

Garrett quietly rolled his chair back to give us space.

Sol looked at him. "David could use some help in the east field."

Nodding, Garrett propelled himself down the ramp and along a narrow path that led into the trees.

I watched until he disappeared into the winter thicket, then shifted my gaze back to Sol. "Where are we?"

He smiled, but his eyes were sad. "Nice to see you, too." He stepped around me, set his hands on the railing, and looked out at the woods. "This place used to be called Weavers Ford—a little community on the northwest border of North Carolina."

"Used to be?"

He nodded. "We're smack dab in the middle of a waste."

I stiffened, looking around again. Wastes couldn't support life. They were dead zones, created when all the ambient energy had been drained out of an area by a massive magical clash. The trees here were bare, but winter bare, not *dead,* and the pines seemed healthy enough. Closing my eyes, I searched for the tingle on my skin that signaled the presence of magic in the air around me. Not only was the tingle there, it was strong, like ants marching over my body.

I shuddered and opened my eyes. "This isn't a waste."

Sol raised one eyebrow but didn't ask how I was so sure.

"I found this place on a survey mission shortly after the cease-fire at the end of the Faerie Wars. This waste stretches from about six miles south of here to seven miles past the Virginia border to the north. It's almost twice as large as the waste in Colorado."

I narrowed my eyes. "This *isn't* a waste. Wastes can't support life."

"Think of this place as an oasis." He lifted a hand to indicate the area around us. "For whatever reason, Weavers Ford was unaffected by the conflict that created the Carolina Waste." He pointed in the direction Garrett had gone, then turned and pointed the other way. "Walk for twenty minutes in any direction and you'll find the dead land you're imagining."

I shook my head. "That's not possible. Wastes draw energy from the land around them. They spread. Even if this place didn't get drained during the initial conflict, it should have equalized with the land around it as the waste drew on it to heal itself."

He shrugged. "It's a mystery, but one that works in our favor. A fully furnished, abandoned settlement no one knows is habitable. I've been using this camp as a hidden base since I found it."

"The perfect end-of-days bunker." I crossed my arms. "How do you get in and out?"

"We've cleared a small airstrip at the edge of the dead zone. And it's possible to drive across the waste, though most people feel pretty sick by the time they come out the other side."

I shuddered at the prospect of driving through a waste. Anyone would be affected by the draining effects of a waste, given a long enough exposure, but magic-users felt it more acutely. And fae, being made of magic, had it worst. If a full fae stayed in a waste to the point where their magic completely disappeared, they'd die. I wasn't sure what it would do to a halfer like me.

I shook my head and looked around again, glancing back toward the house. There'd been several voices in the kitchen. "If you've been utilizing this place for years . . . you expected another conflict."

"Not the conflict you're imagining, but yes. I knew, or at least feared, the day would come when we'd need soldiers and practitioners not bound by the Church or PTF. I made it a point during my career with the PTF to recruit certain like-minded individuals." He nodded toward the trees. "Garrett was my first. Unfortunately, I couldn't save his paladin."

My brain snagged on the word *paladin*. Paladins were the Church's guard dogs, used to leash people with powerful magic. "Garrett's a sorcerer?"

"He was," Sol amended. "Garrett suffered a magical backlash during the war—burned out his powers and left him without the use of his legs. I was his handler. I officially reported him dead from the burnout, like so many young sorcerers those days, but in actuality, I brought him here. I recruited a handful of others in the years after the war, and several more joined me when I left the PTF." He crossed his arms. "We now have roughly two dozen practitioners and thirty human troops, though that's still a far cry from the army I fear we'll need."

"You said the conflict isn't what I imagine. What exactly are you preparing for?"

He removed his glasses, rubbed the inside corners of his eyes, and slipped the glasses back on. "Perhaps you should sit down for this next part. Better yet, we could have some lunch. You must be starving by now."

Mention of food made my stomach contract with a loud grumble, but I shook my head. "Spill."

He settled on one of the rocking chairs, elbows braced against his knees, fingers laced. He looked up at me. "The reason I started this little enterprise, and kept it secret from the Church, the PTF, and the rest of the world, is that those organizations have been compromised by a dark conspiracy festering at their heart. The massacre in Rome was the work of a group of rogue sorcerers led by the strongest practitioner I've ever known."

He sighed and shook his head. "I had a chance to end this threat at its inception." He held up a single finger. "One chance, and I missed it because I hesitated to end the life of a friend. I won't make that mistake again."

I hugged my blanket tighter and sank into the empty rocker, tucking my feet into the trailing blanket ends. "So this friend of yours . . . that's who you're preparing to fight?"

He nodded and fixed me with his flinty gaze. "Alex, the man leading the sorcerers—the one responsible for the fall of the Church—is your father."

Chapter 4

MY CHEST CONSTRICTED. My mouth went dry. "My father is dead. You told me so yourself."

"I also told the PTF that Garrett was dead, but as you can see, he's a lively ghost."

I shook my head, tears stinging my eyes. My heart had broken when I learned Sol was spying on me. I hadn't thought he could hurt me worse than that. "Why would you—"

"Darren Carter died the day he joined the sorcerer troop, just like every other member of that company. Their names were erased from all public records. They were cut off from the outside world. They were given new lives, new purpose, new identities."

I set my hand against the slight bulge of the silver locket with my father's picture in it.

"Darius," I whispered, remembering the name Shedraziel used when she recognized the man in the picture. I'd thought her mistaken at the time, but . . .

Sol frowned. "How did you—"

"Shedraziel said he was a powerful practitioner . . . 'a wonderful adversary,' she called him." She'd also said he survived the war. I hadn't wanted to believe her, because that would mean his continued absence was by choice. But if he was a sorcerer bound by the Church . . . maybe he hadn't abandoned me after all.

"Shedraziel? The fae general?" Deep lines furrowed his brow. "I thought she was locked up in some faerie prison."

I looked away. "Not anymore."

"And she sought you out?"

I didn't bother to correct him, to tell him *I* was the reason she was loose.

He sighed and rubbed a hand over his forehead. "That bloodthirsty witch is the last thing we need right now."

"I agree." I shifted my gaze back to him, eyes narrowed. "Which is why I was on my way to Director Harris. I need to open a line of communication with the PTF before the fae declare war."

Sol pursed his lips. "Harris is a good agent, a good director even—a little too by-the-books to risk inviting into my motley crew, but with the way things are going . . ."

"If there's even a chance the fae aren't responsible for the attack on the Church, the PTF needs to be told." I pressed my fingertips to my temples, trying to massage away a growing headache. "We can still stop this war."

Sol looked across the lawn and up toward the pale sky. "War is coming, though whether the fae will have any part in it remains to be seen." He shifted in his seat, turning to face me fully. "I'm calling in your debt, Alex. Remember the deal? Follow my orders. No questions. No arguments."

The threads of anxiety constricting my lungs pulled tighter. I'd made that deal when I still trusted Sol.

"What exactly are you asking me to do?"

He leaned forward. "Lead my army."

I jerked away. "*That's* why you brought me here? I'm no soldier, and certainly no leader."

"Darius is the most powerful practitioner I ever supervised, and his blood flows in your veins. I've watched you since I grew suspicious of your father, waiting to see if his magic would manifest in you." He gestured to me. "And it did, though you misread it."

"Mis—" A thought clicked into place. "When I told you I was a halfer. That's why you weren't surprised. You thought it was my practitioner magic manifesting. That's why I could handle iron, why no test would spot me as fae. You didn't think I was one."

"People can be fae or practitioners. Not both. I know you've got practitioner blood. And the fact that you can handle iron is proof enough you aren't fae, whatever that roommate of yours might have said to convince you."

"You think Kai tricked me, that he was using me." I shook my head. "Not everyone is like you. I didn't tell you the whole truth back then." I looked him up and down. "And you don't deserve it now."

"Fair enough. But answer me this. Do you possess magic?"

I stared out over the grass and nodded.

"Then my tactic is sound. I need your help to stop Darius."

I rose and started pacing, too agitated to remain in the rocker. I was still having trouble wrapping my mind around the thought that my father could be alive after all these years. The concept was too surreal.

And now Sol wanted me to . . . what? Fight him? Kill him?

"Even if you're right—if my father is alive and well—why would he destroy the Church? Unless . . ." Recalling his intense hatred of the fae, I spun on Sol. "He's planning to blame the fae. He *wants* the war so he can finish what he started." I frowned and shook my head. "But he's weakened the mortal forces. Made it harder for humans to win . . ."

"Your father isn't the man you once knew." Sol rubbed one wrinkled hand over his mouth and jaw. "He may not even be a man anymore."

I stopped pacing. "What do you mean?"

"Darius . . . changed during the war."

"War has that effect on people."

He nodded. "Which is why I could never prove my suspicions. Still can't, in fact. But if I'm right, Darius will make his presence known soon enough. Then we'll know for certain if my paranoia was justified."

I crossed my arms and narrowed my eyes at Sol. "How *exactly* do you think he's changed?"

His jaw tightened. "I think he's been possessed."

I uncrossed my arms, bracing my hands on the railing behind me, recalling stories I'd heard about rifters—practitioners who'd been overcome by demons riding the currents of their magic. I'd experienced enough of demons to know the threat was real, but rifters didn't sit idly by for a decade—the chaotic nature of demons made it impossible. I shook my head. "You said he changed during the war, but he's still alive. Rifters don't last that long. They wreak as much havoc as they can before their host bodies fall apart."

"Usually, but rifters are still something of a mystery to us. They're relatively rare, and the Church's policy is to destroy them immediately."

"Hence the paladins," I said.

"Exactly. Paladins are instructed to eliminate their sorcerers at the first sign of possession. We've never gotten to study the effects of a demon on a truly powerful practitioner. Perhaps someone with a strong enough connection to the magic could survive. Maybe even suppress the demon."

I turned away. The fae had a story about a practitioner possessed by a demon who survived long enough to impregnate a fae woman—thus giving rise to the first vampire. Even now, I had a piece of demon soul inside me, split off from that original source and passed through lines of vampire offspring. Who's to say what was possible when it came to magic?

"What makes you think he's possessed?"

"When your father joined the Church, he was angry. He'd enlisted with the military to fight fae, to eradicate magic on Earth. He was a Purist. So you can imagine his reaction when he tested positive for practitioner magic."

"Actually, I can't," I said. Ever since I first suspected I might have practitioner abilities, I'd been trying to reconcile the idea of my father being a sorcerer with my memories of his unwavering hatred of magic. At first, I'd assumed he hadn't known. Then I learned he was not only an active sorcerer during the war, but a powerful one. War had changed my father all right. I couldn't even imagine the person he'd become.

"He was angry, furious. He insisted it was a mistake. He was retested three times, each with the same result. Then he was given a choice. Use the magic inside him to help chase the fae back to their own realms, or be put down."

"Put down?" My voice cracked on the phrase.

"Soldiers identified as practitioners during the war didn't have the right to refuse to fight. They were considered too much of a threat." He waved my concern away. "Your father opted to use what he'd been given to achieve his goal, but he hated himself—hated what he'd become. He was a difficult man to be around. He was bitter, acerbic.

"Then, after one particular battle, his demeanor changed. He was lauded as the hero who changed the tide of that conflict. After that, he became friendly, charming even. The other handlers believed he'd finally accepted his role, come to terms with his magic thanks to his success, but not me. I could still see the anger in him, simmering beneath the surface. I became convinced he was working toward his own goal—the eradication of *all* magic from the mortal realm."

My head was spinning. "You think that's why he took out the Church? To eliminate the sorcerers?" I frowned. "But that just leaves us vulnerable to the fae."

"If he *killed* the sorcerers," Sol said. "But I don't think he did. The rescue crews have found very few bodies aside from the actual clergy."

"If they didn't die . . ."

"I think he recruited them." He stood up, opened the front door, and retrieved a pair of rubber boots, which he dropped on the porch. "Slip those on. I want to show you something."

I tugged the boots onto my frozen feet, my mind still reeling. My father was alive. He was a sorcerer, possibly a rifter. He'd attacked the Church. "Maybe he just wants his freedom." I looked up at Sol as I pulled on the second boot. "He served his time in the troop. Maybe he just wants out."

"Service as a sorcerer is a lifetime commitment. They can't forget what they know, and their training in destructive arts makes it impossible for them to just register and live under observation like the handful of pacifist practitioners the PTF lets roam free." He shook his head. "There's nothing left for him out here."

The words stung. My father left a wife and child behind with his old life. Getting a new name didn't change that.

"You said the Church erased their old lives when they joined." I bit my lower lip, hating the quaver in my voice. "Does that mean he forgot about me?"

"We can't erase memories." Sol looked away. "But I told him you died in the crash that killed your mother, and I doctored the records to prove it."

I staggered back a step. "You—"

"It was to keep you safe. The Church would have wanted you tested. I hid your identity from the PTF for the same reason. I knew, if your father ever went bad, you'd be my trump card."

I placed one hand over my chest, straining to fill my lungs. My whole life was a sham. And this man, who I'd once believed was my only supporter, the closest thing I had to family, was behind it all. "Was anything you told me true?"

"I know it's a lot to take in." He reached for me, but I jerked away.

He let his hand drop.

"Come on." He walked down the ramp and started along the path Garrett had followed. When he was about ten paces away, he turned and waited.

I stood rooted to the spot. I wanted to run from the house, from Sol, from everything I'd learned since I woke up. But running wouldn't get me anywhere. I'd tried once to hide from who I was. All that accomplished was to put the people I cared about in danger. I wouldn't run this time, no matter what.

Taking a deep breath, I stepped off the porch and followed Sol.

The path wound through the naked branches of densely clustered trees and bushes, stripped of leaves for the winter months. Here and there, pines squatted among their sleeping brethren, adding a splash of color.

After about five minutes, we stepped into a clearing—a long, narrow stretch of grass along the bank of a small river. Men and women wearing black shirts and pants stood in four even lines near where we'd emerged. At the far end of the open space, just before the grass gave way once more to trees, were arranged four targets on stacked hay bales. Garrett and David shouted instructions from behind the lines of marksmen.

The river gurgled merrily in its bed. On the far bank, a similar clearing mirrored the one in which I stood. Beyond that, another line of trees. The trees climbed the side of a small hill. About halfway up that rise, a visual line broke the landscape.

I blinked, confused for a moment about what I was looking at. The gray at the top of the hill was nothing like the natural barrenness of winter. The pale bark of birch trees had become the chalky white of bleached bones. Pine needles were black and brittle, like slivers of charcoal. Massive oaks and towering maples, whose bark should have been deep brown, were washed of color to flat gray.

Halfway up that hill was the border of the waste.

I twisted my hands in the hem of my sweater, feeling unsettled. Wastes drew magic from the world, and from people foolish enough to wander into them, but I wasn't feeling any ill effects save concern at being so close. Perhaps stories of the wastes' ability to drain life from the living had been exaggerated. Or perhaps even this small buffer was enough to protect us.

A series of *pops* yanked my attention back to the people assembled in the near field.

"No, no, Shannon." Garrett shook his head. "Try again. Remember, you have to coil the energy tightly and set it spinning, so the ball holds its form all the way to its destination."

A woman nodded, her short, brown ponytail bobbing. She squared off with the distant target and held her hands in front of her body as though gripping an invisible ball.

I shifted my focus so that I could see the flow of magic, a trick I'd learned from Bael. Unfortunately, seeing magic meant I could also see the demons that seemed to inhabit the same space, slightly out of phase with the physical world.

Drifts of purplish fog floated across the grass, and within those cloudy clusters moved hazy shapes. A clawed hand here, a wing there.

As the woman focused, a ball of swirling blue formed between her hands. Lightning crackled along its surface.

The fog gravitated toward her. Eyes flashed in the darkest patches, fixed on the glowing ball. The mist swelled and spread. More eyes opened, but the concentration wasn't as dense as I expected with this many magic users. The fog that heralded the demons was thin, wispy.

Then the woman sent her little ball of light flying. It zipped across the field, wobbling slightly, and hit the edge of her target, scorching the paper with a black smear.

"Better," Garrett called.

The clustered demons faded away, as though losing interest. The fog became patchy again, pulling back into the trees through which I'd walked, like ribbons carried on a current.

I turned. The demon presence seemed stronger, more concentrated, back the way I'd come. I took a step.

"Not interested in our training grounds?" Sol's voice made me jump.

I blinked, and the misty demon trails disappeared. I was once more seeing only the physical world. I shook my head and turned back toward the group, where the people in front had circled around to the ends of their lines to give others a turn.

"You're training sorcerers."

He nodded. "Garrett was one of the best. He may not be able to access magic anymore, but he knows his stuff. He's trained a number of sorcerers in the past decade, and paladins too."

I swung my gaze to him. "You're still pairing sorcerers with paladins?"

"The Church may have made some mistakes in handling the sorcerers, but the paladins weren't one of them. Demon possession is a real threat, now more than ever. We can't have any of our soldiers succumb during battle. They wouldn't just stop being allies; they'd become enemies."

I hugged myself, remembering the feel of demons surging through my body on rivers of magic. If I'd had a paladin with me, would they have killed me? Or would they have been able to help hold the demons back? "What exactly do the paladins do, besides kill their sorcerers if they go bad?"

"You'll find out soon enough. I'd like you to train with Garrett. He's going to make you a sorcerer, and you'll receive your own paladin."

My throat swelled. A pins-and-needles tingle spread from my fingers up my limbs. A sorcerer . . . like my father. "Magic to fight magic."

He nodded.

I looked down at my empty palms. I'd just started getting a handle on my fae magic. Was I ready to add another layer of complexity? What if there was some wonky side effect to practicing two different types of magic? But then, I'd already tapped into my practitioner abilities on several occasions when my fae magic wasn't enough. Each time had resulted in a battle with demons. Would Garrett know how to keep them at bay?

"Sol!" A man came running up the gravel path. He skidded to a stop, panting. "We've got them."

Sol glanced at me, at the man, and back to me. "Come on," he said, striding back the way we'd come. "Time to see if I was right."

Chapter 5

SOL AND I FOLLOWED the messenger through the trees, past the building where I woke up, to a small house with a ridiculous number of dishes and antennae peppering its roof. The walls of the main room were covered in monitors. Three desks had been set up, each loaded with computer equipment. The man who'd come for Sol pointed at a still frame on one screen. "PTF picked up this footage from LaGuardia. They've crossed the Atlantic."

I squinted at the screen. A man with pale skin and brown hair was descending a set of rolling stairs from a small jet. He wore a dark, long-sleeved shirt, dark pants, dark shoes—his clothes cast a stark contrast to his pallor. I leaned closer, trying to bring the pixels on the screen into sharper focus. The man on the stairs *could* have been my father, but then, so could the man who'd called us there. I hadn't seen my dad since I was a child, and I'd recently realized just how faded my memories of him were. I might not recognize him from three feet away, let alone fuzzed out on some security footage.

I shook my head. "That could be anyone."

"Perhaps," Sol said, "when compared to the memory of a child. But I assure you, that man *is* your father."

I rolled my eyes. "Because your assurances mean so much these days."

Sol frowned and turned back to our guide. "How many are with him?"

"Twenty at least," said a woman with short, dark-blond hair who stepped in from a side room. She was heavyset but muscular. Her brown gaze shifted to me and she smiled. "I'm Nicki. Welcome to camp." She gestured around her. "This is the communication hub, where we monitor the PTF, Church, and various government channels."

I glanced at Sol. "That's how you knew where I was. When and where to attack the convoy."

He nodded. "We'd hoped to reach you before they had you in custody, but"—he shrugged—"they were closer." He turned to address Nicki. "Has the PTF responded yet?"

"They're sitting on their bureaucratic asses, debating the proper course of action, but they've called a meeting of the regional heads. They should all be in Washington by midday tomorrow."

"Any news on the Church?"

"None of it good." The woman sat down at a terminal and started typing. A browser window popped up on one of the screens. She scrolled through online articles about the attack. "Almost all of the higher clergy members were killed, along with at least thirty paladins. Several religious sects are threatening to withdraw from the Unified Church. Others are trying to take over. It looks like Purity is making a play to fill the power vacuum." She enlarged an image of a man with sunburned skin and bleach-blond hair giving a speech on the steps in front of a Purity church. "They're claiming they've found a new option for fighting magic. One that doesn't rely on practitioners."

"Fantasia," I said.

Three pairs of eyes looked at me.

I cleared my throat. "The place where O'Connell held me—where he recorded my confession and Sophie's transformation—they were doing experiments there. They had cages of captured fae. Somehow, they were harvesting their magic, distilling it into drugs that make normal mortals faster and stronger . . . and completely unstable."

"Purity doesn't mention Fantasia," Nicki said, skimming the article. "Most likely, the cases where people went out of control were early field tests gone wrong. They may have found a way to correct the psychological damage."

Sol crossed his arms. "Doesn't matter. No mortal, no matter how hopped up on faerie magic, will stand a chance against Darius and who knows how many trained sorcerers."

"And your troops can?" I asked, recalling the woman's wobbly little lightning ball on the range.

He pursed his lips, clearly uncomfortable with the answer. "No one's guaranteed victory, but in my professional opinion, with you leading the charge, we stand the best chance."

"What about the PTF?" I pushed.

He shook his head. "Their soldiers are trained to fight fae. They won't be entirely defenseless, but iron won't give them the advantage they're used to." He leveled his stare at me. "As I said, the only way to fight magic is with magic."

"Surely *all* the sorcerers weren't in Rome when the Church fell?"

"Dozens were on assignment," Nicki said. "But after this"—she gestured to a screen that showed billows of smoke rising above stone rubble—"the PTF locked down every practitioner they could get their hands on, even the civilians. We snagged a few, but . . ." She shook her head.

I shifted my weight, the beginning of a plan working its way into my mind. I hated to take advantage of a bad situation, but these rogue sorcerers may have given me exactly the leverage I needed to divert a war between the humans and fae, and maybe sidestep Sol's attempt to draft me into his army. But if Sol was wrong about my father being a rifter . . . if the sorcerers were just fighting for their freedom in a system determined to keep them in servitude. . . . "Why not side with the sorcerers?"

Sol looked at me sharply.

I gestured to the image of my maybe-father stepping off a plane. "If the sorcerers were forced to fight and basically enslaved, and you're telling me there's no way the Church would ever give them back their lives, why shouldn't they fight for their freedom? I would."

"You'd murder hundreds, maybe thousands of people?"

I pressed my lips closed.

"You'd destroy the delicate balance of power that keeps the fae at bay and leave the world vulnerable to attack?"

I looked away.

"You'd—"

"I get the idea," I snapped.

Sol sighed. "Even if I'm wrong about your father being possessed by a demon, he's proven he'll go to abhorrent lengths to get what he wants. Which means a lot more people are going to die if he isn't stopped."

I closed my eyes and took a deep breath. Then opened them and fixed my gaze on Sol. "Fine, but if it's magic we need to fight the rogue sorcerers, who better than people with experience fighting those same sorcerers?"

Sol laughed. "The only ones with that kind of experience are—"

"The fae." I lifted my chin and stared evenly at him until the smile left his lips. I'd turned myself over to Harris hoping to broker a deal between Bael and the PTF. Sol had just given me the perfect opening.

Sol shook his head. "Ambitious, but there's no way the fae will help us."

"They might," I countered. "If I'm the one asking."

He frowned. "What are you talking about? I told you, your assumption was wrong. Your magic comes from your father. That's why you can handle iron, why the tests couldn't spot you. You're a practitioner, not a halfer." He gripped my arm. "That roommate of yours was just using you."

"Yes," I said. "And no. You're wrong about people only being one or the other, at least in my case. I wasn't mistaken when I told you I was a halfer. And while Kai may have been using me for his own ends, fae can't lie." I pulled his hand off my arm. "I *am* a fae halfer, and I have access to the Lord of Enchantment. I can convince him to help us put down the sorcerer rebellion in exchange for a new, more lenient treaty. If we show humans the fae can be useful allies, we might be able to stop another war between the races before it starts."

I turned to Nicki without waiting for Sol's reaction. "Can I contact Director Harris from here?"

She frowned. "You *could*, but why?"

"We'll need the PTF's support if we want to bring a fae army into the mix without causing total chaos."

Sol was staring at me. "That's not possible. Practitioners *can't* be halfers. If you really are fae . . ." He shook his head. "I was so sure you'd inherited your father's magic . . . that you'd be able to stop him."

"I've got practitioner magic, too. I'm a unique case."

Abomination. The word echoed through my head. Sol wasn't alone in thinking a halfer-practitioner hybrid was impossible. Magics didn't often mix. The results when they did were unpredictable, and often unstable.

Sol was shaking his head. He seemed older, his skin a little more wrinkled, his back a little less straight. I was still angry about the lies, the spying. This man, who'd pretended to be my friend, my guardian, didn't deserve to know the truth about me. But I wouldn't let the world suffer because I was angry. If there was a chance I could get the fae and PTF to work together toward a common goal, I couldn't let my hurt feelings stand in the way.

I took a deep breath. "I'm not just any halfer. My mother's family is descended from the Lord of Enchantment himself. He and I share a rare kind of magic, which allows me to handle iron. He can, too."

The humans in the room stood wide-eyed, mouths agape.

I held my breath. I could act as a bridge, but I couldn't broker peace on my own. Someone had to be willing to cross that bridge.

Sol blinked. "You really think you can get the fae to back us in putting down the sorcerers? Wouldn't he be more likely to take advantage of their desertion and attack the PTF?"

I bit my lip. Bael wouldn't balk at fighting sorcerers, but getting him to stop fighting when it came to other humans?

"Bael is preparing for war because he can't see any other path forward, but he's proven willing to compromise in the past—he signed the treaty that ended the last war, after all. He'll do whatever is in the best interest of his realm. We just have to convince him that, in the long run, an alliance with the PTF is not only possible but preferable to another war with humanity. In any case, we won't know until I ask, so the sooner I get to a reservation, the better."

Sol began to pace. "Can't you send a message? I need you here, training with Garrett, learning to use your sorcerer abilities so you can counter Darius."

I raised an eyebrow. "It's not like I can pick up a phone and call the Lord of Enchantment. I have to go in person. I can train with Garrett when I get back." I felt like a kid crossing my fingers behind my back. If I could get Bael to sign a new peace treaty, I wouldn't be coming back to Sol's camp.

Sol stopped pacing. He turned to face me. "Alright. You can make your case to the fae. But sorcerer training starts as soon as you get back." He turned to Nicki. "Call Harris."

Nicki raised an eyebrow but set her hands back on the keyboard and started typing.

"Will they be able to trace the call?" I asked.

"Not with Nicki in the operator seat. She'll send their trackers chasing ghosts all over the world." He winked at me. "This isn't our first rodeo."

A muffled ring poured out of speakers mounted on the wall, then a loud click. The ring cut off.

"Harris here."

"Agent Harris," Sol said. "Oh, excuse me. It's *Director* Harris now. Congratulations."

There was a long pause. "Solomon?"

"Nice to know you haven't forgotten my voice."

"I had to listen to enough of your lectures. Why are you calling?"

"I recently . . . liberated an asset you were trying to collect. She has a proposal I think you should hear."

"Blackwood." She said my name like a curse.

"Sorry I couldn't make our last meeting, Ms. Harris. It really was my intention to come in." I glanced at Sol. "I had no idea Sol would attack the convoy."

"Thompson says you tried to run from your rescuers, so I'm inclined to believe you. But I don't have time for you anymore, Ms. Blackwood. I've got bigger fish to fry."

"The rogue sorcerers," I said. "That's why I'm calling."

"How did you—" Another pause. "I should have known you'd still have moles in the PTF, Solomon."

"I like to stay informed."

"The point is," I said, "you've got a bunch of out-of-control magic users on your hands. The very people the PTF would normally call on to deal with magical threats."

"Thanks for that tactical update," she drawled. "I'm aware of the situation."

"So why not call on the people most capable of fighting sorcerers?"

"There's no one—"

"The fae."

Static crackled through the speakers.

I looked at Nicki, who shrugged. The line was still open.

"Harris?"

"You've got to be kidding."

"If I can convince the fae to fight the rogue sorcerers, would the PTF agree to a new, more lenient policy regarding fae segregation?"

"That's a big if."

"Would the PTF be willing to change the treaty?"

"I can't unilaterally make a decision like that. Even if I were willing to entertain your little fantasy, it would require a vote of all the regional heads."

"As I understand it, the PTF directors are meeting in Washington. Will you at least share my proposal?"

I held my breath as the silence stretched.

"Not on your word alone."

I gritted my teeth. "What if I can guarantee fae support?"

"If you had absolute proof the fae would back us against the rogues . . . maybe."

I sighed. I was going to build this bridge if I had to do it one stone at a time. "Fine. I'll get your proof. Expect to hear from me in the next day or two."

"And you'll need to lift the warrant on her so she can enter a reservation," Sol added.

"Deal. But you're not the only ones with a proposal on the table. Don't expect me to wait for you if a better offer comes along."

"Purity's drugs won't save you," Sol said. "No matter how strong or fast your soldiers become, they won't stand a chance against magic."

"That's no longer for you to decide, Solomon. We'll make our decision as soon as the regional heads are assembled. You have until then to bring me proof of fae support."

The line went dead. Nicki, Sol, and the man whose name I didn't know all looked at me.

"Who can point me toward the nearest reservation?" I asked.

AFTER HALF AN hour of planning with Sol, I'd found some lunch and a quiet spot to call James and update him on the situation. I'd had to borrow a burner phone from Sol because David had *destroyed* mine when he snatched me from the PTF. Guess taking the battery out wasn't good enough for him.

I took a bite of my sandwich—turkey and lettuce on dry, sourdough bread—while I waited for James to process what I'd told him about the sorcerers, Sol's request-slash-demand that I help, and my plan to broker a deal between the PTF and fae. I *hadn't* told him about Sol's claim that the sorcerers were being led by my not-dead dad. I still wasn't sure I believed him, and even if I did . . . that was more of a face-to-face conversation.

I rocked slowly as I chewed. The chair creaked against the porch's weathered wood. The sun was high in the overcast sky, a pale glow that sparkled off the lingering snow. There didn't seem to be any birds in the area, but silence was kept at bay by the hum of a nearby generator and the occasional *pop* of distant gunfire as the training troops switched from magic to bullets for their target practice.

"So?" I asked when it seemed James might never answer. "What do you think?"

"I think Bael is a proud man, and the sting of your refusal to fall in line is still raw. If you race back to Enchantment begging for help, he's sure to use your need against you."

I took a sip of cold water. "I know. But I'm not making a personal request, and I'll never get a better opportunity to broker this alliance. Bael has an army experienced at fighting sorcerers. He can easily put down . . . a handful of rogues."

I took another swig of water, trying to distract myself from the image that had flickered through my mind—a man who might have been my father descending the steps of a jet.

"And because the humans need him," I continued, "he'll be in a strong position to negotiate a new treaty, one that puts the fae on equal terms so they don't have to sneak around anymore. Bael isn't stupid. He won't pass up an opportunity like that."

"I don't doubt the Lord of Enchantment will wring every concession he can from the humans," James said. "What I'm concerned about is what he'll ask of *you*."

"Why should he ask anything? I'm just the go-between." But we could both hear the hollowness of my words. James was right that Bael was proud. After our last encounter, he might not even hear me out without some gesture of respect. So the question wasn't, *What would Bael ask for?* The question was, *What would I give to enlist Bael's support?* Fealty? Freedom? I shuddered. An heir? Bael had asked for many things in the short time we'd known one another. So far, I'd managed to sidestep or flat-out refuse his demands. But if I could secure a lasting peace between the humans and the fae . . .

"Peace means nothing if I lose you in the process."

I jolted. Had I been thinking loudly enough to cross our tenuous link, or had he simply guessed where my thoughts had spiraled?

I cleared my throat. "There's no use worrying about what-ifs at this point. We'll just have to see what he asks for."

"If the cost is too great, promise me you won't agree."

The front door of the house creaked. A second later Sol stepped around the corner of the building. "Ready to go?"

"Just finishing up." I took two more bites of sandwich and smiled at Sol with chipmunk cheeks.

"The Humvee's packed." He glanced at the lit screen of the cell phone resting on the arm of my chair, which showed the active call. "We'll leave as soon as you're ready."

I gave an affirmative grunt and he disappeared back around the corner. I choked down my oversized bite, gulped the last of my water, and lifted the phone to my ear, switching off the speaker button.

"How are the kids doing? Any word on the medicine yet?"

"None. The children are . . ." He sighed. "Their symptoms are getting worse. I had to use magic to sedate one of them lest his screams alert the neighbors."

I bit my lip. Even with the time difference between realms, Rhoana had had hours to collect the goblin fruit extract. What was taking so long?

"Sol's taking me to the Appalachian reservation." I dropped my voice, keeping an eye on the corner where Sol had been. "But I plan to come out in Ohio after my meeting with Bael. If you don't have the medicine by then, I'll bring it back with me. "

A twist of guilt rose up at the way I was deceiving Sol. He deserved no better after the way he'd lied to me about . . . well, everything. But he'd also stood beside me at my mother's grave, put me through college, helped me buy my house. Those memories, and the emotions attached to them, were real. I couldn't quite bring myself to hate the man in them, even if it had all been an act. Besides, he'd done what he had because he was trying to save the world . . . just like me. I'd work with Sol to establish peace, but I had no intention of staying under his thumb.

"I'll let you know when I arrive," I whispered. "I'll need a ride."

"I think Morgan will be happy to collect you."

"Morgan? I thought she was in New Orleans."

"When she saw news of the attack on the PTF transport in Missouri, she came back. Apparently we are once again interesting enough to warrant her company."

I snorted. "She may be disappointed. With any luck, I can stay with you and help with the kids while Bael, Sol, and Harris take the reins on the new alliance and deal with the rogue sorcerers."

"I hope you're right." A trickle of doubt clung to his words, tainting them.

"You don't think this will work."

"Let's just say I don't have the faith you do in everyone's desire to avoid a war."

There were plenty of people, both human and fae, who wanted to see the other species annihilated, but I had to believe those warmongers were in the minority.

"I've got to go. Sol's waiting. I'll see you when I get back."

"Good luck," he said. "I love you."

"I love you, too." A thrill of warmth rushed through me as I hung up. It still felt strange to admit those words aloud. Smiling, I rose from the rocker with a creak and carried my empty plate and glass back inside. Then I followed the path Sol had previously indicated would lead me to the camp's garage.

Five vehicles were parked in front of another commandeered building—two Humvees, a van, a topless Jeep, and one sedan. A large generator hummed by the side wall. Sol, David, and two men I didn't know stood in the parking area. They all wore black cargo pants and black shirts, just like the outfit I'd been given to replace my blood-stained clothes. Guess they got a deal buying in bulk. I'd also borrowed a heavy, tan jacket with about a million pockets. Only my boots were my own.

"Hop in." Sol patted the side of one of the Humvees.

I swallowed the lump that had formed in my throat. Sol and I had discussed the effects the waste might have on me, being part fae, but as he'd pointed out, I'd already passed through it once—though I'd been unconscious, and a plane was considerably faster than a car. Still, being partly mortal should offer me some protection.

I took a deep breath and climbed in.

David slid into the driver's seat and was joined up front by one of the unnamed soldiers. Sol claimed one of the back seats. The other soldier held the door for me, so I climbed into the middle position on the back bench. My seat was mounted slightly higher than those on either side, so my head brushed the roof, and I had to fold my legs over the raised floor that filled the space where my feet would normally have rested. There didn't seem to be any seat belt. The final member of our group followed me in. I offered him my hand as the engine turned over and the vehicle pulled out.

"I'm Alex."

"Toby," he said, giving my hand a shake. He nodded toward the front. "Up there's Steve, and I guess you know David. We'll be your escort today."

The man in the passenger seat was middle-aged, though fit and muscular. Toby, on the other hand, looked barely out of high school. His face was narrow and marked with acne.

"You're a soldier?" I asked, unable to keep the skepticism out of my voice.

"Toby's a new recruit to the sorcerer ranks. He was still in orientation stateside when the Church went up in flames. I managed to collect him, three other trainees, and a couple sorcerer-paladin teams out on assignment during the ensuing chaos."

Ignoring Sol's self-satisfaction, I frowned at Toby. He looked a lot like my friend Oz, with wide ears that stuck off the sides of his head like satellite dishes and light-brown eyes. My throat constricted. Oz had been accepting and friendly. He'd also been caught in the conflict between Purists and paranaturals. Now he was dead.

"You don't have to do this," I said. "You can be a practitioner without fighting."

Toby frowned. "Sol told me what's been going on with the sorcerers, what's at stake." He straightened in his seat, puffing his chest slightly. "It's my duty to serve. And my honor."

"Look alive," David called from the driver's seat. "We're about to cross the threshold."

Steve rubbed a hand over the curve of his shaved head. "I hate this part."

Through the windshield I could see a line in the landscape where the color abruptly stopped. A line we were fast approaching.

David stepped on the gas, his jaw clenched tight.

The Humvee raced forward along the deserted road.

I held my breath.

The hood crossed the threshold. Then the air slammed from my lungs as I hit what felt like a solid wall.

Toby grunted beside me and doubled over. Steve braced his hands against the dash. Only David and Sol seemed unaffected.

Sol set a hand against my back. "Deep breath. You'll be okay."

I clutched my chest, struggling against the tight pain there. "You sure?" The ropes around my lungs had stopped tightening. They did not, however, loosen.

"It's twelve minutes to clear the dead zone." Sol said. "We've never had a fatality yet. Though you may lose your lunch."

As if on cue, Toby slapped a hand over his mouth and crunched into a tighter ball.

Twelve minutes. Even full fae could survive in a waste for a few minutes. I could do this.

Gray trees flashed by. Between them, gray bushes blurred with gray grass. Everything looked bleached and brittle—a world of sculpted ash.

A feeling of hollowness spread through me, as though a black hole had opened in my chest and was devouring me from the inside out.

I shifted my focus in the way that allowed me to sense magic. The ambient tingle I'd grown accustomed to feeling against my skin was absent, replaced by a cold emptiness that leached my soul. Beside me, Toby began to moan. Sporadic arcs of blue lightning flashed around him like bursts of static. A similar scene unfolded around Steve in the front seat, and when I looked down at my hands, blue arcs jumped like hungry fish along the surface of my skin. The display grew smaller and less frequent until the air around us remained uniformly gray.

I focused on my hands, clenched into fists on my knees. My skin seemed to glow an eerie white against the black backdrop of my pants. A layer of sweat coated my body, dripping between my breasts and dampening my shirt. My teeth chattered as a sudden chill swept through me. My joints ached. My skin was on fire. My brain felt like it was rattling against the inside of my skull with every bump and dip the Humvee's wheels encountered.

I glanced at the clock in the dash. Six minutes down. Halfway through.

I could do this.

I closed my eyes, blocking out the disturbingly colorless world, and turned my focus inward, toward the tiny pool of ruby glow that was my magic reserve—a product of my fae heritage. I gasped.

The liquid light of my magic was barely a glimmer. I'd never had a whole lot of magic to call my own, but the pitiful display of energy I found within me now made my usual reserve seem like an ocean. As I watched, tendrils of crimson light trickled out of my body and evaporated into the uniform gray around me.

I'd misjudged the speed at which the waste worked. My magic wasn't going to last.

Chapter 6

THE LIGHT INSIDE me dwindled.

I groped for it, cradling it as though shielding a flame from a high wind, but the last few ruby specks snuffed out.

My mouth went dry. I'd known entering the waste would drain my magic, that there was a chance I'd run out before emerging. A full fae would die if their magic was completely depleted, but my human physiology should protect me from that fate. So long as I survived, my magic would recover. . . . I hoped.

I stared at the dashboard, my vision blurred by tears.

Ten minutes ticked over to eleven as I watched. We had to be near the border.

I fumbled for the silvery thread that marked my link to James, desperate for a lifeline in the emptiness, but there was no silver connection to show me the way. There was no blue spark of practitioner magic. There was no warm glow from my fae reserve. There was only gray.

Panicking, I reached out, straining, stretching, searching for a spark of life in the barren waste . . . but there was nothing. A vast emptiness pressed against me on every side. I hugged my ribs and began to rock. This was worse than the shadowy abyss through which Morgan traveled.

A hand touched my cheek.

I jerked, but couldn't uncurl my body enough to pull away.

Sol was speaking. His lips moved, but I couldn't make out the words. The volume of the world had been turned down to a low hum that permeated my mind.

Then all at once the world burst to life around me. A wash of sounds and colors that threatened to overwhelm me as much as their absence had.

I shuddered and gasped, my lungs filling to capacity for one long moment before I exhaled.

Tires screeched. The Humvee shuddered to a stop. Toby threw

open his door and leaned out to dump the contents of his stomach on the asphalt.

I started to straighten, then a wave of emotions slammed into me. *Panic, fear, grief.* I doubled over with a gasp. The silver thread that connected me to James was back. Even stretched thin as it was by the distance between us, the force of his reaction made me cringe. When the link had severed, he'd thought I was dead.

I pushed back, sending as much reassurance as I could muster, praying he wasn't upset enough to call my true name again.

I could feel James's desperation, his desire to communicate in a more precise way. I clapped my hands to the sides of my head and did my best to project calm. *I'm fine. The threat is past. No reason to worry. I'm fine. I'm fine.*

After a moment, the connection settled down to the familiar, comforting throb of *I am here.*

Sol's hand was a warm, steadying presence on my back. "Alex? You still with us?"

I glanced up at him. I hadn't thought the creases around Sol's eyes and mouth could get any deeper. His eyebrows pulled together into a solid black line above his nose.

"I'm fine," I repeated out loud this time. Then, because he didn't look convinced, added, "Just a headache."

I unclenched my fingers, dislodging several strands of hair I'd pulled loose from my head. My hands wouldn't stop shaking.

"That was . . ." I swallowed, unable to put words to the experience.

"Yeah," Sol said. "So I've heard."

"You couldn't feel it?"

He shook his head. "Normal folk aren't affected like those with magic. That's why we drive."

"But even us nobodies get the heebie-jeebies in there," David called over his shoulder. His knuckles were white on the wheel. "That place isn't right."

The Humvee door slammed. Toby wiped his mouth and looked up sheepishly. "Sorry."

His breath stank. Not that I could blame him for tossing his cookies. I was drenched in sweat and twitching like I'd been plugged into an electrical socket.

I wished James was there, his strong arms wrapped around me to chase the lingering tremors away. For one irrational second, I thought about calling him. Morgan could have him by my side in a matter of minutes. Then reality settled in again.

I was headed to Enchantment, a place he couldn't go so long as the demon part of his soul remained. Any comfort he could give would be short-lived and pointless. He was where he needed to be, and I had work to do.

I took a deep, centering breath and refocused my attention, searching for the ruby spark inside me. The silvery thread of my connection to James flared bright when I brushed against it. The ambient tingle of magic against my skin made me itch. I continued to search, dread welling inside me. Then I saw it. A single crimson spark floating deep within— an ember adrift in darkness. I sighed, pressing a hand over my racing heart.

"All good?" Sol asked.

I nodded, though my head was spinning and my insides felt like they'd gone through a blender.

The Humvee started moving again.

I let my mind drift as the Humvee carried us through rolling hills. According to Sol, the reservation was about an hour away. He figured we had a fifty-fifty chance of Harris planning an ambush instead of rescinding my wanted status so I could pass through. I was hoping my promise of fae support, and the fact that she didn't know which reservation I'd be approaching, would skew those numbers a little more in my favor, but I was glad to have backup just in case.

The hills became steeper as we traveled. Pines outnumbered the bare deciduous trees. More snow lingered on the ground, filling every shadow. The Humvee slowed and stopped.

"Checkpoint's over the next ridge." David turned in his seat to look back at Sol.

Sol studied me. "Are you ready?"

I nodded.

He locked gazes with Steve, who nodded and stepped out of the Humvee. Slinging a rifle strap over his shoulder, he jogged toward the trees on the right side of the road.

Toby offered me another handshake. "Good luck," he said, then followed Steve. Toby didn't carry a gun.

When both men had disappeared over the ridge, David started us forward again.

"Remember," Sol said, "let me do the talking."

I slipped into Toby's vacated seat, folded my arms, and stared out the window. Butterflies fluttered in my stomach. This would be the first time I'd ever approached a reservation through the front door. I wasn't entirely sure what to expect. Sol, on the other hand, had a lifetime of experience dealing with the PTF. I was happy to let him take the lead . . . so long as our goals were in alignment. Sol would do everything in his power to get me onto the reservation. He needed support as badly as Harris if he wanted his ragtag group of rebels to stand a chance in the coming struggle. So long as he didn't suspect I had no intention of coming back to join his army, he'd get me where I needed to go.

The Appalachian reservation looked a lot like the one I was used to back in Colorado. Large, black iron rods had been drilled into the ground a few inches apart to create a fence lined with razor wire. David followed a road down into a wide valley through which the snaking fence cut.

The butterflies in my stomach started dive bombing other organs until my whole abdomen was a war zone.

The Humvee's tires rumbled over a bridge. A line of green vegetation wound away to either side, marking and masking the stream. Farther up, the grass was still brown and brittle, waiting for true spring. Partway up the far slope, a PTF guard station sat beside a large, iron gate. Uniformed agents with rifles stood to either side. As we approached, a third agent stepped out of the guard station and motioned us to halt.

The Humvee rolled to a stop ten feet from the gate.

The third guard, a man in his mid- to late thirties, walked up to the driver's side window, which David was already lowering.

"No vehicles beyond this point," the man said, peering over a pair of reflective sunglasses. "Are you folks looking to enter the reservation?"

"Just one of us," Sol said as he stepped out.

The guard's pistol was out of its holster before I could blink, the barrel trained on Sol. "Back in the car, sir."

Sol lifted his chin and gave the guard a withering stare. "I am PTF Commander Solomon Adams, authentication zero, five, seven, three, one." He flipped open a small leather wallet and thrust it into the guard's view with the same efficiency the guard had drawn his gun. Then he snapped it shut and tucked it back in his breast pocket.

By the way the guard's eyes widened, it seemed he didn't know Sol's position had been revoked. Probably a reservation guard was a little low in the PTF hierarchy to be kept in the loop about the decisions of the higher-ups. Of course, if he actually ran Sol's name and number through their system, it would raise all kinds of red flags.

"The young woman with me is on an official mission to speak with the fae on the PTF's behalf. You will let her pass."

Sol gestured for me to get out of the Humvee, though he never took his eyes off the guard.

Taking a deep breath, I slid out to stand beside and slightly behind Sol.

The guard glanced at me, then did a double take. "That's . . . that's . . ."

"The woman who will be presenting our proposal to the fae," Sol said. "Open the gate."

My heart pounded against my rib cage. I imagined Toby and Steve, hidden among the trees, waiting for a sign that the situation had gone south. Their orders were to lay down enough magical cover fire for us to retreat. The rifle was a last resort. We weren't there to kill anyone.

One of the guards by the gate shuffled his feet. His rifle was pointed at the ground, but that didn't make him any less of a threat.

Sol stood statue still, staring down the near guard with a contemptuous glare.

The man's Adam's apple bobbed. He pressed his lips together. Finally, he lowered his gun.

Both sides relaxed with a collective sigh.

The agent tucked his pistol back in its holster. "The detain order was lifted on Blackwood an hour ago. Let her through."

My legs felt like jelly as Sol led me toward the iron gates.

"But first"—the agent pointed to an alcove in the side of the guard station—"you'll need to sign the logbook."

The log book sat open on a counter. A cup full of pens sat to one side. Two cameras were anchored above it. One pointed at the approach, one at the book itself.

The guard went inside and settled at a computer behind a thick sheet of plexiglass.

I licked my lips. Was he going to double check Sol's credentials after all?

"Name?"

I frowned. He obviously knew my name. "Alyssandra Blackwood."

He typed it in. "Purpose of entrance?"

I stared at the little red light on the security camera, considering my words. "To meet with a fae contact and negotiate on behalf of the PTF."

Again the keys clicked.

"Expected length?"

I bit the inside of my cheek. The time difference between realms made such estimates difficult. "A day or two."

More typing.

"And do you expect to return by this same gate?"

I resisted the urge to glance at Sol. "Yes."

"You understand that the area beyond this gate is outside human jurisdiction, and the PTF cannot be held liable for your health or well-being, up to and including physical injury, mental trauma, subjugation, and death. By passing beyond these gates, you take full responsibility for any and all consequences of your presence on fae land. Do you agree?"

I swallowed. "I do."

He pointed to the logbook. "Sign there."

Picking up a pen, I signed my full name and listed the date in the area indicated.

The agent behind the glass motioned for me to proceed to the gate.

As Sol and I approached, one soldier slung his gun over his shoulder and entered a code in the electronic lock. He gripped the gate and pulled until there was a three foot gap for me to pass through.

I paused at the gap and turned to Sol. "Don't let Harris go to war while I'm gone."

"That's asking a lot," Sol said. He opened his mouth again but cut his gaze to the nearby guards and seemed to think better of what he wanted to say. "Call me from the guard station as soon as you return. We'll come get you."

I nodded and stepped onto the reservation. The gate clanged shut behind me.

"Alex."

I glanced over my shoulder. Sol looked like an inmate gripping the bars of his cell.

"Good luck. I'll see you when you get back."

I forced a smile to my lips. If all went to plan, Sol wouldn't see me for a long time.

THE ROAD CONTINUED past the gate for about a mile. Then the asphalt became cracked and uneven. Trees and grass pushed up through the road, splitting it apart.

I couldn't believe I was heading back into that wilderness again so soon. I shook my head, recalling the first time I'd set foot on a reservation. I'd been terrified, curious, and unprepared. Since then, I felt like a bus shuttling back and forth between the realms. I'd thought, after that first trip, that I'd return to my mortal life. But that had never been an option. It was clear now that I was, and always would be, a daughter of two worlds.

A few paces farther, and the only evidence of the road was scattered chunks of concrete and an occasional piece of rebar tangled in the undergrowth. Here on the reservation, nature had reclaimed the land.

With all evidence of human civilization behind me, I stopped walking.

I'd told Sol I could enter Enchantment through any reservation, which was theoretically true. I hadn't mentioned that I had no idea where the portal on this reservation was. Portals to Enchantment required an arch created by the crossed branches of an oak and ash, but I didn't have time to inspect every tree on the reservation.

Taking a deep breath, I braced for the most uncertain part of my plan and called out, "I request to speak with the guardian of this area."

A warm breeze blew through the trees, making the branches groan. Dry leaves tumbled past my ankles. The hairs on the back of my neck stood on end.

"My name is Alex Blackwood, and I seek the portal to Enchantment."

The wind picked up, tugging my hair loose of its ponytail and whipping it into my face. "You come here without knowing how to get out."

I turned to my left, seeking the source of the raspy voice.

"You offer your name to strangers."

This time the voice came from behind me. I spun to face it. The wind was tugging at my clothes and buffeting me enough that I had to shuffle my feet to keep my balance.

"You smell of humans."

I grabbed a handful of my twisting hair and yanked it away from my face. I seemed to be standing in a localized tornado. Snow and dust lifted free of the ground to swirl around me. Twigs and leaves danced through the air, scraping, scratching.

"Only the fae belong here," said the voice.

"I'm part fae," I countered, standing my ground as best I could and shouting into the gale. "Why else would I have called you?"

"You are part human. Humans are cunning. Deceitful. Unwelcome."

The wind picked up again, and the debris caught in its currents pressed closer, tearing at my clothes and skin. I could barely keep my eyes open in the storm. A gash opened on my cheek. I gave up on keeping my hair under control and focused on protecting my face.

"I am kin to the Lord of Enchantment," I yelled.

"Humans lie," the voice hissed.

Dropping my guard, I shrugged out of my borrowed jacket, shoved the right sleeve of my shirt up to my elbow, and extended my arm into the chaos around me.

Slices tore open on my bare skin, but beneath the blood and grime collecting on my pale flesh was the beautifully intricate charm tattooed in a spiral up my arm. I'd been warned to keep the charm hidden because it would give away my lineage to any fae knowledgeable enough to decipher it. I just hoped the fae hiding in the wind hadn't skimped on his education.

The wind abruptly cut off. Sticks, rocks, snow, and dirt pelted the ground around me.

I took a shuddering breath. My ears rang in the sudden silence.

A small dust devil rose in front of me. I took a hasty step back, but the tiny tornado didn't expand or advance. Instead, the top half of it took on the shape of a human—or something like a human, anyway. There was a head, torso, and arms, all formed of swirling winds, visible mostly by the grains of snow and dust swirling through it. It was as though I was looking at a clear mold under which colored specks were in constant motion.

"Your claim is true." This time the voice came out of a mouth, translucent lips moving.

"Glad you agree." I wiped a trickle of blood off my forehead to keep it from running into my eyes, and clapped a hand over the deepest cut on my arm. I was having trouble catching my breath. "I need to find . . . the portal . . . to Enchantment."

"We guard the portals. We do not guide."

"Please. I know the portal lies between an oak and ash. I just don't know which ones. I promise you, I mean no harm. The Lord of Enchantment will be glad you helped me."

"You are part human. Humans lie."

"Humans *can* lie. That doesn't mean I'm lying now."

The figure crossed its arms, creating what looked like a mobius loop of swirling particles in front of its chest.

"What can I do to convince you?" I asked.

The fae's strangely clear eyes stared at me for a long moment.

"Give me a lock of your hair."

I jerked back, surprised. "My . . ." One hand involuntarily went to the tangled nest on my head. "Why would you want that?"

"Insurance," it said. "With a lock of your hair, I will be able to find you. Anywhere. Should you prove false, your life will be forfeit and I will come for you. You will not be able to hide."

I imagined trying to run from the wind itself and shuddered. "So long as I keep my word, and your leading me to the portal doesn't cause trouble, you'll leave me alone?"

The translucent form tucked its chin to its chest. "I will not hunt the honest."

Nodding, I gripped a clump of hair in one shaking hand. "Do you have a—"

A gust blew past my cheek, and the hair I was holding sheared free.

"—knife." I swallowed, my mouth suddenly dry, and lowered the detached clump of hair. The ends were severed in a straight line, and again I thought what it must be like to be hunted by the wind.

Slowly, I extended my hand and opened my fingers so the hair lay exposed on my palm.

A gentle gust lifted the strands, tickling my skin. The lock of hair swirled away to join the chaos inside the airy form. I quickly lost track of it.

I really hoped my meeting with Bael went well. I didn't want to give this bounty hunter any reason to come after me.

"Come," said the guardian.

The elemental's form collapsed, and for a moment I had no idea which direction to walk. Then the wind rose again, blowing steadily from the north. I let the gentle tug lead me into the trees.

Chapter 7

GRAVEL CRUNCHED underfoot. I stood at the top of an outcrop of reddish rocks streaked with sparkling black veins. Ice crowded in the shade of cracks and crevices, but the exposed surfaces were clear and dry. The sun was warm on my face, though it hung heavy above the horizon and the sky faded from pale blue to deep indigo where the first scouting stars marked the advancing night.

I looked around the rocky hill, trying to get my bearings. Pine trees ringed its base in green, blue, and deep burgundy. Between them stretched the bare branches of their sleeping cousins, though clumps of fuzzy buds could be seen on some of the brighter twigs. It seemed spring was coming early to Enchantment. Unfortunately, none of this gave me any idea where I was in relation to Abonaille Malmür—the capital city where Bael's keep was located.

The only landmarks I had were the sun and the mountains that ringed the south and west sides of the expansive forest. My destination was nestled high in the white marble cliffs of those mountains, above a towering waterfall visible for miles, but even those massive markers were blurred to invisibility at this distance.

"Hello?" I called.

Only the rustle of pine needles and the sharp call and reply of a pair of nearby birds answered me.

Bael's guards patrolled the portal entrances at regular intervals, but I had no way of guessing when their next pass might be.

"Guess it was too much to hope for a welcome party," I muttered.

Stepping down from the rocks, I passed into the trees. Every other time I'd come to Enchantment there'd been gaala—six-legged, flying, deer-like creatures—waiting to carry me to the keep. Then again, every other time I'd come to Enchantment, I'd had fae escorts.

Twigs rustled and snapped as I pushed through the trees. I stumbled in a wide circle, searching for signs of mounts. After a few minutes, I tried whistling as I'd once seen a kitsune named Haru do to attract a gaala.

Birds flitted through branches, shaking pine needles and tiny white buds that looked like tufts of snow, but I saw no antlers, heard no scrape of hooves.

The thorny branches of a nearby bush rustled. I froze.

A quivering black nose poked out from beneath the bush and snuffled in my direction. Then a flash of red fur about as tall as my knee streaked to another bush a little farther away, short, black legs a blur beneath it.

I licked my lips. If there were no gaala, perhaps I could convince this pyaku to let me ride it. I'd done so once before, though I'd had the help of a fae guide and a handful of goblin fruit seeds with which to bribe the energetic little furball.

Creeping closer, I got down on my knees and reached an open hand toward the bush, as though offering the treat I knew it wanted.

"Come on," I said softly. "I won't hurt you."

The bush in front of me rustled. Then another, off to my right. A small scuff sounded behind me. I forced myself to hold still and keep my hand steady. Pyaku traveled in packs. Where there was one, there were bound to be others.

"Come on," I said again.

A raccoon-like face framed with shaggy orange fur appeared among the brambles and blinked at me with shiny black eyes.

"That's right," I crooned. "Just a little farther."

The pyaku gave one noisy sniff, cocked its head to the side, then plunged back through the bush and away into the forest.

"Damn." I let my hand drop, fingers scraping the snowy ground.

"Not a bad attempt."

I whirled at the sound of a voice, overbalanced, and crashed to the snow.

Rhoana, the captain of Bael's court guards, was standing behind me, arms crossed over her leather breastplate. A long green cape waved lazily in the breeze, contrasting sharply with the bright red of her braid. She watched me through indigo eyes flecked with silver.

"Who taught you how to charm a pyaku?"

I stood, brushing snow and dirt off my pants. "Mica."

She nodded, lips pursed. My cousin Mica—also known as "the failed prince," and a lot of less friendly names—was not Rhoana's favorite person. He'd helped me break into Bael's dungeon, used his magic to trick Rhoana into letting me return to the mortal realm against Bael's orders, and participated in an attack that incapacitated the guards of a prison outpost—guards under Rhoana's command.

"We didn't expect to see you again so soon," she said.

I nodded. By Enchantment's time, less than a day had passed since the raid on Shedraziel's prison. "A lot's happened since I left. I need to speak with—" I frowned. "How did you know I was here?"

She lifted her chin. "My lord informed me I should come collect you."

"How did *he* know I was here?" I crossed my arms. "I've never used this portal before, and there was no one here when I arrived."

"You'll have to ask him yourself." The corners of her mouth rose slightly. If I didn't know better, I'd think she was fighting a smile. But that would imply the stony-faced guard actually had a sense of humor. "Come."

She spun, her cape whipping around her, and strode back toward the rocky outcrop upon which I'd first emerged.

Waiting in the open space was a tall gaala with thick, dark fur and massive, pale antlers. A smaller gaala with golden-brown fur and a much less impressive rack of antlers was nearly hidden behind it. Rhoana swung up onto the larger beast with smooth grace.

I scrambled onto my mount, balancing on my stomach while I swung my leg into place. I'd never had much experience with horses, and my gaala riding was limited to the handful of trips I'd made to and from the keep. Still, once I was settled with my knees pressed to the beast's ribs and my hands closed around the thin leather reins, I began to relax. Whatever had led Rhoana to arrive when she did, I was on my way to Bael, closer to my goal, and I didn't have to waste precious time wandering through a magical forest full of creatures that might eat me before I could ask for directions.

THE STREETS OF Abonaille Malmür bustled below as Rhoana and I soared toward Bael's keep, tucked back against the white wall of the cliff. The din of haggling, laughing, and yelling voices mingled with the rumble of the river, which sloshed along its carved banks through the center of the city, then plummeted from the plateau's edge. We passed over the high walls that marked the edge of the keep grounds and the sprawling garden maze that ringed the fortress, gaining height until we came to rest in a courtyard at the top of one of the keep towers.

Rhoana was already handing her reins to a waiting groom when my feet hit the stone floor. "Your rooms have been made available. Do you wish to change?"

I shook my head. "No time."

She ran her gaze up and down my black pants and tan jacket but didn't offer her opinion. Instead, she strode toward the stone arch that would lead us into the keep proper.

I'd made this trip several times before, but the architecture continued to astound me. My hand trailed down a stone banister as I descended a spiral staircase supported on pillars carved so thin they looked to be made of spun sugar. At the base, I stepped onto a living carpet of green moss dotted with tiny white flowers. Rhoana crossed the floor without so much as denting the plants, but my mortal footprints remained for a moment before the moss sprang back, marking my passage with a fading trail.

As we approached the pale wooden door bearing Bael's coat of arms—a sword and hammer crossed over a flame—I spotted two fae standing side by side in front of the audience chamber. My foot came down at a funky angle and I staggered to a halt, staring. A knot lodged in my throat.

The man wore the green and leather livery of Bael's court, his outfit a match to Rhoana's, minus the cape. A long, narrow blade was strapped at his waist. Mousy brown hair hung over his forehead and covered the tips of his pointed ears. His pale skin was stretched over high cheekbones and a narrow jaw, and his eyes spun like rainbow galaxies.

Beside him was a tall woman who stood ramrod straight in a brocade dress that looked stiff enough to stand on its own. A frown pulled at the corners of her lips and wrinkled her yellowish-green skin. The dark fall of her hair had been pinned into a braided crown, fully exposing the obsidian glint of her narrow, red-rimmed eyes.

Kai and Hortense. The knight and the tutor. They'd been my teachers, protectors, and friends during my rocky introduction to fae society, and I owed them both a great deal, but it was my debt to Kai that stopped me in my tracks. The last time we stood in Bael's throne room together, I'd cost him fifty years of his life. I'd managed to negotiate his release after barely a month, but still. That's not the kind of sacrifice a person just forgets.

"Bael let you out." I cringed at the inanity of my greeting. Obviously Bael had let him out. He was standing there, wasn't he?

Kai smiled, and the colorful galaxies of his gaze swirled faster. "As I understand it, you didn't leave him much choice."

I took three quick steps and wrapped my arms around him, squeezing until he squeaked in protest.

He patted my back and pulled away. "It's good to see you, too."

"If you've come for the goblin fruit juice, your impatience did little good," Hortense said. "I was on my way to the mortal realm with the medicine when news of your arrival reached me. We could have been treating the children at this very moment, if you'd reined in your mortal need for action."

I rolled my eyes. "Charming as ever, Hortense. But that's not why I came. There's been . . . a development in the mortal realm that has created a unique window of opportunity. I've come to present an offer to Lord Bael."

Hortense sniffed and lifted her chin, eyeing my clothes. "And this is what you wear to petition the lord?"

I glared. "It's been a busy day."

"Do you intend to speak with the lord at this time, or not?" Rhoana asked. She stood with her hand on the handle of the pale, carved door.

"Yes, you oughtn't keep him waiting," Hortense said.

I gripped Kai's hands. "Can we talk after my meeting?"

"Of course." He grinned—the carefree, lopsided grin I'd missed so much since his incarceration—and my heart grew light, as though a great weight had been lifted from it.

"In fact," he continued, "Bael has asked me to attend this meeting. I suppose he thought I might be the reason for your quick return."

Rhoana cleared her throat.

I squeezed Kai's hand once more, then released it. "After."

Straightening my shoulders, I nodded for Rhoana to open the door.

Bael's audience chamber was much as I'd seen it on the day I met my fae relative for the first time. A great expanse of open floor stretched between me and the dais upon which Bael's throne sat, giving him plenty of time to observe me as I approached. Rhoana, Kai, and Hortense trailed a few steps behind, so that I was alone at the head of our group.

My footsteps echoed off the marble floor, which was polished to a mirror finish. The galleries above were empty and dark. The last time I'd made this approach, crowds of fae had been packed at the railings, staring down at my humiliation.

I closed my fists to keep my hands still and resisted the urge to rub my arms as the ghostly memory of that sea of watching fae washed over me. I shivered. Was Kai suffering a similar flashback?

When I was halfway across the vast room, I refocused on the stone dais. It was short and wide, and at its center sat a throne of pure iron—a symbol of Bael's unique ability and a testament to his power. Any fae who approached the lord would have to deal with the gut-wrenching effects of iron exposure. It was Bael's way of reminding petitioners who was in charge.

Bael himself was a less daunting figure, until you looked into his eyes. He wore the body of a lanky teenager, with narrow features and baby-smooth skin, but his eyes. . . . No one could look into those swirling infernos and see a child. Centuries of memory lurked behind the flickering black and gold embers of his gaze.

He shifted as I approached, draping his hands on the throne's armrests.

I shivered, remembering the way the cold metal felt beneath my palms. The way it seemed to leach the warmth from my body.

When I reached the edge of the dais, I dipped in a formal curtsy, moving my hands to grip imaginary fabric as though I was in the fine gown of a courtly lady rather than the borrowed clothes of a soldier. I stared at my reflection in the polished floor. The back of my neck tickled as my hair slid aside to expose it. Hortense and Kai stopped several paces behind me. Each dropped to one knee, heads bowed, in a show of fealty. Rhoana circled around the side of the dais to take her usual position on Bael's left.

"Rise." Bael's voice was as smooth and young as his features.

I straightened and raised my chin.

Bael smiled and leaned forward. Long, intricate braids of purplish-black hair strung with shining gold beads slipped over his shoulders. "You've returned. I hope this means you've reconsidered my offer?"

When I left Enchantment the last time, Bael had offered me a place by his side—an opportunity to learn more about my magic . . . and my family. I'd turned him down, but not without hesitation.

"Actually," I said. "I've come with an offer of my own."

"Oh?" One eyebrow arched in question above his fiery eyes.

I licked my lips and took a deep breath. The future relationship of humans and fae could well depend on my diplomatic abilities in this moment.

No pressure.

"Trouble is brewing in the mortal realm, the likes of which we didn't see coming."

"Perhaps *you* didn't see it coming." Movement drew my attention to the side of the room, where a woman was striding across the marble floor. Her steps were silent on the polished stone where mine had rung out like gunshots. "*We* have been preparing."

I blinked at the newcomer, squinting to make out her features across the wide room. When recognition dawned, I jerked as though I'd taken a taser to the stomach—which I can say from experience is not a pleasant sensation—and stumbled back a step. The woman coming toward me was Shedraziel, who less than a day ago, by her reckoning, I'd had under the tip of a magical blade.

Long falls of layered purple silk swirled around and behind her as she walked, as though gravity had no hold on the beautiful fabric. Her dress complemented the cerulean blue of her skin and the long fall of her hair, which was indigo near her scalp and faded to teal near the tips. She looked like a tidal wave moving across the room.

She strode to the dais, on the opposite side from Rhoana. Then, with her deep-green eyes focused on me, she stepped up. She didn't move any closer to the throne than that one step—unlike Bael and me, she wasn't immune to the effects of iron—but that one step was enough to set her above me. She smiled as the meaning of her not-so-subtle gesture struck home, her green lips splitting over pearl teeth sharp enough to tear flesh.

"I'm pleased you joined us," Bael said, twisting in his seat to address the new arrival.

"Who am I to refuse an invitation from my lord?" She set one delicate hand over her heart. "Though I admit to being weary from the trials of the past day."

"Then we shall keep this brief," he said.

And just like that, Shedraziel had taken control of the room, without even drawing on the enchanting power of her siren voice.

Gritting my teeth at the condescending look that filled her expression as soon as Bael's attention swung back to me, I took a deep breath. Losing my temper would only hurt my case. Kai's presence was a visceral reminder of what the consequences of action without sufficient forethought could be. Only this time, rather than the life of a single man, the fate of a whole realm rested with me. I couldn't afford to fail.

"All due respect." I nearly choked on the idea of offering any respect to this monster who'd kidnapped, tortured, and eventually eaten children like Emma's little sister. It was because of Shedraziel that James and Emma were currently babysitting a dozen traumatized, drug-addicted kids. "But the trouble I'm referring to has nothing to do with the fae."

Bael frowned. "Then why mention it?"

"Nothing to do with the fae . . . yet," I amended. "It's my belief that this trouble will provide an opportunity that could go a long way toward repairing the relationship between the humans and fae, as well as give you the bargaining power to change the regulations outlined in the current peace treaty."

He stroked his clean-cut chin—the gesture of a much older man that looked slightly ridiculous on his boyish features. "I'm always keen for bargaining chips. What exactly is this 'trouble' you've come to tell me about?"

"Around the time that I returned to the mortal realm"—my gaze flicked to Shedraziel to indicate what I'd been returning from—"there was an attack on the Unified Church in Rome."

Bael frowned.

Shedraziel stood up a little straighter, the condescension on her face replaced by curiosity.

"Have you come to accuse me?" Bael asked.

I shook my head. "Quite the contrary. I've come to enlist your services in defeating a group of rogue sorcerers we believe are responsible for the attack."

Bael blinked, his expression blank. Then he threw his head back and laughed.

I glanced side to side. Rhoana was stony faced as ever, but Shedraziel looked thoughtful, and that concerned me.

Bael waved a hand at me as though sweeping cobwebs from the room. "The holy murderers have lost control of their dogs, and you ask *me* to save them?" He shook with another burst of laughter. Wiping a tear from his eye, he smiled down at me. "I haven't laughed like that in years."

"All joking aside," I said through gritted teeth that I hoped looked like a smile, "this is a precious opportunity for you to prove the fae can be strong allies to humanity. If you help them with this problem, you'd be heroes. And that would go a long way toward easing the friction that's been building between the species."

He pursed his lips. "War against the sorcerers to avoid a war with the regular humans?"

"We were preparing to face the Church's sorcerers in battle regardless," Rhoana chimed in. "If we take Alex's proposed path, at least we can assume those troops won't have additional support. They will be a weaker target than we were anticipating."

"But still a major threat," Shedraziel said. "Even a lone sorcerer can be dangerous." She narrowed her eyes at me. "Tell me, do you know which sorcerers have turned on their masters?"

I shifted my feet. Shedraziel had seen my locket, seen the picture of my father. She knew who he was. She'd fought him during the Faerie Wars. "A group of about twenty was spotted in New York."

Bael wrinkled his nose. "Metal, glass, and asphalt. It's hard for the fae to wage battle in such a place."

"Perhaps we could draw them out," Rhoana offered. "The humans have historically avoided fighting in their own cities."

"If the sorcerers have slipped their leashes, we can't assume they'll follow the same patterns," Shedraziel said. "These rogues have already killed some of their own kind." She raised one indigo eyebrow at me. "Correct?"

I squeezed my hands into fists, struggling to keep the annoyance out of my voice. "There were casualties in the initial attack. To the best of my knowledge, no one has died since."

"No one?" Shedraziel's expression morphed to shock. "Surely an historical day for humanity then. It was my understanding that many mortals expire each and every day."

I rolled my eyes.

"If you're quite done with your teasing," Bael said. "This is indeed a worthy piece of news. I appreciate you bringing it to me, grand-daughter."

"Then you'll help?" I held my breath.

Bael leaned back in his seat, settling against the tall back of the iron throne. His lips turned down. A small crease formed between his eyebrows.

"It's true the humans would be in my debt were I to ride to their aid." The index finger of his right hand tapped the iron armrest.

"The fae would benefit from a new treaty," Rhoana said. "Which you would be in a position to negotiate, with the promise of our forces in the balance."

Shedraziel snorted. "Negotiation is just another form of retreat."

Bael looked at her sharply.

My heart sank.

If there was one word that would make Bael shy away from this plan, it was "retreat." As a rule, the fae did not approve of weakness—the Lord of Enchantment less than most. Shedraziel had been Bael's general for years. Even without using magic, she knew exactly which strings to pull to make him dance.

Light flashed in the murky green depths of her eyes, and her voice took on the smooth, mesmerizing quality that made men leap to their deaths to please her. "The Bael I knew didn't compromise." She took a step closer to the throne. She had to be feeling the effects of the iron at that distance, but if she was suffering any discomfort she wasn't showing it. She extended her hand palm up. "Deliverer; Slayer of Ancients; Dragon Killer; Lord of Enchantment. These are not the titles of a man who compromises with mortals. They belong to a man who decides what he wants . . ." Her fingers snapped closed like the jaws of a trap. "And takes it."

At the words "Dragon Killer," my gaze jumped to the red door behind the throne. That door led to Bael's private workshop, where he'd helped me hone my imbuing powers and taught me to see in the magical spectrum. The walls of that room were lined with shelves stacked high with projects in various stages of completion. It was also where he kept the small silver box my friend Aiden had been murdered for—a magical artifact Bael had used to decimate the dragon homeworld, then tricked the other fae lords into believing he'd destroyed.

Bael stroked his chin. Shedraziel couldn't compel him. That didn't mean she couldn't persuade him. Fiery light danced in the crimson depths of his narrowed eyes. I couldn't tell if Shedraziel's words had pleased or enraged him, but I was definitely losing control of this conversation.

"Those are the words of a person who cares for nothing but herself," I said, risking a step onto the dais to put me on level with Shedraziel.

Bael did not object.

I pinned Shedraziel with an angry glare. "This woman was locked away specifically because she refused to compromise at the end of the last war. Do you really want to take advice from someone whose selfishness landed her in prison?"

"*Compromise?*" Shedraziel sneered. "That treaty was nothing more than glorified surrender. And what did it accomplish?" She spread her arms. "Are you not here, groveling before the lord, because those with magic and those without are once again at each other's throats?"

"What it accomplished was over a decade of peace."

She waved my words away. "The blink of an eye."

"And how fast did that blink pass for you?"

She flinched at the barb in my words.

Guilt plucked at the pleasure her reaction gave me. It was petty to bring up her torture—being trapped in an unchanging world where time stretched endlessly before her. The years she'd spent there had extended into centuries, locked away with nothing but cold stone and the sound of her own voice. Then again, she hadn't stayed alone. She'd managed to destroy lives even from within her cage. I recalled the glazed eyes of the children I'd put in James's care, and the prickle of guilt faded. A few cutting remarks was far less than this woman deserved.

"Enough." Bael didn't raise his voice, but it resounded through the chamber as though shouted through a megaphone.

I realized I was leaning forward on the balls of my feet and settled back on my heels, berating myself for getting goaded into arguing with Shedraziel when my focus, my only concern, should have been Bael.

Bael tipped his face toward Shedraziel. "Alex isn't wrong. Even the best of us must sometimes compromise for the greater good."

Hope swelled in my chest, speeding my pulse.

He turned his blast furnace gaze on me. "Shedraziel is also correct. The compromise we struck with the mortals to end the war was a mistake. The fae have chafed under it since its signing."

"That's why this is such an important opportunity," I said. "You'll have the bargaining power to forge a new treaty, with regulations the fae can more comfortably live with."

"You think the humans would keep their word when given under duress?" Shedraziel shook her head. "Your granddaughter is naive. But she has indeed brought us news of a unique opportunity. The mortals are weak, distracted, and our army is already preparing for war."

Bael's frown deepened. "What, exactly, are you suggesting?"

"A wise general takes advantage of any weakness."

"A preemptive attack." Bael pursed his lips. "While the PTF scrambles to deal with the sorcerers they hoped to use against us."

Now my pulse raced for a different reason, as Sol's concern played out in real life. This was *not* the way this meeting was supposed to go. I took another step toward Bael but stopped when his gaze swung my way.

"War will only bring more war," I said. "What we need is to find a way for the two species to coexist."

"We'll coexist just fine," Shedraziel drawled, "once the sorcerers are gone, and the mortals are put in their place."

A vision of bloodied flesh puppets dancing themselves to death for Shedraziel's entertainment flashed through my memory. I clenched my fists, slamming down on the shudder that wracked me.

"There's more to be gained from this than a new treaty," I blurted.

"Oh?" Bael raised one eyebrow and waited.

I took a deep, shuddering breath. I'd known when I came that Bael would press his advantage, that I might have to make a personal concession. I licked my lips and tried to push aside the image of James that filled my mind, the memory of his arms around me, his lips on my skin . . . the hurt and accusation I could picture in his pale-blue eyes.

I was grateful the distance across dimensions muted our link so he wouldn't know what I was considering. Still, I erected a mental barrier, cutting myself off as much as I knew how—shielding him from the turmoil of my thoughts, and me from his disapproval.

I lifted my chin. "We would need to work out some details"—like ensuring my vampire lover could come for visits lest we be condemned to the most impossible long-distance relationship in history—"but in exchange for your assistance, I'm willing to stay here . . . in Enchantment . . . with you."

A small gasp escaped from Kai.

Bael sat up a little straighter, hands braced on the edges of his throne. A throne that, so far as I knew, I was the only other person to ever sit on.

I recalled Bael's words during that first encounter, when he had me take his place on the iron throne. *I had to be sure you belonged.*

His every action since then had been geared toward getting me to remain by his side. He'd bribed me, threatened me, tricked me. Now, it seemed, he would finally get what he wanted.

Kai's voice rang in my memory. *In the end, the lord always gets what he wants.*

Chapter 8

"YOU WOULD SWEAR fealty to the court? To me? Give up gallivanting in the mortal realm?"

I swallowed twice, trying to work moisture into my suddenly dry mouth. I'd said, "stay." Fealty was another matter altogether. Fealty meant giving up control and doing what you were told—something I'd never been comfortable with. And my comfort wasn't the only consideration.

If the cost is too great, promise me you won't agree.

Even if I managed to imbue James so he could enter Enchantment, he'd never be safe at court without Bael's approval. And I doubted Bael would approve of my having a vampire lover, considering his hope that Mica and I would produce an heir. Despite my offer, I'd hoped to retain some level of autonomy. If Bael's wishes became iron-clad commands, James and I would be trapped on opposite sides of a magic portal neither of us could cross.

I shuddered. If I agreed, I might lose James forever. But letting the world fall to war wasn't an option either.

I'd been a teenager during the first Faerie War, struggling through middle and high school as soldiers died on battlefields. Still, I'd watched enough news reports and special announcements to understand the cost of the conflict. I'd seen the memorial—the wall of engraved names. And of course, I'd lost my father . . . or so I'd thought.

I had to do all I could to make sure history didn't repeat itself, and thanks to my mom's inability to stay in one place, I was a master of uprooting my life and starting over somewhere new. Granted, a fae realm was a little newer than the next state over, but I could do it. I could pack up my trinkets and my studio. I could say goodbye to Emma—who would have her hands full with May—and David, whom I hadn't quite forgiven anyway. I could even handle the loss of Maggie, knowing she and her baby would be safer with me gone. What I couldn't imagine was never seeing James again.

After a lifetime of isolation, I'd finally found someone worth hanging on to. Someone who'd seen me at my worst and hadn't run. Someone I could count on when the world fell apart. I wouldn't give him up. I just had to be smart about my offer.

"If you back the PTF against the sorcerers and forge a new peace treaty, I'll stay with you. I'll learn magic. I'll serve your interests to the best of my ability. But I won't give up the right to make my own decisions."

Shedraziel gave in indelicate snort. "A half-hearted promise laced with resentment. Such an oath is worth less than nothing. Fealty is about love and loyalty. Concepts you clearly don't understand."

"Says the woman imprisoned because she refused to follow orders," I snapped.

Bael waved us to silence, then pursed his lips and leaned back in his seat. "An interesting concession. But if the humans go to war with their own magic users, you'll likely end up seeking sanctuary here regardless of my actions. After all, if the PTF starts hunting sorcerers, you'll hardly be allowed to remain free." His finger tapped the armrest again. "Tell me, is Darius part of this little coup?"

His words were a bucket of ice water dumped over my head. My muscles cramped. My fists clenched. My lungs seized. My jaw locked shut.

Bael knew about my father . . . about my mixed magic.

I glared at Shedraziel. She'd been the first one to tell me my father was a sorcerer. Had she told Bael too? Or had he known all along?

Shedraziel made a noise like a purr. "If that's the case, maybe we *should* help." She pinned me with her hard green gaze and slowly licked her lips. "It's been ages since I saw that man."

Bael cut her a look and she fell silent, but mirth continued to dance in the depths of her eyes.

He turned to me. "Is residency and limited allegiance the best you have to offer?"

I choked down the knot that lodged in my throat. When we'd first met, Bael had made it clear what his ultimate goal for me was. For all that he talked about teaching me magic and getting to know each other, what he really wanted was an heir, which he'd been unable to produce on his own despite centuries of trying. So far, his best bets were Mica—a powerful enchanter who, sadly, lacked the ability to imbue—and me. No matter how strong my magic became, or how far my tattooed charm shifted the balance of my blood, the fae court would never accept a human-raised halfer on the throne, to say nothing of a mixed-magic abomination like myself. I'd be lucky if they didn't come after me with torches and pitchforks when they learned the details of my tangled family tree.

But Bael was convinced that if I conceived a child with Mica, he would at last have a mostly-fae child with the ability to imbue—a true heir. Of course, that had been before I'd learned the truth about my father. Surely he didn't still want an heir from me, knowing my dad was fae enemy number one from the Faerie Wars? Then again, Bael wasn't a man who'd turn away power, no matter its source. If the child was raised in a fae realm, cut off from mortal influence . . . a smattering of sorcerer blood might not be a deal breaker.

I frowned.

Risking my freedom and happiness was one thing. I was already screwing with James's life, whose future had become entwined with my own. I wouldn't subject an innocent child to the machinations of the fae court and its constant power plays. A baby was not a bargaining chip. Not even when it could stop a war.

I shook my head and settled my gaze on Bael. "My presence, my loyalty, and my gratitude. That's all I can offer."

Bael's finger was tapping again. "I appreciate your bringing this information to my attention, but I'm afraid I must refuse your request."

My heart was a cold stone in my chest. I knew Bael wouldn't agree without demands, but I *had* thought he'd agree. I thought he was only preparing for war because he believed it was inevitable, that he'd choose peace, given the option.

"While having the humans in my debt would be nice, having them at my mercy will be better." He turned to Shedraziel, who was beaming with all the radiance of a summer sun. "Prepare your troops. We'll march against the PTF as soon as their conflict with the sorcerers is decided. With any luck, they'll have wiped each other out and left the realm defenseless."

The ice in my chest spread to the rest of my body. I couldn't believe what I was hearing. I took a stumbling step on numb legs. "You can't!"

Bael's head whipped around. The fire in his eyes was cool, the black and gold embers nearly still, but a simmering heat lay just beneath the surface of that calm, ready to ignite.

"Excuse me?" He drew the words out. A small muscle in his cheek twitched.

"I only meant . . ." I couldn't think what to say, so I dropped to one knee and dipped my head. "Please. Don't do this."

Bael pushed to his feet and stepped toward me. An oppressive silence settled over the room.

At first, I hoped the quiet was because he was reconsidering. But as he moved closer, I realized my mistake. I'd let my emotions dictate my actions, first in my outburst, then in my groveling. Without thinking, I'd done the one thing I shouldn't have. The one thing a fae would never do.

I'd shown my weakness.

And in doing so, I'd lost the last of my leverage.

"Rise." Bael's voice was laced with disappointment.

I didn't want to stand, to face the finality of my failure. I wanted to crawl under a rock and die. But I rose, unsteady, to my feet.

Bael set his hand on my shoulder as one might to console a child who couldn't understand the full scope of what was happening around them. The gesture seemed ludicrous since Bael, in his teenage body, had to look up slightly to meet my gaze.

"I understand this is difficult for you, given your background. But it will, ultimately, be for the best. With the human threat quelled, and me to thank, all the realms will be at peace." He tightened his grip. "Returning to the mortal realm will only hurt you. Stay here, where you're safe."

I shook my head, but I didn't have the confidence to shake off his hand. I'd gambled everything on being able to convince Bael, and I'd lost.

"Just the night then. You look ragged and weary. Rest one night and make your choices in the morning."

Time. He was bargaining for time. The thought made the stalled engine of my brain turn over and start working again.

Even one night in Enchantment might be long enough for me to miss the PTF's meeting, maybe even its counterattack on the sorcerers. More importantly, a night in Enchantment would mean delaying any warning about Bael's decision and the coming attack. Bael didn't care that I was tired. He cared about keeping me out of the way until he'd won his war.

This time I did shake loose his hand.

He frowned.

"If your answer to my request is no, there's no reason for me to stay." I inclined my head in a perfunctory nod and backed off the dais. Thanks to the oath I'd extracted as part of the deal for sparing Shedraziel's life, Bael couldn't keep me in Enchantment against my will. Though, come to think of it, I never did find out how he'd known I was back in Enchantment to begin with.

I glanced at Rhoana, who was staring unhappily ahead, then back at Bael. "How did Rhoana know where to find me when I arrived?"

Bael's expression closed down. "You think I don't know what happens within my own realm?"

A question for a question. I was beginning to recognize that as a standard fae misdirect when they were trying to avoid a lie. Since Bael hadn't seemed to know when I was coming or going during my little escapade to infiltrate Shedraziel's prison, I had to assume he wasn't all-knowing, even within the bounds of his realm.

"I think you knew exactly where and when I showed up here," I said. "And I want to know how."

"You also want us to fight your battles for you, then roll over like good little pets and let the humans continue to kick us," Shedraziel said with a sneer. "The Lord of Enchantment doesn't answer to the likes of you."

Bael raised one hand between us like a knife cutting a line. "A precaution. A simple adjustment to your charm."

I gripped my right forearm with my left hand, imagining the curving tattoo branded there. What else could he make it do?

"A precaution you'd think she'd be grateful for." Shedraziel spoke to the room in general, careful not to look at me. "Without it, who knows how much time she would have wasted, lost in the forest. That the lord himself would bestow such favor upon a mortal . . ." She shook her head, leaving everyone to come to their own conclusions about my ingratitude.

Anger and resentment boiled inside me. Bael had once again marked me with magic without permission. This time, without my knowledge even. At least the fusing of the original charm to my skin had been impossible to miss. He must have added the tracker spell after my fight with Shedraziel, while I was tired and distracted by the dozen damaged children I'd just taken responsibility for.

"Can you undo it?" I asked.

Shedraziel tsked, implying by that small sound that I was being petty.

Bael nodded. "But I won't. The spell is for your own good as much as my peace of mind, as evidenced today."

While the benefit to me might be even with the "peace of mind" Bael had in knowing where I was, I didn't doubt the larger part of the spell's purpose was to ensure I didn't attempt any more surprise invasions, as I had against Shedraziel's prison.

My body tensed. I wanted to argue, to demand he remove the

charm entirely if that's what it took to regain my autonomy, but as this whole encounter had just proved, I was in no position to make demands.

I'd come to Enchantment full of hope for a human-fae alliance that would usher in a new era of peace between the realms. Instead, I'd handed Bael the information he needed to wipe the floor with the PTF and subjugate the human race. And his army would be led by Shedraziel, his psychotic, blood-thirsty general, who was only free because I had made a choice to save the broken kids she'd stolen.

My body sagged, as though gravity had suddenly quadrupled its pull.

Every choice I made, every person I tried to save, seemed to make matters worse. Maybe I should have let Bael keep me in Enchantment—not for my protection, but to ensure I didn't do any more damage.

Keeping my expression as close to neutral as I could, I sucked in a deep breath that did nothing to cure my lightheadedness, then turned away and began my slow retreat across the ballroom. I'd failed, but my work wasn't done. At the very least, I had to warn Sol and Harris— anyone who might stand a chance of fixing my mistake before Shedraziel was given free rein across the mortal realm.

Kai's arm shot out when I pulled level with him and Hortense. The two were still kneeling on the hard floor. His fingers wrapped around my wrist and squeezed, halting my sullen march.

"Humblest pardon, Lord," he said, looking up at Bael. "But the mortal realm is no safe place for such a vulnerable member of your family right now."

I blinked, shocked. Was Kai suggesting I be detained?

"I agree," Bael said. "But she has my word. I'll not keep her against her will. If she insists on risking her life by returning, I cannot stop her."

I exhaled, my pulse returning to normal. Whatever Kai's play, Bael's hands were tied by his promise.

"Then let me accompany her as a guard." Kai placed his free hand over his heart. "I swear on my life I will let no harm befall her."

Bael pursed his lips. "A guard seems prudent, but you're still inexperienced, and my granddaughter holds an unbecoming amount of sway over you. Rhoana would be the wiser choice."

From as close as I was, I could see the tension in Kai's face, but he kept his expression neutral. "Have I not proved my loyalty?"

During my first, blundering visit to Bael's court, I'd made a simple but deadly mistake. I'd lost my temper while talking to a pair of malicious courtiers. Kai had willingly accepted fifty years of incarceration, not just to save my life, but to allow Bael to save face in front of the court. Then, when I'd attempted a rescue, he'd made the choice to serve his time with honor rather than run from his duty. Kai might have been young by fae standards, but he lived his life by the knightly codes of duty, honor, and loyalty. To question his competence as my guard was an insult.

I bit my lip, quashing the urge to defend Kai. Such a display would only prove Bael's point.

"With war so close at hand, my service would be put to better use in the training yards," Rhoana said.

I glanced over my shoulder. Rhoana still stared straight ahead, her expression stony. I couldn't tell if she'd spoken to lend Kai her support, or if she simply didn't want to get stuck babysitting me in the mortal realm.

Bael's gaze flicked to her, to me, and down to Kai. "Very well, Malakai. I charge you with my granddaughter's safety. You will lay down your life to protect her, if need be."

Kai bowed so low his shaggy brown bangs swept the floor. "On my honor."

"And Alex," Bael said, focusing on me, "if the situation becomes dire, please come to me. We may walk different paths, but I would not see you harmed."

We stared at each other for a moment, but I couldn't find words to express what I was feeling.

A sad smile creased Bael's lips. He returned to his throne, settling on the cold, hard iron as if it were the most comfortable seat in the world. "You are dismissed."

"See you soon." Shedraziel's voice coated me like honey, smooth and sticky. Those words would remain with me.

Kai released my wrist and stood beside me. Hortense rose on my other side. Together, the three of us made our silent way out of the audience hall.

When we were all out, I pushed closed the white wooden door to the entry room. Then my knees turned to soup, and I sank to the springy, green moss of the carpet. This close, the tiny white flowers smelled like nutmeg. I brought both hands up to cover my face.

I'd failed to bring peace to the two halves of my heritage, and it seemed more and more likely that I would be forced to choose a side.

Strong fingers squeezed my shoulder.

I looked up, expecting to see Kai, but it was Hortense attached to that squeeze.

"Come," she said. "This is not the time or place for wallowing."

Kai was several steps ahead, watching the comings and goings in the entrance hall past the arch where we were concealed. His stance was alert. His hand rested on the hilt of his sword.

"Take her to the tower and prepare three gaala," Hortense said to Kai's back. "I will meet you there."

I looked up sharply. "You're coming with us?"

Her dark, red-rimmed gaze settled on me, and her thin lips turned down in a frown. "Don't you ever pay attention?"

Matching her frown, and feeling a surge of familiar annoyance at her condescension, I pushed to my feet so I didn't have to look up at her.

"I told you I was on my way to the mortal realm with the goblin juice when you arrived." She crossed her arms. "My orders haven't changed."

Gratitude swept through me. Hortense was a stodgy pain in the butt who made me feel like a clump of dirt brought in on a shoe . . . but she had my back.

Shifting my frown to something closer to neutral, I nodded. "We'll meet you at the tower."

"After a trip to the armory," Kai added over his shoulder.

My lips tugged into the barest smile. As terribly as this trip had turned out, at least it wasn't a total loss. I might not be returning with an army, but I had allies. That thought sent a warm surge of hope through my limbs . . . for about a second. Without a fae army, I had nothing to offer Harris, or Sol. I was going to have a lot of explaining to do when I got back, and it wouldn't be pretty.

ICY SLUSH CRUNCHED under my boots as I stepped through the portal to the Ohio reservation. I tipped my face to the silvery light of the waning moon and took a long, deep breath of smog-laced air. The sky was a cloudless stretch of stars streaked by the pale ribbon of the Milky Way. I was back in the mortal realm, though still far from my Colorado home.

Kai had gone through first and was watching the forest around us with intense concentration. As Hortense exited the portal, I located a large, dry rock to sit on. Now that I was out of Enchantment, I had some important decisions to make.

"What are you doing?" Hortense asked when she saw me sitting.

"Thinking." I sighed and stared up at the waning crescent of the moon. Would Marc and the other werewolves who'd fled to the backcountry to avoid the PTF's roundup be running on four feet tonight despite the moon not being full? I shook my head. "I really thought Bael would choose peace, given the option."

Kai, apparently satisfied that nothing was going to jump out of the darkness, settled by my side. "From Bael's perspective, I think he did choose peace. Just not the peace you were hoping for."

"How can you say that?" I twisted to look at him.

"Did you know Bael was once a great hero among the fae?"

I shook my head.

Kai tipped his chin up so the moonlight lit his face. "Many centuries ago, he overthrew a powerful, ancient fae who'd lived so long and become so strong, he'd gone mad with his own power. That fae was a danger to all the realms, and many tried to stop him. Bael was the one who finally succeeded."

I tried to picture Bael riding to battle, sword raised, in the shining golden armor he'd worn when he came to negotiate for Shedraziel's life. In a few days, I might see just that.

"Defeating such a powerful enemy earned Bael a great deal of fear and respect from the other fae. That's one reason the realms have been at peace so long. No one dared upset the man who'd defeated an ancient. But as I said, that was centuries ago. While the fae do not age, they sometimes forget, and many have been born since those times. To them, the stories are just stories."

I snorted. "He made a magic box that destroyed the dragon home-world, and from what you've said, that wasn't so long ago. I'd think they'd still find him plenty scary." I shivered and rubbed the goose-bumps on my thighs. "I know I do."

Hortense shook her head. "While he made the artifact that struck the final blow, the war against the dragons was a group effort supported by many realms. Bael cannot take unilateral credit for their defeat, any more than your Mr. Oppenheimer can take credit for ending the Second World War because of his work on the atomic bomb."

I blinked. "You know about human history?"

She gave me a withering look. "I'm a scholar. I study the histories of *all* the realms."

"Right." I shook my head, pulling my thoughts back to the flaw I hadn't realized existed in my original plan. "So Bael wants to reassert his position among the fae—to be a hero again—and for that he needs to demonstrate his power." And I'd handed him an easy victory. I dropped my head into my hands. "I'm so stupid."

"You are young." Hortense wasn't looking at me. She too, was watching the stars. "And your heart was in the right place. But your faith in the goodness of others is naive."

"Maybe," I whispered. "But the fae aren't all bad." I bumped Kai's shoulder and offered him a smile.

He smiled back.

"Bael isn't the only lord," I said. "Maybe I can find someone more willing to help. Someone not so obsessed with their own importance that they're willing to sacrifice innocent lives."

Kai and Hortense shared a look.

"Anika, the Shifter Lord, seemed reasonable. She helped me rescue the kids from Shedraziel."

Hortense sighed. "While the Lord of Shifters may be willing to side with humanity against the sorcerers, she would not risk upsetting Bael's plan to invade. The shifters, while many, are not very strong among the fae. Their talents lie in stealth and secrets, not open conflict."

"What about the Shadow Realm?" I asked, thinking of Morgan's offer to call her brother.

Kai shifted his weight, looking uncomfortable. "Lord Dimitri and Lord Bael have something of a rivalry between them."

Hortense nodded. "Meeting with Lord Dimitri would be dangerous. If you walk into his territory, he might kill you just to spite Lord Bael."

Kai sat up straighter. "Maybe not. Alex, do you still have that token Galen gave you?"

I shook my head and rubbed my bare wrist where the black silk ribbon—the token of Galen's debt—was once tied. "I used it to call him a few days ago."

Kai paled. "Why would you . . . ?"

"A lot's happened since you got locked away," I said. "I had Galen open a path to the fae naming trial, so I could get a true name to protect me from Shedraziel's ability to command people, in order to infiltrate her prison and save the kidnapped kids."

Kia stared at me for a moment, processing the torrent of words. Then he blinked. "Oh."

"We heard about some of your exploits upon Bael's return to the keep," Hortense said. "And some we could guess from Shedraziel's presence, Kai's release, and the fact that I was ordered to bring you goblin juice. But apparently there were . . . gaps . . . in the narrative."

I gave them the quickest possible version I could of my hunt for the missing children, my defeat of Shedraziel, and the deal I'd made with Bael—to spare her life in exchange for the freedom of the kids, Kai, and the people who'd helped me.

"For which I'm grateful," Kai said when I finished my story. "And I'm immensely impressed you succeeded in gaining a true name."

"Indeed," Hortense said with an expression I didn't recognize. Could it have been pride?

"But with Galen's debt paid, I'm afraid you've lost your best chance to gain the Shadow Realm as an ally."

"Maybe not," I said. They both looked at me. I smiled. The short version of events hadn't included the fact that Galen's twin sister was currently bumming around the mortal realm in search of adventure.

Closing my eyes, I reached for the silvery thread that connected me to James and thrummed the line. I frowned. The connection was stronger now that we were in the same realm, but still stretched thin by distance. Thinner even than when I'd been in Sol's secret compound. I could feel him at the other end—a warm anchor to which my heart was tethered—but I couldn't hear him.

James should only have been a few miles away, in the cabin with the kids, but his continued silence told me he wasn't where he was supposed to be.

My heart thudded faster as my mind presented possibilities. Had the cabin been discovered by the PTF? Was James in custody? Emma? I bit my lip. If I didn't get Hortense's goblin fruit treatment to the kids soon, they'd die.

Opening my eyes, I shook my head. "I can't reach James."

Hortense raised an eyebrow. "Reach?"

I looked at Kai, who gave a subtle shake of his head.

"It's a long story," I said. "Can you use the glass marble Rhoana gave me to track him down?"

"Of course." Hortense's intense gaze lingered on me for another moment, as though she might be able to pry my story out by force. Then she walked over to a shallow puddle of smooth ice.

I stepped close and peeked over her shoulder as she mumbled over the ice. The surface, which had been rather milky, became a perfect mirror. Then smoke swirled beneath the surface, and a face appeared that wasn't either of ours.

"Hello?" Morgan's bright amber eyes blinked in her gray face.

"Morgan," I called, pressing closer to Hortense so I'd be in the picture. "Where's James?"

"In the vampire nest."

Her words hit me like a sledgehammer upside the head. My thoughts whirled without purchase.

"You ready for your ride?"

I moved my lips, vaguely aware I was supposed to respond, but my brain just wouldn't engage. James was in a nest? Which one? Why? When? Were Emma and the kids there too?

"Yes," Hortense said beside me. "We require transport."

"Right. I'll be there in a couple minutes. Head for the spot we came in last time."

Morgan's face blurred and disappeared before I could ask any of the questions swirling through my head.

Hortense swept her hand over the ice, turning it mottled and milky again. Then she twisted to look at me. "I see the company you keep is as eclectic as ever."

"Indeed," Kai said. "Was that Galen's sister?"

I nodded.

Kai crossed his arms. "You really have to tell me *everything* that happened while I was gone."

Chapter 9

TEN MINUTES AND several stories later, we were standing by the side of the lake where Morgan had brought me to the Ohio reservation, two days and a lifetime ago, on my way to Shedraziel's prison. I'd told Kai about my abduction by O'Connell and his Purity friends, about the video confession and its subsequent release, about May being kidnapped and the struggle to find her, about my naming trial and the ghosts I'd faced. I even told him about my failed attempt to use my imbuing magic, which allowed me to change the nature of objects, to change James enough to pass through the portals between realms.

Hortense, who listened to all my stories along with Kai, gave a soft snort at that last. "As if a child with no knowledge of her own powers could manage such a delicate undertaking."

I frowned. "You sound as if you believe it's possible . . . or would be for someone with more experience."

She looked away from my inspection. "I don't claim to be an expert on imbuing, but I've studied magic and its application my whole life. There are very few things it cannot do, given enough knowledge and power." She met my gaze. "You have a surprising amount of power for a halfer."

I pressed my lips together as the gift and burden of my mixed magic settled heavier on my shoulders. "So what I lack is knowledge."

"Always," she said.

There was a subtle shift in air pressure that made the hairs on my arms and neck tingle. I turned in time to see Morgan materialize in the shade of a large pine tree. Her boots settled on the silvery snow, barely denting the surface. Above the boots, she wore tight black pants and a high-collared, midnight-blue blouse with billowy sleeves and lacy cuffs. Her ashen skin glowed in the moonlight. Reaching up, she tossed her hair—bound in a dozen or so tiny black braids—over her shoulder and pinned me with her amber gaze. "It seems you're not done being interesting after all."

"Morgan, this is Kai and Hortense." I indicated the two fae beside me. "Guys, this is Morgan, Galen's twin sister."

Morgan, Kai, and Hortense all bowed, each to a different height. None lowered their eyes.

When the three fae straightened, I turned to Morgan. "Why is James at a nest? And which one? Are Emma and the kids with him? Are they okay?"

She rolled her eyes and said, "They're all fine." Then she seemed to think better of her statement and said, "Well, they're all alive at least."

I gritted my teeth. "What happened?"

"Some of the kids were getting"—she wrinkled her nose—"loud. They were attracting attention."

"James said he used magic to sedate one of them."

"One, sure. But then there were two, and three, and . . . you get the idea." She gestured to indicate the continuing sequence. "Anyway, Mr. Vampire couldn't keep them all quiet on his own, and the neighbors were starting to take notice, so he made a few calls and arranged to stash the kids at the bloodsuckers' sanctuary in Denver."

"You took the kids on the shadow roads while they were in that condition?"

She snorted. "I'm interested in entertainment, not slaughter. Your boy James snagged a private plane and flew everybody to some rinky-dink airport out by Boulder. Then they got in vans with thrall drivers who took them to the nest."

"What did he have to promise Victoria in return?"

She shrugged. "I didn't stick around long enough to be out-numbered by vampires. Whatever deal he struck, you'll have to ask him when you see him." She pulled the glass marble from her pocket and tossed it to me. "He gave me that for safekeeping, figuring whatever fae came with the medicine wouldn't make a house call to a vampire nest. But since it was you who called . . ." She shrugged again. "Ready to go?"

I hated that James had turned to Victoria for protection. Her interest in him had been frustratingly obvious the one and only time I'd met her, but James had insisted he had no intention of joining her, either as a lover or an underling.

Hypocrisy burned like bile in my throat as I recalled the way I'd considered Bael's deal. I had to trust that James had assessed all the options and done what was necessary. I just hoped he hadn't sacrificed too much. But before I could confront James about the cost of Victoria's sanctuary, I had to know if there was any chance of a fae alliance, and Morgan was my best bet.

"I assume you've heard about the attack on the Unified Church?"

"Rogue sorcerers. Mass casualties. PTF running scared of their own dogs." She inspected the long, sparkly purple nails on one hand while she spoke.

Her blasé attitude toward the carnage in Rome brought me up short. "Um . . . yeah. I'm looking for fae who'll back the PTF in stopping the rogue sorcerers."

"Still trying to forge a new treaty?" She glanced at Kai and Hortense. "I take it you didn't get what you hoped for from Enchantment."

"Bael won't help," I said. "Do you think your lord might?"

She pursed her lips and looked up at the stars as though divining an answer. "Doubtful."

My chest tightened, but she hadn't said no. "Would you take me to ask him?"

She shook her head and the braids lashed her shoulders like angry snakes. "Not a good idea. Walk into Dimitri's court, and you won't walk out."

"If he wants me dead," I countered, "why've you been helping me? Aren't you loyal to him?"

"Second in line to the throne, thank you very much." She lifted her chin. Her ash-gray complexion was hard to focus on when she moved— sections seemed to shift and disappear in the shadowy moonlight. "Doesn't mean I'll hand you over and end my fun. As to helping you, all I did was sneak you into Enchantment behind Bael's back so you could stir up trouble with Shedraziel. Nothing my lord would disapprove of."

"If you say so." I turned to Hortense. "Isn't there some protection for traveling ambassadors?"

"Of course," she said. "Else how would warring lords ever speak with one another?"

"So I claim that."

"Which would stop him cutting off your head or locking you in a cage as soon as you said hello," Morgan agreed. "But I still can't see him agreeing to your plan, even with the perk of gloating over Bael."

"That's *Lord* Bael to you," Kai said. He was shifting his weight back and forth, clearly uncomfortable with the direction this conversation had gone. "I don't think we should involve another lord. Especially Lord Dimitri. The risk is too high."

Ignoring Kai's comment, I focused on Morgan. "Why wouldn't he agree?"

"You don't have anything to offer him . . . other than yourself.

Would you be willing to swear fealty to him?"

I recoiled. I'd been nervous enough offering my oath to Bael, who seemed to have at least *some* affection for me. No way would I hand my life over to a total stranger.

"Didn't think so," Morgan said.

"But I could make him the same offer I made Bael. He could negotiate a new, more lenient treaty for the fae."

Morgan screwed her mouth up, crinkling her nose. "Bael might have been able to negotiate, then make the other realms fall in line. Without Enchantment, you'd need at least half the realms behind you to have enough sway to make that kind of decision. More than half if Enchantment is opposed to a new treaty, since they have the largest standing army."

"She's right," Hortense chimed. "So long as Lord Bael is against renegotiating, you won't be able to bring enough fae to the table to ratify a treaty."

"And he won't negotiate until he has the humans right where he wants them," Kai said.

"Argh!" I paced back and forth, shaking my hands to loosen my knotted muscles. "Not only is Bael unwilling to work with me. He's standing in my way of getting anyone else to help."

"Well," Morgan said, "not *everyone*."

I looked at her sharply. "You want to help fight the sorcerers?"

She smiled and shrugged. "I said I wanted excitement."

Kai crossed his arms. "Even knowing your lord wouldn't approve?"

She gave him a flat look. "Better to beg forgiveness than ask permission. So long as he doesn't order me otherwise, I'm not breaking any rules." She fixed her amber gaze on me. "Do you want my help or not?"

"You'd be risking your life. That goes way beyond boredom. Why are you really doing this?"

One side of her mouth lifted in a wry smile. "You speak of boredom like a blind man describing the sky. You've been alive for, what, a few decades? Talk to me in a few centuries."

I stared at Morgan, and for a moment I felt like I was looking at Mica—Bael's almost-heir, the failed prince. He'd been raised in the hope of ascending the throne, but a fluke of genetics made him not quite worthy in the eyes of his lord. He was set aside, but not freed. Now he wandered the halls of Bael's keep in a pixie dust-induced stupor, kept on hand in case a more suitable candidate couldn't be found.

Morgan's brother was heir to the Shadow Realm. Her twin brother. Had she missed that appointment due to the order of their birth, her gender, or some other tiny factor? Did she, like Mica, long for distractions to pass the time and forget her disappointment at coming so close to greatness and falling short? Did she chafe under rules designed to hold her in reserve like a trinket on a shelf?

"Who am I to turn down help when it's in such short supply?" I grabbed Morgan's right hand and gave it a firm shake. "Consider yourself conscripted."

It was an effort to keep my smile from wobbling as my insides roiled with anxiety. I'd promised Harris and Sol a fae army. What I had was a single bodyguard, one rebellious shadow walker, and a hag with a penchant for lengthy lectures. I wasn't going to get to hole up with James in a secluded corner of nowhere and let Bael and Sol mount a defense against my father.

My father. . . . I'd done my best to think of the enemy force as rogue sorcerers, careful not to put a face or name to their leader.

Even without Bael's troops, the PTF wasn't helpless. And Sol's backyard practitioners could lend support. And maybe Sol was wrong about Purity's super soldiers. Maybe they'd worked out the kinks in their drugs and those soldiers would be enough to subdue the sorcerers. Not that I wanted Purity gaining any more power, but at least if they were successful it would mean I didn't have to fight.

I felt as if a bucket of worms were wriggling around my insides. There were no clear answers. My mind was running in circles.

"You ready to hit the road, or what?" Morgan asked.

I heaved a tired sigh. I'd lost half the night already, which made it midday for the vampires. But hey, who needed sleep? "Take us to the nest."

WHEN I STEPPED out of the shadows beside a graffitied brick wall in Denver, I was shaking like a leaf and ready to puke. We'd split the trip from Ohio to Colorado into four legs, but even short exposures to the empty space between shadows was hard on a mortal system.

Morgan released my sweaty palm and wiped her hand on her hip. Her outfit hadn't changed, but her ears were rounder, her skin was pale pink instead of gray, and her eyes were hazel. Kai had adopted the human glamour he'd worn when we first met—a thin, rosy-cheeked human in his twenties with light-brown eyes instead of rainbow galaxies. The green and leather livery of his knight's uniform had been made to look like simple tan pants and a green sweatshirt. Hortense had undergone the biggest change. Her green flesh had become pale, thin, and marked with age spots. Her black hair had turned steely gray. The elegant brocade dress she'd worn at court now looked like a simple long-sleeved maxi dress. The distinguished fae tutor had become someone's doddering grandmother.

Morgan patted the bricks of the apartment building beside us. "This is where I've been staying since we arrived." She pointed up the street. "Abandon's just over there."

"Why not take us straight inside?" I asked.

"I'll not set foot in the place where my brother was held and tortured." She crossed her arms. "The nest may be under new management, but monsters are monsters. You want to deal with them, that's your business. I'll wait out here."

"Right." I rubbed the back of my neck and turned to Hortense. "There are some things you should probably know before we head inside."

"Like how the last time I was here, you infiltrated the local vampire nest and overthrew its master in a foolhardy attempt to rescue your vampire lover?" Hortense's expression could have cleaned up at a poker tournament.

Mine, not so much. I snapped my jaw closed. I'd suspected Hortense might have figured out some of what was going on at that time, but she was way better informed than I'd imagined. "So you *did* know about the plan when you helped me make that stealth charm."

"If I had *known* about such a plan, it would have been my duty to report it to the lord." She tipped her chin away, a small smile curling her lips. "My *suspicions* were never substantiated . . . until now."

Chuckling, I shook my head. Hortense was stiff and condescending, but also surprising, and not nearly so rigid in her thinking as she let on.

"I will also remain here while you"—she looked up the street in the direction Morgan had pointed—"assess the situation. Your friend didn't know we'd be with you when he struck his bargain, and I'll not trust myself to the innate hospitality of vampires."

I nodded and glanced at Kai. "Perhaps it would be best if you all stay here."

He opened his mouth, but I held up my hand to forestall him.

"Hortense is right. I don't know what deal James made with Victoria to keep the kids here, but I guarantee he'll have arranged for my safety as well. I can't say the same about yours. Let me get the lay of the land. Then we can reconvene and decide what to do." I turned to Hortense and held out my open hand. "The goblin juice?"

She shook her head. "Not until I've assessed the children for myself. Your bumbling might well make them worse."

I let my hand drop. "Fine. Wait here."

Kai looked unhappy, but didn't try to follow when I moved away from them. Morgan was gesturing toward the building's door as I turned the corner. I probably should have asked for her apartment number before I left.

A block away, the colored lights of the vampires' dance club flashed through the stained-glass windows of a repurposed church. The thrum of deep bass vibrated my bones, pulsing through the night like ocean waves slamming against a shore as I strode over the cracked asphalt toward its source.

There was no line outside the building tonight, and the parking lot to the side of the club was only half full. I glanced up. The moon was still high in the sky, though many of the stars had been washed out by the light pollution from the city. Dawn was a long way off, but last call was probably right around the corner.

I walked up the wide stone steps to the church's front door. A man sat on a stool to one side of the entrance. He wore an outfit that matched my own—dark cargo pants and a black T-shirt that stretched tight over the muscles in his arms and chest.

He looked up as I approached, did a double take, and frowned as he took in my outfit. Guess muddy boots and cargo pants weren't exactly standard clubbing gear. Then he saw my face and his frown deepened.

"I'm here to see James," I said, stopping on the second-to-top step.

He pressed a hand to the wired device in his ear and said, "Ms. Blackwood is here."

He continued to watch me, though his eyes took on a slightly unfocused quality as he listened to whoever was on the other end. Then he nodded and lowered his hand.

"Wait here. Someone will collect you shortly."

I ascended the last step and took position on the far side of the door from the bouncer. While I waited, a group of three young women stumbled out and down the steps. They wobbled on impractically high heels, and the sight of their short skirts and bare legs made me shiver. One went down on the steps. The other two helped her back to her feet, teasing their companion about her inability to hold liquor. Their laughter rang through the night.

I'd come to clubs like this in college, with my friend Maggie. We danced, drank, laughed. I rubbed my hands over my arms and hugged myself tight against the seeping cold the inebriated women didn't seem to feel. I couldn't remember the last time I'd heard such a carefree laugh.

The most coordinated of the bunch pulled out a cell phone and called for a ride. I pressed my lips tight and turned away from the women, trying not to picture Maggie sitting in a windowless PTF detention cell.

"Not exactly dressed for the establishment," said a deep, quiet voice beside me.

I jerked away and glared at the tall, broad-shouldered man who'd snuck up on me. Bryce had been the former master vampire's lieutenant. He'd done Merak's dirty work. He'd attacked me, tricked me, tortured me. My hand involuntarily moved to cover one of the many scars left over from the feedings I'd suffered as Merak's prisoner. Bryce had been demoted when the nest was put under new management, but he still had entirely too much freedom for my liking.

His wide smile showed too many teeth, shining in stark contrast to his dark skin. The smile also pulled at the edge of a long scar across his cheek and eye. The skin of his eyelid puckered, and Bryce stared at me through a milky-white orb that was the complete opposite of his healthy eye, which was so dark it looked black. My fingers twitched, wishing for the hilt of the light-imbued knife I'd used to make that wound.

"You look more like a soldier than a party girl," he continued.

"Then my clothes are appropriate. Where's James?"

"Indisposed at the moment." His smile took on a leering quality. "Entertaining the master."

The insecure, jealous part of me tapped my link to James before I even realized what I was doing. But James had walled off his end. Beyond the steady reassurance of his presence, I found only silence.

Taking a breath, I chided myself for letting Bryce rattle me. Yes, Victoria was beautiful and powerful . . . and James's ex. But I trusted James.

I matched Bryce's smile with one of my own. "Then take me to Emma while I wait."

His smile evaporated like water in the desert, but his mouth didn't seal. The scar curled one side of his upper lip in a permanent snarl. "I don't take orders from you."

"Then what are your orders? Because I know you were expecting me."

He narrowed his eyes, but the scar made his glare lopsided and a little silly looking.

My smile became easier to hold at the thought that I'd ruined Bryce's scary scowl.

"Follow me." His voice rumbled from the deep cavern of his chest.

Inside, the pulsing of the music was deafening. Each beat shook me to my core. Only a handful of dancers occupied the large open space in the middle of the main room, twirling and swaying in time to the music. Above them, in a railed balcony, the DJ spun discs on his turntable. Higher still, lights flashed in the vaulted ceiling, casting rainbows of color on the people below.

There was a lull in the music, and a woman's voice overlaid the pulsing beat for a moment. "Last call. The club will be closed in twenty minutes."

Many of the dancers continued to gyrate, oblivious. Some dashed to the bar for one last refreshment before being turned out into the night. Knowing what this place truly was, I wondered how many of those stragglers would actually find their way safely out of the club at closing time, and how many would wake up with the worst hangover imaginable and a nasty case of anemia.

I followed Bryce past the dancers and drinkers to an arched corridor filled with dim, purplish light. Bodies slouched on cushioned benches along the outer wall. Some might have succumbed to drink alone, but I was betting most had had a little help on their way to oblivion.

A young man and a scantily clad woman were making out in one shadowy corner. The man's eyes were closed, but as I passed, the woman looked up at me. Her eyes flashed gold under the black lights. Her skin glowed. She smiled, and I saw teeth longer and sharper than any human's. She bent toward the man's neck and he gave a little moan.

I hesitated. The man wasn't unhappy. According to James, vampires could magically induce any number of states in their victims, including lust and euphoria. Not that I'd experienced anything but pain each time I was bitten. But then, no one was trying to keep what they were a secret from me. My fear and anguish had been part of the meal.

Bryce cleared his throat. He'd stopped walking and turned back to see what had distracted me.

I took one last look at the man's rapt expression. Victoria didn't let her vampires bleed humans dry the way Merak had. She had more of a "catch and release" policy. That was one of the reasons James had wanted her here. Her philosophies were more in line with his own. But she was still working on converting her adopted underlings to the new way of feeding.

I spent a moment memorizing the guy's features. If he became a missing person, I'd know who to talk to.

"Like watching, do you?" Bryce asked quietly as we approached the door at the end of the hall. "Does it bring back memories?"

I took a breath and relaxed my expression. I wouldn't give Bryce the satisfaction of seeing my discomfort.

When he glanced over his shoulder, I smiled.

He grunted and pulled open the heavy security door marked *Employees Only*.

The space beyond the door was even darker than the black light corridor. Anyone allowed in that section would have the unparalleled eyesight of a vampire.

Bryce moved to one side, watching me. "After you. Unless, of course, you'd like me to carry you."

This time I couldn't stop the flinch.

Bryce smiled.

Lifting my chin, I reminded myself that I was there voluntarily. That James and Emma were inside, waiting for me. That Bryce answered to a new master these days, and Victoria had no reason to attack me. But nothing would change Bryce. Given half a chance, he'd chain me back in the pit where he'd tormented me after my first trip down these stairs.

I took several shallow breaths, then stepped past Bryce into what looked like a broom closet. The back wall opened onto a flight of stairs leading down. Bryce followed immediately, pulling the door closed behind us and cutting off the last of the light. He pressed close against my back for a moment. I jumped away, moving so the solid comfort of a wall was behind me.

"After you," I said.

I couldn't see well enough to make out his expression in the darkness—even my heightened fae vision couldn't match that of a vampire—but I would have bet good money he was grinning.

His clothing rustled. A hand brushed my cheek.

I jerked away, bumping my head on the wall.

His laughter filled the tiny room and fled down the stairs. "Come on then."

The presence in front of me suddenly vanished.

I turned toward the back of the closet, stretched my arms out in front of me, and slid one foot forward. Then another. I knew there were lights that *could* be turned on in this section. Bryce was forcing me to grope through the dark for his own amusement.

My toe hit open space. The top of the stairs. I set my foot on the top step. Hands still stretched before me, I made my way down into the nest.

"Nice of James to deliver all those tasty little morsels to us."

My foot missed a step and I stumbled against the wall. The silence had been so complete I hadn't realized Bryce was still so close.

"You haven't fed from them," I said.

"What makes you so sure?"

"James." I regained my balance and continued walking. "He would never let you hurt them."

"You think you know him so well?"

For a moment, my mind wandered to the memories James had hidden from me the first time I tried to imbue him—the dark patch in his soul to which I couldn't gain access despite the link that bound us. But those were just memories, events that shaped him. I knew who he was *now*.

"I can't wait to see your face," Bryce said.

"Excuse me?"

"When you learn what he's done."

My breath stuttered as a thread of doubt twisted through my chest. Had he sworn fealty to Victoria after all? "What did he do?"

But there was only silence on the stairs. Either Bryce had gone ahead, or he was holding his tongue.

I stumbled again at the bottom of the stairs, and firm fingers wrapped around my wrist. I gasped and tried to pull away, but couldn't break the grip.

"Do you want a guide, or not?" Bryce asked.

I stopped struggling. The vampire nest was designed as a labyrinth. Even if I could see, the only places I had any idea how to reach were the throne room and the dungeons. I had no idea where Emma and the kids had been put, but I desperately hoped I wouldn't find them in either of those locations.

Bryce tugged at my wrist and, gritting my teeth, I trotted along behind him like a good dog.

We made several turns until, finally, light bloomed ahead, and we stepped into a brick passage lit by overhead lights.

I yanked my arm. Bryce resisted for a moment, then let me go. Now that I could see, there was no reason to let Bryce touch me.

"How much farther?" I asked.

He turned another corner, then stopped and pointed up the hall. "Third door on the left."

He crossed his arms and stared at me.

Bryce was large enough that I had to scrape my back against the bricks to squeeze past him without risking contact, but the snags on my clothes were worth keeping my distance.

Once I was past him, I forced myself to turn and walk down the hall normally. The hairs on the back of my neck prickled. A spot between my shoulder blades started to itch, as though his gaze was a physical pressure building there. I kept my pace even, resisting the urge to look back.

When I reached the third door on the left, I turned, placed my hand on the doorknob, and finally risked a glance toward Bryce.

The hallway was empty.

Releasing a deep breath, I rapped sharply on the door and let myself in.

Chapter 10

THE SMELL HIT me first and stopped me in my tracks. Sharp and sour. Bile, sweat . . . the smell of sickness. The room was large, but so packed with bodies it seemed cramped. Soft moans came from every corner. A queen-sized bed pressed against one wall held two girls, including Emma's sister, May. A sofa against the far wall held a boy with blond hair plastered over his flushed face. The center space was filled with cots with narrow passages between. Within those gaps was an assortment of buckets, trashcans, and other objects capable of containing vomit.

Emma was kneeling between two cots, wiping a wet cloth over Cari's forehead. The four-year-old was whimpering and shaking, rolling her head from side to side. Her tiny hands clenched and unclenched over her stomach.

I stepped fully into the room and pushed the door closed behind me. The heat was oppressive. It had to be at least ten degrees warmer in the room than the hallway.

I shook my head, my mouth dry. "How could they get so bad so fast?"

Emma whipped around. "Thank goodness!" She sprang to her feet. Navigating the thin corridors between cots, she grabbed my arm, pulled the door open again, and dragged me out of the room.

When the door closed, she gave me a quick hug, then gripped my shoulders and held me at arm's length. "Did you bring the medicine?"

"I knew they were getting sick, but . . ." I stared at the door to what I could only think of as a recovery ward. At least, I hoped they'd recover.

"After you left, things went downhill fast. The kids were screaming in pain. James tried to keep them sedated with his magic, but after the fifth or sixth kid, he couldn't keep them all quiet. Two neighbors came to investigate, and James did what he could to placate them, but that used *more* magic." She wrapped her arms across her chest and shook her head. "We couldn't stay there. Please tell me you brought the treatment."

I nodded. "Hortense has it. She's waiting outside."

"Then bring her in." She shifted her feet as if she couldn't bear to hold still. Her face was pale, except for the bruised bags under her eyes.

"Are *you* okay?" I asked.

She blinked. A shadow of a smile played on her lips for a moment before giving up. "I haven't slept since we got here. Between the kids and . . ." She glanced up and down the hall. "I don't like this place."

"Why are you and the kids all crammed together? Surely Victoria could have spared more than a single room."

"We started with three to a room, but as the kids got sicker it was too hard for me to run between them. They need constant supervision. Though there isn't much I can do besides try to keep them comfortable." Her voice cracked slightly. "I need to get back to them. Just . . . bring the medicine."

She slipped back into the children's sick room and closed the door.

I took a deep breath. Now that I knew what was behind the door, I could smell the sick even from here. Was that why Bryce had stopped at the end of the hall? At least being sick ensured the kids wouldn't be appetizing to their vampire hosts.

I turned left, back the way I'd come, and paused at the intersection where Bryce had abandoned me. I wasn't sure how to reach the exit from where I was, and I could spend the rest of the night wandering the halls if I walked aimlessly. I needed to get Hortense, but first I needed to find James.

I plucked at the silver thread wrapped around my core. James had dampened our link so I couldn't hear his thoughts or feel his emotions, but I could still feel *him*—a constant presence that pulled me like a lodestone.

I stalked the halls, hunting the source of that pull. Twice I encountered vampires I didn't know. Each time I froze, wishing I had my stealth charm to hide me as I had the only other time I went bumbling through these corridors. My heart sped at the sight of the unfamiliar faces, drawing their attention. On both occasions the vampires looked me up and down, hunger clear in their expressions, then quickly moved away. No one spoke to me. And happily, no one tried to eat me.

The pull grew stronger as I walked, until I turned a corner and found James striding toward me, clean, groomed, wearing dark jeans and a navy-blue shirt. He paused when I stepped into view. Then smiled and continued forward. We had a lot to discuss—my failure to sway Bael and what that would mean for our plans, the sick kids and what James had promised in exchange for their safety, the fact that my father was apparently alive and well, and leading the rogue sorcerers—but all those thoughts skittered away at the sight of him. Warmth swelled in my abdomen and rushed through my limbs. My cheeks tingled. A wide grin sprang to my lips. I crossed the last few steps at a run.

A burst of emotion punched through James's mental barrier as the distance between us shrank—relief, anger, happiness, regret, desire— too much for even him to suppress entirely.

Our bodies slammed together, arms wrapping tight. Relief turned my legs to liquid. I'd convinced myself I could survive being locked away with the PTF. Then I'd gambled my freedom with Bael. I hadn't dared hope I'd be back in James's arms so soon. Now that I was, I couldn't believe I'd been willing to risk being separated from him, necessary though it had seemed at the time.

I tangled my fingers in his long dark hair, dislodging the silk ribbon that held it back, and guided his lips to mine. An electric charge raced through my body as though I'd completed a live circuit. Our breath mingled in quick bursts and my heart began to race.

My back was suddenly against a wall. James's hands moved down my sides. His lips left my mouth, blazing a trail of kisses along my jaw and down the side of my neck.

Then he reached the slightly puckered patch of skin where he'd once fed from me, and I abruptly recalled where we were. With that awareness came the image of cots full of suffering kids waiting for relief. My own needs were a raging fire inside, but that thought dampened the flames enough for me to think clearly.

Sliding my hands to his chest, I forced some space between us. "Wait."

His kisses stopped, but he didn't straighten. He exhaled noisily and rested his forehead against my shoulder. "You are going to be the death of me."

I smiled and patted his cheek, enjoying the way his jaw fit so perfectly into my cupped palm. "You've lived for centuries. I'm sure you've met worse than me."

The emotions flowing between us abruptly cut off, as though he'd plugged a leak. Bracing his hands on the wall to either side of me, James pushed himself upright and took a heavy step back. His eyes were bright, his cheeks uncharacteristically flushed. "I'd offer the use of my room, but I take it privacy isn't all we're waiting for."

"The kids," I said. "We need to bring Hortense in to treat them."

He frowned. "The court tutor came with you?"

"Just to treat the kids. And Kai's here too, as a bodyguard."

He took another step back and crossed his arms. "Housing fae in the nest might be a problem."

"They don't need to sleep here. They can stay with Morgan. The fae rules of hospitality should keep them all civil long enough for us to make more long-term plans. For now, Hortense just needs access to the kids. Can you keep her safe if she comes inside?"

He nodded, pulled a cell phone from his pocket, pressed a button, and held it to his ear.

"Bring the tutor." James slid the phone back into his pocket, then took my hand and started walking.

My palm grew warm against his. I tightened my grip, marveling at the simple pleasure of holding his hand. "That wasn't much of a conversation."

"Morgan had me set up an old answering machine in her apartment—the kind that plays as it records. She never answers the phone, just listens."

The brick corridors of the nest all looked the same, so I was surprised when James turned a corner and I was standing at the bottom of the stairs to the club after far less time than I'd spent wandering the halls with Bryce. I was also pleased to see the lights were on this time. Maybe they always had been. Bryce could easily have created the illusion of darkness with his magic so he could watch me stumble around blindly.

When I passed through the *Employees Only* door again, the club was silent. The dancers were gone and the lights were dimmed. A single worker—I couldn't tell if he was human or vampire—was wiping down the bar. James and I pushed through one of the large front doors to find Hortense, Kai, and Morgan standing on the steps.

Morgan was shifting her weight from foot to foot as though dancing on hot coals, but she was careful not to move beyond the shadow of the doorway. Kai's hand rested on the hilt of his sword. His gaze swept side to side, scanning for threats. Only Hortense seemed at ease. . . . Or as at ease as she ever seemed with her stiff posture and stern expression.

"What's our status?" Kai asked when we emerged.

"Safe enough for the moment, so long as you don't do anything reckless." James looked pointedly at Kai's sword.

Kai released the hilt and lifted his chin. "James."

"Malakai."

"Where are the children?" Hortense asked.

"Inside," James said. "I'll take you to them."

"And I'm out," Morgan said. She gave me a level look. "Give me a call when you're ready to have some fun. Until then . . ." She gave a little finger wave and stepped back, dissolving into the darkness of the arch.

I crossed my arms, staring at the place where she'd vanished. "And here I thought she liked living dangerously."

"Craving adventure and overcoming fear are two very different things," Hortense said. "Now"—she turned to James—"take me to the children."

JAMES HESITATED in front of the door behind which the children waited. Stepping past him, I turned the knob. The stifling heat and rancid smell slammed into me as soon as I entered. Kai and Hortense pressed in behind me.

Emma was helping a girl of about ten back from the bathroom. The girl was pale and sweating, huddled nearly double as she shuffled slowly between the cots. Emma spared us a glance, but didn't speak until the girl was safely back to her bed. Then she nodded to Kai and extended her hand to Hortense. "I'm Emma. Nice to meet you."

Hortense shook the offered hand. "Hortense. I've come to help."

"We could sure use it," Emma said grimly.

"So I see." Hortense rolled back the cuffs of her dress, exposing papery white skin covered with splotchy age spots. She really went all out on her glamour. She looked around the room, assessing. "Let's start with a full dose to alleviate their symptoms. Then we can wean them slowly. It will probably take several weeks to bring them down safely." She turned to Kai. "You will assist me."

"We all will," Emma said.

Hortense pursed her lips. "If either of you"—she swung her finger between Emma and me—"ingests so much as a drop of goblin juice, you'll be in the same wretched condition as these kids." She eyed James, who remained in the hallway. "I'm not sure about the vampire."

"It's not worth the risk," Kai agreed.

"Besides," I chipped in, "you're exhausted."

"But kids get stressed around strangers." She glanced at Hortense. "And fae . . ." Her gaze cut to May. The unspoken fact that it was a fae who'd done this to them in the first place hung heavy in the air.

"I'll stay with the kids while they get treated." I set my hand on Emma's elbow and steered her out the door. "Get some rest."

I caught James's eye. *Can you take her?*

James nodded and escorted Emma away. He looked relieved to have a reason to avoid entering the sickroom.

"Stay if you must," Hortense said. "Comfort the children, but I'll not let you handle the juice."

I raised my hands. "I'm just here to keep them calm and give Emma some peace of mind."

"We'll start in the back corner." Hortense pulled a small vial from a hidden pocket at the waist of her skirt and headed for the bed where May was sleeping.

May was curled in a tight ball, stick-thin arms wrapped around her middle. She shook slightly and made soft whimpering noises.

I whispered her name.

Her eyes fluttered open.

"Alex?" Her voice was hoarse and gravelly.

I forced a smile and nodded.

"I hurt."

"I know." I pushed a strand of sweat-matted hair back from her forehead. None of the kids knew they were addicted to magical faerie fruit. We'd erased their memories of the time they spent in Shedraziel's realm—quick and dirty therapy so they didn't have to face what had been done to them. That also meant they didn't know why they were sick. "We have something to take the pain away."

I nodded to Hortense.

Kai placed his hands on May's shoulders. "Lie still."

Hortense unstoppered the vial. A whiff of sweet aroma drifted out.

May stiffened. The eyes of the girl in bed beside her snapped open and rolled in our direction.

"You'll be next," I promised. My own stomach growled. My mouth started to water. No wonder Hortense hadn't trusted Emma or me to handle the juice. I wasn't even addicted, but my body was desperate to get to the sweet nectar. I couldn't imagine how much worse it was for the children.

Hortense lifted an eyedropper of liquid out of the bottle and moved it carefully over May's mouth.

She strained against Kai's grip, arching to lift her head as close to the dropper as she could get.

"Open," Hortense said.

She obeyed, and three shiny drops of pink liquid fell onto her tongue.

May strained until the stopper was back in the bottle. Then she snapped her lips closed and fell back against the bed. The tension eased out of her muscles. The lines around her eyes and mouth relaxed. She took a deep, calm breath. When her eyes opened again, I got the feeling she wasn't seeing me, or the room, or anything real. She was wrapped in the dream of the goblin fruit.

The bed's other occupant rolled over and started climbing over May's unresponsive body to reach the bottle in Hortense's hand.

"Hold her back," Hortense said, rounding the bed.

I pushed the girl's shoulders to the bed while Kai pinned her legs. She was small, about twelve years old, and like May she was all skinny sinew. Still, she struggled with the force of an adult in her desperation to get at the drug.

Other faces turned in our direction as more kids became aware of the goblin juice. I only hoped they were too weak to do more than look.

SHAKING DROPLETS out of my damp hair, I pulled a towel tight around me and padded across the thick, gray carpet of James's bedroom. A shower had done wonders to settle my mood, but my eyelids drooped and I couldn't stop yawning. I sank into the black leather of the couch and rubbed a set of swollen scratches where a little boy had raked my wrist with his nails. My cheek ached thanks to a surprisingly strong left hook from an eight-year-old, and I had an imprint of human teeth on my forearm. The waiting kids had grown more impatient with every dose given, and while they'd seemed barely able to move when I first arrived, they were practically throwing themselves at Hortense once they noticed the goblin juice.

I picked up a leather-bound journal from the coffee table and flipped it open. My own face, rendered in charcoal, stared back. James's signature was scrawled at the bottom.

"I see you've found your gift."

I startled, slamming the journal shut on the ghostly portrait.

James closed the door behind him. "Kai and Hortense are safely delivered. She promises the next dose will be easier."

I nodded. Once the children had settled into their drug-induced sleep, Hortense outlined a three-week treatment plan of regular, decreasing doses. The kids would always be addicted, but since the fruit didn't grow anywhere in the mortal realm, they'd be able to get through the rest of their lives without more than an occasional, unfulfillable craving.

I set my hand on the cover of the journal. "I didn't mean to snoop."

"The sketchbook is for you." He smiled and joined me on the couch. "I know how artistic expression settles you, and with your supplies out of reach . . ." He shrugged.

My heart ached at the idea of never seeing my studio again—my sanctuary from the world. Even if I somehow managed to get my life back, would I ever feel free there as I had before, now that the police and PTF had ransacked it? I cleared my throat and pushed the thought away. "And the drawing?"

"A lonely heart passing time until your return."

"It's beautiful."

He caressed my cheek. *It doesn't do you justice.* He plucked the book from my hands and set it on the coffee table. "Now our duties are done, what say you to a proper hello?"

"My duties are far from done. I still need to talk to Harris." My shoulders sagged. "She needs to know that not only will the PTF have to stand against the rogue sorcerers without fae backup, but now Bael has decided his best bet to establish a new order in the mortal realm and regain his status as a hero among the fae is to strike while the human defenses are weakened. I mean, what am I supposed to say? 'The fae army I promised is totally coming, but instead of helping you, they plan to wipe you off the face of the Earth once you're worn out from fighting the sorcerers.'" I rubbed my hands over my eyes and groaned. "Somehow, I don't think that'll go over very well."

"You did what you could."

"And made things worse."

He shook his head. "Bael has spies everywhere. If he did not already know of the sorcerer's rebellion, he would have soon."

I sighed and pinched the bridge of my nose. "I really thought Bael would choose peace over war if I gave him the alternative."

"Believing the best of people is nothing to be ashamed of." He kissed my jaw just below my left ear and whispered, "I'm just glad you came back to me in one piece."

I bit my lip, thinking of how close I'd come to agreeing to stay in Enchantment.

James stilled as he caught my stray thought.

"I considered staying," I whispered. "For the good of the world. But I couldn't. Not if it meant losing you."

He stared steadily into my eyes. Then he smiled. "You kept your promise."

I studied his smile, wishing more than anything I could feel those soft lips again and forget everything, at least for a while. But I wasn't the only one who'd been making deals. Now that we were talking, there was one more topic that had to be addressed—one more confession between us. "So did you."

His smile faltered.

"Morgan and Emma told me what happened with the kids—why you had to leave the cabin—but why *here*?"

Annoyance flitted through our connection. "In case you've forgotten, I'm a wanted fugitive. My assets are frozen. And while I might have been able to call in enough favors to buy myself a comfortable hidey-hole, I could hardly accommodate the dozen sick and screaming kids you left in my care. Victoria had the means to transport, house, and suppress the symptoms of the entire group."

"At what cost?" I searched his face. "There's no way Victoria would shelter you out of the goodness of her heart."

Sighing, he reached up and undid the top button on his shirt, then the next, and the next, until the silky fabric parted over his bare chest.

I frowned, thinking he was trying to distract me, but the emotions leaking through our connection swirled with worry.

Then I understood. I flattened my hand against the naked skin where his yellow pendant should have hung. "You gave Victoria the necklace that let you walk in daylight."

"She demanded either my charm or my oath. I gave her the item of lesser value."

Relief and anxiety warred inside me. I'd been dreading the news that James had sworn himself to Victoria, that he'd be taking orders from her just as Bael had wanted me to take orders from him. That he'd given up his freedom to keep his promise to me. The fact that he hadn't was like a deep breath of fresh air after being submerged too long.

But that necklace had been made by Bael himself to protect James from the destructive power of the sun—payment for services rendered a long, long time ago. It was the only one of its kind. Without that necklace, James would be bound to darkness like the rest of his kind. No more afternoon walks or picnics in the park. No more freedom to live as he chose. No more pretending to be human.

"I'm sorry," he said, responding to the loss pouring through me. "I wasn't strong enough to keep the children safe on my own."

"You did what you had to." I shoved aside my disappointment at having a boyfriend who could never stand under the sun and cupped his cheek. "If you're bound to the night, so be it. I'll become nocturnal."

He covered my hand with his, sandwiching it against his cheek. "I fully intend to walk under the sun with you again."

I frowned.

A ripple of . . . trepidation? . . . swept through our connection.

"Victoria did not take as much as she believes from me. The pendant, while powerful, is nearly at the end of its use. Of the thousand days of sunlight Bael imbued that charm to absorb, there are perhaps only one hundred left. And I want so much more than that with you." He pinned me with his gaze. "I want you to try again to change me with your magic—to shift my nature."

Chords of anxiety squeezed my chest. James had almost died during my first, and only, attempt to change his essence with my imbuing magic. I wanted to try again, to change James enough that he could walk in daylight, pass through fae realms, and be free of the constant unraveling of his soul that required him to feed on mortal lives to counteract the damage. But I wasn't sure imbuing a living person was even possible. I might be risking his life for nothing. "I don't know."

"You *can* do this. What happened last time . . . it was my fault." He lifted his chin. "But I understand now."

"You do?"

"Marron said you had to know who I was and who I wanted to be in order to change me."

"Marron also built an army of paper critters, brought them to life, and had them march into a fire while she did cartwheels around the room. She's batshit crazy."

"The last time we tried, I . . . blocked you . . . from certain memories."

When I'd finally pierced the shell of James's innermost core, I'd been bombarded by memories and emotions, but James had shielded some, pushing me away.

"Those memories are a big part of who I am. Without them, your magic couldn't work properly."

I'd come to the same conclusion after our failure, but knowing the problem and being able to fix it were two very different things.

"Are you willing to share those memories now?"

"The thoughts I hid from you are from a time I've done my best to forget." Fear leaked through our link, though I could tell he was trying to hold it back. "You may not look at me the same way after seeing what I've done. You may want nothing to do with me."

I set my hands on his thighs and leaned in until our noses nearly touched. "Whoever you were, whatever you've done, I know who you are now, and I love you."

"You gave me your name—opened yourself to me fully despite a lifetime of mistrusting those around you." He smiled, but his eyes remained haunted. "I will do the same."

"You're sure?" I was thrilled James was willing to share the entirety of his being with me as I had with him. But if there was any doubt, any reservation, the magic would unravel as it had last time, and maybe this time the demon would take over. We were gambling with his life.

"I'd say we could do it right now, if you didn't look as though you'd fall asleep halfway through."

I shook my head. "Performing surgery on your soul isn't something we should rush. Besides . . ." I traced my fingers over his bare chest and pushed the edges of his shirt until the fabric slid off his broad shoulders. Worries about Harris, Bael, rogue sorcerers, failed imbuing, and a life without sunshine still swirled through my mind, but it was nearly four a.m. and there was nothing I could do about those things at the moment. The liquid heat rising in me as I shifted to straddle James's legs, however, that I could deal with. "I still owe you a proper hello."

Chapter 11

SOMETHING NUDGED ME.

I snuggled deeper into the solid warmth at my back.

"Alex." Hairs tickled my neck as they were moved aside, pulled back to expose my face. "It's time to wake up."

I grumbled and groaned. Then drifted back to the border of sleep. "Alex."

"*You* get up."

A rumbling chuckle vibrated against my back. "I will. But you made me promise before I turned out the light that I wouldn't let you sleep in. You need to call Harris."

My eyes snapped open. Shit. Harris. The PTF conference. The sorcerers. Bael. It all came back in a rush that chased the contented fog from my mind and left me cold.

I pulled the edge of the pillow up to cover my face, wishing today had never come.

James's arms tightened around me, one under my neck and across my chest, the other draped over my side. The pressure and warmth of him almost made waking up tolerable. But he'd have to let go soon enough.

"Can't I just stay in bed?" I mumbled into the pillow. Then I twisted slightly so I could speak over my shoulder. "*You* could call Harris. Just tell her I'm a failure, and the PTF should expect a war with the fae as soon as the sorcerers are dealt with. That should go over well."

James shifted, and his icy-blue gaze peeked over my shoulder. "Okay."

I stiffened. "Wait, really?"

"If that's what you want." He kissed my bare shoulder. "You know I'd do anything for you."

"In that case, how about arresting the rogue sorcerers and making Bael back down from war with the mortals?"

He nuzzled against my neck. "While I'll gladly attempt the impossible for you, I'm afraid even I can't take on an army of sorcerers by myself, to say nothing of an army of fae."

I smiled. "If only I had an army of *you*."

"I'll just have to do what I can on my own." His mouth found mine and set off a series of fireworks throughout my body. But my brain kept turning over the image of an army of Jameses, faster and stronger than any mortals.

James pulled back from his kiss, a crease between his dark eyebrows. "What's wrong?"

I shook my head, unwilling to let the idea go, but not yet ready to voice it.

An army of vampires could take on the rogue sorcerers . . . probably . . . maybe. But why would they? They were still in hiding from the PTF, and judging by the conflict with the fae and the current hunts being run across the country for the recently outed werewolves, they'd want to stay safe in the shadows. But the fae were coming, and the fae knew about vampires. Knew about, and hated. The fae had tried to eradicate vampires once before, when they were first created. They'd failed, but who's to say they wouldn't try again if they took control of this realm? Maybe I could convince Victoria it was in the vampires' best interest to side with the PTF?

I laughed at the idea, shocked by my own desperation. Sure, Victoria had proven more reasonable than the last master of Denver, but she'd required payment just to shelter a group of drug-addled kids. I couldn't image the price for buying her allegiance in a war. Still, a vampire army would make Bael think twice. And vampires weren't the only paranaturals in the mortal realm. Werewolves. Practitioners. Sol already had a group of would-be-sorcerers training at his camp. And unlike the vampires, most werewolves felt a certain loyalty to the humans they started out as. I might be able to provide Harris with an army after all.

"It could work."

I jerked, startled out of my thoughts. James was squinting at me, a deep frown on his face. He'd been using the link to eavesdrop.

"Well, you weren't being very forthcoming," he said with a shrug.

"Do you really think it could work?"

He rolled off me and tucked one arm behind his head. "An army of werewolves and practitioners could certainly rout the rogue sorcerers . . . if there were enough of them."

"And the vampires?" I prompted. "Would they cooperate?"

"Unlikely. Not without a clear gain."

"Do you think the practitioners and werewolves would be enough to deter Bael from attacking?"

"I suppose that depends on the state of them after dealing with the sorcerers, assuming you can even get them to agree. The mortals haven't exactly made the werewolves feel welcome."

My brain was chugging away, fitting thoughts together like puzzle pieces. The more I thought about it, the more I liked the idea. I'd believed having the fae come to the aid of the humans in their hour of need would build a bridge between them. The same logic should hold true for paranaturals living in the mortal realm. If they stood with humanity not only against the rogue sorcerers, but also the fae . . .

Now I just had to figure out how to contact them. The werewolves had gone into hiding when shit hit the fan with the PTF. But I knew at least one person who could find them—assuming I could get him out of prison.

THE STREETS AROUND Abandon were just that, abandoned. Not a lot of traffic around the nightclub once the sun rose. Most of the apartments in the neighborhood were held by single people struggling to make ends meet. No kids playing. No pet owners out walking their dogs. No open spaces for locals to congregate. Just a few commuters rushing to or from their jobs and the usual assortment of newspapers and fast-food wrappers blowing through the streets.

The steps of the church-slash-club were cold enough to leach the heat out of my butt and thighs, but at least they were dry. Scattered patches of ice and slush collected in the shadows of nearby buildings and clogged the gutters where they'd been heaped by careless plows, but most of the ground was clear. Colorado snow didn't last long at this altitude, even in the heart of winter.

The sun shone from a clear blue sky, and all around me the sounds and smells of city life filtered in—steel, smog, and too many bodies. Engines rumbled, horns blared, a bridge rattled with the passing of the light rail. Everything seemed . . . normal.

Sighing, I closed the sketchbook I'd been doodling in while I gathered my thoughts, slipped it in one of my jacket's oversized pockets, and pulled out the phone James had given me—the latest in a long line of burners he'd been using and disposing of. I pressed the dial button and tipped my face toward the sky, closing my eyes against the glare of the afternoon sun. What would I do if James couldn't be changed? Could our relationship survive the limits of dusk and dawn?

The phone rang and rang. I frowned and opened my eyes.

Without a direct line to Harris, I'd called Maggie's house as I had the other times I'd needed to get in touch with the PTF director. But either the agent assigned to the Hawthorne residence was sleeping on the job or they'd withdrawn in light of my amended status. After all, what reason did they have to monitor Maggie's calls if I was no longer a fugitive?

But if the PTF occupation had ended . . . why wasn't Charlie answering?

Shaking my head and doing my best to ignore the icy weight that settled over me, I disconnected and pulled up the number for the Denver PTF office. I hit zero as soon as the standard automated response started reciting menu options.

"PTF, Denver office. How may I direct your call?"

"I need to speak with Director Harris."

"Director Harris is unavailable. I can transfer you to her voicemail."

"My name is Alex Blackwood. Director Harris is expecting my call. I need to speak with her directly."

There was a beat of silence as the operator processed my words, then, "Hold please."

Classical music blared through the speaker.

A moment later, a man's voice filled the line. "Ms. Blackwood?"

"Who are you?"

"Agent Weatherly. I'm currently in charge of the Denver office. I understand you're trying to reach Director Harris."

"That's right. She's expecting my call."

He cleared his throat. "Would this have anything to do with your sudden pardon?"

I opened my mouth, then closed it, registering his tone. Had Harris gotten in trouble for clearing my name and giving me access to the reservation? "I have information she needs. Time-sensitive information."

"I see." There was a pause. "Give me the information and I'll see that she gets it."

"Not gonna happen."

"Ms. Blackwood, if—"

"Get Harris on the line, now, or you'll be responsible for the consequences of this delay."

The silence stretched.

"All right, Ms. Blackwood." He snapped off the syllables of my name. "If that's how you want to do things."

The line went dead for a moment, and I feared I'd miscalculated. Then the speaker crackled and another voice came through. "I was beginning to think you'd stood me up." Harris's voice was tight with stress. "I'm told you're being routed through the Denver office. Why didn't you call me directly?"

"I'm not with Sol right now, and I don't have your number. I tried calling via Maggie's wiretap like I did before, but—"

"Mrs. Hawthorne was released yesterday when I cleared your warrant. The surveillance agents were recalled."

So Maggie was free. A weight lifted from my chest. At least she wouldn't be delivering her baby in a PTF prison camp because of me. But then, why hadn't anyone answered the phone?

"The PTF heads are meeting in less than an hour. I hope you've got good news for me."

My relief was short lived as her words hit me. "I thought you weren't scheduled to meet until this evening?"

"Our timetable's moved up. We can't afford to delay after this morning's events."

"What—"

"Are the fae on board?"

I snapped my mouth shut so fast my teeth hurt. My news couldn't be called "good" by any stretch of the imagination. But my epiphany this morning had provided a silver lining, so at least it wasn't all bad.

"Not exactly. But there's another group who might be willing to help."

There was a beat of quiet. Then, "Another group strong enough to stand up to a unit of elite sorcerers? Who?"

I bit my lower lip, took a deep breath, and said, "The paranaturals."

"You mean Sol's little band of rebels?"

"Not just them. There are others. Like the werewolves."

Silence stretched over the line. "We've already got a group of crazed magic-wielders on our hands, and you want to set loose a bunch of angry monsters?"

"Angry maybe, but they're not monsters."

"I saw the footage of that wolf using you as a chew toy. The whole world saw it. And from what I understand, she was your friend."

I winced. The video that had gone viral was definitely not the best way the werewolves could have come out of the paranatural closet. But done was done. "That was a very specific situation. The man she loved had just been shot."

"By a PTF agent," Harris pointed out. "You really think they'd forget that little detail and run to our rescue?"

I pictured Marc, the Rocky Mountain pack alpha. Every decision he made was for the good of the pack, even if it caused suffering on an individual level. "If it means the difference between running forever, hunted by the PTF, or returning to some semblance of peace and a normal life? Absolutely. But I need something. Or, more specifically, some*one*."

"Surprise, surprise, another favor."

"The wolves have gone into hiding. In order to find them, I need you to release a practitioner you're holding named Luke Miller."

"No. No way. I took a big gamble on you and you didn't come through. I'm not making that mistake again."

"But—"

"Purity gets their shot. Maybe *they* can deliver."

"But—"

She severed the connection.

I lowered the phone, stunned. I hadn't even gotten to deliver my warning about Bael.

"Alex."

I jumped, fumbled the phone, and twisted to see James peeking through a tiny crack in the doorway. A small overhang created a lip of shadow over the portal, but I was sitting in full sun. There were only three feet between us, but without his necklace we might as well have been on opposite sides of the Grand Canyon.

I stood, brushed off the seat of my pants, and crossed the threshold from light to dark.

James stepped back to let me in, or maybe to ensure no light struck him when I pushed the door wider. "How'd she take it?"

I grunted. "Pretty sure she won't be taking any more of my calls. They're gonna let Purity's super soldiers have a go." I pushed the door closed behind me, cutting off the light in the entryway.

"Fools," he said. "They're running scared after what happened this morning."

I froze. "Harris mentioned something had moved up their timetable. What happened?"

"That's what I came to tell you." James pulled the phone out of my hands, typed something in, and handed it back. "Victoria just showed me this. It's all over the internet."

I pressed a button to skip the ad on a video labeled "Liberty in

Death." When the footage started, I was looking at a two-story building supporting a domed clock tower against a backdrop of more modern high-rise buildings. A balding man in a brown suit stood under a statue of George Washington, droning on about the highlights of Independence Hall.

"If you look over—" The guide lifted one arm to gesture, but stopped mid-motion. "Hey! What do you think you're doing?"

The tour guide stomped off the side of the screen. The camera swung to follow, blurring past a wide stretch of brown grass to a steel lattice structure attached to the corner of a glass and brick building. The nearest side was faced with a wall of windows, the lowest of which had been smashed.

The tour guide was running. "Stop. Stop. What are you— " He froze mid-stride, one fist raised in the air, and toppled onto his face as though he'd become one of the bronze castings he'd been describing.

A collective gasp came from the group my cameraman belonged to. The video jostled as people moved to get a closer look at the downed tour guide. Every hand held a camera.

"Did he have a stroke?" asked a girl's voice.

"I don't think so. He—"

"Come, children. Let me continue your education." A cold shiver twitched down my spine. I knew that voice, though I thought I'd forgotten it years ago. When the video lifted from the prone tour guide, it settled on a face I had, before yesterday, believed I'd never see again.

My father wasn't a tall man, nor was he notably broad, but his lithe frame held a coiled tension that reminded me of a hunting cat. His hair was dark brown and his skin pale but weathered. Unlike the blurry image from the airport, I could clearly make out the details of the man in front of the shattered glass wall. He was, without a doubt, my father.

"What's wrong?" James's fingers gripped my shoulder, strengthening the bond that let him feel my sudden emotional upheaval.

I shook my head, pushing my reaction down. "I need to see the rest."

The tour group gathered around my dad, just as he'd asked. Whether that was some spell he'd cast or just natural teenage curiosity I couldn't tell.

He stepped over the threshold of the window, his boots crunching thick cubes of tempered glass, and stopped in front of an old copper bell in a wooden frame. Two lines of words ringed its top. I'd never seen the historic Liberty Bell in person, but the crack splitting its surface was unmistakable.

Two uniformed guards ran toward my father from the interior of the building. But like the tour guide, they toppled before reaching him. He spared them barely a glance, then turned to address the gathered teens, waiting until every smartphone was centered on him.

"You do not know us," he said, and again his voice awakened memories I'd thought long forgotten. "We are shadows, ghosts, men erased from this world. You do not know us . . . but you should. For years, we have stood as your shield against the darkness. But no more. I warn you now, make what peace you can. For the darkness is coming."

Turning, he placed one hand against the side of the Liberty Bell. A dim ringing noise filtered over the audio, growing louder and louder. People at the edges of the video covered their ears. A few moved away.

"Liberty," he said, "in death."

The crack on the side of the bell climbed up the side, splitting wider. The audio feed was a solid, high-pitched ring. Then the entire bell, along with the yoke to which it was bolted, sheared in half and fell to the marble floor with a final, deafening *clang*.

A rush of wind erupted from my father's still extended hand, visible only by the dust and debris pushed in its wake. Then the image flipped end over end as the camera tumbled away. Screams burst and were silenced as the world spun. The ground rushed in, and the screen went black.

"Apparently the footage was taken during a school trip to Independence Hall," James said.

I backed the video up, paused it, and pointed to the frozen image of my father's face. "Do you know this man?"

"Not personally," he said. "I believe he was one of the sorcerers from the Faerie War, but I stayed as far away from that mess as I could."

I took a deep breath and let it out slowly. "He was. He's also . . . my father."

"Your . . . But you said he—"

"Died in the war." I nodded. "I thought he had. Yesterday, Sol told me Dad was leading this charge, but part of me believed he was making that up—saying what he thought he had to in order to manipulate me. Again." I wrapped my arms around my torso and squeezed. "But he wasn't lying this time."

James pulled me into a cocooning hug.

I stood there for a moment, my forehead against his shoulder, breathing in the scent of him. Then I stepped away. Much as I wanted to let him comfort me, I didn't have time to fall apart right now. "Sol wants me to train as a practitioner . . . a sorcerer." I shivered. "I'm not going to be able to sit this out."

The corners of his mouth turned down. "You have no obligation to Sol, or to your father. And certainly none to the PTF."

"But I do have an obligation to the world, and to the human race, even if I'm not strictly a part of it anymore. You saw that footage. Whatever my father is planning, he's only just begun. He's already killed who knows how many people in Italy. If I can stop him . . . I've got to try."

James pursed his lips. His consciousness trickled through our connection, testing my resolve, sharing his concern. He didn't bother stating his arguments. He could already see that my worries matched his own, but I wouldn't be swayed. "Then I'm coming with you."

I shook my head and gripped his arm. "I need you here, with Emma and the kids. I don't care what Victoria promised; they wouldn't be safe in the nest without you."

"Then I suggest you make other arrangements, because I'm coming with you. I've watched you walk into fire time and again, and it's shredded me every time. But this time, you're not going to another realm where I can't follow. If you want me to watch you walk away now, you'll have to kill me, because I'm not leaving your side."

"But you gave up so much to find the kids a safe place to recover. It will have been for nothing."

"From what I understand, Sol's compound is at least as hidden from the PTF as this nest, so the children will be as safe there as anywhere. As to what I've sacrificed."—he took a deep breath and set both his hands on my shoulders—"the loss of sunlight would be nothing compared to losing you. Please, don't ask me to risk that."

I stared into his pale-blue eyes and found a resolve equal to my own. If I asked him to stay behind this time, I would break our relationship beyond repair.

The fight leached out of me.

Part of me was happy James had won the argument. Despite the danger, and the complications his presence would add to an already difficult situation, I wanted him with me.

"You can't travel in daylight anymore," I said.

He smiled a sly smile. "I survived centuries before earning that trinket from Bael. I'll manage."

Chapter 12

I PAUSED IN FRONT of the curtains blocking one of the stone arches that led to Victoria's throne room. My skin itched at the memory of that place. A place where I'd been tortured, where I'd nearly died. For a moment, I wished I'd accompanied James and Hortense to treat the kids. Facing the horror of their addiction might have been easier than walking into that room alone. But despite James's confidence that I could imbue him to walk in sunlight, I couldn't leave without at least *trying* to get his necklace back. And James's skepticism notwithstanding, it couldn't hurt to test Victoria's interest in an alliance. Even one vampire nest could make all the difference in deterring Bael.

Crossing the threshold was like stepping into a sauna. The air beyond the curtain was thick and warm. It wrapped around me like a lover, and snaked inside me with every breath.

I steadied myself on the wall, suddenly lightheaded.

Bodies lay in tangled heaps around the long room. Not corpses, as I would have expected from the old master. These people writhed and wriggled not in pain, but pleasure. Victoria sat upon her throne in a gown of shimmering white that hugged her ample curves and covered just enough of her buttermilk skin to be enticing. A man knelt before her, buck naked and excited to be there.

Victoria leaned forward, long hair falling around her shoulders in an ebony cascade. Her crimson lips parted, revealing teeth too sharp to belong to any mortal. I wanted to recoil, but I couldn't tear my eyes away.

Her lips sealed over the man's neck. He gasped and moaned, the sounds of his pleasure mingling with those around me.

Victoria's gaze flicked up, meeting mine. Her eyes flashed like emeralds. Desire flooded me, warming my muscles, fogging my mind—infecting me like a contagion. I scratched at a persistent itch on my right arm.

One set of lithe fingers snaked around the man's back, kneading deep into his muscles. Victoria's other hand stretched out, open, to me.

I was three steps into the room before I realized I was moving.

Then the itch on my arm turned to a tingling burn as my tattoo's magic alert system kicked in. The fog in my mind lifted. I stopped. Victoria's call was potent, but nowhere near the crushing dominance of Shedraziel's command or the irresistible control James had over me when he invoked the power of my name. Compared to them, Victoria was a gnat buzzing in my ear.

At least, that's what I told myself as I turned away and sucked in a deep, ragged breath.

A thin leg the color of nutmeg bumped my ankle as a woman rolled into me. Her ribs rose and fell quickly, as though she couldn't quite catch her breath. Her eyes were unfocused. Another woman, this one with pale-blond hair streaked across her sweaty face, arched on the floor. Above the blond was a man with a wide, muscular back. Warmth swelled inside me as Victoria's magic continued to pound against me.

"Alex." Victoria's voice slid through the room like silk over bare skin.

The man who'd been kneeling in front of Victoria was lying on a fur rug just to the side of her throne. Sweat slicked his body. His eyes were glazed, staring at nothing. A stoner smile parted his lips.

Victoria followed my gaze. "My lieutenants and I were just having a nightcap before turning in for the day." She gestured around the room. "You're welcome to join us."

"No, thank you. I don't care for the flavor of captivity."

"Everyone here is a willing participant." She gestured to the man at her feet, content in his stupor. "And happy to be here."

"Would that still be true if not for the magic filling this room?"

Her smile stayed in place, but her gaze turned cold. She lifted one shoulder in a delicate shrug. "I'm only setting the mood."

"Well could you set it to something a little less 'brothel'? We need to talk."

She pursed her lips. For a moment I thought she would tell me to leave. Then she stood, the satin folds of her dress falling straight to drape her hips. Her dark hair flowed around her like a cape. Every face in the room, vampire and mortal alike, turned toward her. She was beautiful, perfect. The air grew warmer, and I once again felt the tug of desire. But I was on guard this time. The tingling sensation in my right arm increased as Victoria's magic swelled around me.

As one, the room's occupants let out a collective sigh of release and settled back on their cushions and carpets, eyes rolling up, bodies going slack.

I shivered.

Standing on the dais in front of her throne, power rolling off her, Victoria was every bit as scary as Merak had been on his mountain of bones.

The pressure in the room eased. My arm stopped tingling.

She stepped off the dais like a goddess descending from the heavens and made her way to an arch on the far side of the room. She parted the curtain, cast a brief glance over her shoulder, and passed through.

I hurried after.

She pushed open a heavy wooden door and led me into a room that smelled of sweat, sex, and a heady floral fragrance that made my nose itch.

"You don't approve of my feeding methods."

I kept my mouth closed. I was there to ask a favor, after all.

"Vampires need to eat, just like humans. I've made the process as . . . enjoyable as possible. I should think you, of all people, would appreciate that." She smiled. "James does."

My experiences with vampire feedings had been anything but enjoyable—both at the hands of Merak and when James had taken the energy he so desperately needed to keep us both safe. But James assured me that wasn't his normal modus operandi. Like Victoria, he preferred to keep his donors happy.

"The shadowed places of this world are shrinking around us," Victoria continued, a far-off look in her eyes. "In this age of forensic science and facial recognition, we can no longer cull a population under the guise of a plague and just move on. We must change our hunting strategies if we are to survive. A truth the more traditional among us are slow to embrace." She sighed. "But surely you didn't seek me out to debate the ethics of carnivorous feeding. What is it you want to discuss?"

"Plans have changed," I said. "James and I will be leaving your nest tonight, along with all the sick kids he brought."

"That was a short visit. Shorter than James implied when he begged sanctuary."

"Exactly. Which is why I'd like you to return the necklace he gave you."

She pulled her hair into a twist and turned her back to me, then peeked over her shoulder. "Would you mind?"

I glanced at the crisscross of ribbons lacing her dress closed and pursed my lips. She was clearly trying to push my buttons, make me feel inferior, but if playing the handmaid to Victoria's queen helped grease the wheels of her agreement. . . . I stepped forward and tugged the first silky tie loose.

The fabric strained under my fingers as Victoria filled her lungs. "The deal James and I made has already been struck. If he wishes to abandon the protection I offer, that is his choice. The payment remains the same."

"But that necklace paid for months of sanctuary—"

"Which I shall provide, regardless of whether you and your companions choose to take advantage of it."

I gritted my teeth and yanked viciously at the next two bows. The necklace was a temporary fix, but temporary was all I needed. Once the sorcerers were subdued, I could focus on creating a more permanent change in James. "What can I offer in its place?"

The final ribbon slipped free and the white satin fabric slid off her shoulders to a pale puddle around her ankles. She tossed her long, black hair over her shoulder to hang free, then crossed the room and opened a drawer in a dressing table with a mirror that threw her reflection back to me from three angles—proving once again that not all stories about vampires were based on fact.

She reached in the drawer and pulled out a long silver chain. A pale-yellow crystal in a silver setting that resembled an inverted sun swung from the bottom.

"This is no mere trinket you bargain for." She cradled the pendant in her free hand, gazing down at it as though she'd just unearthed a key that would unlock all the secrets of the universe. "You don't understand what a gift James had in being able to walk the surface during the day. The tactical advantage it gave him. Not to mention . . ." Tears formed in her eyes, shimmering for a moment before she blinked them away.

"I went outside yesterday." She met my gaze. "I felt the sun on my skin for the first time in centuries. You think I'll give that up just because you asked nicely?" She set the necklace back in the drawer. "James made a foolish bargain. Foolish and, it would seem, fruitless. He gave away a treasure like no other, blinded by his need to prove himself worthy of the trust you placed in him." She pushed the drawer closed with a solid *thunk*. "A pity you couldn't have known him at the height of his glory—powerful, beautiful—instead of this pale imitation groveling for the approval of a mortal in a desperate attempt to deny who he really is." She chuckled and shook her head. "As though diminishing himself now could change what he's done."

I bit my cheek to stop from blurting that *she* was the fool. That the necklace she'd so coveted would burn out soon—maybe even while she was wearing it—leaving her as vulnerable as ever.

Her comments about James bartering away his necklace for the sake of his promise to me stung, but the way Victoria talked about him—who he was and what he'd done—like she knew him so much better than I did, twisted like knives in my heart. She made it sound as though the James I knew was just a coat he wore, hiding the person beneath. Worse, was the nagging voice at the back of my mind telling me she was right.

"The necklace is not for sale." She leaned against the dressing table. "If there's nothing else . . ."

I sighed. Getting the necklace back had been a long shot. I'd just have to trust in James's confidence that he could make do without it.

"There is one other matter I'd like to discuss."

She raised an eyebrow.

"I have an opportunity for you—a partnership that would let vampires come out of the shadows, so to speak."

"I'm listening."

"The fae are coming, and with the sorcerers rebelling, the PTF won't have the magic to make them back down. Or to fight if it comes to war."

She laughed, a sound like Christmas bells. "You want us to make friends with the PTF? To be their magic shield now that their dogs have turned on them?"

I licked my lips and took a deep breath. "You said yourself, the shadowy places where vampires hide are shrinking. You have to change your strategy if you want to survive. And there's no love lost between vampires and fae."

Victoria pursed her lips. "Once the mortals know what we are, humans will pose just as much of a threat to vampires as the fae. Perhaps more since we're stuck here together."

"Not if you have a treaty. If you negotiate with the PTF and help them with their sorcerer problem—"

"It will take more than the promise of a bureaucrat to drag the vampires out of the shadows."

I glanced at the drawer where she'd tucked James's necklace and thought about the look of rapture on her face when she talked about walking in sunshine. "Like a magic necklace that protects you from sunlight?" I shifted my gaze back to her. "What if I could make more?"

Promising a new necklace was a long shot. The magic woven into that pendant was mindbogglingly complex. Chances were, I could try my whole life and never successfully make another functioning amulet. But maybe the possibility would be enough to spur the vampires into action.

She crossed her arms. "If you can make another, why beg to get this one back?"

"I'm not certain I can do it. To even try I'd need to study the original."

She frowned. "What you're asking isn't something any one vampire can decide. Not without serious repercussions. Such an alliance would require consent from the Council of Sin."

"What's that?"

"I see James still keeps *some* secrets." Her lips curled up. "All species have a hierarchy. The fae have their courts, the humans their governments, and the vampires . . . we have the council." She studied her nails, as though searching for imperfections in the polished enamel. "If you want the vampires, as a whole, on your side, they're the ones you'll need to convince."

"And here I thought 'master' was more than just a title."

She narrowed her gaze at me. "Make no mistake, masters wield great power. But even we yield to the will of the council. Well . . . most of us." She glanced toward the door. "Too bad your lover no longer craves power. Otherwise, he might be able to help your cause."

"James is doing everything he can."

"Is he?" She quirked an eyebrow.

I lifted my chin. "If the fae take control of the mortal realm, how long do you think it will be before they come after the vampires? Fae may think of humans as lesser beings, but they consider vampires vermin. Sooner or later, they'll exterminate you."

She stared at me for three pounding beats of my heart.

"Five day-walking pendants, and I'll arrange a meeting with the council."

"Five charms just for an introduction? That's ridiculous."

She shrugged.

I gritted my teeth. "Fine. But delivered *after* the meeting, and with the promise that your nest will back me against the fae no matter what. And I need the necklace you have as a template."

She pursed her lips. "I'll send a liaison with the necklace. Convince him you can deliver on your promise and I will stand with you against the fae, but I'll not partner with humans without the council's consent."

I wasn't sure I could make even one day-walking pendant, but if I could. . .Victoria's support might make Bael reconsider his plan. What did I have to lose?

"Deal."

"Good. Then it's time for me to turn in for the day." She moved to the middle of the bed and stretched like a cat in a patch of sun. "Care to join me?"

I let my gaze run over the full length of her body—her smooth, tight skin, her well-toned muscles—but all I felt was irritation. Without her magical intervention, the pull of my desire was a fading memory. She was still a beautiful woman, in the way an exotic spider was beautiful—best observed from a safe distance. But this was a spider I needed. As much as I might like to squish her, I had to play nice.

"James won't mind," she purred. "After all, we've spent centuries sharing our conquests—body and blood." The corners of her mouth curved up. "He taught me everything I know."

I turned away, too unsettled even to voice a rejection.

I FOUND JAMES and Emma standing like guards outside the children's sick room.

"How'd your chat with Victoria go?" James asked.

"Fine."

James narrowed his eyes. "Something happened."

"She was just being her usual creepy, slutty self." I crossed my arms, shutting the doors in my mind as best I could. I'd told James I was going to inform Victoria we were leaving. I didn't want him to know about my failed attempt to reclaim his necklace, or how much Victoria's comments had rattled me. "We'll have an extra body when we leave. Victoria and I made a provisional deal for support."

James frowned. "What kind of deal?"

I looked away with a small shrug. "If I can make more necklaces like yours, she stands with me against Bael. If not"—I shrugged again—"we're on our own."

Agitation rippled through our connection. "I wish you hadn't bargained with her on your own."

"It worked out. We've got nothing to lose and everything to gain."

He shook his head. "There is *always* something to lose."

Sighing, I gestured to the closed door. "How are the treatments going? Did you talk to Hortense about moving the kids?"

"She says they should be fine to travel," Emma chimed in when James remained silent. "They're much calmer today."

I nodded. "I have an errand to run before we go." My unanswered phone call to Maggie's house gnawed at me. I couldn't leave without seeing for myself that she and Charlie were okay. Besides, I owed her an apology . . . and a goodbye.

James, still frowning, said, "You can borrow one of the nest's cars."

"If you're going out," Emma said, "I've got an errand to run, too."

I raised an eyebrow.

She glanced at the closed door. "Mom and I might not be on the best of terms right now . . . but she deserves to know May's safe."

I patted Emma on the arm. 'Not the best of terms' was putting Emma's clash with her mother lightly. "We'll leave in twenty minutes."

Chapter 13

I SHIFTED MY FEET on the postage stamp porch in front of Maggie's narrow townhouse and studied the dry brown twigs in the planters lining the rail. They'd be full of blooms in the spring. Right now they were just lifeless shells, waiting for the world to be safe again. I stomped my feet on the welcome mat and glanced over my shoulder.

Emma was waiting behind the wheel of the Lincoln Continental James had borrowed for us. We'd agreed on the way to Boulder that she would drop me off and take the car to visit her mother so she'd have a quick escape should she need it. She was watching through the passenger side window to see if someone answered the door before driving off.

Taking a deep breath, I pressed my thumb to the doorbell and prayed the TARDIS-blue door would open.

The sun shone dimly behind the clouds that had rolled in with the afternoon. Maggie's street was quiet, but rather than feeling peaceful I got the impression of a storm building beneath the surface, waiting to break. The entire city of Boulder felt subdued—not a word normally associated with the boisterous college town.

There was a *creak* from inside, a moment of silence, then the door swung wide and Maggie tackled me like a linebacker, giving me a face full of stiff black curls. We slammed into the white rail, rattling the desiccated stalks.

"Ohmygodohmygodohmygod! Alex, are you okay? Where have you been? This bloody intense woman kept asking me questions about you. I didn't tell her anything, I swear. Then she just up and cut me loose." She paused for breath, stepping back to hold me at arm's length and look me up and down. Tears welled in her green eyes, but a wide smile stretched her lips. "I'm just so chuffed to see you." She glanced up and down the street, as though registering for the first time that we were standing outside. Her gaze settled on the Lincoln. "Is that Emma?"

"Yeah." I turned and waved, signaling Emma that all was well and she could get on with her own dramatic reunion.

"Well, invite her in. She—" Emma waved back and pulled away from the curb before Maggie could finish.

"She has somewhere she needs to be, but you can say hi when she picks me up."

She nodded and pulled me toward the open door. I let her, limp with relief that she was, despite everything, all right.

"Fancy a cuppa?" She headed for the kitchen, tugging me along without waiting for an answer. In Maggie's opinion, "no" was not an option for an offer of tea.

We passed through the living room, stepping past wood slats, tools, hardware, and part of a crib that was either halfway through being built or in the process of being destroyed. It was hard to tell which.

"Charlie's at the hardware store buying wood glue," Maggie said without slowing. "And maybe a pint. He's been trying to build that thing for hours. I think my mother bought us the most complicated crib she could find just to torment him."

The kitchen was more crowded than usual, with an ornate wooden highchair shoved in one corner and something that looked like a coffee maker but had the words *Baby Cook* printed on the front claiming a good portion of the limited counter space.

"More gifts from your mom?" I guessed, gesturing to the culinary appliance and the hand-carved flowers on the back of the high chair.

"You know her," she said, pulling a teapot out of a cabinet. "Never met a brand name she could resist."

I smiled and sat at the small, round table that took up half the tiny kitchen. "Yeah, your baby's gonna have Armani onesies and Gucci burp cloths."

Maggie's mom was a socialite back in London—a life Maggie had no interest in sharing. Maggie took more after her father, who spent his time gallivanting around the world on research digs to uncover the secrets of forgotten civilizations.

"Will she visit when the baby's born?" I asked.

"Who knows." She set a cup and saucer in front of me. "I guess it'll depend on how the delivery date fits into her calendar."

I nodded. "And your dad?" My voice cracked slightly on the word.

She smiled. "He's been sending me articles on birthing traditions from various cultures to 'help me prepare'." She dropped her voice and made quotation marks in the air. "Did you know that ancient Anglo-Saxons had pregnant women do a ritual dance over a dead man's grave before giving birth to ensure an easy delivery?"

I blinked. "No, I definitely did not know that."

"He's in Sudan right now, but he says he'll come once the baby's born." She grinned. Maggie saw her parents almost as rarely as I saw mine, which was impressive since hers were both alive.

"That's great," I said, but my voice came out tight and tinny.

She narrowed her eyes at me, finished setting the table, and sat down in one of the two remaining chairs. "What's wrong?" She wrinkled her nose, as though she didn't like the flavor of her words. "Other than everything. What *specifically* is bothering you right now?"

"*Other* than everything?" I traced my fingers over a copy of *What to Expect When You're Expecting* that was lying on the table. "Parents."

She frowned. "What do—"

"I'm home." Feet stomped in the entryway. A second later Maggie's husband, Charlie, stepped into the kitchen, proudly brandishing a bottle of wood glue. His freckled cheeks were stained a rosy red that matched the plaid of his lumberjack fleece. "And I got the . . ." His voice trailed off as he registered my presence.

"Hey, Charlie." I gave him a little finger wave.

The wood glue hit the floor. Before I knew it, I was on my feet, wrapped tight in Charlie's hug.

I gave him an awkward pat on the back and waited to be released.

"We thought they must have caught you." He stepped to arm's length. His eyes were bright with tears. "When Maggie was released, we assumed . . ."

"I'm fine." I set my hand on his arm. "Really. Harris and I came to . . . an arrangement. I'm not a fugitive anymore." I frowned, realizing that I wasn't sure what my status was with the PTF at the moment. I'd earned a reprieve while I was on my mission to recruit allies. Now that I'd failed, would I be wanted again?

"What's that face for?" Maggie asked.

I glanced at her, shook my head. "Long story."

"Then I'd better pour the tea."

Charlie finally released me. He pulled a third cup and saucer from the cabinet and wedged himself in at the table while Maggie brought over the teapot, cream, and sugar. The way his eyes followed her around the room made my chest ache. Charlie had lost weight since I'd seen him last. Nothing he couldn't afford to lose, but the folds of his skin hung loose off his frame. Shadows drooped under his eyes. Even the bright orange of his hair seemed somehow subdued. Maggie's incarceration had clearly taken a toll.

Maggie, for her part, seemed as chipper as ever as she bustled about the kitchen. But her hickory skin seemed oddly pale, and her hands shook enough to rattle the spoon in the sugar jar. When she resumed her seat, she scooted close enough to Charlie that their shoulders touched.

"I'm sorry." The words were out of my mouth before I realized. I cleared my throat. "It's my fault you—"

"Don't." Maggie lifted her chin and stared at me imperiously. "Don't you dare get all mopey and self-recriminating. What happened happened. No harm done."

I watched the way Charlie's pale fingers brushed Maggie's on the table, and bit my lip. Harm had been done. Nothing permanent. Not this time. But definite harm.

"I should go," I said. "I just came by to check you were all right since you didn't answer when I called this morning."

I pushed back from the table and started to rise, but Maggie's hand darted out to cover mine, pinning me to the table.

"If you want to make it up to me," Maggie continued, "talk to me. Tell me what's really bothering you, because I can tell something is." Her eyebrows puckered, creasing her forehead. "No more secrets."

I dropped back into my seat.

Maggie knew what I was, but it had taken her almost dying for me to finally come clean about my mixed heritage. I wouldn't make that mistake again. If there was one thing I'd learned over the past few months, it was that I was stronger with friends by my side than I could ever be alone. And with everything that was happening, and likely to happen in the near future, I couldn't afford to be weak.

So I told her the truth . . . about everything. I told her where my fae heritage came from and the truth about my "road trip"—the cover story I'd used for my first trip to the Court of Enchantment. I told her about my mistake and Kai's sacrifice. I told her about Emma's sister getting kidnapped and how it was my fault. I told her about Shedraziel and her demented circus of tortured children. I told her what I knew about my father, the sorcerers, and the fae who would follow in their wake.

Maggie and Charlie sat quietly through my explanation, only their eyes and the tension in their faces betraying their surprise, disbelief, and fear.

"So your dad," Maggie said in a hoarse whisper, "is alive?"

"And leading an army of angry sorcerers in a coup against the PTF."

"And your grandfather is the ruler of a fae realm."

"The Realm of Enchantment."

"Who intends to attack humanity once the sorcerers and PTF have softened each other up."

"That's the gist of it, yeah."

She sank back in her chair, a stunned look on her face.

Charlie slid his arm around her shoulders. Then he looked at me. "What are you going to do?"

"Whatever I can." I leaned forward so my elbows rested on the table and twisted my teacup around and around on its saucer, watching the liquid swirl. "At least some of what's happening is my fault. Especially Shedraziel. I had the chance to put her down, and I didn't. Then there's my dad. Maybe I can reach him, talk to him . . . or maybe I'll end up fighting him. Plus, I'm one of the only people who knows about Bael's plan and might actually be able to do something to stop it. I can't walk away from this. I can't stick my head in the sand and hope everything turns out okay, because it won't."

"What about the kids you rescued from that crazy fae?" Maggie asked. "Where are they going to be? Who's going to look after them?"

"James insists on coming with me, and the place where they are isn't safe if he's not around, so they're coming too. We'll find them a space in Sol's compound where they can recover, and Emma and Hortense can continue to take care of them."

Maggie studied the tea in her cup for a moment, then sat up a little straighter. "I'm coming too."

"What?" I said, at the same time Charlie jerked and asked, "What?"

He twisted to see his wife more clearly. "You want to go to an army camp?"

"I want to help look after those poor lost children until they get back to their families." She wrapped both arms around her own unborn child. "And I want to support Alex." She looked at me. "What you're doing is important. I don't want my child growing up in a world of persecution. You're going to make the world a better place, for all of us. I know it."

"Mags, your baby will be human. You don't have to worry about—"

"What if he wants to have fae friends? What if he wants to date a practitioner? You think being strictly human will protect him? Just because a person doesn't carry the labels of the persecuted doesn't mean they won't be affected by those labels." She took a deep breath. "The bookstore I spent my whole life working to open is closed indefinitely because it's not safe anymore. I had bricks thrown through my windows and threatening messages painted on my walls. I was arrested and held without trial just for employing paranaturals and being friends with a halfer." She shook her head. "People are turning on each other over the smallest hint of strangeness, magical or otherwise, and the agencies that are supposed to protect us aren't. This world is broken, Alex. It isn't safe for any of us, no matter what camp we stand in. So if you've got a plan for fixing it, no matter how bonkers, we're in."

"But you're . . ." I gestured to her swollen belly.

She rolled her eyes. "I'm pregnant, not an invalid."

I turned to Charlie. "And you're okay with this? Uprooting your life, walking away from your job, to follow a bunch of social pariahs on a crazy crusade to unite the warring factions of Earth?"

"Well, when you put it like that . . ." He laughed. Then his expression turned somber. "I was let go from my job shortly after Maggie was arrested. And my life"—he tightened his arm around Maggie and pulled her to his side, wrapping his other across her belly to complete the hug—"is wherever my family is."

Maggie smiled at her husband, then turned her gaze back to me. "I don't have magic, and I'm not good in a fight, but I can look after the kids, I can cook, and if you need research done I'm your girl." She reached across the table and gripped my forearm. "Let me do what I can do so you can focus on making the world safe . . . for all of us."

I looked between the two of them—the three of them, including their unborn child—and felt my resolve crumble. Charlie and Maggie had more invested in the future than anyone else I knew. Who was I to tell them how best to protect it?

"Support only," I said, lifting one finger for emphasis. "And if shit goes sideways, which it probably will—"

"We'll bugger out faster than you can blink."

I glanced at the clock on the microwave. "Emma should be back to pick me up any minute. If you're coming, you'd better get packed."

Chapter 14

WHEN I PUSHED through the front door to Morgan's apartment, Kai was on the couch, slurping down a bowl of chocolate ice cream in front of the TV. Morgan was perched in a window seat, staring through the glass. Both turned when I entered. Kai raised his spoon in greeting, then froze as Maggie and Charlie filed in with their luggage. Emma came in last and pulled the door closed. The apartment felt tiny with all of us crammed in the living room.

"What's going on?" Kai asked with chocolate-smeared lips. Thankfully, his glamour was already in place, so what our guests saw was a thin man in his early twenties with tousled sandy-brown hair, light-taupe skin, and russet-brown eyes. He sat cross-legged on the couch in a pair of baggy sweatpants and a loose T-shirt advertising a local brewery.

"Where'd you get those clothes?" I asked.

"Morgan made a run to a thrift store this morning." He set his unfinished ice cream on the coffee table and switched off the TV. "What's with the company?"

I rubbed the back of my neck. "You remember Maggie, from the bookstore?"

He nodded.

"This is her husband, Charlie."

Kai stood, unfolding his long legs like a spider. "But what are they doing *here*?"

I pulled out the phone James had given me. "Hang on. I'd rather not go through this more than once."

"Was Maggie safe?" James asked as soon as the call connected.

I looked at Maggie. "She's fine. If the kids are secure for the moment, I need you and Hortense at the apartment."

"We'll be right there."

I tucked the phone away.

Maggie shifted her weight. "Not to be a pest, but is there anything to nosh?"

I glanced at Morgan, who waved to the fridge and said, "Help yourself."

James and Hortense walked in while Maggie was raiding the fridge. His gaze swung from her to Charlie, who sat at the little dining table. "Margaret. Charles." He nodded to each in turn, then shifted his focus to me and dropped his voice to a whisper. "I thought you went to say goodbye."

"I did." I crossed my arms and stared at the frayed beige carpet between my boots. "But when I told them what was going on, they insisted on helping."

Morgan strode across the living room and said at a normal volume, "What exactly do you imagine a couple of humans can do?"

Maggie froze on her way to the table with a load of sandwich fixings. Charlie pushed back his seat and stood. I caught his gaze and shook my head.

"You underestimate them," I said. "Humans can be just as useful as fae, or practitioners, or anyone else."

"Maybe. But the mess you're caught up in is dangerous. If they're your friends, I'd think you'd want to protect them."

"I do." I met Maggie's emerald gaze. "But I made the mistake of trying to shield them once before. I won't be that stupid again. Maggie and Charlie—all the humans—deserve to know the truth about what's happening around them. The whole truth. Then they can decide what they want to do for themselves."

Kai quirked an eyebrow. "You planning to broadcast another confession?"

A strained chuckle built in my chest. "Maybe I should. But for now, I'll settle for letting the people around me make their own choices, just like I expect them to let me make mine, foolhardy though they may be."

I looked at James. "Any luck arranging transport for tonight?"

"With Victoria's help, I've secured a Gulfstream jet, along with two vans that will be waiting at our destination. Her liaison will meet us at the airfield." He looked around the room. "It'll be tight, but should suffice."

"We won't all be on the jet." I took a deep breath. "Some of us are going to break Luke out of PTF custody."

The room erupted in voices.

Kai shouted, "Are you insane?" at the same time Morgan whooped, "Finally, some action!"

Maggie and Charlie started babbling questions.

Hortense asserted that such an attempt was "beyond foolhardy."

Only James held his tongue, but I could feel him prodding my thoughts.

I laced my fingers with his and opened myself up, giving him access to my plan. If he was going to tell me I was being stupid, better it happen in the privacy of our link.

Reckless, dangerous . . . but not stupid. We'd lose days trying to locate the werewolves without Luke. He squeezed my hand. *I've got your back.*

Thank you. Out loud I said, "Even if Purity and the PTF can somehow overpower the rogue sorcerers, there's no way they can stand alone against the fae who'll be coming in their wake. It was a fairly even fight during the Faerie Wars, but that was *with* the sorcerers. Without magic, the humans don't stand a chance. But maybe, with the help of the local paranaturals, we can make a strong enough show of force to deter Bael."

Hortense stepped forward, her expression as sour as ever. "You say 'we' but you're not human. You could be royalty among the fae. Why side with the mortals?"

Her words twisted in my heart. "I'm not strictly fae either. 'Abomination.' That's what Shedraziel called me. A mix of magics that should never have existed."

"*She's* the abomination," Emma hissed.

I nodded. "But she's not wrong. I'm not human, or fae, or practitioner. I stand in the space between them." I hugged myself, trying to put my thoughts into words the others would understand. "I thought I could build a bridge . . . be the link that would connect the species and bring them together." I sighed and shook my head. "I'm still hoping for that, someday. But in the meantime, if the humans and fae aren't ready for a bridge to bring them together, I'll build a wall to keep them apart."

"A wall?" Maggie asked.

"The so-called peace we've had since the Faerie Wars wasn't really a peace so much as a temporary cease-fire," I said. "Both sides were biding their time, looking for an advantage. The sorcerer rebellion has unbalanced the human defenses—like a game of chess where one side only has pawns. We need to rebalance the board."

Kai pursed his lips. "You intend to fill in the missing manpower—or in this case magic power—with the werewolves?"

"Not just werewolves. Every paranatural local to the mortal realm." I looked at James. "All those who'll join anyway."

"Easier said than done," Kai countered. "You're talking about uniting people who hate each other."

"It's not the *people* who hate each other." I pointed at Maggie and Charlie. "Human." I swung my arm to indicate Hortense, Kai, and Morgan in turn. "Fae." I centered my finger on James. "Vampire." That made Maggie and Charlie jump, but I moved on to Emma. "Practitioner. The people standing in this room are proof that peace *is* possible. We just need to create an environment where everyone can actually see each other as *people*."

They all looked at each other, then back to me.

"So," Kai said, "how do you propose we add werewolves to this motley group?"

I turned to Maggie. "What do you remember about your time with the PTF?"

I DROPPED TO MY knees, sinking slightly into a layer of mud before hitting the frozen earth beneath, and sucked in great gasps of the cool, crisp air that had seemed absent from the shadowy world through which Morgan traveled. The ground was sloped. Not so much that I was in danger of sliding, but enough that I'd pitched forward when my foot made unexpected contact as I stepped out of the shadow of an enormous cottonwood.

James knelt next to me on one knee, his gaze fixed forward. On the other side of him, Kai slunk up the hill on his stomach and forearms. He'd changed back into his green and tan uniform, sword strapped at his side.

Morgan dropped down beside me. "This is as close as I can get until you're ready to make your move."

Shrugging off the backpack I'd brought with me, I tucked it into the dry branches of a bush at the base of the tree towering over us. With any luck, I wouldn't be the one wearing it when we left. I inched forward, copying Kai, and peeked above the lip of the narrow gully. We were crouched in a cluster of trees just north of a little town called Genoa. The dry creek bed we were using for cover was the only natural landmark on the wide, flat plains that swept out around us. I could imagine herds of buffalo and wild horses grazing this land before the humans came. Now, a prison complex dominated the landscape—a fae internment camp left over from the war. Supposedly they'd all been decommissioned after the peace treaty was signed, but it hadn't taken much to get it up and running again. According to Maggie, that's where we'd find Luke.

Above me, the star-studded Milky Way was a bright streak across the sky. Even the floodlights illuminating the compound weren't enough to erase it out here in the open.

I looked to the east. Somewhere in that sky, eleven sick kids were flying toward an uncertain sanctuary with their caretakers and Victoria's vampire liaison. The plan was to rendezvous just outside the waste in North Carolina once I freed Luke. Then we'd cross to Sol's secret base together. I dug my fingers into the cold soil. If I was caught here, they'd have nowhere to go at the other end of their flight.

I focused my attention ahead. A razor-topped chain-link fence cut across the field about one hundred meters away, its metal illuminated by floodlights along the perimeter. Beyond the fence, a squat, concrete building hunkered in the night, its dull-gray walls lit by another set of floodlights pointing in. Several outbuildings dotted the compound.

I pulled a folded sheet of paper out of my back pocket and smoothed it on the ground, comparing the building to the rough sketch Maggie had made. She hadn't been captive long, but long enough to get the lay of the land. "Mags said the fae and practitioners are kept in the east wing, while she and the other humans were on the west side." I turned to Morgan. Her amber gaze shone like a cat's in the night. "Now that we can see what we're up against, any chance you can get us in through the shadows?"

She shook her head. "Those walls are lined with iron. Even if I had enough strength to get in, I wouldn't make it out."

I frowned. "Maggie didn't mention iron in the walls."

"It's a fae internment camp. They're all built the same."

I blinked, struck by the realization that my companions had not only been alive during the previous war between fae and humans, they'd actually *lived* it. What had been news articles and classroom lectures for me was memory for them. Had Morgan spent time in a camp like this? Had Kai?

Setting that thought aside, I pointed to the side of the main entrance where a dark metal mesh covered one corner of the building. "That should be the backup generator." I glanced at Kai. "Can you take it out?"

"Not quickly if that mesh is iron, which I assume it is."

"So even if we cut power to the building, we'll only have the few seconds before the generator kicks in." I twisted to Morgan. "How many of those floodlights could you take out in that time?"

She pursed her lips. "Maybe a third? Enough that I'd be able to move around the area freely."

I checked the map again, then looked up to study the reality in front of me. I pointed to two small outbuildings near the back fence. "Is there enough darkness in the space between those sheds for you to shadow walk?"

She followed my finger to the indicated space. "Should be."

"According to Mags, there are guard stations at either end of the cell blocks." I tapped a spot on the drawing that we couldn't see from our current position. There were no external doors in that section . . . but I didn't need a door. "If I can alter the density of the wall in this back corner enough for us to pass through, we should enter directly into one of the guard rooms." I looked up again. "And that's not far from those sheds."

Kai snorted. "You think you can change the properties of the outer wall in the thirty or so seconds before the power turns back on?"

"No, but the darkness will give me a head start. And when the power comes back, the guards will have their hands full with you."

He raised an eyebrow. "A diversion?"

I nodded. "Morgan will get James and me in place between the sheds. Then you cut the main power." I pointed to the wires drooping between poles along the narrow road leading to the prison. "Morgan takes out as many lights as possible before the backup kicks on, and I go to work on the wall." I glanced at Morgan. "Is there a limit to the number of consecutive times you can use the shadow roads?"

"The only limit would be my stamina." She waved a hand. "But this is nothing."

"Good. Then you grab Kai and take him to the generator as soon as the lights come on. Even if you can't disable it, the attack should keep the guards distracted."

James nodded. "With the main power down, they won't risk losing their backup. And while the guards focus on the obvious threat, you and I can slip in the back."

"We'll subdue the cell block guards and get our key for these inner gates Maggie mentioned." I pointed to the dotted lines on the map. "And hopefully the cells."

"There will be security cameras," Kai said. "Even with the distraction, you won't go unnoticed for long."

A dull ache squeezed my heart. Dealing with security systems was the kind of operation my techno-wizard friend Oz had excelled at. I blinked away a sheen of tears. I couldn't afford to get distracted. I wouldn't fail anyone else the way I'd failed him.

"I'll take care of any opposition we meet inside," James said. He set a hand on my back, soothing my nerves and bolstering my confidence.

I refolded the paper and stuffed it in my pocket. "We don't know where we'll exit the prison or what condition Luke will be in, so keep close watch." I met Morgan's gaze. "As soon as we clear the building, get us out of there."

"Yeah, yeah." She waved a hand. "Taxi cab Morgan is on the job."

"Seriously," I said. "If we get caught, this adventure is over."

She smiled. "Don't you trust me?"

I gave her a flat stare. The truth was, I barely knew Morgan—just that she was a bored fae noble with a thirst for adventure. But who's to say she wouldn't find watching us wage a losing battle against the PTF guards just as entertaining as watching us fight rogue sorcerers? "We're putting our lives in your hands," I said. "Don't let us down."

Her smile froze, then faltered. She looked away. "I won't."

"And remember"—I glanced around the group—"no killing."

Chapter 15

THE SHADOWED space between the two outbuildings was barely wide enough to stand in without both my shoulders brushing the walls, and the floodlights that lit the rest of the compound couldn't penetrate the narrow gap. We slunk to the mouth of the alley, Morgan in front, James behind me. A line of small, mesh-covered windows was set high up on the nearest wall. The last window in the row—the one I hoped led to the guard station—was blocked with curtains.

I tapped James and pointed over Morgan's shoulder to indicate the back edge of the building and whispered, "We'll go in on the north side so we're out of sight of the generator."

James pressed close, his warmth a solid pressure at my back, to see the spot I'd selected.

Because of the harsh lights, I couldn't see anything beyond the perimeter of the compound, but somewhere out there Kai was getting in position to—

The lights cut out.

Morgan was gone before the darkness fully registered. James swept me off my feet an instant after. Wind rushed past, stinging my cheeks. My feet hit the ground and I reached out to steady myself. My palm connected with concrete.

The sound of breaking glass erupted from my right, followed by voices. Then more glass breaking as Morgan took out another light.

Focusing on the rough texture beneath my hands, I reached for the magic buried deep within me. To access it, I had to pass through layers of thought and emotion that encased my core like wrapping paper on a birthday present. My doubts. My fears. My hopes.

For years I'd tried to contain those emotions, relegating them to a dark corner of my psyche. But all magic had a cost, and for me that cost wasn't just the gnawing hunger and physical drain of burning too much energy. For me, the cost was facing those inconvenient truths I'd rather avoid.

Would Harris ever trust me after I went behind her back to spring Luke? Would

Luke be able to find Marc's werewolf pack before the PTF had their showdown with the rogue sorcerers? Would the werewolves be able to set aside their rage and fear long enough to negotiate with Harris and the PTF, or was I just creating more conflict by trying to force the groups into an alliance?

Those questions and a million more flitted through my mind like ash on a dry wind as my magic swelled inside me.

I poured my magic into the concrete, feeling the iron bars encased at its center to keep the fae weak and incapable of performing magic. I sifted through labels like stone and metal, diving deep into the core of the material. The wall was solid. Rigid. Impenetrable. I picked at the threads in the wall's core properties, nudging them toward a more flexible nature.

Smoke. Mist. A form without substance.

The wall gave a little under my hand. Not enough to pass through, but a step in the right direction.

Lights flashed on around me, blinding me, but their coverage wasn't total. Long shadows streaked the ground. The voices from before rose to shouts. Gunshots rang out. I cringed from the noise, but no bullets pierced my body, so I wasn't their target.

Pressing my hand more firmly against the wall, I concentrated on shifting its density.

Fog against my skin. The cold tingle of matter that parts around me and reforms in my wake.

The resistance beneath my palm disappeared. The new truth I'd written into the wall spread like a virus, infecting the surrounding area until a patch of wall large enough for a person to pass through was convinced it had no more substance than a cloud.

I withdrew my hand, breaking off the magic and ending the expansion. Sweat chilled my skin. I was breathing hard.

James flowed through the section of wall I'd altered in a black blur without needing to be told the work was done. He'd felt my triumph at the same moment I did.

I glanced at the corner of the building that blocked my view of the front of the compound, where the sounds of conflict were growing more intense. How long could Kai and Morgan hold out against guards trained to fight fae?

Shaking my head, I followed James through the breach. All I could do was find Luke as quickly as possible.

The scent of nature vanished, replaced by stale air and sweat. A desk sat in the middle of the guard station, topped with two monitors, a pile of paper, and a romance novel with a tattered cover and dog-eared pages. A chair was toppled behind the desk. Between the two pieces of furniture was a uniformed man lying on his side, limbs draped like a discarded doll. A trickle of blood leaked from the ridge above one closed eye.

On the far side of the room, tucked out of sight of the bars that would expose him to the hallway, James had his arm around the neck of a second guard. The shorter man's face was turning an unhealthy purple color as he groped for purchase on James's forearm. His feet flailed half an inch above the floor.

The man stopped struggling. His eyes closed. His arms fell slack at his sides.

James held him a moment longer, then lowered him gently to the ground and pulled a set of metal keys and a key card from loops on the guard's belt.

"I'll take care of the guards at the far end," he whispered. "You find Luke's cell."

He unlocked the cage door that led to the rest of the prison and flowed away. By the time I exited the first guard station, James was through the door of the second.

I jogged down the wide aisle, glancing side to side through prison bars. Men, women, even children were stirring on the narrow benches that passed as beds. Most were fae stripped of their glamour by the toxicity of the iron in the walls, too weak to keep up appearances. I raced past wings and scales, green skin and purple, sparing barely a glance before moving on.

I slowed at the cells that appeared to hold humans, but only long enough to know they weren't Luke. A blond woman with dark-brown eyes and a bandage on her cheek blinked back at me from one cell, perhaps believing me a dream. The next cell held a boy of about twelve who sat in the farthest corner with his back to the wall. I thought he was human until he looked at me with mirrored eyes.

Halfway down the hall and still no Luke. The inmates started getting restless, finally registering the sounds of conflict as possible freedom.

A nixie stepped up to a set of bars on my left. She was barely four feet tall. Patches of what looked like algae clung to her yellow-green skin, and hair like dark fern leaves hung to her knees. "Are you here to free us?"

I shook my head mutely, unable to voice the truth that I'd be leaving her behind. But I hadn't come to free the fae. Breaking Luke out was a risk, but a necessary one if I wanted to reach the werewolves in time to stand against Bael's army. Staging a full-blown prison break and freeing dozens of fae? The PTF would never forgive that, and I could kiss any hope for an alliance goodbye.

Three cells later, I drew up short when I saw a shock of familiar orangey-red hair.

"Targe," I said, stepping up to the bars even as my brain registered it was a bad idea.

The owner and operator of the fae bar Crossroads—as well as the uncle and guardian of a friend of mine—watched me approach. He seemed even larger than I remembered, but maybe that was because of the small space he was in. His wide chest was covered in rust-colored curls that stood in stark relief against his pale skin. His hands rested on his knees. The skin on his forearms was red and blistered, and around each wrist was a thick metal bracelet. It seemed iron walls alone weren't enough to subdue truly powerful fae.

He stared at me with eyes the color of cut grass, but didn't shift from his seat on the bed. A small frown creased his face. "What are you doing here?"

"I need to find a practitioner named Luke."

His gaze cut to the right. "Six cells down."

I glanced to the side. James was walking toward me, slow enough to be seen. His face swung side to side as he looked in each cell as he passed. The guard station behind him was quiet.

I turned back to Targe. "I'm sorry. I can't afford to—"

"Did Ava make it out?"

I'd last seen Targe during the PTF raid on Crossroads that inter-rupted Ava's wedding celebration. She and Jynx had been married less than five minutes when all hell broke loose and Targe had gone down with a tranquilizer in his arm. A lot of fae had been captured that day. I would have been too, if not for Ava.

"She opened a portal for us," I said. "She didn't want to leave you."

"She's safe?"

I nodded. "She's with Jynx in the Shifter Realm, planning a second wedding reception."

His mouth twitched up at the corners. "Good."

I glanced at James again; he was nearly to the cell Targe had indicated. I hadn't planned on freeing any fae. I also hadn't planned on running into any I knew, which was stupid. Of course Targe had ended up here when he was arrested. Targe's fate, and the fate of the other fae captured at Crossroads, just hadn't been a consideration for me. Now that I was face to face with him though. . . . Could I face Ava if I left her uncle in a PTF prison?

"Give me a minute to—"

"You should go," Targe rumbled in his deep bass. "Tell Ava to stay safe."

I bit my lip.

He narrowed his eyes at me. "Go."

Spinning away from Targe's cell, I raced past the next five and came to a stop in front of the sixth. Luke was on his feet, pacing a tiny circle. His sneakers made a soft squeak on every other step. He was dressed in a pale-gray jumpsuit and what looked like a metal collar. His dark skin made his expression hard to see in the dim light that shone through the high window, but his eyes were easy enough to focus on when they found mine through his thick-framed glasses.

"Alex!" He grabbed the bars between us. "What are you doing here?"

"Getting you out." I turned to shout for James, but he was already beside me, sliding a key into the lock. He pulled the door open and I stepped inside. "Come on, we need to—" I grunted as James shoved me roughly into Luke's arms, stepped in behind me, and pulled the cell door closed, trapping us all inside.

I spun on him. "What are you—" His hand closed over my mouth, sealing my words and drawing my attention to the agitation pouring through our link.

Guards have arrived from elsewhere in the compound.

We knew they would, I reminded him—reminded myself—fighting a wave of panic. Somewhere in the building was a control center with security monitors where our infiltration would have been plain as day.

"We're not getting out the way we came in," he whispered. "Not without killing anyone. I'll keep them distracted while you work on the wall." He tipped his chin toward the back of the cell, then removed his hand and focused on the hallway beyond the bars. A little way up the hall, half a dozen uniformed men and women surged through the security gate from an adjoining section of the prison, guns raised . . . and stumbled to a stop. They blinked and looked around as though they'd suddenly found themselves on the vast plains of an alien world—which probably wasn't far from the truth.

Trusting James's illusions to keep the guards off my back, I shoved past Luke and slammed my palms against the prison wall. My muscles ached, my energy was flagging, but adrenaline coursed through my veins.

"What are you doing?" Luke asked.

I didn't have time to explain—to tell him about my convoluted heritage or the rare magical gift I'd been granted. Blocking out his question and the doubt in his wide, worried eyes, I once again drew on my magic. My insecurities swelled as I tapped into that most central part of myself, becoming walls in their own right that I had to smash to dust and rubble before I could focus on the physical barrier before me.

Was I a fool? Maybe. But the future I wanted was not just a pipe dream. Even if my plans crumbled and my proposed alliance tore itself apart . . . I had to believe a world of tolerance was possible.

The warm tingle of my magic rose to my call.

I might fail to convince the werewolves or the PTF to join forces. I might fail to stop my father. I might fail to deter Bael's invasion. But those were obstacles for the future. I would *not* fail today.

My magic grew alongside my confidence, providing the "way" to my "will."

Wishing I had more the flash-bang variety of magic, I dredged up a memory of mist rising off a lake in wispy tendrils. We were well past subtlety, and all I really needed was to make a hole in the wall, but imbuing was what I had to work with, so I used my scalpel even though a sledgehammer would have done better.

Luke let out a startled yell and dropped to the floor, then his lips clenched together to strangle the sound. His body was rigid. His fingers clawed the cement beneath him. Thick tendons stood out on his neck.

James dropped to one knee and grabbed the metal collar around Luke's neck with both hands. He hissed when his skin made contact, but a grunt and snap later and the two halves of the collar hit the floor.

Luke went limp. He panted and shook worse than the kids in withdrawal.

I turned back to the wall and focused on turning the concrete as insubstantial as smoke. Not long ago, I'd stumbled through clouds of billowing black as fire climbed the walls and rafters of a burning church. I'd felt the particles against my skin, the sting in my lungs, but the smoke had no strength to hold me.

The wall started to give.

Footsteps. The guards were moving closer, but slowly, probably directed by someone in the control room whom James's illusions couldn't reach. Would they stop in front of our cell and open fire without being able to see what they were shooting at? Probably. These guards were trained for combat with fae, which meant not always being able to trust their senses.

I pictured the way my breath clouded as we crouched in the ditch just outside this compound—puffs of warm air visible in the night. I leaned forward until my nose brushed the barrier. Then I exhaled. My breath hit the wall and rolled back against my face, but I wove that breath into the core of the concrete and iron. My hands sank through the wall.

"Grab Luke," I said, and stepped through.

A dozen guards stood shoulder to shoulder about thirty yards to my left, blocking access to the steel mesh that housed the generator. Their guns were trained on the dark patches of unimpeded night created by the broken lights. Several officers were on the ground—I hoped only unconscious.

One of the guards spotted me. His dark eyes went wide. He swung his rifle in my direction.

Kai burst from the shadows. His silver blade arced. The gun barrel pointed at me was redirected skyward as the shot rang out. He spun and clipped the guard's knees with the back of his blade, toppling the soldier. Kai's leather boot made contact with the next guard's gut before the first man hit the ground.

"'Bout time," Morgan stood a breath away. Blood smeared her cheek and she was holding her arm like it hurt.

James stepped through the wall, Luke supported on one arm. Luke's feet scraped the ground as he shuffled forward.

Kai downed a third guard, but took a shot in the leg.

I slunk under Luke's other arm, taking his weight from James, and nodded to Kai. "Help him."

James blurred and was gone, a dark streak rushing toward the fight.

I grabbed Morgan's hand, tightened my grip on Luke, and said, "Get us out of here."

Morgan stepped into the shadow of the prison. I followed her into that darkness and a moment later tumbled to the embankment of the dry creek. The gunshots that had been deafening up close were pops in the distance. I turned and opened my mouth, but she was already stepping back into the shadow of the cottonwood.

Luke dropped to his knees, gasping.

"Deep breaths." I grabbed the backpack at the base of the tree and slid the straps over my arms. By the time the bag was in place, James, Kai, and Morgan were on the hill beside us. I pulled Luke to his feet.

"One more jump."

I ducked under one arm. James supported Luke from the other side. Kai sheathed his sword and took my hand, then grabbed Morgan's with his other. Together, the five of us left the echo of gunfire and the smell of burnt powder that drifted across the plains for the empty darkness of the shadow road.

LUKE STUMBLED as we exited the shadows. He dropped to his knees with a groan.

I released him and braced against the trunk of a dormant aspen tree, fighting my own dizziness. "The funky feeling will pass in a minute. It's a side effect of traveling the shadow roads." I glanced at our companions and added, "At least for mortals."

James nudged me and pushed something into my hand. A Snickers bar.

"Where'd you get this?"

"Stole it from Kai," he said. "Just be sure to eat a real meal once we reach Sol's base. You used a lot of energy back there."

I smiled, tore the wrapper, and passed half the bar to Luke before shoving the rest in my mouth. The candy bar tasted like heaven itself, and the shaking in my limbs subsided. "I needed that." I licked my fingers clean. "Could you guys give us a minute?"

James nodded and ushered the others a few steps away.

I slipped the backpack off and dropped it at Luke's feet. "Feeling better?"

He nodded. "Thank you." He glanced toward the others. "All of you. Really. That place was . . ." He rubbed his neck, as though still feeling the sting of the control collar James had torn off him.

I nodded and tried not to picture Targe in his cell, iron bangles burning his wrists. "Glad we could help."

Luke let his hand drop and fully met my gaze. "Grateful as I am to be out of there, this was clearly a targeted rescue. I'm guessing you're looking for more than a thank-you and my charming company."

I studied the bare branches of an aspen behind him. "Before the PTF started their crusade against all things paranatural, Marc invited me to join the pack at a . . . safe house. I refused at the time, but—"

"You've changed your mind."

"I never got the directions. I figured if anyone knows where his mountain retreat is, it's you."

He nodded. "Not the specifics, but I know the general area the pack will be in. It'll take me a day or two to find them."

I nodded to the backpack on the ground between us. "The supplies in there should last a week if you stretch them. There's also a burner phone. Never been used. Untraceable. There's a number programmed in it under my name that goes to another burner I'll keep with me. Have Marc call me as soon as you find him. We're running out of time."

He nodded. "I'm sure Marc will grant you and your friends sanctuary with the pack."

"That's not why I need to talk to him."

He frowned.

"How much do you know about what's been happening out here?"

"Not much, I'm afraid." He grimaced. "No TV in the prison cells."

"The Church's sorcerers have rebelled. They've killed the leaders of the Unified Church, along with most, if not all, of the paladins."

Luke rocked back on his heels as though he'd taken a blow.

"And that's not the worst of it," I said. "Even if the PTF or Purity manage to put down the rebellion, the damage is done. There's blood in the water and the fae are circling. No matter which side wins, the sorcerers will be decimated and the authorities left in disarray. The fae intend to strike while there's no one to protect the mortal realm."

The exposed whites of his eyes glowed in the pale starlight. "You're sure?"

"Heard it from the horse's mouth, so to speak."

He shook his head. "What's any of this got to do with the werewolves?"

"The only thing the fae respond to is power. Whatever happens with the sorcerers, we need a sufficient show of force remaining to make the fae think twice about invading. That's where Marc and his wolves come in."

"You think the werewolves will fight the fae for the sake of humanity?"

"I think some of the werewolves still think of themselves as human, but regardless, they'd be fighting for their own sake as well. If the fae succeed at invading this realm, it won't be long before they turn their attention to the various paranatural races here, and there's no love lost between the wolves and the fae."

"The werewolves may not be enough to deter a fae invasion."

"I know," I said. "But I have to start somewhere. And if the werewolves help the PTF subdue the rogue sorcerers, we may be able to show people the wisdom of an alliance." I looked up. The sliver of moon glowed like a scratch on the sky, nearly overwhelmed by its twinkling companions. "Even if the PTF refuses to cooperate, we've already got some practitioners on our team—people Sol hand-picked from his time with the PTF. He's training them to be sorcerers and paladins. Emma and I are going to fight too. And once you've delivered my message to Marc, I'm hoping you'll join us."

He stiffened. Luke was a healer—he'd spent his life proving to the PTF he was no threat despite his practitioner abilities—the idea of using his magic to fight probably sickened him. But we all had to do things we were uncomfortable with if we were going to survive what was coming.

"Practitioners, werewolves, and the PTF?" He braced his hands on his hips and shook his head. "That's quite the mix. Chances are it'll blow up in your face."

"I'd actually like to get the vampires onboard too, but since they're still keeping their secret . . ." I shrugged. "We'll see."

He laughed, a wild, strangled sound. "I don't know if you're crazy or brilliant, but you certainly do dream big."

"Anything less and I might as well give up. But with a little luck and a lot of help, I think we can forge an alliance that will ensure no one else ends up in a prison cell with a collar around their neck just for being different."

"Yeah." He tugged the front of his shirt as though it was suddenly choking him. "That's a goal I can get behind."

"Take care of yourself, Luke. And travel fast."

"You too. And thanks again." He hefted the backpack onto his shoulders and took a couple steps through the underbrush. Then he paused. "When you see Emma, remind her to set her filter well before casting magic, and sip, not gulp. She tends to get carried away." He tipped his face up. "Tell her I'll see her soon. In the meantime, take care of each other."

Chapter 16

THE SKIES ABOVE North Carolina were solid black when I stepped out of the shadows behind Morgan. James and Kai were right behind me. The sparse clouds that had decorated the stars back in Colorado were thick and heavy overhead, but even the lack of starlight couldn't entirely blot out the pale landscape of the waste from my fae-enhanced vision. The stark line where living plants and fertile soil met withered husks and dry sand was only a few feet away, and at the place where the asphalt ribbon crossed that border, two black vans waited. Their head-lights cast a warm glow over a small section of empty road.

As I stepped away from the trees and trotted down the hill on which we'd emerged, the side panel of one of the vans opened, revealing the sleeping forms of children snuggled together on rows of bench seats. Emma disentangled herself from her sister's grip and stepped out beside Maggie, who'd climbed from the passenger seat. They both raced to meet me by the side of the road.

I embraced one, then the other, and we all three laughed with relief that we'd made it back to one another.

"Did you find Luke?" Emma asked. "Where you able to free him?" She peeked around my shoulder as though hoping to find her mentor strolling down the hill behind me.

"He's on his way to Marc's pack. With any luck, we'll hear from him soon." I squeezed her shoulder. "In the meantime, he said to remind you to set your filters well, and sip, not gulp . . . whatever that means."

Splotches of red bloomed on Emma's cheeks.

James reached the base of the hill and stilled beside me. He was staring toward the vans.

I glanced in that direction as another figure stepped into the head-lights of the rear van. James's day-walking pendant glinted yellow around Bryce's neck.

My mouth went dry. "You?" My voice cracked. "Victoria sent *you* as her liaison?"

The curve of his lips as he enjoyed my reaction didn't match the dark look in his eye or the tension in his stance. Joining my merry band clearly hadn't been his preference either.

I glanced at James. *Did you know?*

The stiff set of his jaw as he glared at Bryce was answer enough.

"Considering our . . . rapport, Victoria thought my presence would encourage you to work quickly." Bryce spread his hands. "Until you produce what you promised, I'm going to be your shadow."

Charlie and Hortense emerged from the rear van while I struggled to get my emotions under control.

Bryce strolled over to the line where brown bark and pine needles turned to bleached bones and ash. "I've never seen a waste this close before. Good choice for a rendezvous though." He gave an exaggerated shiver. "No one gets near one of these that doesn't have to."

I took a deep, steadying breath. Sure, Bryce was one of my least favorite people in the whole world, but if keeping him close was what it took to convince the vampires to join us, he was a necessary evil. Repulsive though I found his presence, I could tolerate him for the sake of peace. "You're about to get a whole lot closer."

The scar across his face puckered as his eyes widened.

"Here's the deal." I turned to the rest of the group. "We have to cross this waste to reach the rebel camp."

Several voices piped up in distress, muddling their comments into a cacophony of concern.

I held up both hands, and the group quieted down.

Bryce planted his feet and puffed his chest. "I'm not crossing a waste."

"Scared?"

Childish though the taunt was, it made me feel stronger to know I'd done something that had a monster like Bryce shaking in his shoes.

"Self-preservation isn't the same as fear. Only an idiot would welcome death."

"You won't die." I rolled my eyes. "I'm not that lucky."

While I would have liked nothing better than to watch Bryce stumble around the waste and wither to nothing, I couldn't afford to lose my connection to Victoria.

"Anyone who wants to leave, should turn back now. I won't blame you." I glanced over my shoulder at the barren landscape. "Once we cross the waste, we'll be part of Sol's rebel army."

James took my hand. "I go where you go."

Kai nodded. "Me, too."

Hortense lifted her chin. "I shall remain with the children until my duty is complete."

Emma draped her arms over Maggie's and Charlie's shoulders, inserting her face between theirs. "We've got your back, Alex." She looked from side to side. "Right?"

Charlie nodded.

Maggie grinned. "Absobloodylootely."

Gratitude welled in my chest and clogged my throat. I'd spent my whole life running from commitments, pushing people away to save myself from the pain of abandonment—causing the very pain I sought to avoid. But these last few months had changed me. I wasn't running away anymore. I'd opened up to the people around me, and I hadn't been abandoned. I'd been embraced. There'd been loss, and heartache, but on the whole, we were stronger together. I just hoped we were strong enough for what was coming.

I looked at Bryce, who looked away. He wasn't there by choice, but he wouldn't be leaving any time soon. Not if he wanted to stay in Victoria's good graces.

I focused on Morgan. "It's about five miles through the waste. Can you shadow walk it?"

Morgan glanced at the alternately bleached and charred landscape, then at me. She tipped her head to one side. "What will you do if I say I'm out?"

I stiffened.

She laughed. "Relax, it was rhetorical. I intend to get much more excitement out of this arrangement before I leave."

I blew out a noisy sigh. "Careful what you wish for."

She continued to smile. "As long as there's magic on both ends, and I don't stop anywhere between, I can travel through the waste."

"With passengers?"

She nodded.

"Good. Then everyone with an ounce of magic will go with Morgan." I turned to the only human adults present. "Maggie, Charlie, we need someone to drive the vans with the kids. The waste won't affect you as bad as us, but it *will* make you feel sick, and . . ." I glanced at Maggie's swollen stomach. "I have no idea what it will do to an unborn baby. So if you'd rather, I can call David to drive and you can—"

"I'm not taking her through the shadows," Morgan interjected. "Those roads are no place for something so . . . malleable. No telling what the magic might do."

Hortense cleared her throat. "So long as there is no magic in the child, it should not be harmed by a short time in the waste."

I looked from Maggie to Charlie. "You'll have to drive fast on curvy roads, and keep your focus despite the discomfort. Can you do that?"

Charlie's skin was ghost-white, but he nodded. "Gotta pull my weight where I can."

Maggie gripped her husband's hand and gave me a weak smile. "We can do it."

I nodded. "The rest of us will meet up with you on the other side. Stop as soon as you're clear of the waste. We'll enter the camp together."

Maggie and Charlie embraced, climbed aboard, and set off with their precious cargo. I watched until the taillights of the two vans vanished from view, then borrowed James's phone and dialed the number Sol had given me. I didn't want his soldiers shooting us because we drove up unannounced.

"Alex?" Sol's gravelly voice came through the line, heavy with relief. "I'm glad you're back."

Guilt twisted through me. I hadn't intended to come back. But since I had, Sol didn't ever need to know how close I'd come to breaking my promise.

"But I'm afraid you're late," he continued. "The PTF has approved the deployment of Purity's super soldiers. We'll need to act fast if we want an invitation to the party. I'll send David to pick you up."

"I'm not at the reservation."

There was a crackle of static as Sol processed my words. "Where are you?"

"The southern border of the waste. I'll be at camp in twenty minutes, and I'm bringing guests."

"You were successful in recruiting the fae?" The hope in his voice stabbed my heart like shards of ice.

"I'll explain when I see you."

I SQUINTED THROUGH the windshield from the passenger seat of the lead van as it slowed and stopped. Four figures were illuminated in the headlights. David and Sol stood in the middle of the road. They each held a flashlight trained on the ground. Two guards, a man and a woman, both in black clothes and holding rifles, stood a dozen or so paces behind them.

Charlie glanced at me from the driver's seat. His knuckles were white on the wheel, and he was even paler than usual, but he'd insisted he was good to keep driving.

"Wait here." I unlatched my seat belt and opened the passenger door.

Behind me, the van's side panel slid open. James reached my side before I'd cleared the front of the van.

I shook my head, but didn't comment.

David's attention swung from me to James, and stuck. There was a moment when I could almost see the cogs whirling in his brain as he placed the gallery owner he'd done security for in Boulder into this new context. "James? What are you doing here?"

"Alex has recruited me. It seems she was in need of a friend."

Both David and Sol stiffened at the implication.

David shifted his focus back to me. "This isn't a weekend picnic, Alex. War is no place to bring your boyfriend."

It was James's turn to go still. "I fully understand and accept the risks of what lies ahead." His voice was low and dangerous. "I will remain at Alex's side, no matter what."

The two stared at each other for a moment before David looked away.

I laced my fingers with James's. "Don't worry about James, David. He can take care of himself."

"Does he know the whole story?" Sol asked.

"Everything," I confirmed.

He nodded and glanced at the vans behind me.

"Your mission was a success?"

I shook my head and gave Sol the Cliff Notes version of my failed negotiation.

When I finished, he looked troubled, but not surprised. "Tactically speaking, a reactionary fae invasion was always a possibility. The only unknown variable was the lord's disposition toward *you*. Given your claims, I'd hoped your being the one to make the offer would sway him, but I can't say I'm surprised by the outcome." He shook his head. "We'll continue with the original plan. You'll lead the practitioners we've gathered when we join forces with the PTF."

Lead? James's question came through on a wave of concern. *You didn't say anything about leading this charge.*

I told you Sol wanted my help in stopping my father.

Help, yes. But it sounds like Sol wants you to be the figurehead of his army.

While I shared his concerns, the idea that James was doubting my ability pissed me off. *What's wrong with me leading?*

Nothing, came his quick reply, *if that's what you want. But figureheads have a tendency to get cut down.*

A memory trickled through our link—blood-stained hands cradling the pale cheeks of a woman with staring, glassy eyes the the clear blue of a mountain lake. Streaks of crimson dyed her wheat-blond hair.

James slammed the door on that memory. *I don't doubt your ability. I just don't want to see you get hurt.*

"Given your failure to negotiate an alliance," Sol said, unaware of the conversation between James and me, "I take it these vans aren't full of reinforcements." He gestured to the vehicles. "Who's in them?"

"A dozen sick kids and their caregivers."

David blinked wide eyes. "Sick kids? Are you serious?"

"Dead serious. They need a safe place to stay." I pinned my gaze on Sol. "Somewhere the PTF can't find them."

"Are they fae?" he asked.

"No."

"Then what interest does the PTF have in them?"

"Right now, none, and I want to keep it that way. But they were kidnapped by a fae. That alone would be reason enough for the PTF to get involved, and if these children are taken into custody, they'll die."

"Who are these kids to you?"

"Strangers, mostly. One is the sister of a friend. That's how I got involved in the first place." I studied Sol's face. He'd been a general in the Faerie Wars, attached to the sorcerer troop. He'd been at the front lines, fighting the fae. "You wanted to know how I met Shedraziel? She took these kids. I rescued them, but she escaped her prison. She'll be leading the fae invasion force."

His jaw slacked. His shoulders slumped. "Then the peace truly is over."

"The current treaty is over," I corrected. "That doesn't mean there has to be another war."

He rolled his head side to side. "You're naive. If Shedraziel is out, she won't stop at anything short of slaughter. That woman is more demon than fae."

I pictured Shedraziel as she'd been the first time I met her—an exiled queen ruling over a court of blood and horror. Even now that she was free, madness danced in her eyes. I shuddered. "She's a problem for another day."

Sol sighed heavily and looked back at the vans. "A training camp is no place for children."

I squared my shoulders. "You want me? This is the package."

Sol glanced from me, to the vans, and finally to David. "Prepare a house for Alex's guests."

Chapter 17

THE WORLD WAS shaking. No. That was me shaking. *What?*

"Alex."

I gasped and jerked awake from the first decent sleep I'd had in I didn't know how long. At least, I thought I was awake. Cotton seemed to fill my head the way darkness filled the room. I groped for the hand that was bouncing me like a basketball.

"'M up," I slurred.

"Come on." David's voice emanated from the blurry form next to me. "There's something you need to see. Now," he added, yanking back my covers.

I shivered as the cold night slammed into me. I was still wearing the borrowed black T-shirt, but the cargo pants were on the floor. Goose-bumps erupted across my bare legs when the air hit them.

James sat up beside me, unabashed by his nakedness.

David's focus shifted. His gaze slid appreciatively over James's alabaster skin before he shook himself and recentered his attention on me. "Get a move on."

"Can't this wait till morning?" I mumbled.

"No." David grabbed my wrist and tugged until I was on my feet beside him.

Once my eyes adjusted to the dim light filtering in from a nightlight in the hallway, I could make out deep lines furrowing the skin at the corners of David's eyes, across his forehead, and around his mouth. He shifted his weight from foot to foot.

I rubbed my eyes, grabbed the discarded pants, and pulled them on. James slipped into his shirt and jeans as I slid my boots on without socks. As soon as my second heel hit the floor, David shoved a coat into my arms and pulled me out the door. We trotted down the creaky stairway of the building our group had claimed, past rooms of sleeping kids and caretakers, and out the front door before I was able to get my balance.

David jogged toward the communications room I'd been in

before—the room where I'd seen my father's face for the first time in decades and foolishly promised Harris a fae army to stop him. He pushed open the front door, and I was momentarily blinded by lights. I stopped on the threshold and blinked. The room was packed. The monitors and computer equipment lining the walls made the room feel small, but the number of bodies packed inside made it a sardine can. James pulled the door closed, and I experienced a momentary rush of claustrophobia.

Nicki, the communications operator, was sitting at a keyboard. She held one side of a pair of bulky headphones to her ear, presumably listening to the monitors' missing audio feed. Garrett sat beside her in his wheelchair, dark curls flattened on one side of his head from sleep. Sol was on her other side, staring at the screens. Behind them stood three men and two women in the black clothing that seemed standard issue for the troops.

Off to one side, as far from the other people as she could get, was a woman in faded blue jeans, a bright-yellow sweater with a stretched-out collar, and a black leather jacket. She was slouched against the wall, but I got the impression she'd barely come up to my shoulder standing straight. Her wavy brown hair had a single streak of white running through it—like Rogue from an X-Man comic.

Her dark gaze locked with mine for a moment, then drifted over my shoulder to James. Her eyes widened. She frowned and turned back to the monitors.

David pushed his way to Sol's side and beckoned me to join him. "Any change?"

Nicki shook her head. "Cops are evacuating the buildings near the barricades, but it's slow going. A few people in the center buildings tried to make a run for it. They didn't get far."

I wedged myself next to Sol. The monitors displayed several different angles of the same scene. A group of six individuals—four men, two women—stood in the middle of a wide, dimly lit street. They wore a hodgepodge collection of clothing, from a three-piece suit to a pair of overalls and a plaid button-up.

"Are those the sorcerers?" I asked. "I thought there'd be more."

"A good gambler doesn't show his hand until all the bets are in, and neither does a good general. They're probably traveling in small cells," Sol said.

Cars sat at odd angles along the street, as though the people had stepped into traffic, and drivers coming from both directions suddenly stomped their brakes or swerved.

At the edges of the traffic jam were rows of police vehicles. Most had their doors open with uniformed officers standing behind them, guns leveled. The group was caged on the remaining sides by buildings—what looked like three-story row houses crammed between skyscrapers of concrete and glass. Street lights cast a golden glow around the lower levels while many of the upper windows were lit from within and held silhouettes of faces. There were a few bodies in front of the buildings closest to the sorcerers. People who'd tried to run and died for their efforts.

I scanned the shadowy figures, but couldn't make out their faces. "Where is this?"

"Wilmington, Delaware. The police swarmed in as soon as Darius was identified," Sol said. "Local LEOs are holding position for now, hanging back so Purity can have first crack at these guys with their super soldiers." His lip curled.

"You still don't think they have a chance?"

"A chance? Sure. But using people with mismatched magic patched into them through pharmaceuticals is like sending in kids wielding aluminum foil armor and cardboard swords. Purity's hatred of magic has left them impotent. Darius is the real deal, and only real magic—strong magic—will be able to stop him."

I dug my fingers into the back of Nicki's chair. If only I'd thought of enlisting the local paranaturals sooner, rather than wasting my time on Bael, we might have had the werewolves onboard already. But we couldn't wait. We'd just have to hope Sol's half-trained sorcerers and superior numbers would be enough to sway the battle.

"We should get going," I said. "Fit however many you can in your plane. I'll meet you there with James and Kai."

Sol shook his head. "Even if I wanted to, there isn't time."

"Even if . . . What do you mean? Isn't this the battle you and your renegade practitioners have been training for?"

"This isn't going to be a battle," Sol said quietly. He gestured to the group on the screens. "Look at them. They're calm. Darius and his men are drawing Purity's soldiers out like pawns in chess, clearing the board for the big play that comes after. I'll not lead my troops to slaughter just because Purity is too blind to see their own shortcomings."

"So you're going to let the PTF and Purity troops fight alone? With *no* magic backup?"

"If I thought we could make a difference, I'd join them, but I won't throw my troops' lives away on a desperate gamble. If Darius keeps his current pace, we've still got time before he reaches D.C., and I intend to use every second of it."

A sudden, powerful downdraft fluttered the sorcerers' hair and clothing, signaling the arrival of a helicopter. Seconds later, a spotlight lit the group from above. One woman had an olive complexion and short black hair. The other was pale and blond. Of the men, one was Caucasian, one had dark skin with coppery highlights, and two were shades in between. The man in the center of the group had brown hair flattened to his scalp by the press of the helicopter's wind. He looked up. My heart stuttered. Three different angles of my father's face filled the screens as the media zoomed in on his features.

I set my hand over the silver locket beneath my shirt, pressing it against my sternum. I wanted to rip the locket open, compare the man on the screen to the picture from my youth, but I didn't need to. Even my faulty memory could recognize the truth now. Darius was Darren Carter. My father was leading the sorcerers.

"I should be there." The words were out of my mouth before my brain had a chance to process them. "Maybe I can talk him down before things turn bloody."

Sol shook his head. "Not a chance."

I turned to look at him. "He's my father."

"Exactly. You're too important. No way I'm risking you here."

The muscle under my right eye twitched. "That's not your call to make. If I can convince him to negotiate, maybe we can stop this fight before it starts."

"We're well past that." Sol set his hand against my shoulder and squeezed just hard enough to be uncomfortable. "I know it's hard to accept, especially since you just learned he's alive, but your father is gone. Perhaps it would be best if you keep thinking of your father as a casualty of the war—look at Darius as a different person."

"They're moving in." Nicki's words ended any further debate. "I'm turning on the audio from one of the news feeds."

"—as local law enforcement continues to evacuate buildings on the surrounding streets," said a man's voice. "For those of you just joining us, the Wilmington police are in a standoff with a group of terrorists suspected of yesterday's attack in Philadelphia, as well as the devastation of the Unified Church in Rome. A group of Purity operatives has just arrived on the scene, along with several dozen PTF officers in full riot gear—though what use anti-fae armor will be against practitioner magic is anyone's guess."

One of the zoomed-in frames showed my father's lips moving. The figures in the middle of the street raised their arms parallel to the ground. I unfocused my eyes, hoping to see what magic they were weaving, but the smoky tendrils that accompanied practitioner magic weren't visible through a camera lens.

There was a sound like thunder.

Several cameras panned sideways, blurring the scene. Others stayed fixed on the sorcerers.

One of the buildings near the police barricade twisted. Its steel frame bowed. Glass burst, showering the street below. There was a moment of silence as the building rested against its neighbor like an old man on one knee catching his breath for the next effort. The trickle of people exiting the compromised building became a flood. Officers shouted and waved for them to keep moving.

The supports buckled. The building shifted with a massive groan and tipped toward the street. Floor after floor shattered in a wave of glass, metal, and concrete that smashed against the ground, crushing those who couldn't get clear. A cloud of dust and debris billowed out from the impact like shrapnel from a mine, enveloping the fleeing people. A piece of metal skewered one woman's shoulder like a javelin. A chunk of what might have once been street flew out of the dust and slammed into a man's back, knocking him to the ground. The audio was saturated by screams. The image on one of the monitors—the one showing the closest shot of the falling building—swayed wildly, presumably as the camera operator ran. Then it went black and switched to the colored bars that signified a loss of signal.

The camera angles still focused on the sorcerers showed they hadn't moved except to lower their arms. Dust from the collapsed building billowed through the street, but stopped short of enveloping the sorcerers as though it hit a wall.

I clenched my jaw and glared at the man in the center of the group. I could understand wanting freedom, resenting a lifetime of being used as a tool for the Church. But to bring down a building of innocents?

There was movement on the roof of one of the shorter buildings next to the sorcerers. I squinted. A man crouched at the edge of the flat roof. Then he jumped.

I gasped. My hand flew up to cover my mouth as I watched the man's suicide. Except he didn't go splat when he hit the ground. He landed beside one of the sorcerers, and it was the street that buckled.

The man raised his fist as he straightened and caught his targeted sorcerer, a Middle Eastern looking man, under the jaw. The sorcerer toppled backward.

The black-haired woman dodged her falling companion and kicked out at the man from the roof, who grabbed her leg and, with a spin, sent her sailing into the facade of the building he'd jumped from.

A man built like a bodybuilder with broad shoulders, a thick neck, and a blond ponytail, stepped past the police barricade on the side of the street not affected by the downed building. He grabbed the front bumper of one of the parked cars. The little blue Civic had its doors open. Whoever had been inside must have run. I hoped they'd made it. More likely they were on the ground somewhere, laid out like the poor souls on the sidewalk. Muscles bulged in the man's arms. Tendons stood out on his neck. He jerked, and the car flipped into the air.

The sorcerers scattered like cockroaches to avoid the incoming automobile.

Three more men ran onto the field, dodging cars so fast I had trouble tracking them. They closed the distance to the sorcerers at close to vampire speed.

The blond woman thrust her hands toward the charging soldiers. The air rippled like heat waves over asphalt in August, and the front runner was thrown off his feet. A sorcerer with tan skin and a dark goatee that made him look like Dr. Strange charged the remaining two.

Each monitor showed a different scene of the chaos, and my attention swung from screen to screen as I tried to process what was happening. The audio was useless—saturated by shouts, sirens, settling debris, and the thrum of helicopter blades.

I scanned the screens, searching for more newcomers, but there was no one else. "Five?" I asked. "That's it? That's all Purity has to show for their experiments?"

Sol shook his head. "Purity didn't know where the sorcerers would be spotted. Most likely, small groups were stationed in all the likely cities so they could respond quickly."

Two cameras tracked the jumper who'd dropped from the roof. After laying out the Middle Eastern man, sending the woman flying, and avoiding friendly fire from the Civic, he'd closed with Darius. The man's hands and feet were a flurry of attacks, but my father blocked every one. He did not, however, get a chance to strike back.

One of the remaining cameras zoomed in on the dented wall where the dark-haired woman had been thrown. She was standing up, brushing herself off. She looked at the man who'd tossed her aside, but seeing he was engaged with Darius, she turned instead toward the man who'd thrown the Civic. She squared off against the gorilla of a man and raised her fists. The man hesitated, perhaps caught off guard by his petite opponent. Then he howled like a berserker and charged the tiny woman.

She sidestepped his attack and brought both hands down in a double fist on his back. Her hands never made contact, but the charging man dropped as though a sledgehammer had come down on him. If I'd been there in person, I was sure I'd have seen a glow of magic around her fists.

The car-throwing man turned as he fell and punched the woman's forward leg—the one holding most of her weight. His fist connected with her knee. I winced as the joint bent sideways. The man followed up with a kick to the woman's ribs. The angle and timing were off, but the force of the hit was enough to knock the woman off her already unsteady feet.

A series of gunshots rang out. PTF snipers had taken up positions on the roof where the jumper had come from and were giving the Purity soldiers cover fire. But none of the bullets made contact. Bursts of light erupted about ten feet above the street.

I scanned the screens and found the blond woman had her palms stretched toward the sky. She stood with her knees bent, her limbs shaking as though she was supporting something immensely heavy. She must have erected some sort of barrier to stop the bullets, but the limitations of technology meant I couldn't see the magic she wielded.

Closer to the camera, the goatee guy was dodging hits from a Purity soldier who bounced around him like a ping-pong ball. The sorcerer swung his arms as though throwing invisible knives. Tears appeared in the soldier's clothes, quickly turning dark with blood. Then the sorcerer slipped on a piece of debris and took a hit to the chest that sent him spinning into the windshield of a nearby pickup truck.

As the sorcerers were drawn into battle, the people still alive in their cars took the chance to get clear of the war zone. First one or two. Then, when they weren't struck down, more slunk from their cars and raced for the police line. The police from the barricade moved in, using the cover of the abandoned cars, calling to the civilians, tightening the noose around the sorcerers.

Despite hating where Purity's soldiers got their super strength and speed—namely the distilled magic of kidnapped fae—I had to admit they seemed to be holding their own against the sorcerers. "They might actually win this."

Sol shook his head, eyes fixed on the screen where Darius continued to counter the attacks of the man from the roof. "The sorcerers aren't using their full potential." He leaned closer, squinting at the monitor. "What are you up to?"

I rolled my eyes. I'd always known Sol was cautious, but perhaps I should change that to "paranoid."

The Middle Eastern man who'd taken the first hit and the sorcerer with skin the color of asphalt and a dark fauxhawk flanked the remaining Purity runner—a tall, thin man in a button-up shirt and a cowboy hat who pulled a pair of metal whips off his belt. One whip arced toward the darker man, causing him to stumble back.

The Middle Eastern man darted in. The second whip looped around to encircle his neck, cutting into his flesh. He managed to pull the cord off, but was tackled from behind by the soldier who'd been knocked aside by the blond woman on the initial approach.

The Purity soldier rode the sorcerer to the ground and brought his fist down on the choking man's face, sandwiching it against the pavement.

The whip-wielding cowboy spun back toward his second opponent, but Mr. Fauxhawk snatched the tip of the whip out of the air. Blood ran down his arm. He smiled.

The cowboy tugged, but couldn't get the whip back. He lashed out with his remaining weapon, slicing a bloody line across the sorcerer's arm.

Fire erupted around the sorcerer's fist. It raced up the whip and engulfed the cowboy.

The soldier's mouth opened wide, but the audio we were getting was from a different source, too far away to isolate his scream. He dropped the burning whip, but the fire continued to spread. The cowboy dropped to the ground, rolling over and over. When he stopped, his skin was black.

I gagged, imagining the smell of charred flesh—a scent I was far too familiar with.

The cowboy's companion continued to pound the tackled sorcerer with bloody fists. Then the ground bucked and both men popped into the air like popcorn. The Middle Eastern man came down on his side. A large section of his face had been crushed, leaving his skull concave on one side. His mouth was open, revealing a bloody mess of missing teeth.

His eyes were closed. He didn't move.

One down.

The soldier landed on his stomach, but instead of a hard stop when he connected with the ground, the asphalt parted around him like corn syrup. He flailed, groping for solid ground, but continued to sink. His head vanished beneath the street. The surface of the road rippled, then stilled.

The man who'd taken out the cowboy looked down at the smoldering corpse, the sinkhole, and his fallen comrade. He seemed calm. He wasn't even breathing heavily. He took a step toward the advancing police. Then he stumbled, slapped a hand over the side of his neck, and looked up. Blood oozed between his fingers. A second wound appeared in his thigh, and he went down to one knee.

I scanned the screens.

The blond woman was down.

The goatee-sorcerer rolled off the pickup truck's dented hood and tackled the Purity soldier standing over the fallen blond, but the damage was done. The force field, or whatever she'd created to block the bullets, was gone—Purity's human backup was no longer impotent.

Bullets rained down, tearing flesh and sending chunks of asphalt flying from the street.

Mr. Fauxhawk raised a hand toward the roof with the snipers, fingers outstretched. A bullet ripped a hole in his shoulder. Then he closed his fist. Fire erupted along the roof—a tiny supernova that caused a whiteout of the camera feed. When the glow faded, the roof was in flames. Several of the snipers had fallen to the street below, blackened and unmoving. The rest were just gone.

The car-flipping strongman looked up at the conflagration, and in that moment the dark-haired woman he'd knocked flat swung her fist. She was too far away to make contact, but blue lightning lanced from her hand like bolts in an Arizona storm. The Purity soldier reeled back and collapsed to the ground, twitching. Smoke curled off his body.

The woman climbed to her feet, one leg still bent at a wonky angle. She turned toward the open end of the street where the police had closed in to provide cover for the people fleeing their cars. She nodded to the man who'd ignited the sniper nest. He swung his arm toward the advancing police. This time the fire didn't hit the men directly. A wall of flame swept across the street, blocking the only escape and trapping both the cops who'd moved closer and the civilians who'd been too slow to clear the battleground.

The dark-haired woman tugged her injured leg straight, forcing her bones back into alignment, and limped toward the caged-in people. As she passed the Middle Eastern man whose face had been crushed, she reached out.

The sorcerer I'd thought was dead clasped her wrist and stood up. He opened his eyes. The collapsed ridge of his left socket was no longer malformed. Olive-colored skin sealed over a section of exposed bone and shiny sinew in his cheek. He spat a gob of bloody mucus and grimaced, showing a full set of teeth.

My gaze flicked toward the back of the room, where James stood by the door. I'd only ever seen one thing heal that fast.

"If there was ever any doubt," Sol said, "there isn't now. They're rifters. And not just Darius. All of them."

I shivered. Rifters—sorcerers possessed by demons. I stared at the figures on the screens and bit my lip, remembering the feel of demons inside me as I struggled to control my magic—the sensation of them hooking their barbs into my flesh, searching for places to hang on. Was that how I'd end up if I kept drawing on my practitioner magic?

The limping woman and the man with the new face stopped beside their companion, who seemed to have recovered from his bullet wounds. The woman raised one hand to the sky. Blue lightning danced on her fingertips. The light arced to the nearest parked car, then the next, and the next. Then it jumped to a cop using the car for cover. Then it skipped to a woman in a business suit who'd been cowering near the back wheel. Then another cop. On and on, until every human between the wall of fire and the fallen building was on the ground, twitching and smoking like the Purity man. Two more camera feeds went dark, fried by the lightning.

"You were right," I whispered. "They never stood a chance against these guys."

No one does. I pushed the thought away. If I let myself believe that, everything I'd fought for was already lost.

The man with the goatee was still grappling with the Purity soldier who took out the blond. He kicked the soldier in the gut, opening a space between them, and extended his arm, fingers splayed. The soldier flew back and slammed into the side of the overturned Civic, but he didn't fall. Blood seeped from several points in the man's torso. He groped at something above the first wound, wrapping his hands around an invisible shaft that pinned him to the car.

The man who'd started this battle by jumping from the roof was the last super soldier standing. He continued to hammer away at my father, sweat pouring from him, fatigue clear in every punch, every kick. He still hadn't landed a blow.

My father didn't block the next punch that came in. He stepped to the side and grabbed the man's wrist. Then he brought his free hand up and slid a knife across the younger man's throat. A line of crimson appeared on the pale skin.

The man stumbled back, both hands closing around his neck, trying to hold in the precious liquid draining from him. He dropped to his knees, then flopped to his back.

Purity's soldiers were down. The police were down. The PTF snipers were down. Dizzy sparks danced in my vision. I was having trouble breathing. The fight had only lasted a couple of minutes.

Darius raised his hands. The other sorcerers—rifters—turned to face him, but didn't otherwise move. He stood like a statue, arms stretched to the heavens as dust continued to billow around his ankles from the fallen building. Fires crackled on the roof and at one end of the street.

He dropped his arms to his sides.

Silence filled the communications room as we all studied the monitors, searching for some indication of what he'd done.

Then the man with the sliced throat sat up, a dazed expression on his face. He looked up at Darius. Blood still streaked his neck, but the gash was gone. He pushed to his feet.

"Oh my God," Sol whispered.

The man with the goatee gestured, and the soldier pinned to the Civic slumped to the ground. Then he stood, rubbing his chest where the invisible spikes had impaled him. He too wore a dazed expression.

One by one, the people on the battlefield stood up. Not just the Purity soldiers, but the police, even the civilians. They all stood up, looked around, and waited.

My father didn't look at any of the cameras. He didn't make a speech. He just walked to the end of the street with the burning cop cars. As he passed, the people on the battlefield fell into step behind him. The flames blocking the street flickered and faded as he approached. Then he stepped past them and walked into the dark night beyond, his resurrected army following.

Chapter 18

SOL TAPPED A button on the keyboard. The screens went blank.

I couldn't tear my gaze away from the empty monitors that now reflected my own shocked expression. I couldn't process what I'd seen . . . what it meant. "If they were that powerful, why drag out the fight? Why not just kill the police when they first hemmed them in and be done with it?"

"Darius wanted the Purity soldiers, wanted to see what they could do."

"You think he got cornered on purpose?"

"I think that situation played out *exactly* the way Darius intended." Sol patted me on the back, then turned to address the people gathered behind us. "He's not just a rifter. Darius is a necromancer. Which means every battle he wins, every person he kills, makes him that much stronger." He looked at Nicki. "It also means we need to account for every body missing from that mess in Rome."

I hugged myself. My limbs felt weak, my torso hollowed out. How could we stop someone who could raise the dead? I looked at the ceiling, vaguely aware of the shuffle of feet behind me as the other watchers exited the room.

The first vampire was born from a necromancer father, and all the later vampires shared a piece of that original demon-tainted soul. That's how they healed so fast, and why they had to drain the life from others to survive. Did being a necromancer mean my father was basically a vampire now? Was he absorbing the lives of innocents to keep himself strong?

I turned and found James staring at me. Our link was muted, but the steady reassurance that I was not alone let me breathe a little easier. I crossed the room in three long strides and stepped into his open arms, relishing the illusion of safety as he wrapped me up and squeezed me tight.

Sol expects me to stop him. I buried my face against James's chest. *Even if Marc brings the werewolves . . . Even if the PTF sends every agent they have . . .*

Even if Sol's practitioners can hold off the rest of the rifters . . . He expects me *to deal with my father.*

An image flashed through my mind of James writhing on the ground as he and his demon nearly tore their shared body apart when I disrupted their delicate balance. Would that same type of disruption, done on purpose, work against a necromancer? But it wasn't just the thought of *fighting* my father that made my heart race. Demon-possessed megalomaniac or no, now that I knew he was alive, I was filled with a gnawing desire to speak to him—to say all the things I'd been too young to say when he left.

The door closed behind David as he followed the other watchers out of the communications room, deep in conversation with Sol. Nicki and Garrett remained, talking in low tones. The woman I'd noticed earlier was still slouched in the corner with her arms crossed.

James glanced at her. *Who is she?*

Let's find out. I gave him one more hug, then stepped back, breaking the circle of his arms. Together, we approached the mystery woman, who regarded us with narrowed eyes.

"Hi." I offered my hand. "I'm Alex."

She looked at my hand, but didn't extend her own. "Mira." She tipped her chin toward the blank screens. "You're the necromancer's kid?"

My blood froze, then started racing.

You're crushing my fingers. James's voice in my head snapped me back to the present. I forced my hand to relax.

Someone cleared their throat behind me. We all turned to look. Garrett rolled up beside us. "My apologies, Alex. I told Mira about you to help explain our situation." He gestured to Mira, who still hadn't uncrossed her arms. "I asked her here to share her expertise."

I frowned at the young woman. She was short and muscular, but with some definite curves. Her smooth skin was a warm beige—the kind that tanned rather than burned in the sun. This close, I could see that her eyes were slightly different shades of brown. Her right eye was milk chocolate, while her left was closer to the color of thick honey. "What exactly are you an expert in?"

"Demons." She shifted her gaze to James. "And those possessed by them."

This time it was James who squeezed a little too tight, making my fingers go numb.

"She's agreed to help train the practitioners," Garrett said into the silence that followed Mira's pronouncement. "And specifically, you."

I reluctantly shifted my gaze away from the woman who suddenly felt like a threat. "I thought *you* were going to teach me to use practitioner magic."

"I, and the other practitioners here, can give you basic training. But if you're going to defeat Darius in our limited time frame, you'll need more than just the basics." He gestured to Mira. "That's where she comes in."

I turned back to Mira. She couldn't have been older than twenty-five, but there was a weight in her mismatched eyes that spoke of horrors witnessed . . . or committed. "You're a practitioner?"

She shrugged. "Meet me in the field behind the old church just south of here at dawn. We'll see if you stand a chance against that." She finally uncrossed her arms to indicate the blank screens. Then she pushed off the wall.

James and I backed up a pace to give her room to pass.

She kept her gaze on James until she reached the door, then shifted her attention back to me. "Come alone. And don't be late." She yanked the door open, stepped into the wind that rushed in, and pulled it shut behind her without waiting for a response.

"Charming," I muttered.

Garrett laughed. "She grows on you."

PALE STREAKS OF peach blossomed on the eastern horizon as I stepped onto the porch of the house where I was staying. I took a deep breath of the lingering night air until the cold ache in my chest was too much to hold, then blew it all out in a noisy sigh. I took a bite of the bagel I'd snagged from the dark kitchen on my way out. The camp was still asleep, all its soldiers tucked in their beds.

I glanced at the window blocked with cardboard and duct tape where James would be spending his day. He'd been crawling out of his skin to join me, but until we either changed his nature or made a new necklace. . . . Meanwhile, Bryce would be free to wander the compound, safe with James's pendant around his neck.

I took another bite of my bagel, but the bread turned gummy.

I had to believe it was possible to change James despite Bael's insistence that it was impossible to imbue living things. I'd changed myself after all—twisted that piece of vampire James used to bring me back to life so it was unrecognizable to fae wards. My first attempt to change James failed due to lack of experience, pure and simple. Once I had a better handle on my magic it would work. It had to.

Turning south, I crunched along the frozen gravel by the side of the road. Shaggy pines dotted the landscape, but most of the trees were bare, their bark coated with frost. My breath puffed out in little white clouds. My fingers went numb in their gloves. January was almost done and February fast approaching. Hopefully, that meant this seemingly endless winter was almost over.

I passed more abandoned buildings. Most of the houses near the center of Sol's camp had been claimed and turned into bunk houses, though a few had been renovated for other purposes like the communications room. The farther I got from that command center, the more deserted the town felt. The houses were spaced far apart, each sitting on at least an acre of land, and the farther south I walked, the fewer houses there seemed to be. The road split, and I followed the more southern path, winding through a forest of naked trees until I came to a little white building with a small field behind it. There was a blank LED sign near the road that probably used to display the name of the building, but all I had to go on was the golden cross above the door.

Stuffing the remaining bite of bagel in my mouth, I scooted around the outside of the church. In the field around back, I found a dented, white, U-Haul-style truck, a grumbling generator, and a black and silver motorcycle. No Mira.

I continued around until I was back in front of the main entrance. I looked up at the golden cross.

Abomination.

I'd been called that by humans, fae, even a manifestation of my own memories. When the fae first came out of hiding, the Unified Church declared all magic demonic in origin, but even they couldn't condone all-out genocide without proof. So they'd allowed certain practitioners to exist—those they trained as sorcerers and kept under lock and key, and a handful of pacifist practitioners, registered and carefully watched for signs of aberrant behavior or development of advanced magic— tagged animals released into the wild for observation and analysis, with the understanding that if they stepped out of line, they'd be put down. It was no wonder the sorcerers at the center of that system rebelled, or that Sol managed to recruit so many discontents. If Purity managed to take the reins of the broken Church, they'd make the previous rules regulating magic look lenient. Given that kind of authority, they'd hunt down every magic user on the planet.

My palms started to itch as I pulled open the heavy wooden door.

Churches made me uncomfortable long before I discovered I had magic. Before Dad died and Mom stopped attending. Ever since Mrs. Henderson made me stand in a corner when I was six years old because I asked too many questions in Sunday school. Apparently, "Because the Bible says so," was supposed to be answer enough.

I sighed and stepped over the threshold. I was a grown woman now. Old enough to realize mean old Mrs. Henderson was just trying to cover up her own ignorance, maybe even her own doubts. As a child, I'd believed grown-ups held all the answers. Now I knew better. We were all just children stumbling through the dark, doing the best we could to find meaning and comfort in a crazy world.

The church smelled of wood, dust, and furniture polish.

Opposite the main entrance, two large stained-glass windows glowed in the early morning light, casting swaths of pink, orange, and yellow across the walls and two rows of dust-covered pews that filled most of the space. I shivered and tried not to see the warm light as flames closing in. The last time I'd been in a church, it had burned down around me. I'd also been kidnapped, shot, and lost a friend, to say nothing of the torture taking place in the church's basement—the same torturous experiments that led to the magically enhanced Purity soldiers and the street drug Fantasia.

At the end of the aisle, centered between the stained-glass windows, was a small wooden altar below a painting of the Virgin Mary and baby Jesus. And kneeling before that altar was Mira. Her jeans might have been the same ones from last night, but a bright-pink shirt covered her bent back, and her hair looked like it was still damp from a shower. Unlike the rest of the church, the altar was free of dust. Two lit candles in polished holders flickered at either end, along with a single red votive in the middle.

Once my surprise faded, I folded my hands and bowed my head, not wanting to intrude on Mira's prayer.

She stayed kneeling for another minute, then slowly stood and turned to face me, tucking a silver necklace into the collar of her sweater as she did. "Thanks for waiting."

I nodded toward the painting. "I'm surprised to see you praying, considering the Church's stance on practitioners. If Purity got their hands on you, no amount of praying would save your life."

One corner of her mouth curved up. "Being a practitioner is the least of my sins."

I frowned. "Then why would you—"

"Purity is not the Church. And the Church is not my faith." The other side of her mouth curled up, turning it into a full smile. "The beliefs of some frightened few can't change my relationship with God."

I shook my head, amazed by her conviction.

She walked up the aisle, gave me a slap on the shoulder, and continued to the exit. "Let's get started."

I followed her outside and back around the building to the truck and motorcycle. She opened the door on the back of the truck. Inside was what looked like a tiny apartment just tall enough for a person to stand upright in. Cabinets and shelves had been mounted to both walls, their contents anchored in place with straps to prevent them shifting while the truck was in motion. A folded futon was tucked into the space above the cab. Mira stepped inside and pulled a can of ground coffee out of a cupboard. "You want some cafe con leche?"

"Sure."

She pulled two cups off hooks in an overhead cabinet. "Garrett said you're new to your powers."

I nodded.

"And you haven't had any instruction."

I nodded again.

"What are you able to do?"

I pressed my lips together. Much of what I could do was tied to my fae magic—it was hard to tell where one ability stopped and the other started—and I wasn't sure how much I wanted to share with this stranger. But how could she train me without the whole truth?

"We've all got secrets," she said, as if reading my thoughts. "I can't help you control your powers unless you trust me." She bustled around her tiny kitchen as she spoke, heating coffee and milk on a small propane burner. Then she sighed and said, "We should probably go first."

I frowned. "Excuse me?"

She shook her head. "I don't like it either, but we've got the upper hand here. It's only fair."

"Um . . . Mira?"

She jolted as if surprised to find me standing there. A blush flooded her cheeks. "Sorry. I was just . . . never mind." She poured the coffee-milk mixture into the mugs and handed me one. "If we're going to work together, there's something you should probably know about me. So let's make a deal. I won't blab your secrets if you don't blab mine."

I chewed my lip. Most of the world had already seen the recording of my confession, incomplete though it was. And I needed to know how to use my practitioner magic if it came to a fight with my father, which seemed to be the way things were going.

I offered Mira my hand. "Deal."

Stepping out of the truck, she set her steaming mug on the metal floor, wrapped her fingers tightly around mine, and gave one stiff downward yank. Then she took a couple steps away and looked up at the sky, hands on hips. "Your boyfriend from the computer room last night . . . you know what he is?"

"Do you?"

She glared at me. "This is no time to be cute. If you can't trust me, that's fine. Your lessons end here."

I glared back, then sighed. "He's a vampire."

She nodded and went back to watching the sky. "You know what makes a vampire? What keeps them alive and forces them to feed?"

"Part of a demon soul."

She lowered her gaze and the intensity in her eyes made me take a step back. "Have you seen it?"

I swallowed, picturing the writhing silvery-black mass that lived deep within James. "Yes."

She smiled. "Good." She planted her feet wide, took a deep breath, and said, "Look at me the way you looked into him."

Setting my coffee aside, I unfocused my eyes in the way that let me see magic. The world took on a washed-out quality, as though all the color had been bleached by the sun. Except Mira. A hazy sheen of teal light clung to her.

"I can see your magic," I said.

She crossed her arms. "Is that all?"

Frowning, I narrowed my focus, searching for the threads that made up the core of her being. More teal mixed with red, gold, and white, and through it all were ribbons of pure black. I traced them to their source and found a dark shadow nestled in Mira's heart, like the silver-eyed demon that dwelled within James.

I gasped and let my vision return to normal. "You're a vampire, too?"

She chuckled. "Hardly. The demon within a vampire is a tiny sliver of the original, like a copy of a copy." She pressed her hand flat over her chest. "This is pure."

My mouth opened and closed a few times before I finally managed to get out the words clamoring through my mind. "You're a rifter."

She touched a finger to the tip of her nose. "Bingo."

"But—" I gestured toward the end of town where Sol's practitioners would be waking up to begin their daily training.

"Garrett knows what I am," she said with a small, sad, smile. "That's why he asked me to come. Figured if anyone could teach you how to take down a rifter, it'd be me."

"But why would you? You're—"

"Evil?" she finished. "Let's just say I'm not your typical rifter."

I looked her up and down once more, from her wavy brown hair and mismatched eyes to her curvy hips and tiny, sneaker-clad feet. She was maybe five-foot-four and a smidge over one twenty. Despite clearly living out of the back of a truck, she seemed healthy and respectable in her Levi's jeans and pink cardigan—the kind of person you wouldn't look at twice if she passed you in a department store. Her image definitely didn't scream demon-possessed evil sorcerer.

I shook my head. "If you're able to control the demon inside you, maybe the other rifters can too. Maybe Sol's wrong about my dad being beyond reason. Maybe—"

"Stop." She raised her hand. "I told you, I'm not typical. I've been a rifter for half my life. Most burn out within a month."

"Exactly. Sol said my father changed years ago, during the war. So he must be like you."

Some of the color left her cheeks and her gaze slid to the ground. "Maybe, but considering what he's already shown himself capable of, that just makes him more dangerous. He won't wreak a little havoc and burn out. He's going to do serious damage if he isn't stopped. Holding out hope for anything else will just make your job harder."

"But—"

"Trust me. I know what I'm talking about." She returned to the truck, picked up her drink, and sat down on the bumper. "So there's my secret. Your turn."

Chapter 19

SITTING BESIDE MIRA on the bumper, I sipped my coffee and gave her a brief recap of my life since October—Kai's arrival and finding out I was part fae. Discovering I could relive other people's memories if there was a strong enough emotional connection. Fighting a vampire master and using my imbuing magic to craft a knife that harnessed the power of sunlight.

"Do you still have it?"

I shook my head. "Confiscated by the PTF."

"Too bad. Rifters aren't as sensitive as vampires, but sunlight weakens a demon's hold."

"Could a light-imbued knife kill a demon?"

She sipped her drink. "A strong enough concentration might dislodge a weak demon, send it scurrying back to the rift . . . but not someone like Darius. He's got a high-level demon riding him. Maybe even stronger than mine."

"Well, the knife was enough to distract Merak so James could take his head off, but not before he gutted me." I rubbed my abdomen. "James brought me back by giving me a piece of his soul."

She lifted an eyebrow. "So you've got a bit of demon in you, too?" She narrowed her eyes and looked me up and down. She frowned.

"Maybe not anymore. When I traveled to Enchantment for the first time, the portal reacted to that piece of James inside me. I changed it to hide it from the magic trying to destroy it."

Her eyes widened. "You *changed* the demon?"

"A little piece of demon, but yeah. In fact"—I rolled the coffee cup between my palms—"I'm going to try it on a larger scale . . . to change James so he's not a vampire anymore." I studied her out of the corner of my eye. "If it works, maybe I could—"

"No." Mira stared into her drink. "Maybe I didn't ask for this bonding, but it's a part of who I am now. I don't need, or want, to change that."

I nodded, once again amazed by the strength of her convictions.

This was a person who knew who she was and what she wanted to do, whereas I spent half my life second-guessing myself.

"So you tweaked the demon out of your soul so you could visit a fae realm. Then what?"

I told her about meeting my grandfather for the first time and the basic training he'd given me about imbuing magic—how to change the nature of things—and the various ways in which I'd used it. I also told her about Bael's insane ex-general who'd kidnapped children and was now building a fae army. I pulled the silver locket with its engraved "A" out of my collar and told her how Shedraziel recognized my father as the sorcerer she'd fought during the war.

"I wasn't sure until Sol confirmed it, but . . ." I shook my head. "Some of the things I could do with magic just didn't mesh with what Bael taught me."

"Like what?"

I set one hand against my chest. "Fae magic comes from inside, but when I needed an extra boost, I was able to draw magic from the air around me."

"Definitely a practitioner trait," she said.

"But when I did that . . ." I shuddered.

"Demons came?"

I nodded.

She downed the last of her drink and set it beside her, then slapped me on the back and stood up. "Let's start there. What did it feel like when you drew power from the air?"

I set my empty cup aside, thinking back. "There was a tingling all over my body. Then the energy sort of . . . leaked in. Once the flow started, it was all I could do to keep from drowning."

She pursed her lips. "Did you pull from everywhere evenly? Or one specific place?"

I frowned, trying to remember the sensation. "All over, I guess."

"That's dangerous. Opens you up to all kinds of nasty. Let's teach you to focus your draw point. You won't be able to draw as quickly, but you're less likely to get overwhelmed and suffer a burnout. Plus, a single point of entry makes it easier to guard against demons who might try to possess you."

I cast her a sideways glance, recalling the shadow anchored inside her.

She caught the look. "Yeah, I was wide open and drawing like crazy when I got my passenger. Lucky for me, she's not so bad."

"There's one more thing," I said as I joined her. "When I move the energy from outside my body through my fae magic, it changes."

She tapped a finger against her chin. "We'll experiment with that." She gestured for me to proceed. "First, show me what you've got."

"HOW'S IT GOING?" Emma poked her head around the side of Mira's truck-slash-home and grinned at me. "We come bearing lunch." Stepping fully into the field, she lifted a large wicker basket as evidence. She was wearing black combat boots, green corduroy pants, a black-and-white striped shirt, and a military-green jacket. Her teal hair showed black at the roots, and the shaved side was now long enough to hide her scalp. Her many piercings caught the light like winking stars.

Garrett wheeled around the corner right behind her with a blue blanket tucked around his legs and a heavy coat to protect him from the winter chill. He lifted one hand in greeting. "Thought you two could use some fuel for your training."

I wiped my forehead. The noon sun was shining brightly in a sky broken by scattered clouds, but it wasn't heat that was making me sweat. I'd channeled more magic in my few hours with Mira than I had in my entire life. My limbs were shaking with fatigue, and my stomach rumbled long and loud in response to the promise of food.

"But first"—Garrett pointed a narrow finger at me—"let's see what you've learned."

I sagged, then straightened. Much as I hated the role of trained monkey, the sooner I showed him my progress, the sooner I could eat.

Mira caught my eye and gave a slight nod as she moved to join the others in the audience.

Sighing, I settled my stance to make sure I was grounded and focused on my breathing. I felt for the tingle against my skin that represented the energy in the world around me. Unlike the wild grasping I'd done when I'd been desperate for that energy, I didn't just pull it into my body. Instead, I opened my left hand and created a tiny vortex above my palm. Blue light swirled like water in a drain, flowing through my skin. The trick was to keep the flow constant.

The rivulets of sweat I'd wiped away dripped once more into my eyes and down my neck and back as I pulled that current of energy through the "lint trap" Mira had helped me create with my fae magic. As it turned out, all practitioners had to create a filter for the magic coming into their bodies, but they had to set it up with a small portion of the energy they were absorbing before turning up the flow. I could use my innate fae magic to filter the influx and save time.

Once I'd drawn the magical energy through the filter, I channeled it through my body to my right hand, where I created a glowing orb of light that hovered just above my palm. I counted the seconds until the surface of the orb began to deform. The light burst and scattered. My record for the morning was twenty-three seconds. This time I only made it to eight before my concentration gave out. I really was hungry.

Emma set her basket down and clapped like a kid at the circus. "That was amazing, Alex."

I gave her a weak smile. "It's a light bulb. Hardly worth a standing ovation."

"For a single morning of training?" She placed a fist on her hip and glared. "It took me almost a week to focus my energy like that."

Garrett gestured to Emma. "I thought it might be useful to train Emma as a paladin so Alex could focus on offense, but it seems you've got her protection pretty well covered."

Mira shook her head. "A paladin is a good idea, if only to give her a boost."

I frowned. "I've never been entirely clear what paladins were for . . . other than killing sorcerers who got out of hand."

Garrett looked at Mira, who snatched up the picnic basket and said, "All you, dude. I'll serve lunch." She retreated to the back of her truck.

Garrett sighed, but there was a softness in his eyes as he watched Mira. I wanted to ask how they knew each other, but I bit the inside of my cheek. Their past was none of my business.

Turning his attention back to me, Garrett said, "Paladins act as a sorcerer's shield so the sorcerer can focus on the spells they're casting. I'm sure you realize how difficult it is to both safely channel the energy you need and direct its manifestation at the other end."

I nodded. When I'd pulled magic from the air before today, I'd been working entirely on instinct. I'd drawn as much power as I could all at once so that I could cast the spells I needed. Maintaining a steady flow was an entirely different experience. It was the difference between slamming a steel bar with a forging hammer and tapping out a pattern with a set of chasing tools.

"Lucky for Alex," Mira called from inside the truck, "she gets to cheat a bit."

"Cheat?" Emma asked.

I lifted one shoulder. "My fae magic filters the outside energy naturally, so as long as I pull everything I gather through my innate magic, I don't have to create the elaborate magic filter Mira explained most practitioners use."

Emma made a sour face. "No wonder you got it so fast."

"The point is," Garrett said, "while sorcerers focus on learning attack spells, paladins dedicate themselves to defense. During battles, paladins act as filters for their sorcerers, purifying the energy before it's passed on and protecting from demonic possession."

I frowned. "Then how did Dad and those others end up as rifters? As Church-sanctioned sorcerers, they all should have had paladins assigned to them."

"Maybe he did magic in secret. Or maybe his paladin fell down on the job. I know Darius lost at least two paladins during the war because they couldn't cope with the amount of magic he was drawing through them."

Emma went pale. "They had burnouts?"

Garrett nodded. "Neither survived." He held my gaze. "Perhaps your father was infected during one of those times when he was left exposed, but whatever the case, the cause of his corruption doesn't change the present situation. Darius is dangerous. He has to be stopped."

"I know." But I looked away as I said it.

"If Alex's fae magic means she doesn't need a paladin, what should I do?" Emma asked.

Mira stepped out of the back of the truck holding two plates, each with a roast beef sandwich and a handful of potato chips. "Alex is going to have her hands full with casting if she's fighting a trained sorcerer. The less she has to focus on filtering, the better her chances of winning." She handed one plate to Garrett and the other to Emma, then went back for the other two.

Emma stared at her sandwich. "If she's drawing that much power, couldn't I burn out like Darius's paladins?"

Garrett nodded. "You could."

"Then no way," I said. "I'll filter my own magic. If I draw more than is safe, I'll accept the consequences myself."

Emma shook her head. "Whether or not I end up filtering your magic, I'd like to learn how to be a paladin. There are going to be a lot of practitioners fighting when we face your dad. Being able to draw a little extra energy at the right moment might make the difference between victory and defeat."

"But—"

"It's my choice." She fixed her brown gaze on me, then turned to Mira. "I'll train as Alex's paladin."

"Good." Mira shoved a plate of food into my hands. "Everybody eat up. We've still got a lot of ground to cover today."

BLADES OF DEAD, dry grass prickled my neck as I stared at fingers of orange and purple clouds stretched across the sky. I was lying spread-eagle. My heart pounded. Puffs of condensed breath rose from my mouth like exhaust from an engine. Beside me, Emma collapsed into a similar pose.

"So," Garrett said from his place near the edge of the field, "what do you think?"

Mira made a noncommittal noise. "They might not die in the first thirty seconds."

Emma continued to stare at the clouds. "My training with Luke was tough, but nothing like this."

"Your previous training was for a career as a healer," Garrett said. "This is war. We're teaching you to stay alive."

Mira walked over to us. "The basic attack spells you learned today earn you the title 'sorcerer,' but don't limit yourself. Practitioner magic is all about imagination—the ability to clearly picture what you want to have happen. Great sorcerers can accomplish almost anything." She pulled me to my feet. "Given enough time, you could be great."

I frowned. "Thanks." But of course we didn't have "enough time." We had no idea when the rifters would make their next move. Every second counted.

I nudged Emma's leg with my foot. "Ready to go again?"

"Are you serious?"

Most of our day had been spent learning to work in tandem, with Emma siphoning and filtering magic while I cast—and casting was definitely easier with someone else managing the flow. But, at Garrett's insistence that Emma not be helpless if we were separated, we'd spent the latter part of the day on opposite sides, launching attacks at each other and deflecting them. The sleeve of my coat was singed from one of Emma's fireballs, and her hair had a little extra body thanks to an electrical shot she hadn't managed to repel.

Emma had been reluctant to learn offensive magic at first, no doubt cautioned by Luke about the strict pacifist rules imposed on free practitioners, but she'd proved a natural. Still, once she'd learned even a single attack spell, she'd become a sorcerer in the eyes of the PTF. If we failed to establish an alliance, she and all the practitioners training with Sol would be seen as a threat to be collared or killed.

I sighed. "We need all the practice we can get."

"You also need to eat," Garrett said. "And sleep."

Mira nodded. "Killing yourselves in practice won't do anyone much good. We'll start again at dawn tomorrow." She crossed her arms and waited beside Garrett until I nodded, helped Emma to her feet, and the two of us began the walk back to camp.

"You coming, Garrett?" I called over my shoulder.

"I'll be along later." He turned to Mira as I passed the corner of the church, and again the softness in his expression made me wonder what kind of relationship the two of them had.

Emma laced her fingers and stretched her arms above her head, making her bones pop. "I'm starving."

I nodded. We'd been using magic nonstop all day. I felt hollow, like a plaster cast with nothing inside. My eyelids drooped as I shuffled my feet over the road. If Dad attacked tonight, I wasn't sure I'd have the energy to raise my hand, let alone my magic.

As we got closer to the main camp, the sound of small explosions came through the trees that hid the large training field Sol showed me when I first arrived. I turned down a narrow dirt trail toward the noise.

"Where are you going?" Emma asked.

"Detour. I wanna take a peek at what the other sorcerers-in-training are working on."

"Ugh. We've been at it all day and you want to do *more?*"

I chuckled. "Not do, watch. Go ahead, I'll be along in a minute."

She rolled her eyes. "Whatever. I'm hungry."

I pushed through bare brambles that snagged at my pants and came to the edge of the clearing where Sol's troops were preparing for war. Dozens of men and women were in the field, using the last of the light to hone their skills. Some were human soldiers working on their aim or hand-to-hand combat. Others flung magic back and forth as Emma and I had been doing for the last several hours. I shifted my focus to see the flow of their magic. Before the ball of fire or arc of lightning left their hands, the energy was pulled through a glow I now recognized as a filter spell. Wisps of ethereal smoke swirled and drifted across the field, but that smoke wasn't as demon-laden as it had been where Emma and I were working. Or maybe these sorcerers just weren't as appetizing.

I rubbed my hands over my upper arms, remembering the faces in the smoke during practice. Mira assured me that so long as my magic filter was in place, the demons wouldn't be able to crawl inside me as they had before. And true to her word, the demons kept their distance. They didn't even speak to me as they had on our previous encounters. They'd simply hovered in the fog that wasn't fog and watched me train with their flat, glowing eyes.

I blinked, and the empty haze faded away.

In the center of the field, David directed people firing spells or bullets at targets set along the riverbank. At the far end of the field, people clashed with blades and brawn. Kai and Morgan whirled amid the mortal soldiers, swords flashing.

All that training was an impressive sight. But as I watched, I couldn't help thinking, *It isn't enough.*

How could we defeat an army that could get back up after we killed them? Even if the remaining Purity soldiers and PTF troops joined us . . . even if the werewolves and vampires joined us . . . how were we supposed to fight an enemy that wouldn't stay dead?

Kill the necromancer.

I shuddered and wrapped my arms tight, squeezing my chest.

"Alex!" David came up at a trot, one hand raised in greeting, the other resting on his holstered gun.

Kai was also jogging toward me, sword sheathed, showing no signs of his injury from the PTF raid.

"How'd your first day of sorcerer training go?" David asked.

"You knew about that?"

"Sol told me you and Emma were getting a crash course from that new girl Garrett brought in."

"Mira. Do you know her?"

He shook his head. "She arrived last night, just after you did."

"I'd like to meet her," Kai said. "In fact, I'd like to join your training session tomorrow. As one of your teachers, and the knight responsible for your safety, I need to assess your new skills."

I tried to picture Kai's reaction when he realized my newest teacher had a demon living inside her and nearly choked. No, Kai meeting Mira would *not* be a good idea.

"Sol says you're more useful here." The way David growled the words made me think these two had butted heads quite a bit today.

"I've fulfilled his request to strengthen your troops' fighting skills, but I am not a member of your army. My primary concern is Alex's safety."

"Then you should want the troops as well trained as possible."

"Guys." I held up my hands to stop either from saying more. "Kai is right that Sol can't command him like a common soldier." Kai smirked, but his smile faded as I turned to him. "But I'm asking you to help here with the sword training. Having you around while I practice my practitioner skills would distract me, and I can't afford that right now."

"Why would my presence be a distraction?"

Because a fae would no doubt notice that my teacher had a demon inside her.

I set my hand on his shoulder. "Just trust me on this, okay?"

He grumbled, but nodded. "We should brush up on your sword skills, too. Did you practice while I was . . . away?"

I appreciated him not saying something like "rotting in prison thanks to your short temper."

"Umm . . ."

"You didn't, did you?"

"What about your shooting?" David asked. "Have you been using the gun I gave you?"

I bit my lip and studied my boots. My gun and sword were sharing space in a PTF evidence locker. "In case you haven't noticed, I've been a little busy."

David and Kai both crossed their arms and skewered me with matching scowls.

I raised my hands in surrender. "I promise to practice my sword skills and my shooting as soon as this mess with my dad is over. But right now, going up against a necromancer, the magic lessons are more important."

David uncrossed his arms. "Don't underestimate the impact of a well-placed bullet."

"But Alex is right," Kai said. "With a necromancer in play, magic is our best bet. Kill a demon's host and the demon will just keep coming, or jump into the next available corpse. You'll run out of bullets before Darius runs out of bodies. Dismemberment will slow them down more than a bullet, but even a sword can't affect the demon inside."

I turned Kai's words over in my head, picking at a thought that had started to form. "What if they could?"

Both men frowned as though I'd spoken gibberish. Then Kai asked, "What if *what* could *what?*"

"Bullets," I said. "Swords. What if they could affect the demons inside?"

David looked at Kai. "Is that even possible?"

Kai opened his mouth, but didn't answer.

I shrugged. "I am an imbuer, after all."

Closing his mouth, Kai swallowed and said, "Let's go talk to Hortense."

Chapter 20

WE STEPPED OUT of the trees near the house where I'd woken up on my first day in camp. Sol was sitting in one of the wooden rockers on the wraparound porch. Toby—the young man who'd accompanied me to the reservation—was in the other. Between them was the chess set I'd made for Sol.

Toby looked up and waved. "How was your first day of training?"

"Tiring." I nodded toward the chessboard. "How's your game?"

"Ugh." Toby shook his head. "I only have three pieces left."

"Would you like to play when we're finished?" Sol asked.

A memory bubbled up of Sol and me playing chess on the balcony of an apartment in L.A. when I was fifteen years old. We'd sipped cold drinks—root beer for me, real beer for him—and sweated through the hot, humid, July afternoon while we waited for my mother to get home from work. We played seven games that day, and about a million since, and I'd never beaten him. Not once.

"Another time," I said, and continued past Sol's porch toward the house where we'd stashed the kids.

Bryce was lying on a picnic table in the front yard. He wore no coat, and his sleeves were pushed above his elbows. The last of the evening sun cast rich, golden highlights over his skin. He breathed deep and smiled as I approached. "Been a long time since I did this."

I stared at the pale-yellow stone around his neck and wondered what would happen if I couldn't duplicate it before it burned out. "Victoria didn't send you here to sunbathe."

He sneered and nodded toward the blacked-out window. "How is James enjoying his room?"

Ignoring both Bryce's jibe and David's quizzical look, I pushed through the front door. Kai and David followed me inside. Two large tables had been placed end to end in the main room, and all the children were seated around them eating dinner. The clank and clatter of dishes was accompanied by boisterous chatter and occasional laughter that made my heart soar with hope. Despite all they'd been through, all they continued to go through, these kids could still laugh. While still disturbingly thin, most had color back in their cheeks. Most importantly, the flat shadows had lifted from their eyes, bringing them back to life.

Maggie, wearing a checkered apron and thick oven mitts on both hands, set a pan of sizzling ribs in the middle of one table while her husband deposited its twin on the other.

I slapped her on the back. "Quite the feast you've prepared."

"Just doing what I can." She smiled, and her eyes lit up like I hadn't seen since before the bookstore closed. "Take a seat anywhere. I've got more coming."

She pushed a stray curl off her forehead and trotted back to the kitchen like a woman on a mission. Nursemaid was a far cry from bookstore owner, but taking care of these kids seemed to have given her a new sense of purpose.

Emma was sitting beside May in front of a plate piled high with cleaned bones and a heap of potatoes drenched in gravy. She dropped another bone onto the plate and grabbed a roll from a nearby basket.

My stomach growled.

Kai cleared his throat and tipped his chin toward the east wall.

Hortense was standing near the edge of the room like an overseer watching the factory floor. She either wasn't hungry or had already finished.

Doing my best to ignore the mouth-watering aromas and the twisting hunger in my gut, I walked over to her. "The children have their appetites back. I'm impressed how fast they've recovered."

"They're not recovered," she said. "They are simply suffering less."

"Well, they look happy. And right now I'll take any win I can get." I gestured to the door where Kai and David were waiting. "Could you step outside for a moment? Kai and I have something we'd like to discuss."

Hortense followed me to the porch as the last glow of the sun vanished below the horizon. Kai and David took up positions opposite each other like pillars holding up the roof. As soon as the door closed behind her I asked, "Is it possible to imbue a weapon to affect demons?"

She stared at me, frowned, and said, "Yes."

I blinked. I'd expected a long exposition about magic theory and all the variables involved, not this uncharacteristically straight answer.

David grinned and leaned forward as if he didn't want to miss what was said next.

Kai gaped. "How are you so certain?"

"Because it's been done before." Her gaze rested heavily on me. "Once."

"By Bael," I guessed.

She shook her head. "By Marron."

It was my turn to gape. Bael's niece was the only living imbuer besides him and myself. I'd met her once, briefly. She was insane.

I waved a hand inarticulately. "I thought she was too . . . you know . . . to be effective at stuff like that."

"She wasn't always as she is now. And even now, what she is isn't well understood. Many among the fae believe Marron looked deep into the heart of the world and now sees too much truth for the rest of us to understand her. Some even revere her as an oracle. But at one time she was Bael's apprentice, and a talented imbuer in her own right. She crafted a sword that could cut through the rift to those shadows who live on the other side."

Kai, David, and I were all leaning forward now. "How?" we said together.

She shook her head. "I only know that it is possible."

"We could ask her to show you," Kai said, turning to me.

"We don't have time for a trip to Enchantment right now. Not with the rifters so close to D.C. If we left now, the whole conflict could be over before we made it back."

David slumped against the railing. "Well, it was a happy thought while it lasted."

I glanced to the south. Mira had trusted me for the sake of success; maybe I could convince her to trust a few more. . . .

"There's someone else who might be able to help." I looked at Kai. "I think maybe you should meet my practitioner instructor after all."

David gestured to the path we'd just come up. "Let's go."

I took a step, wobbled, and grabbed the rail, suddenly dizzy.

"It's because you haven't eaten." James's breath tickled my neck.

David jumped back, but Kai and Hortense didn't move. They knew what James was.

David lifted his chin. "'Bout time you showed up. I stopped by earlier to invite you to train, but your room was empty."

I raised an eyebrow at James.

I hid.

"I realize you're a high society muckety-muck," David continued, "but if you want to stay by Alex's side, you'll need at least basic combat training. Do you even know how to fire a gun?"

James smiled. "I'll manage."

I stepped between them. "We've been discussing the possibility of making anti-demon weapons. I need to talk to Mira."

"You need food."

"James is right," Hortense said. "You're no good to anyone if you collapse. And if you discover a way to make the weapons you're proposing, you'll need your strength."

"I need to secure the range and get a little something myself," David said. "Let's meet at Mira's truck in half an hour." He gave James a wary look, stepped off the porch, and headed back toward the training field.

"Malakai," Hortense said, "lend me a hand."

Kai followed her inside without objection.

James traced his fingers over my cheek. "You're losing weight."

"Magic burns a lot of calories."

"All the more reason to be diligent about your meals."

"Am I interrupting?" Bryce sauntered up to the porch, hands in his pockets. James's pendant rested against his chest, glowing slightly with residual light. Smiling at James, he held his bare arms out, turning them to show off his dark skin. "How do you like my tan?"

James's weight shifted toward Bryce, but I pulled him back.

Don't let him goad you.

Anger, frustration, humiliation, rage. James's emotions boiled just beneath the surface of his stony expression, spilling through our connection.

I know how you feel, but we need Victoria's good will if we want any chance of forging an alliance with the vampires. Right now, that means putting up with Bryce.

Bryce laughed and continued past us. At the corner of the building, he raised a hand and called, "Enjoy the night."

I kept my hand against James's chest until Bryce was out of sight.

James inhaled, a long, shuddering breath. "It's been a long time since I've felt this . . . helpless." He shook his head. "Even with the necklace, there were plenty of days I didn't set foot outside. I didn't want to use up the pendant's allotment. But somehow, knowing that I *could* made it bearable. Today? With you and everyone else working so hard while I was trapped . . . Knowing *he* was out here . . ." He glared after Bryce. "I need you to change me, Alex."

"And I will, as soon as I can."

"I can't be this useless when you face your father. I . . ." His voice cracked. He took a deep breath. "If you can't change me before your father attacks, I'll kill Bryce and take the necklace back."

I stiffened. "Much as I'd love to never see Bryce again, that would destroy any chance at building an alliance with Victoria. Besides, according to Mira, the attack will probably happen at night. Rifters aren't big fans of sunlight either."

"Still, I'll not risk your life in the hopes of gaining a future ally. Besides, Victoria doesn't care about Bryce. His death won't stop her from making a deal with you, so long as the pot is sweet enough."

I groaned. "Magic necklaces I can't actually provide . . . Sweet, but empty."

He lifted my hand and kissed my palm. "Don't tell Bryce that."

With his lips pressed against my pulse I could feel his hunger rising. Vampires could go quite a while without feeding, but the longer they went, the more likely they'd lose control, and I'd brought two to this closed community. Another reason to change James as soon as possible, and get rid of Bryce.

I sighed. At least my own hunger was something I could take care of.

IT WAS FULL DARK when I led James and Kai back to the little church. I tucked my gloved hands under my armpits. The sun had sucked the remaining heat away, like the undertow of a sinking ship pulling down survivors. Hortense had stayed behind to give the kids their evening treatment. There was no sign of David yet, so I circled around to Mira's campsite.

". . . going to notice." Mira's voice drifted through the night, growing louder as we approached.

"There's going to be a smorgasbord. You really think you can pass that up?" A pause filled only by the hum of a generator, then, "She's not ready."

I hadn't heard any response. Was she talking to Garrett? Were they talking about me? I slowed down to listen more closely.

"Yeah, if it comes to that I guess we'll have to. But don't come crying to me when the PTF—"

A twig snapped under my boot.

Plastering on a customer service smile, I rounded the corner and raised my hand in greeting. Mira was illuminated by the light shining out of the back of her truck. She was the only person present. My smile slipped. "I thought I heard you talking. Is Garrett around?"

A hint of color crept into her cheeks. "Just me. Why are you back?"

She placed a fist on her curvy hip. "I thought I told you to get some food and rest?"

"Food I did, but I have a question for you."

Her gaze shifted over my shoulder. Lines of tension appeared around her eyes and mouth.

"This is Kai," I said, indicating him. "And James. Don't worry, he's not like most vampires."

James's eyes widened slightly. *What are you—*

She already knows. She can see the demon inside you.

He stiffened. *Is that a trait common to practitioners?*

I frowned. "I don't know."

As I said those words out loud, I realized who Mira must have been talking to, both when James and I walked up and when she'd said nonsensical things during training. She was communicating with the demon inside her.

"I haven't had much interaction with practitioners," James said. "Can you all see demons?"

Mira shook her head. "It takes a special talent."

"A talent you clearly have." James stared at Mira, waiting.

Mira crossed her arms.

"Yo." Behind me, David strolled around the corner of the church. He looked between James, stiff and glaring, and Mira with her arms crossed, and asked, "Did you start the party without me?"

I made a "wait" motion and crossed the remaining space to Mira, who was now staring at the group behind the church as if they were a force of invaders. In a low tone, I whispered, "I didn't tell them about you, but working together would be a whole lot easier if they knew. We've come because we have an idea, but you're the only one who can tell us if it will work." I stepped back. "Please."

She raised her gaze to the dark sky. "I knew coming here was a bad idea." She sighed, releasing some of the tension from her stance. "You trust all these people?"

I glanced at David and chewed the inside of my cheek. He'd lied. But I believed him when he said he only meant to protect me, that our friendship was real.

"I do."

"What's your idea?"

"I have the ability to change the properties of an object. I want to change something like a bullet or a sword so it can affect demons."

She rubbed one hand over her mouth and jaw and stared into

empty space for a moment. "That might be possible."

"We know it's possible," Kai said. "It's been done before."

Mira crossed her arms again. "Then what are you asking me for?"

"It's the *how* we need to work out," I explained.

She shook her head. "I can help with demons and practitioner arts, but I have no idea how your other magic works."

"I'd like—" I winced apologetically. "I'd like to study you."

She gave me a blank stare. "What am I, a lab rat?"

"If I could just take a look at your . . . friend . . . maybe I could figure out what kind of change I need to make to the weapons."

She gestured to the group behind me. "And these guys are what? Moral support? Eye candy?"

"Kai's fae. You said yourself, you don't know anything about my other magic. If I run into trouble with the imbuing, I'll need his expertise. David's in charge of the human troops who will be using the weapons I imbue if this works."

"And the vampire?"

I glanced at David, who—to his credit—didn't move away from James, but was now looking at him as one might a poisonous snake that had slithered into his bed. I turned back to Mira. "He *is* my moral support, but I'd also like your advice on the change I plan to make inside him. Last time, his demon surged and nearly killed him. We've got a theory how to avoid that, but I want to run it by you before I give it another go."

She stared at me for a moment, then said, "I'll make some coffee," and climbed into the back of her truck.

The group split apart with a collective exhale. Kai paced the field, muttering to himself and casting furtive glances at Mira's truck. James moved so he could study the stained-glass windows in the back wall of the church, and I wondered if it was the artistic or religious aspect that drew him. Had he been a religious man when he was human? It had never occurred to me to ask.

David came over and bumped my shoulder with his. "So . . ." He gestured toward James. "Vampire."

"Yep."

"And I thought admitting I was gay was hard." He shook his head. "Does Sol know?"

"No. And if you really are my friend, he never will."

He gave James's backside a long, assessing stare. "What's the sex like?"

I choked, punched him in the arm, and we both laughed. When the laughter died out, I said, "I've missed you."

He hesitated, then wrapped one arm around my shoulders and gave me a squeeze. "I'm sorry."

"Me too." We stood quietly for a moment, then I said, "If I can't make an effective weapon against the demons, I don't want you to come when we fight the rifters."

"Because I'm just a human?"

I bit my lower lip.

"If our roles were reversed, and you didn't have magic, would you be okay just sitting back and doing nothing while others fought for your future?"

"Hell yes," I said. "If I didn't have magic, I'd still be holed up in my cabin in the woods, happily twisting metal into interesting shapes and selling it for obscene amounts of money."

He smiled. "Liar."

I sighed and thought about the way Maggie had insisted on coming with me despite being mortal. *Let me do what I can do.* "If the people I cared about were going to fight, I'd want to be there . . . even if I couldn't do anything but cheer them on."

Mira climbed out of her truck with a tray of six steaming, mismatched mugs full of cafe con leche, and everyone drifted to the center of the illuminated area to claim a cup. I burnt my tongue on the first sip. James downed his like he was doing shots.

"How do you want to do this?" Mira asked.

I turned to James, who had the best vision in the dark. "Could you find some steel I can work with?"

"Any steel?"

I nodded, and he walked away.

Turning back to Mira, I said, "Get somewhere comfortable. I'm . . . basically just gonna stare at you for a minute."

She raised an eyebrow, but settled on the back bumper of the truck, coffee mug cradled in her lap.

I sat down in the grass. Cold immediately seeped through my pants and into my butt and thighs, but I pushed the sensation aside. I shifted my focus and found the shadows near Mira's core, as I had that morning. Unlike the silver streaks of James's demon, Mira's had shimmers of gold and pearl that cascaded over its surface like ripples on a lake.

While James's demon was an angry bundle trapped inside him, the presence in Mira was more of a hazy cloud overlapping her. The demon seemed to pass through Mira in most places, but there were small anchors—points of connection that didn't shift. Those were what I needed to focus on.

I reached out with one hand and set my fingers over Mira's wrist. We didn't have the kind of bond I shared with James, so there wasn't a sudden rush of clarity, but the edges of the demon became slightly easier to see.

I prodded the places where the demon came into direct contact with the mortal world, testing the connection. What was different? Why did it pass right through in some places but not others?

I sharpened my focus further, as through increasing the magnification on a microscope. Ribbons of white and gold mingled with red, and threads of teal twisted through them both.

I ran my tongue back and forth over my teeth, thinking. The energy practitioners pulled into their bodies to create magic was the same energy the demons lived in. That's why it was easiest to possess practitioners wielding more magic than they could safely handle—or fools like me who didn't know how to filter the energy they were drawing.

There was a metallic groan and a loud *crack* that echoed through the night and broke my concentration. I blinked at Mira, and saw only a twenty-something-year-old woman with slightly narrowed eyes and a small pucker on her lips. A moment later, James came around the corner of the church.

"Will these do?" He extended his hand. On his palm were several pieces of metal ranging in size from coat hanger wire to a six-inch chunk the width of my wrist. One item was clearly the peg from a door hinge. Another looked like it had been snapped off a large, grime-crusted rod.

I lifted the hinge pin from the pile and turned it over in my hands. "Perfect." I looked at Mira. "I think demons are anchored to the physical world through the magic practitioners use."

"Fireballs and plasma bolts won't kill a demon," Mira said. "Trust me on that."

"I'm not talking about the finished spells practitioners cast, I mean the raw energy we pull in to create the magic."

Kai nodded. "Rift energy—the chaotic energy demons live in and are composed of. But that energy has to be channeled into some kind of order to take shape in this world."

"At which point it stops affecting them," Mira finished.

I lifted my arms, palms up, as I had when I demonstrated drawing energy into one hand and creating light in the other for Garrett and Emma. "We need to find the balance point. The place where chaos becomes order, but both still exist."

"A decent theory," Mira conceded. "But you're talking about stopping a spell halfway while still holding it together. Any aborted spell you're channeling will blow apart if you cut off its outlet. You'd be risking a serious backlash."

"But I *am* going to give the energy an out. I'm going to channel it into this." I held up the hinge pin.

Mira blinked. "You've lost me."

Kai nodded. "You want to embed the partially converted energy into the pin the way we once attached a light spell to your knife to make a weapon against vampires."

"Exactly." I looked around the group. David looked confused but hopeful. Everyone else wore thoughtful expressions. "Do you think we can do it?"

James patted me on the back. "Only one way to find out."

I closed the fingers of my right hand around the steel pin. With my left, I started pulling energy out of the rift.

ATTEMPT THIRTY-SEVEN.

I felt like one of those people who snaps a black-and-white slate board to signal a movie scene is about to be recorded. Of course, I also felt like the actor who couldn't remember my lines, hence having to record thirty-seven takes.

I sighed and stared at the pin cradled in my hands, cleansed once more after my last failure. My arms hung like tubes of boiled pasta, limp and lifeless. My breath puffed out in a growing cloud of steam as the night grew colder. James had found a folding chair so I didn't have to kneel, but my legs were still numb. The moon, which had started its trek across the sky shortly before dinner, had reached its zenith. The silver sliver faded in and out behind wisps of cloud.

Beside me, Kai sagged in a chair of his own, one hand wrapped around my left wrist. I'd run out of energy to repeat this test after my sixth try. Since then, Kai had been funneling magic into me, just like a paladin tending to his sorcerer. But in Kai's case, he wasn't siphoning rift energy. He was feeding me directly from his own supply—the magic that kept him alive. Even so, the weight of my dinner was gone. My muscles felt wrung out. My eyelids drooped.

Taking a deep breath of ice-laden air that stung my lungs and momentarily shocked me into wakefulness, I settled my focus on the metal pin and sifted through the labels at its core—the properties that made it what it was. Then I pulled a thread of energy from the pool Kai was supplying and used my imbuing to add an extra attribute to the pin, just as Bael had taught me. Just as I'd done thirty-six times before. I shifted the refinement of the magic a little further than I had on the previous attempt, as I had on every one that came before, searching for the correct balance.

When the newly introduced magic was anchored to the pin's core, I lifted my weary arm and, watching the dark shadow that overlapped the tiny woman, touched the steel to Mira's chest for the thirty-seventh time.

Mira gasped and jerked back, falling to the truck bed. Her brown eyes were wide and ringed with gold.

The steel pin dropped from my frozen fingers, falling silently to the dead grass.

James's hand closed on my shoulder, squeezing just shy of pain. *Did it work?*

"I . . . I think so." I couldn't tear my gaze away from Mira's startled expression. "Are you okay?"

She sat up and rubbed the point where the pin had made contact as though she ached there. "I think so." She took several deep breaths. "There doesn't seem to be any damage. I think she was just startled by the sensation."

"She?"

"My demon."

Setting the matter of demon genders aside for the moment, I asked, "Do you think a bullet or a sword with that balance of magic inside it could hurt her?"

She pursed her lips and tipped her head as though listening to a voice only she could hear.

"I don't know what kind of damage it would do, and she isn't willing to let you test that on her, but even the sensation of impact might be enough to send a lesser demon scurrying back into the rift." She rubbed her chest again. "It was . . . unsettling."

"Sorry for your discomfort." I grinned. "But thank you . . . and her . . . for helping. This could make the difference between life and death for the humans on the front lines."

I glanced at David, who was snoring softly with his chin on his chest, his back propped against the wall of the church. Watching me stare at a hunk of metal for hours on end had apparently not been riveting enough to stave off sleep. As I watched his chest rise and fall, my own exhaustion settled around me once again, damping the excitement of success.

I patted James's hand and said, "Could you wake David? He needs to know we've succeeded."

"Finally." Kai was smiling, but he sagged in his chair like a crayon left to melt in the sun.

As James moved away, I leaned forward and scooped up the steel pin. Thirty-seven attempts and more energy than I'd been able to provide on my own, but I'd done it. I found the right balance of order and chaos that could allow something to exist both in the mortal realm and the rift where the demons resided. We had a weapon against the rifters.

David stumbled over, rubbing his eyes. "You've done it?"

I held up the steel pin, which looked exactly the same as it had before I'd started my experiment. "I have."

He squinted at the metal. "Really?"

"If you hadn't nodded off, you would have gotten to see the result," I said with a sniff.

"Fair enough." He raised his hands in surrender. Then he tipped his chin toward the pin. "Now you can make my gun shoot magic bullets?"

"It'd be nice if I could just imbue the gun," I said with a sigh, "but that wouldn't help unless you clubbed rifters over the head with it. I'll need to imbue the actual bullets or blades. In any case, I'll need more energy. Even with Kai donating, I won't be able to imbue many objects before I'm too tired to function."

"What about the other fae that came with you?" he asked. "Can they . . . donate?"

"Hortense might," I said. "She's proven willing to help me in the past."

"I doubt Morgan will," Kai said. "As a member of the Shadow Court, such an act would be . . . distasteful. But the fae aren't your only option."

I nodded. "Garrett said paladins feed energy to their sorcerers, so maybe Emma and the other practitioners could help."

"But if they're all exhausted when the call to arms comes . . ." David squeezed the back of his neck as though working out a kink. "Having a way for the humans to be more effective is great, but not if it means we lose our magic attacks. As it is, I don't know if Sol will agree to this after seeing how spent you are. You're supposed to be our trump card against your father."

I looked away. I still wasn't sure I could face my father on a battlefield. . . . I definitely didn't want to.

"Perhaps the humans could provide the energy to fuel their own weapons," James said.

I twisted to look at him. "What do you mean?"

"The fae have, in the past, used ritual magic to drain energy from large groups of mortals to fuel their spells."

We all looked at Kai, who pulled back. "Sure, but that's high-level magic. I don't know how to do that."

"Hortense probably does," I said. "She *is* a court tutor after all. It's her job to know stuff like that."

James turned to David. "Do you think the humans here would be willing to exchange energy for the chance to inflict real damage?"

David nodded. "I guarantee it."

"I'll go speak with Hortense." Kai groaned as he rose out of his chair.

"Sleep first," I said. "We can talk to Hortense and Sol in the morning to get everyone on the same page."

Kai grunted and shuffled toward the side of the church. David nodded to me and James, glanced at Mira, then turned and said, "Wait up, Kai. I'll walk with you."

I frowned. David didn't like Kai—blamed him for the spiral my life had taken since he showed up in October. But David was practical. If Kai could help keep David's soldiers alive even a second longer, David would be his best friend.

I turned back to Mira, who was sitting cross-legged on the floor of the truck.

"You okay?"

She nodded, but her silence worried me.

James set his hand on my back, his fingers brushing my neck. *We should go.*

I want to get her talking first.

Would you like privacy?

No. In fact . . . I cleared my throat. "Do you have any more of that cafe con leche?"

Mira looked up. Her eyes still held a golden sheen, sort of like the silver that swirled through James's blue when his demon was taking over. She tucked her loose hair behind her ear.

I frowned. The white stripe seemed wider than before.

"You should sleep," she said. "From the sound of it, you'll be busy again tomorrow."

"I'm too excited to sleep," I lied. "Besides, there's still the other matter I wanted to discuss with you."

A wrinkle creased her forehead, then her eyes widened and she looked at James. She laughed, loud and long. "Demon-killing weapons not enough for you? You want to save the hosts too?"

"I don't need to kill James's demon. I want advice on how a person can coexist with one."

That stalled her laughter. She looked from me, to James, and back to me. "I'll make more coffee."

Chapter 21

I DRIFT IN GRAY fog, weightless. I can't tell if my eyes are open or closed. There's no light. No shadow. No sound. Then the soles of my bare feet touch solid ground and I have a body again. The fog continues to swirl around me, but the mist no longer feels empty. The back of my neck tingles. I'm being watched.

"Alyssandra."

The name rasps against my nerves and makes the muscle under my eye twitch. No one calls me that anymore. Not since I was a child. Not since. . . . I turn to face the speaker.

My father wears the fog like a cloak. The smoky forms of demons coil around him, clinging like children to a parent.

Dad's eyes, the same blue-gray as my own, stare into me. Deep lines crease his face with age, strain, and worry. Gray-brown stubble shades his narrow jaw. He is smaller than the giant from my memories—the man who carried me on his shoulders and sheltered me in his arms—yet so much larger too, full of details I've long since forgotten.

"You've grown." His voice is not deep, but my bones shake as though his words are inside me.

"Almost twenty years . . . it was bound to happen."

"Solomon told me you were—" He looks away and takes a shuddering breath. "He said you died in a car accident . . . with your mother."

I bite my cheek. "Only Mom died."

He closes his eyes. Perhaps he hoped Sol had made up the accident, that I'd tell him Mom was fine. "I'm sorry I wasn't there."

"You hadn't been there for a long time."

His gaze returns to me. "I'm here now."

"No you're not." I look around. "This is a dream. My father is miles away, waging a war against humanity."

"This is a not-quite-dream. A place where the lines between energy and matter blur and bend." He takes a step toward me and reaches out. His fingers brush my cheek, warm and solid. "A place where practitioners can walk . . . if they're strong enough."

I stumble back a step and shake my head. He looks more believable than the patchwork of memories wearing my father's eyes I faced during my fae naming trial, but

I could have picked those details up when I saw him on the television earlier. "Dreams can feel real. You're just a manifestation from my subconscious, brought on by the stress of what's coming."

"August seventeenth."

I frown.

"That's the day I became a rifter. It was on the fields of Aubrac in Southern France. Check with Solomon when you wake up. He can confirm I was there."

My mouth is too dry to form words. Has my mind invented a random date to fool me? Or is my father really speaking to me through some form of astral-projection or dream telepathy? I can't deny the possibility . . . and I've never even heard of a place called Aubrac.

"Let's say I believe you."

His posture relaxes slightly.

"Why now? Why not come to me before?"

"I only learned you were alive after your rather controversial confession was broadcast."

"That was a week ago."

"A very busy week."

"Yeah, I guess killing all those people didn't leave much time for dream chats."

"I'm not a monster, Alyssandra. I simply want my freedom. Freedom for all of us with magical potential. A world where we can be who we are without the fear of being caged."

"You brought down a building full of innocent bystanders."

"After giving the police ample time to evacuate it."

"Not everyone got out." Tension sings through my muscles. I struggle not to curl my fingers into fists. "And what about the people on the street? The ones who died as they ran from their cars?"

"They aren't dead. I brought them all back."

"As what? Demon puppets?"

"See for yourself. You can meet them, talk to them."

My mouth drops open, but I can't think of a response. My thoughts swirl with confusion.

He looks to the side, as though his attention has been caught by something only he can see. "The sun is rising."

"So?"

"Meet me in Baltimore today at noon. Seventh and Chesapeake. Come alone."

"What? No. I—" This is my chance to talk to him, to find a solution that doesn't involve bloodshed. And if that isn't possible . . . it's an opportunity to face my father without an army standing in the way. Morgan could have me there in moments, but then what? Am I really ready to face him in the flesh? If I can't talk him down,

am I ready to fight? "—I need more time."

The corners of his mouth turn down. "Surely Solomon is keeping you in striking distance of D.C.*"*

"Give me a day. I promise, I'll be there."

He drums his fingers against his thigh. "One day. No more. The natives are getting restless."

I nod. "Tomorrow at noon."

He stares straight into my eyes. "I'll be ready for an ambush."

I force myself not to blink. "I'll come alone."

Cold air surged into my lungs as I jackknifed into a sitting position with a gasp. James's arm around my waist was all that kept me from falling out of the narrow bed.

Sitting up beside me, he tucked a sweat-damp strand of hair behind my ear. "What is it?"

His steady presence helped calm my racing heart.

A nightmare. A bad dream. But not a dream. "My father came to me . . . in my dream. He wants to meet in person."

He didn't laugh or tell me I was crazy. He just stared at me with that serious, stern expression he got sometimes when his thoughts were far away. "If he can appear in your dreams, what need is there to meet in the physical world?"

I frowned. "Honestly, it all happened so fast . . ." The memory of my meeting had blurred a bit since waking, but it didn't fade the way dreams usually did. "I didn't ask. And now it doesn't matter. I've already agreed."

"That doesn't mean you have to go."

"I know that. But this could be my only chance to meet him face to face before . . . whatever he's planning."

He studied my expression. "Meeting him could be a trap. A way to take you out of the equation."

"Maybe . . . probably . . . but that works both ways. And he seemed genuinely relieved that I was alive. I don't think he intends to hurt me."

"He's killed."

I met his gaze. "So have I." A tightness spread through my chest with the weight of those memories. "The sorcerers are basically treated like slaves by the Church and PTF. They're given new names, told where to live and what to do, and when something dangerous comes along they're sent to fight and die as if their lives don't matter. Can you really blame them for wanting their freedom?"

"You're forgetting about the demons. Your father and his companions aren't just sorcerers anymore. They're rifters."

I pictured Mira, and the shining darkness within her, as she sipped her coffee and answered my questions after the others left last night. What made her so different from other rifters? And was that difference in her, or her demon? But even she had insisted that Darius needed to be put down.

"I'm not saying the demon in him isn't a problem, but the fact that my father didn't immediately go on a rampage like most rifters . . . Maybe he's strong enough to fight it, control it even. Like you do."

"I have barely a sliver of demon within me, not a whole separate consciousness. You're comparing controlling an instinctive impulse to resisting compulsion from a powerful being full of malevolent intent."

I took his hands in mine. "I lost my father once before. I can't lose him again without at least *trying* to save him. I need to see if he can overcome his demon."

And if he can't?

I took a deep breath and squeezed his fingers. *Then I'll kill him and end this fight before he can attack D.C.* "I bought a day. Hopefully I'll have some demon-killing magic bullets by then."

"We still don't know for certain how many rifters there are to deal with, or what will happen if Darius loses control of them."

"True, but if they don't have a necromancer bringing them back from the dead, and we can get the werewolves mobilized, we've got a shot. Of course, we'll still have Bael and *his* army to deal with." I rubbed a hand over my forehead, trying to ease the dull ache throbbing behind my eyes.

"One threat at a time. If you're going to meet your father, you'll need backup."

I shook my head. "I promised to go alone."

"And I swore not to leave your side." His grip on my hands became a vise, trapping me. "I'm going with you."

A wave of resolve poured through our link.

The thought of having James by my side when I faced my father made the tightness in my chest ease slightly, but. . . . I looked him square in the face and said, "I'm meeting him at noon."

Silver swirled through the ice in James's eyes—a clear sign of agitation. "Then change me. Now."

My palms started to sweat. "We're not ready."

"We'll never be one hundred percent ready."

"If I get it wrong again, I could kill you. Or you could be overtaken by the darkness inside you."

"We know more than we did last time, and you have better control of your magic. Just today, you figured out how to make weapons that can cross the boundaries of physical existence." He raised our joined hands to his chest. "If Mira and her demon can attain a stable symbiosis, and you truly believe your father can be talked down from the blood-stained path he walks, surely one more miracle isn't impossible."

Strength and confidence poured through our link—a silent, *I believe in you*, that was hard to argue with no matter how unfounded it seemed.

"I *would* feel better having you nearby."

He leaned over our joined hands and found my lips with his, melting my thoughts and concerns away in a liquid warmth that sloshed around my insides and made my skin tingle. I pulled my hands from his and slid them over the muscles of his bare abdomen.

James made a sound that was half groan, half sigh, and tipped his chin up with a gasp like a drowning man coming up for air. "Wait."

I nipped the side of his exposed neck.

His shudder rippled under my palms. He caged my wrists and pulled my hands off him.

I settled back and glared, caught between frustration and rejection.

Silver and blue swirled in his eyes as he struggled to control the impulses I could feel raging through our connection.

"Why did you stop?" My words came out husky and annoyed.

"Because there is precious little time before the day starts and you are whisked away by the demands of others." He was slightly breathless, but his gaze was solid blue. "If you're to have a chance at changing me, you need to do it now, before training and imbuing drain you beyond function."

"And here I thought immortals were supposed to be patient."

"Patience, not procrastination. There is no reason to delay at this point."

I pouted. The heat in my muscles disagreed.

He smiled, lifted one of my hands, and brushed his silky lips over my calloused palm.

I shivered.

"There will be time enough for pleasure once the work is done."

I groaned. "Fine."

He scooted back enough to fold his long legs into a cross-legged position. The sheet draped across his lap couldn't quite hide the evidence of his arousal, which made me feel a little less rejected.

I shook my head. Immortality really did seem to grant a super-- human amount of patience and self-control . . . or maybe that was just James.

Pushing back the unruly tangle of my hair, I shifted so I was sitting knee to knee with him. The loose T-shirt I'd gone to bed in wasn't enough to chase back the chill of the predawn morning without the flames of passion to supplement it, so I gathered the quilt and tucked it around me.

"You're absolutely certain about this?"

"I'm certain that I can't spend another day trapped in the darkness while you face unknown threats and challenges out of my reach." He squeezed my knee.

I nodded and set my hands against the bare muscles of his chest. This time, when I made contact with his skin, it wasn't the flames of passion that filled me, but the cold wash of anxiety.

We know more than we did last time, and you have better control of your magic. I repeated James's words in my head like a looped recording.

I have better control. I can do this.

"Try to relax." I wasn't sure if I intended the words for James or myself, but he gave me a nod and closed his eyes. He trusted me. Despite the fact I'd almost killed him the last time we did this, he still trusted me. I took a deep breath and let my focus shift.

I followed the threads of James's soul back to their core and found the silver-lined darkness that waited there. It had no face, no eyes, but I could feel it watching me, waiting to see what I would do. It would strike at me if I gave it an opening, tear free of its prison and take control. If that happened, would James cease to be a vampire and instead become a rifter in the traditional sense? I pushed the thought aside. I couldn't afford distractions or doubt.

I can do this.

Swallowing my doubts, I pushed ahead into the core of James's soul. Images flew past. I saw myself among his memories, mixed with friends and strangers, as I walked the timeline of his life in reverse. The faces I recognized were quickly replaced by ghosts from his past—armies of acquaintances that flashed through my awareness. The memories slid by faster and faster, until James's life was a blur around me. My heart pounded as dozens of mixed emotions slammed through me, battering my concentration. Pain, pleasure, sorrow, joy, grief, love, anger, fear, pride. . . . I was drowning, pulled into the undertow of centuries of expe- riences—more than one person was ever meant to have.

Darkness swirls like mist around me, solidifying into stone walls. Four cloaked figures sit in tall-backed chairs on either side of me. Two chairs stand empty. My pale fingers tighten on the dark wood of my arm rests. The edge of a hood obscures my vision, narrowing my focus to the pitiful man kneeling on the floor.

"Wrath?"

I look at the man to my right. Heavy jowls wobble as he tips his head toward the cowering wretch on the floor.

I breathe in the air I'll need to make my pronouncement. The room reeks of fear.

"Kill him."

The room melted away as James's life continued to rewind. Screaming faces, piles of corpses, fields on fire, and blood . . . so much blood. Regret filled me—James's regret—but beneath that regret was anger, simmering and raw, looking for an outlet.

The stream of images slows again, and pauses on a scene stained red. Drapes of cloth that should have been white flutter around me, splattered crimson. Blood so deep it's almost black pools beneath my knees. The mattress squelches as I shift my weight.

I stare into eyes as blue as my own. A strand of golden hair rests against her cheek.

My heart pounds as it hasn't since I was human. Tears spill down my cheeks to splash against the knife still clutched in my cramped fingers. The knife I used to kill her. The pale skin of my arms and chest is streaked pink where her bloody fingers clung to me . . . until they fell away.

A scuff near the doorway.

I turn to see Victoria, her emerald eyes wide as she stares at what's left of our mistress. Her gaze moves to me. I have no time left for tears. Tangling my fingers into the golden hair, I step off the bed with my trophy. My bare feet leave perfect prints stamped in blood across the floor.

The scene dissolved. The reel continued to spin. Images flashed past of Victoria, as beautiful as I remembered but with softer eyes than she'd had when I met her. And with her was the blond woman, alive and vibrant. She shone like the sun in James's memories. Visions flashed past of lust and luxury. Beds, couches, carriages, women, men, and the feeling that I would never want for anything. The tastes and textures of James's many exploits enveloped me, and the burn that nearly overwhelmed me just a few moments ago was like a match against the wildfire of his uninhibited passion. This was a James I'd never seen, reckless and free. How many centuries ago was that?

"Have you made your decision?"

I look up from the grave marker—a simple wooden cross that would crumble to dust long before the bones of my son buried beneath it. He rests now between his sisters.

Rain mingles with my tears, blurring the woman beside me. The top of her head barely reaches my collarbone. She looks barely out of childhood . . . but I know better.

"Can you promise I'll never suffer like this again?"

She leans into me, the golden curls of her hair pressing flat against my arm. Droplets cling to the strands like diamonds. "I promise you'll never be alone."

I wrap my arm around her, feeling like a traitor for the comfort I find in that contact. My gaze flicks to the rough stone that marks the first grave on the hill. Rainwater pools in the shallow channels of my wife's name.

"I accept your offer."

She turns her sapphire gaze up to me and smiles with teeth like tiny blades. Then she rises onto her tiptoes and whispers in my ear, "Then I claim you."

Pain tears through me, dropping me to my knees with a muddy splash. My veins are full of fire. My muscles shred—tearing apart and stitching together over and over. I can't inhale to scream, so I writhe in silent agony.

Is this what my promised eternity will be? Is this punishment for turning my back on God? If I could, I would laugh, but all I can do is huddle around my pain. A fitting end for a wretch like me.

My heart broke the day my father walked out of my life, and it broke a little more every day after until the news came that he was dead. I hadn't thought I could feel worse than I did at that moment . . . until the night I begged my mother to get the Christmas tree she'd promised and she ended up in a pile of twisted metal and bloody glass by the side of the road. I knew the pain of loss and despair. I'd lived with those feelings for most of my life. I still wasn't prepared for the shock of emotion that tore through me as I stood over the graves of James's children.

James was a ball of grief, and I was standing at his center, a witness to the pain he'd tried to deny. But I couldn't pull back from the memory. This was part of who James was, who he would always be, and I needed to embrace that if I was going to succeed in changing him.

The rain turned to sunshine around me, and the grass that clung stubbornly to the top of the hill, everywhere but the mud puddle of freshly turned earth, spread into a sea of green dotted with bright-red poppies that shone like rubies under the summer sun. The graves disappeared.

I sit under the dappled shade of an old oak, a leather-bound book open on my lap. Laughter draws my attention. My son is running through the field, keeping just out of reach of his baby sister.

"Mother says it's time for supper." My oldest daughter holds the hem of her dress to keep from tripping as she crests the hill. "She's sent me to fetch you."

I glance past her, down the hill and across the field. Smoke rises from the chimney of our stone cottage.

Closing my book, I press two fingers to my lips and whistle. My son, startled by the sound, is captured by his sister. He breaks free and they both charge up the hill.

I scoop my youngest child up in one arm and reach for my son's tiny hand. His pale skin disappears beneath the olive tan of my fingers. I smile down at the face that looks so much like his mother's except for the pale-blue eyes he inherited from me.

"Let's not keep Mama waiting," I say in a language the part of me who is Alex doesn't recognize. The sun is warm on my face as I lead my family home.

The memory freezes in place, a glitch in the film, and the James of here and now steps onto the field. He casts a long, dark shadow over the happy scene.

"This was your mortal life," I said, struggling to separate myself from the pull of the memory.

"The hills of Tuscany." He pointed toward the setting sun. "The village of Cafaggiolo is just over that rise."

I stared at the little cottage at the base of the hill. "You lived here with your family."

"This is where I was born." He let his arm fall. "And born again."

I studied the man who once was James . . . but I didn't recognize him. His skin was suntanned olive, and his eyes reflected the summer sky rather than the glacial ice I knew. He wore a beige tunic that fell to his knees and—I chuckled silently—were those tights?

"His name was Niccolo," James said, nodding toward the man.

"Your name, you mean."

He shook his head. "Niccolo died on this hillside . . . along with the rest of his family. I'm what came after."

But that wasn't right. Deep down, James still remembered what it was like to live a mortal life. He remembered the feel of sunlight on his skin. If I could bring those feelings to the surface, I could make him that way again.

The colorful hillside faded around me. The movie was over. We'd reached the beginning, and I'd seen all there was to see.

To change someone's core, you have to know who they are and who they want to become.

James's manifestation and my own faded with the memory so I was once again staring at the colorful threads that made up his being, each representing some aspect of who he was. Carefully, I sorted through the strands that felt like Niccolo, the ones that felt like James, and the silvery threads of the demon. Calling up my fae magic, I began to braid, and as I braided, I imbued.

I couldn't go backward, couldn't erase the demon from James's soul—to try would have denied Niccolo's choice. I could feel James's discomfort when I pressed the threads together—red, blue, and silver, the three aspects of his personality—and smoothed them into a single unit. Niccolo's presence molded in my hands like clay. He'd long ago given up caring what became of him. James and his demon, however . . .

As I focused on the traits I wanted to encourage, the silver threads of the demon whipped and whirled as though caught in a storm. The threads snapped at me and pulled free—spreading, swelling, trying to take control as they had last time.

Blue surged around me, filled with James's convictions and desires—a simple life, the power to protect those he loved . . . and penance. Deep down, James could not forgive himself for what he'd become. He'd faced his past, but simply facing it wasn't enough. He had to embrace it—both the pain and helplessness of Niccolo and the callous selfishness of his vampire persona.

Pushing back against the blue were the feelings of reckless freedom I'd glimpsed in his memories. The unwavering certainty that he could do anything at all, consequences be damned. This aspect of James did not want to give up the taste of blood and the sweet power that it held. He would not become weak like Niccolo, or self-recriminating like James.

The threads I was weaving frayed and pulled apart as silver and blue rejected each other. James was going to war with himself, body and soul. Again.

I growled at the stupidity of it. He'd wanted this, begged for it even, but he couldn't stop hating himself long enough to find a balance. The image made me think of the alliance I was trying to create between the human PTF and paranaturals. They all came from the same place, but could they stop hating each other long enough to band together? Or would we end up destroying ourselves? Maybe the fae wouldn't find anyone left to fight by the time they got here. . . .

I shook my head. No time for pessimism. I had to find something, anything, that James and his silver-eyed alter ego could agree on before he tore himself apart. James wanted control. The demon wanted freedom. But there was one thing they both craved.

Sunlight.

I pictured Bryce sitting in the sun with James's pendant around his neck . . . but that was just a crutch. Even if James still had the necklace, it wasn't a permanent solution.

I thought of Mira training under the afternoon sun, the demon within her integrated so fully that it was protected by Mira's mortal body. It seemed unlikely that James and his demon could reach Mira's level of balance . . . but perhaps they could blend enough to reach this one goal.

The blue and silver storm around me stilled. They'd heard my thoughts, my proposition. They were considering. James would have to give up some of his control, the demon some of his recklessness. But in exchange . . . sunlight.

Do it. James's voice held a strange echo that I interpreted as the demon giving his assent.

I exhaled. James's warring personalities had called a cease-fire to give me a chance to work, but I could feel them watching me. If I failed, or tried to alter something in a way either didn't like, the war would resume, and it wouldn't end until one completely dominated the other or they were both destroyed in the struggle.

My physical body was a distant impression as I floated in the center of James's soul, surrounded by the multi-colored threads of his being. Dimly, I could feel the mattress beneath my legs, the shaking in my limbs as I struggled to find the energy to continue, but they were like memories of sensation faded by time.

Drawing as much power as I dared through the palm of my left hand as Mira had shown me, I bolstered my fae magic. Smoky shapes moved at the edges of my awareness. The tingle of being observed made my skin itch, but I couldn't afford to be distracted. I needed to focus on one element, one change, one last push.

You can do this. Again James's voice carried that strange echo. Both parties were in agreement. They believed in me. Trusted me.

I started merging the threads once more.

It was Niccolo we needed for this—the part of James that was purely mortal. I wrapped the silver strands in sleeves of red, shielding them, spreading them throughout the whole of James's body. For this to work, the demon had to be integrated, not a being apart, trapped and contained. James reluctantly stood down his guard, though I could feel his coiled energy like a fighter bobbing on the balls of his feet. The demon's desire to surge forward and claim the entirety of James's body was palpable, but it . . . he . . . restrained himself.

I continued to twist and braid, smoothing the newly integrated strands. Now that the individual personalities weren't pulling my magic apart as fast as I could weave it, I could see more clearly the effect of what I was doing. When the silver and blue were no longer distinct colors, but a diffused mix of light that sparkled like dawn mist throughout

James's core, I released the last trickle of my magic.

My awareness slammed back into my physical body like a punch.

James's arm shot out, cradling my head so I didn't smack it on the bed frame when I fell.

"Did it work?" I whispered. My vision swam in and out of focus. My stomach cramped and growled with painful hunger.

"We'll find out soon enough," he said.

I smiled up at him, but my gaze settled on eyes that weren't quite the right color. Not the cold blue of glacial ice, nor the silver of his demon. The pale blue sparkled like aquamarine gemstones under the soft glow of moonlight. I thought about that color as I lost the battle to keep my eyes open. Maybe it was just my imagination. . . . At least I hadn't killed him.

Chapter 22

MY HEAD WAS pounding, my limbs were shaking. My stomach was cramped, but the smells of coffee, bacon, and melted cheese that filtered through my muddled senses were enough to make me open my eyes. The room was dark, but not dark enough to thwart my fae vision. I blinked a few times until the details came into dim focus.

I was lying on the narrow bed I'd been sharing with James. A tray sat on the bedside table, and on it was the source of the smells. My mouth watered.

"I took the liberty of fetching sustenance while you recovered." James stepped into view, fully dressed.

I sat up and a wave of dizziness slammed into me. "Is it morning? Did you—"

"I stuck to the shadows." James shifted his weight from foot to foot and rubbed his hands as though cold—a gesture totally out of character for the self-assured immortal. "You definitely changed *something*." He looked at the floor, at the ceiling. He didn't look at me. "I still feel the need to feed, the constant drain of being pulled apart and stitched back together. Though even that feels . . . different. I considered testing myself against the sunlight, but . . ." Echoes of fear and doubt trickled through our connection. "I would appreciate your company."

I pushed the covers off my legs and rose to unsteady feet.

"Once you've eaten." He pushed me back to the bed. The mattress squeaked under my butt.

I glanced at the tray of food and my curiosity was overwhelmed by baser needs.

Pulling the tray into my lap, I shoveled in heaping forkfuls of scrambled eggs topped with cheddar, strips of crispy bacon, toasted sourdough slathered with butter and raspberry jam, and dark, rich coffee that burned all the way down.

"Feel better?" James stood near the end of the bed, his expression halfway between amusement and horror as he watched me inhale my breakfast.

I licked sticky residue off my fingertips and sighed contentedly. "Much." I glanced toward the blacked-out window. "What time is it?"

"Time for others to be starting their day. I'm sure Kai and David will be here shortly to collect you for your imbuing experiment."

I frowned at the empty tray. "I might need another breakfast. But first"—I stood again, pleased by how stable I felt—"we have an experiment of our own to finish."

I dressed quickly in the borrowed cargo pants that probably could have done with a wash and a fresh T-shirt the same black as the one I'd slept in. I stepped into my boots, stuffed gloves and a knit cap in my coat pockets, and crept downstairs with James. Creaking floorboards and soft voices came from some of the rooms we passed, but most of the children were still asleep. Water squealed through neglected pipes as a toilet flushed on the second floor. Metal clanked in the kitchen. I peeked in to see Maggie in her checkered apron whisking a huge bowl of frothy eggs.

She beamed at me. "Breakfast will be ready in two shakes."

"Sounds great." I set the empty tray from my first meal on the counter by the sink.

Maggie raised an eyebrow, but didn't ask about the dishes.

I rinsed my plate, set it in the drying rack, and fled Maggie's domain as she poured the eggs onto a hot skillet. Just past the kitchen was the large common room where the tables had been arranged for dinner. Watery, orange light drifted through the eastern windows, creating patches of contrast on the floor and furniture.

James froze in the doorway.

I took his hand and was surprised to find it slick with clammy sweat. "You okay?"

I am afraid. He sounded almost awed by the admission.

I squeezed his hand. *I'm here.*

He nodded and stepped into the room. We traveled along the western wall, keeping clear of the streaks of sunlight shining on the floor, until we reached the front entrance at the far end.

I grabbed the doorknob. "Ready?"

Muscles and tendons stood out along his jaw and neck. His Adam's apple bobbed. His grip tightened on my hand, grinding my fingers painfully.

He nodded, and I opened the door.

The porch was half in shadow, cut diagonally by the edge of the building. James took one step outside, stopping just shy of the line of contrast where day met night. His breath puffed in the cold air as he stared at the orange light beyond the tips of his shoes. Fear and hope swelled inside him, leaking through our connection, mixing with my own until I couldn't tell which emotions were his and which were mine. Then he reached out with his free hand until the dawn illuminated his fingertips . . . his knuckles . . . the back of his hand.

I stared at his naked flesh, searching for any sign of charring, any curl of smoke.

He turned his hand over, exposing the palm. His fingers trembled, flexed, and closed as though he could trap the light inside.

Releasing my hand, he took three stumbling steps off the porch and turned to the east. Sunlight bathed his face. Tears streamed from his closed eyes. He dropped to his knees and raised his arms to the dawn.

I covered my mouth, choking back a sob, and grabbed the porch post for support as relief washed through me and turned my legs to rubber. It had worked. I'd changed him. James could walk in the light.

"What the hell?" Bryce's voice tore through the early morning like an alarm, startling the birds to silence. He was sitting on the picnic table again. His mouth hung open. His eyes were wide and fixed on James, kneeling in the sunlight.

I scrambled to get my emotions under control, my thoughts in order. I'd promised Victoria pendants that could protect vampires from sunlight in exchange for her support. I hadn't shared my theory about changing a vampire's core. If she knew that was a possibility, she wouldn't be satisfied with limited-use magic trinkets. She'd want the real deal.

I stepped off the porch. "Still doubt me?" My words came out in a cloud of steam that mixed with the morning fog.

Bryce's gaze swung to me, seething with hatred. "What did you do?"

"Exactly what I told Victoria I would." I moved to stand at James's back, but resisted the urge to touch him. He hadn't moved since falling to his knees. Hadn't responded to Bryce. He was drowning in his emotions. They radiated off him, pounding against the barrier he was trying to hold between us. If I touched him, I'd be overwhelmed. "I said I could make more artifacts like the one you're abusing." I tipped my chin toward the pendant shining against his chest. "And I did."

"But you've barely looked at the necklace since we got here. You said you needed—"

"Guess I'm better than I thought."

He hopped off the table and took a step toward James.

I moved to block his path. "Tell Victoria I've held up my end of the bargain. I expect her to hold up hers."

Bryce's upper lip curled back in a snarl that would have looked more at home on a muzzle than a mouth. He spun and stomped away, pulling a phone from his pocket. He'd tell Victoria about my success, and eventually I'd need to deal with the consequences of my lie, but hopefully I'd have vampire backup when it came time to face Bael . . . assuming I survived that long.

I turned back to James. Tears sparkled on his cheeks. The morning light was struggling to pierce the mist that clung to the forest, but it was enough to give his skin a warm, orange tinge. I squinted into the growing light. "Others will be up soon. While most won't think twice about you being out since they don't know what you are . . . or were . . . what should we tell Kai and the others about your sudden immunity to sunlight?"

"The same thing you told Bryce." He climbed to his feet. Two ovals of damp darkened the knees of his pants. "At least for now. Better they believe you've performed a known act than that they report to Bael what is truly possible."

I shuddered. While I didn't think Bael would be able to duplicate the process without consent, he'd certainly try, and who knew what that kind of experimenting would do to his guinea pigs.

James blinked in the sunlight, wiped his cheeks, and looked at me.

I stiffened, unsettled by the feeling that his eyes weren't quite the same as they had been. A shade or two difference in eye color was a small change, but one I hadn't intended. What other "small changes" might I have made without realizing?

"We should . . . assess . . . your changes. Make sure you're . . . okay." I forced myself to smile, to keep my concerns in check. James was James. Just different. Like we wanted.

I reached out.

He moved back before I could touch him. I could feel him strengthening the wall between us. He didn't want me accessing our link right now. Still, some of his emotions were seeping through. Confusion. Joy. And despite his new freedom to walk in sunlight, he felt vulnerable.

The wall became a mountain.

I need some time alone.

His need pressed against me like a physical weight. I wanted to be with him, to help him sort through what was happening and what it meant for his future . . . for *our* future. But I wasn't the one who'd just been unmade and put back together.

When I'd discovered I was part fae, I'd felt like a stranger to myself. The whole world had seemed different. I could understand needing time alone to come to grips with a new reality. Much as it hurt me, I smiled and nodded. "Of course. I'll be here when you're ready."

"Thank you." He watched me for a moment with those not-quite-James eyes, then turned and stepped into the forest.

He didn't blur with speed, but walked at an even pace until the many trees obscured him from view. He couldn't go far, enclosed as we were by the cage of the waste, but as soon as he was out of sight, an aching loneliness settled through my frame like a flu. Granting him the ability to walk in sunlight was supposed to make us closer, to give us the ability to stay together despite our different natures. . . . So why did James feel farther away than ever before?

Bryce cleared his throat. I jumped. Angry lines outlined his frown and pulled the scar across his eye into a pucker. He held out his phone. "Victoria."

I lifted the phone to my ear.

"I understand you've won our little wager." Victoria's voice was sweet as antifreeze. "When can I expect delivery?"

"After the fae back down. I can't spare the energy right now."

"*If* the fae back down. I told you my nest would stand with you, but I expect payment no matter the outcome."

"What about bringing my proposal of a paranatural alliance before the vampire council?"

"Once I have my artifacts."

So . . . never. Unless I really did manage to unravel the spell Bael imbued at the heart of that light-absorbing pendant. Oh well. At least Victoria wouldn't know her payment was a lie until after Bael made his move. At that point, we'd either be at peace or so busy fighting the fae that my lies wouldn't matter.

"Then I look forward to seeing you when I face Bael." I ended the call and tossed the phone back to Bryce. "Looks like you're on standby until this mess with the sorcerers is over."

He wrinkled his nose. "My orders are to keep you alive until you've made your delivery."

I blinked, then smiled. "Then I guess we've got another soldier."

I SCRAPED UP THE crumbs from my second serving of breakfast—third if you counted the meal I'd had in the bedroom—and reached for another cinnamon roll from the tray Maggie set in front of me.

"Which one of us is eating for two here?" she said, rubbing the stretched fabric over her stomach.

"She's going to need it," Kai said as he took two cinnamon rolls for himself, ignoring the more savory dishes. "Even if David does round up the volunteers he promised."

"He will." I bit into the sweet bread. David and Sol were traveling from house to house this morning, requesting help from the human soldiers, though I had a feeling Sol's idea of asking was more like ordering.

Grabbing a piece of bacon for the road, I chugged the last of my juice and pushed back from the table. Kai followed suit, licking glaze off his fingers.

"Are you sure you don't want me there?" Emma asked. "I'm happy to be your battery."

"Duly noted, but your time will be better spent with Mira and Garrett so you can back me up in the field if it comes to a fight."

"I'll send Charlie with a snack in a bit, in case you get peckish," Maggie said.

"Thanks, Mags." I gave her a hug and headed for my rendezvous with David, Sol, and the troops who were going to donate energy for today's imbuing.

When I stepped outside, I glanced at the place where James had walked away from me. I scanned the forest, hoping to see him, but the only motion was the gently swaying branches of evergreens. I prodded the link between us and hit a solid wall. I could still sense the quiet resonance that whispered *I am here*, but his thoughts and emotions were closed to me.

"Alex?" Kai raised an eyebrow and motioned toward the narrow track that would lead us to the main training ground.

I pulled on my knit hat and gloves to cover my hesitation and headed for the path.

Lightning and fireballs streaked the far end of the field as practitioners honed their skills against scorched targets. Closer, a group of about twenty men and women milled about near the gun range. The area where Kai and Morgan had been teaching swordplay now had a large circle with symbols around its edges burned into the dry grass—the ritual circle Kai and Hortense had set up before breakfast. Just outside the circle, beside one of the charred runes, was a small card table and a pale-green lawn chair that looked totally out of place on the brown, frost-coated grass.

David and Sol broke off from their group and joined us.

"This is everyone I can spare," Sol said as I approached. "I'll not risk depleting my forces entirely while Darius is within striking distance of D.C."

I bit the side of my cheek to resist telling him we had at least a day and a half. If Sol learned of my intended meeting, he'd either try to stop me or insist on a shoot first approach that would ruin any chance I might have of bringing my father in alive.

"Without Alex's intervention, the bullets these people shoot will be little better than mosquitoes to the rifters," Kai said. "And the more people there are, the less we'll need to drain from each individual."

"As I understand it"—he glanced at David—"you're not even sure this will work."

"It'll work." I was still abuzz with my success from that morning, so I met Sol's stare with a smile. Sure, James's imbuing hadn't been a *complete* success—he'd still be sucking the life out of mortals for the foreseeable future—but I'd used my magic to accomplish something even Bael—the freaking Lord of Enchantment—thought was impossible. What was altering a few hunks of metal by comparison? "You'll have weapons that can kill demons by the end of the day."

Sol didn't look convinced, but he gestured for us to proceed.

"I figured we'd start with guns, since most of us non-magic folks aren't as comfortable with swords," said David. He pointed to the table and chair. "The ammo's set out for you there."

"You get settled," Kai said to me. Then he bumped David's arm and nodded toward the milling people. "Help me corral these volunteers into the center of the ritual circle."

"Are you staying to watch?" I asked Sol as the others trotted off.

He shook his head. "Curious as I am to see this . . . imbuing . . . at work, I have a campaign to run. Darius's attack could come at any moment. I need to get my troops in place."

"You're sending them to D.C.?"

"We'll move the first wave into position today, hide them amid the population. With any luck, they'll be near enough when the rifters attack to hold the lines until backup arrives."

Backup . . . meaning me. I swallowed the lump in my throat and took a step toward the card table, then paused. Without looking at Sol, I said, "One of the practitioners was telling me about a battle in France, in a place called Aubrac. It got me wondering . . . did my father fight there?"

I held my breath and watched Kai and David directed the people in the field.

"He was there." Sol's voice was oddly flat. Did he suspect that was where my father became a rifter?

I could feel Sol's gaze on my back as I walked away. My heart was pounding. I'd been ninety-nine percent certain my father had really appeared to me last night, but there'd still been a nagging doubt that maybe I'd made the whole thing up—that the arranged meeting was just a fabrication from my subconscious to satisfy the desires of a little girl who'd spent her childhood sitting on the front steps of a dozen different houses, hoping her father would come back for her. But Sol's confirmation silenced that doubt. My father was waiting for me in Baltimore. I'd see him tomorrow, for the first time in nearly twenty years.

The thought made my knees shake.

"You okay?" Kai gripped my arm just above the elbow and walked with me to the little folding table at the edge of the ritual circle where all the volunteers, including David, were now gathered.

I nodded, sat down in the lawn chair, and pulled the steel hinge pin I'd successfully imbued out of my pocket. "Just nervous."

"You've got this." He knelt on a folded blanket next to the table.

"Your legs are gonna get sore."

"I'll live." He set one bare palm against the ground on top of a large black symbol. "Ready when you are."

On the table were several boxes of ammunition in a variety of calibers. Setting down the pin, I grabbed a box of 9mm—the size that fit into the Ruger LC9 David had given me to protect myself when he thought I was only human. That gun was now sitting in a PTF evidence cabinet back in Colorado, beside my silver sword and light-imbued knife. I sighed. Magic was impressive, but a solid blade and a trusty gun could be just as important. I'd ask David for another weapon when we were done today.

Pulling off my gloves, I lifted the first cartridge out of the box and held it at eye level. Then I took Kai's free hand with mine and opened myself up to my magic.

Kai began to chant. A dull amber light filled the space inside the circle. Sparks of blue and green shed from the volunteers and drifted through the air to the sigil Kai was touching. Energy flowed into Kai's fingertips, swirled through his body, and poured into me.

I focused on the balance I'd found last night—the point where rift energy became practitioner magic—and poured a single drop of power into the bullet, anchoring it to the core of the lead. I shifted my gaze to the pin on the table, comparing the threads of magic and matter between the two pieces of metal, tweaking the balance until they matched. Then I set the round back in the box.

One down.

Wisps of smoke curled around the edges of the clearing as I worked on bullet after bullet. Faces watched from the fog, just as they'd watched during my training with Mira. They didn't close in around me. They didn't speak. They just . . . watched. Could they understand what I was doing? Would they warn my father?

I finished the box of 9mm and opened a case with *Winchester M855* printed across the top. These rounds were longer and the bullet tips were green. Clouds rolled in as the sun climbed higher. Winter in North Carolina wasn't as bitter as in the mountains of Colorado, and I was plenty warm in my borrowed coat, but my bare fingers were stiff with cold, and I fumbled several cartridges by the time I was through the second box.

The third box I grabbed held .45 caliber rounds. I was halfway through the contents when my pocket vibrated. The cartridge I was holding slipped from my numb fingers.

"Damn it." I tugged Kai's hand. "Stop the energy transfer."

The flow of energy slowed to a trickle, then stopped. Kai was breathing heavily and sweat stood out on his forehead, but he seemed no worse for wear.

"Are you done?" David asked, coming to the edge of the circle.

"No." I pulled the buzzing cell phone out of my pocket.

David scowled. "You're stopping to take a phone call?"

Ignoring him, I walked toward the trees on legs that tingled with each step. Only one person had this number. I couldn't afford to miss this call.

"Marc?"

"Hello, Alex." Marc's voice was strong and deep, but also tired. He and his pack had been hiding since the PTF declared it open season on werewolves. "Luke delivered your message, though he was . . . a bit vague."

"Thank you for calling." Hope and relief swelled in my chest, choking off my words for a moment. Marc was my best chance to establish a unified, mortal realm, paranatural coalition. Even without the vampires, if practitioners and werewolves stood together, we'd have the negotiating power to make the PTF acknowledge paranaturals as legal citizens with the same rights as other humans. And maybe, just maybe, we'd have the clout to make Bael think twice about the mortal realm being easy pickings.

"I need your help," I said.

"So I gathered. Something about helping the PTF fight sorcerers?"

"Yes and no. Siding with the PTF is supposed to be a sort of olive branch to open negotiations for widespread paranatural rights, and the first step toward unifying the mortal realm." I held my breath. As the seconds ticked by in silence my heart beat faster.

"That's a . . . lofty goal."

"I know. But not impossible. The PTF has been backed into a corner by their own shortsightedness. Purity has already failed, leaving an opening. If we want to establish a new balance in the world, this is our chance. We solve the PTF's sorcerer problem and establish ourselves as allies. They call off their werewolf hunt and agree to treat paranaturals as people with equal rights. A new, more balanced system that benefits both sides."

"But the PTF *doesn't* see us as people. You really think they'd negotiate with us?"

"I had a regional director of the PTF willing to negotiate with the fae in exchange for firepower. They're desperate."

"What happened with the fae?"

I pursed my lips, wishing I hadn't broached that particular subject. "My plan backfired. But that doesn't make the premise any less solid. The PTF needs support, and you're in a position to offer it."

"Not alone I'm not."

I frowned. "What do you mean?"

"Wolf packs are territorial, and my pack lives in Colorado. I could give you backup here, but from what I've heard, *here* isn't where the sorcerers are heading."

I paced from a shaggy pine to a bare birch and back. "Can you call the other packs? If we want to make this a large-scale alliance, we'd need their support anyway."

"I can get in touch with the Appalachian pack alpha, but this is the kind of pitch you'll need to make in person. Where are you?"

I glanced at David, who was glaring at me from beside my

abandoned card table. "North Carolina. How do werewolves do with wastes?"

A moment of silence, then, "About the same as regular humans."

"The practitioner camp where we're building our force is circled by a waste. That's how we've stayed off the PTF's radar. If he's willing to make the trip, he can tour our camp, meet the practitioners and humans already working together here. Then we can contact the PTF director I intend to negotiate with." I really hoped Harris would still take Sol's call.

"A human-paranatural alliance granting equal rights to all parties." His words were thoughtful. A sigh drifted across the line, muffled halfway through as though he'd covered his mouth with a hand. "Give me the directions to your camp and I'll see what I can do."

I told him the shortest path through the waste to reach Weavers Ford. "If you call me when you get to the edge of waste, I'll arrange an escort for you—someone used to driving through the dead zone." I rubbed my chest, remembering the sensation of passing through that barren land. "It can be a shock if you're not used to it."

"First let's see if I can convince Ken to come," he said. "I'll call you later."

I hung up and turned toward the card table and ritual circle. Many of the volunteers were sitting despite the dusting of snow on the frozen grass. David, however, stood with his back straight and his arms crossed, one foot tapping.

With Victoria's promise of aid against the fae and Marc bringing the Appalachian alpha, the prospect of a paranatural alliance was finally looking like a real possibility. But if I was going to convince the werewolves to trust humans, or the PTF to see paranaturals as partners instead of prisoners, there was someone I had to get on my side first.

Heading back toward the group, I waved my arm to get their attention. "Take a break, guys. Eat a snack, recharge, and meet back here in half an hour." I stopped in front of David as the volunteers shuffled out of the circle. "I need to talk to Sol."

Chapter 23

"YOU WANT TO DO *what?*" Sol's eyebrows slid up his forehead and his eyes grew wide behind his glasses.

"Form a coalition of all the paranatural beings in the mortal realm and negotiate with the PTF for equal rights—like a labor union."

He stared at me for a moment, then he laughed.

I balled my fists. "I'm serious."

"I can see that," he said, shaking his head. "But you're naive. This mess with the rogue sorcerers is going to convince people more than ever that Purity is right and all magic needs to be contained or eliminated."

"If anything, this rebellion proves that those methods *don't* work." I gestured to the far side of the field where Sol's army was training. "Do you think these practitioners who are learning advanced magic to combat the rifters will let themselves be caged once the fight is over? That they'll give up their lives and their freedom to take the place of the sorcerers they put down for the PTF?"

Sol's gaze slid away from mine.

"And what about the werewolves?" I pressed. "Right now they're just trying to stay out of humanity's way, but if the PTF backs them into a corner like they did with the sorcerers, what do you think is going to happen?"

"So we form this . . . coalition . . . and offer the PTF our assistance only if they agree to grant equal rights to paranaturals?"

"We'll never be in a better bargaining position than right now, while the proof of the current system's failure is looking the PTF right in the face. And it's almost the same deal Harris was willing to back with the fae alliance, except this group has a vested interest in humanity's well-being."

"Even if Harris goes for your plan—and that's a big *if*—do you really think you can convince the PTF to just . . . *ignore* people's special powers?"

"Not ignore. Incorporate. Werewolves, practitioners, halfers . . .

other beings . . . they just want to live their lives. That means being able to hold any job, live in any city, attend any church. They . . . we . . . want the same rights that every minority group has struggled to achieve."

"Except having different colored skin doesn't make you able to shoot lightning from your fingertips or rip someone's throat out."

"And having magic doesn't make someone a psychopath any more than being human makes them a saint. Regular humans have probably killed more people than all the paranaturals combined." My mind flashed momentarily to the blood-soaked images buried in James's past and I silently amended, *except maybe the vampires*.

"You asked me to help solve the problem with the rogue sorcerers." I lifted my chin. "Well, this is me helping. Even if we beat the rifters, there's no going back to the way things were. We have to find a new path forward. A better one."

Sol sighed, took off his glasses, and rubbed the lenses with the hem of his shirt. "You're not wrong about the current system's shortcomings . . . or the culpability of the PTF and the Church for using the sorcerers as we did." He slid his glasses back into place. "If you can actually convince the werewolves to join this . . . alliance . . . I'll call Harris. But unless you can give the humans some concrete benefit to this deal . . ." He shook his head.

I crossed my arms. "Humanity has more to gain from this partnership than anyone."

"THAT'S ENOUGH."

I jerked my eyes open, focusing on the cartridge in my hand. David was standing beside my card table. I squinted at him. The dusty orange of approaching twilight had set in without me noticing.

Kai had called it quits after the seventeenth box of ammo, saying we'd taken as much energy as we safely could from the volunteers. I'd pushed through two more boxes on my own.

David plucked the round from my fingers. "These bullets might keep our troops alive, but they aren't what'll win this fight."

The unspoken "you are" was a pressure in my chest that wouldn't ease.

David took the imbued ammo to a shed near the edge of the field and came back with a Ruger and a box of ordinary 9mm. I hadn't even needed to ask. He also handed me a Ka-Bar folding blade to keep in my pocket.

"Let's see what you remember."

Nodding, I grabbed a pair of earmuffs off the stack and lined up with the troops who hadn't felt too sick to keep training. The fact that we only had a limited number of bullets capable of damaging demons had encouraged them to work on their marksmanship—that and David's not-so-gentle suggestion that they do so.

Squaring my stance, I sighted down the barrel of my new gun. Fluffy snowflakes drifted through my vision.

Deep breath in. Aim. Exhale. Squeeze. Repeat.

The Ruger kicked against my palm as I unloaded its magazine into the target. I'd never cared for the flash and bang of guns, but the weight of it in my hand felt good.

"Your aim's improved," David said when I pulled off the muffs.

"Enough guns." Kai approached on my left. Powdered sugar ringed his mouth and speckled his shirt. He carried a half-eaten jelly donut in one hand. He offered me a plate with two more—a chocolate and a plain glaze.

I set the safety on my gun, tucked it in its holster, and took the chocolate. He hesitated a moment, then offered the remaining donut to David.

I devoured my sugary confection in five bites and licked my fingers clean. "I should check in with Mira and Emma, see how paladin training's going."

"No more magic," David said. "We need you rested."

"We could always work on your swordplay," Kai suggested. "Goodness knows you need all the practice you can get in that department."

"Ha ha," I deadpanned.

My pocket vibrated. I pulled out the burner phone to answer Marc's call.

"Ken and I are at the edge of the waste on Grassy Creek Road." Marc sounded even more tired than he had that morning.

"I'll send an escort."

"No. He wants to meet you before committing himself to your hospitality."

I wrinkled my nose, but I was fairly confident Morgan would jump at the chance to leave camp. "Okay, I'll be right there."

"Bring Emma."

"Why?"

"Just do it." He hung up.

"Need a driver?" David asked.

"Or backup?" Kai added.

I shook my head. "Find Sol. Tell him company's coming."

I retreated along the snow-dusted path back to the main camp and out the other side toward the house Morgan had claimed as her own. Other than popping in to spar with the troops for a few hours, Morgan had mostly kept to herself since arriving at camp.

As I walked, I scanned the trees around me.

James? I probed along the silvery link anchored in my soul. The connection felt . . . different. Not weaker exactly, but not as solid. *I'm going to meet Marc and another werewolf to discuss the alliance.* Nervousness crept into my heart as I sent the thought out and held my breath for a reply. James had been silent since we parted company that morning. Not that silence was anything new, but it felt more . . . distant . . . than usual.

Take care.

I closed my eyes and tried to follow the words back to their source, but the connection faded to a distant thrum that told me only that James was somewhere to the southeast.

The cold that stung my nose and cheeks seemed to grow a few degrees colder.

"It's dangerous to walk with your eyes shut."

I opened my eyes.

Morgan was sitting in a swing with rusted chains—part of a cedar playset that dominated the yard beside the small, blue, single-story house. The boundary line of the waste was close enough to throw a rock at.

I tipped my chin toward the bleached grass. "Doesn't it bother you to be so close?"

She shrugged. "It's not killing me, if that's what you mean." She dragged her toes through the gravel, making shallow tracks. "Have you come to save me from this tedium?"

"Depends," I said. "Do you fancy meeting some werewolves?"

She kicked her feet up and did a little back flip out of the swing. "Why not?"

"We need to pick Emma up first. She's just south of here."

"Training with the rifter?"

I stumbled. "How did—"

"I popped in on you yesterday."

I hadn't noticed Morgan during my training with Mira. But then, Morgan could watch from the shadows without ever stepping fully into view.

"I like her," she continued. "She might be even more interesting than you."

I bit my lip. "You're not planning to . . . tell anyone, are you?"

She shrugged.

I shook my head and started walking again. "There's another—" I snapped my mouth shut on the word "favor;" favors were dangerous commodities among the fae. "—adventure I want to invite you on. A *secret* adventure."

She smiled. "I love a good secret."

"I need to be in Baltimore tomorrow at noon, and I don't want anyone to know. Can you get me there and back?"

"What will you do in Baltimore?"

"Hopefully, end this conflict." *One way or another.*

Her gaze cut over to me, assessing. "Secret mission? High stakes?" She grinned. "I'm in."

MORGAN, EMMA, and I climbed the gentle slope beside the abandoned barn where we'd emerged from the shadow road. The winter sun sat low on the western horizon, casting long shadows across the land. Full dark would be on us within the hour. I slipped twice on the slick snow that was starting to collect on the ground before reaching the bright-red F-150 that sat in the middle of the road.

Marc slid out of the driver's seat as we approached, but he left the door open and the engine running. He wore blue jeans, a plaid fleece, tan work boots, and a strained expression.

I raised a hand in greeting. "Long time no see, Marc."

He smiled, but it didn't reach his hazel eyes. "There was a time I went out of my way to see you, Alex." He ran a hand through his hair, mussing his copper waves. "But when I see you these days I get the unshakable urge to run in the other direction."

"Good survival instincts," Morgan said.

"This is Morgan. Bit of a smart-ass, but she's proven reliable."

Morgan gave Marc a sloppy salute.

"And of course, you know Emma."

"Hey, Marc." Emma offered a little finger wave, but didn't look him fully in the face.

I craned my neck to see into the cab. Luke was in the passenger seat. He looked leaner than when he was in prison, and his clothes were rumpled. He held a bundle of gray fabric on his lap and stared through the windshield as though half-asleep.

No sign of the new alpha.

Marc moved to the end of the truck and lowered the tailgate. He motioned me over.

Five enormous wolves were lying in the bed. There were two with dark-gray fur, one that was pure white, one tawny brown, and one the color of rust. Each had paws the size of my face and muzzles the length of my forearm. Their eyes ranged in color from pale yellow to practically black, and every gaze was locked on me.

The wolf in the middle—dark gray with a black patch on its back and eyes like slate—stood up. Standing in the back of the truck, he was a whole head taller than I was.

I swallowed what felt like a golf ball and took a small step back. I'd been on the receiving end of werewolf teeth and claws before. Even though I knew the wolves weren't there to hurt me, my fight-or-flight response was screaming at me to run.

"Alex Blackwood," Marc said, "meet Kenma Hayashi, leader of the Appalachian pack."

The big gray wolf hopped off the tailgate and stalked forward. On the ground, his shoulders came up to my hips.

His gaze didn't waver as he approached. Was I supposed to stare him down? Or look away? Could I appear strong without picking a fight?

In my peripheral vision, I noticed Marc was staring at me too.

When the wolf was close enough to lick . . . or bite me, he bared his teeth. A deep rumble rattled out of his chest like thunder across the desert.

I flinched—I couldn't help it—and once our eye contact was broken, I couldn't work up the nerve to meet that stony gaze again.

There was a wet snort.

When I risked looking, the wolf's thick gray tail was disappearing around the far side of the truck. The passenger door opened. Luke stepped out.

I glanced at Marc. He was staring at his feet.

There was a series of wet popping noises and a groan from behind the truck, then some shuffling. No one else seemed perturbed by the sounds, so I did my best to ignore them. A few moments later, a short Japanese man in a slate-gray business suit that perfectly matched his eyes came around the back of the truck. He stopped in front of me and bared his teeth—this time in a smile instead of a snarl—and extended his hand. "Call me Ken."

Ken's hair was jet black on top and feathered with gray on the sides, much like his werewolf pelt. I gripped his hand and gave it a shake.

"I apologize for the theatrics," he said, "but I find intimidation is the most expedient way to assess character."

"And what did you . . . assess . . . about me?"

"That you're sincere."

"I assume Marc told you my plan?"

"To offer a helping hand to the humans while they're weak in exchange for equal rights."

I nodded.

"Bold." He clasped his hands behind his back. "Foolishly so."

My hopes sagged. But Ken had come, so there was still a chance. I gestured toward the waste. "Let me show you our camp, introduce you to the practitioners and humans we have training here."

Ken nodded. "Your companions will wait here, with mine, while you accompany me." The four remaining wolves hopped out of the back of the truck and padded toward Emma and Morgan, forming a loose circle around them.

Emma went very pale and still.

Morgan seemed only mildly interested in the proceedings.

I glared at Marc. "That's why you wanted Emma here? So she could be a hostage?"

"Only a fool would walk into a possible ambush with no contingency plan," Ken said.

I rolled my eyes. "You're gonna get along with Sol just fine."

"I'll stay too." Luke stepped around the back of the truck. "Emma and I have some catching up to do."

I looked at Emma, shivering in the snow, then at the idling truck. "At least let them keep the truck. Otherwise Emma will have frostbite by the time we get back."

Ken frowned. "You wish to cross the waste on foot?"

"I don't wish to *cross* the waste at all." I gestured to Morgan. "You've heard of shadow walkers?"

His upper lip pulled back. "I will not trust my life to a fae."

I clenched my jaw to cut off my first response. Many werewolves blamed the fae for their condition—their curse, as they sometimes called it—because a fae shifter created the first werewolf. But that act had been one of love, not malice. Still, centuries later, there was a distinct anti-fae vibe among the werewolves. Ironic if that turned out to be the common ground that brought the wolves and PTF together.

"Shadow walking is the fastest, and safest, way through the waste."

"I'm in no rush." He narrowed his eyes at me. This time I dropped my gaze right away. No more staring contests with the alpha.

"Fine." I'd survived the passage before, I could survive again, though even the thought made me nauseous. "But don't blame me if I barf in your lap."

Chapter 24

I CLUNG TO MARC'S arm as I climbed out of the cab on shaky legs. I'd avoided hurling or passing out as he raced the truck along the curving road to Weavers Ford at breakneck speed, but the shock of having my energy sapped was no less traumatic for being less of a surprise this time. Once again, the ruby ember of my fae magic had flickered and faded into oblivion, and the tingle of energy I should have felt on my skin was replaced by an icy emptiness that drew my strength like a syringe drawing blood. By the time the truck stopped, my vision was bursting with colored sparks against a dark backdrop, my shirt was drenched with sweat, and I was shivering so hard my bones felt like they would shake apart.

My werewolf companions stepped onto the street at the edge of camp with little more than pale cheeks and grim frowns. I wanted to punch each of them in the gut so they'd know how I felt.

"Welcome to camp." I stepped away from Marc and spread my arms. "Training ground for renegade practitioners, disillusioned PTF agents, and an array of misfit paranaturals like myself."

Ken looked around. "And you're in charge here?"

I shook my head. "Sol's the one who put this group together. He's been recruiting discontents from the PTF ranks for years."

Ken raised an eyebrow. "Just in case?"

"I like to be prepared." Sol stepped onto the road. "The situation with the sorcerers was volatile from its inception. It was only a matter of time before they rebelled. And when I realized how powerful Darius had become . . ." He glanced at me, then strode up to Ken. "My name is Solomon Adams. I lead this group."

"Kenma Hayashi," Ken said. He didn't extend his hand. Neither man blinked. Neither looked away. My muscles tensed as my fight-or-flight response rose in response to the tension between the two men. If an insect had dared cross their locked gazes, it would have been vaporized.

Ken smiled. "I like you." He extended his hand.

Sol shook it, but didn't smile. "Alex has a dream about paranatural rights. I've got a dream about not seeing the world overrun by demons in practitioner skin-suits. If you can help with the latter, I'll see what I can do about the former."

"What makes you think your team, even with our support, can stop sorcerers the PTF and Purity's abominations couldn't defeat?"

"We have the one person in the universe Darius might actually hesitate to kill."

Sol looked at me. Everyone else looked at me. I resisted the urge to hide.

"Our job is to create an opportunity," Sol said. "Alex will finish the job."

"Without hesitation?" Ken asked.

I raised my chin, forcing myself to meet his gaze. "I *will* bring an end to my father's violence, one way or another."

He pursed his lips, then gestured to Sol. "Show me the rest of your facility."

I CLOSED THE DOOR to the darkened room I shared with James and leaned against it. The back of my head thumped gently against the wood.

"How'd your meeting go?"

I twitched. My gaze zeroed in on James, who sat in a wicker chair in one corner.

"Not bad." I kicked off my boots, draped my coat on the dresser, and sat on the edge of the bed. "Not great either. Ken—the leader of the Appalachian werewolf pack—hasn't given his answer yet. Says he needs to sleep on it. He and his entourage are squatting in a house north of here."

James nodded. "Change can be hard on those of us who've been around for a while. Even change for the better. I'm sure what you're proposing . . . the hope of living openly with humans . . . must seem too good to be true."

I rubbed my hands together, more for a kinetic outlet than a need for warmth. "How was your walk?"

He smiled. "Different."

I studied his face and waited for more.

"I'm not sure I can describe it." He leaned forward so his elbows rested on his knees. "I thought I remembered what sunlight felt like. After all, I've enjoyed the benefit of Bael's charm for years. But I was wrong. What I felt wearing the necklace was muted, dull—it only felt intense compared to the darkness that came before. But today?" He shook his head and spread his hands. "My skin was on fire."

I snickered at his look of euphoria. "Most people would interpret a sunburn as a bad thing."

"Most people don't know what a *true* sunburn feels like." He looked to the ceiling with a sigh. "But it wasn't just the sun. The earthy smells of the damp soil and decomposing leaves. The brush of snowflakes carried on the wind melting against my cheeks. The song of a goldfinch calling for its mate. Everything felt . . ." He shook his head again.

I worried my lower lip between my teeth. The world felt different because *he* was different. But how different?

He looked down and met my gaze with cornflower blue. *I'm sorry you felt excluded.*

I forced a smile. James's emotions were guarded, but I could feel him well enough to know much of the turmoil from the morning was still there. "I just . . ." I stared into the familiar yet alien eyes. "You're not the only one feeling things a little differently today."

He frowned. "You're afraid."

I inhaled and used the moment to take stock of what I was feeling. Fear? Yes. But fear of what exactly? I'd wanted James to change, to stop being a vampire, so why was a shade or two difference in eye color throwing me for such a loop?

"A great many things about me may have changed. Some obvious, some subtle. Some we may not discover for a while yet. But one thing has not . . . *will not* change." He crossed the room, wrapped both hands around mine, and let down his guard. Warmth enveloped me like a quilt keeping a child's nightmares at bay. "I love you, Alex Blackwood, in every version of my existence."

Pouring my response through our connection, I pressed my lips to his, breathing in the scent of winter forest that clung to his skin. *I love you, too.*

The warmth filling me shifted, growing strong enough to burn. My skin prickled with it. My muscles twitched to respond.

James's lips parted. Our tongues touched, tasting. His hands left mine to travel up my thighs. When his fingers reached my shirt, they slid under. I shivered as the night air kissed my skin.

James crashed over me like a wave, tumbling me back onto the mattress with our mouths still connected. His hands moved from my sides to my breasts. His mouth traveled down my neck. I gasped. What-ever change I'd seen in his eyes, this was not the touch of a stranger.

He pulled back for a moment, and our hands flew in a mad race to remove our clothes. When the last article hit the floor, I shoved James, rolling him over, and climbed on top. The walls between us crumbled. I responded to his desires faster than thought. He reacted to my every cue. The bed frame squeaked and bumped the wall, but I was too lost in the moment to care.

He grunted. I shuddered. We both arched back in a moment of shared release.

Diminishing waves rippled through me like aftershocks. My muscles were warm and slack as I collapsed.

I rested my cheek against James's chest and listened to the comforting rhythm of his heartbeat. His thoughts and feelings swirled through me, lazy and slow.

I closed my eyes and tried to let the sleepy contentment rolling through James seep into me, but the concerns I'd momentarily pushed away were once more piling up in my mind—not just the issue of how I was going to convince Ken and Harris to work together, but anxiety about my impending meeting with my father. The warm haze I'd been enjoying couldn't hold back the twisting cramps of stress as my mind cataloged every possible way the next day could go wrong.

A soft snore escaped James.

I smiled in the darkness. At least one worry had been crossed off my list. Whatever changes I'd inadvertently made, James was still the man I loved.

Carefully disentangling myself, I slipped off the bed and draped the skewed covers over James as best I could. Then I pulled my clothes back on, grabbed my sketchbook, and left the room.

"CAN'T SLEEP?"

I looked up from the seventh sketch I'd started since sitting down at the kitchen table. Maggie was standing in the doorway.

"You either?"

She snorted. "I'm pregnant." She went to the fridge and pulled out the makings of a roast beef sandwich. "I have to pee twenty times a night, and I'm always hungry." She set bread, meat, cheese, and mayonnaise on the table. "You want one?"

I shook my head.

"Guess I should get used to it," she continued. "From what I've read, I'll be up every two hours with the baby, so nights of uninterrupted sleep are a thing of the past."

"*Your* past maybe. I can't even remember my last night of uninterrupted sleep."

"Speaking of . . ." She tapped my sketchbook. "What're you working on?"

"Just doodles. I was hoping if I got my thoughts out on paper they'd stop swirling around my head."

She pulled the sketchbook toward her and flipped back a page. "This one looks like an M.C. Escher drawing."

I glanced at the sketch—a twisted collection of bridges and walls in a variety of styles all jumbled together, the whole mass teetering on a precipice above an abyss. "I'm trying to build all these bridges." I leaned back in my seat and stared at the ceiling. "But everywhere I turn I find more walls."

Maggie continued to flip back through the pages of the sketchbook. She paused on a collection of faces, portraits of people I'd observed around camp. "Have you shown these to anyone?"

I raised an eyebrow. "My doodles? No. Why would I?"

She chewed her bottom lip for a moment, then pushed the sketchbook back across the table and started building her sandwich. "Sol brought you here to stop your father. I get that. But you're not a soldier, Alex. At least, you weren't."

"A lot's changed in the past few months," I said.

"That's what I'm worried about." She slathered mayonnaise on her bread and slapped a piece of cheese on top. "You've never been great with words and, let's face it, charisma's not your strong suit." She chuckled. "I don't think I've ever seen anyone as uncomfortable at a party as when you were rubbing elbows with the posh folks at your first gallery exhibit."

"Gee, thanks."

"But you never sold your art with words or smiles. Your sculptures sold because they showed an idea that resonated with people."

I frowned, thinking back to October, when I learned I'd been accidentally imbuing my art. I'd felt like a fraud until I remembered that art was just a means of expression, a way to communicate ideas visually, viscerally.

Maggie tapped the sketchbook. "You're not a soldier, Alex. So stop coming at this problem like a soldier. Making people see new aspects of the world, helping them understand . . . that's a job for an artist."

She set a stack of meat on the second slice of bread, pressed the two pieces together, and took a bite.

I looked from her, to my sketches, back to her, and smiled. "You're right. Dealing with people like Sol, Bael, and Harris . . . I've been losing myself."

She swallowed and grinned. "Glad I tagged along now?"

"Beyond glad," I said.

"I can't stop sorcerers, or convince werewolves to work with the PTF, or stop a fae invasion. But you can. I know you can."

"We each do what we can do," I whispered.

I flipped to a fresh page in my sketchbook and started drawing. I wasn't an illustrator—I preferred to work in three dimensions—but every sculpture started with a sketch, an idea. When this was over, I'd build a monument. In the meantime, I poured all my hopes for the future into the graphite streaks on the page.

Maggie chewed contentedly on her sandwich and watched me work.

A SCUFF. THE CREAK of wood. Noises filtered into my groggy awareness.

My cheek stuck to the kitchen table when I lifted my head. I wiped the dampness off with stiff fingers and opened my eyes. Tangerine light filtered through the sheer curtains above the sink. I smacked my lips, trying to dislodge the flavor of moldy cotton balls. The gears of my brain clunked and clanged as they tried to spin up to actual thought.

My gaze drifted to the right—the direction of the sounds that woke me.

Ken's hip rested against the edge of the table. He was once again in the slate-gray suit he'd worn last night. His dark hair was combed back, exposing the gray on the sides. My sketchbook was balanced in one hand. He flipped a page. Flipped again.

"Marcus said you were an artist."

"A metalsmith usually, but"—I gestured to the drawings—"I use what's available."

He turned the sketchbook toward me, opened to the drawing I'd fallen asleep making long after Maggie returned to her bed. The picture was incomplete, last in a long series of concept sketches, but all the important elements were there. Six paths of different materials spiraled toward a central point. There, they twisted together in the same way I'd woven James's three selves, combining to form a spire from which a single alloy emerged and folded back in a dozen ribbons to create the longitude lines of a sphere. High walls separated the six starting materials, petering away to nothing as they moved toward the center.

Ken tapped the page. "What's this?"

"My vision for the future."

He laid the sketchbook on the table and turned back a page, studying the smaller components I'd detailed there.

"You really think the different species can become a unified whole?"

"I know they can." I set my hand over my heart. "I'm proof of that."

He frowned.

"How much did Marc tell you about me?"

"That you're a friend, an artist, fond of the outdoors, loyal, and brave."

"That I'm a halfer?"

Ken pursed his lips. "Halfers are no more responsible for their parentage than werewolves are for their disease. I'll not hold that against you."

I took a deep breath and blew it out slowly. If I was going to convince Ken, Harris . . . my father . . . I needed them to trust me, to believe my vision was possible. That meant putting all my cards on the table. "I'm not just a halfer, I'm granddaughter to the fae Lord of Enchantment. I'm also a practitioner, daughter of the necromancer we're trying to stop. I've been bitten by a werewolf and share the soul of a vampire. And as my friend Maggie reminded me last night, despite all of that, I'm still the same person I was when I thought I was human and nothing more.

"This"—I tapped the sphere in the center of my drawing— "doesn't represent the world. Not really. It's the center of a single person, the core of their being, because that's where the change needs to happen. We start with treaties and laws to make space for peace." I pointed to the picture. "But that's the goal. A fundamental change on an individual level. That's how we bring peace to the world."

"Every ethnicity, every religion, every minority throughout history has made the claim that we're all the same inside. That there's more uniting us than dividing us. And those were humans trying to convince other humans." He shook his head. "Even setting the fae aside, do you really believe people can accept someone who grows fur and runs on four feet once a month?"

"I think deciding they can't makes *you* as bigoted as you fear they are."

He stiffened. His gaze drifted back to my drawing. Tracing the ribs of the sphere, he unwound the path back to the highest wall and whispered, "A fundamental change on an individual level . . ."

I chewed my lower lip.

"I think you're crazy," he said. "But I won't be the individual who stands in the way of peace." He looked up. "The Appalachian werewolves will ally with the PTF for the greater good of the mortal realm."

Chapter 25

I STARED AT THE BLANK monitor with Sol, Marc, Ken, and Nicki the tech queen. I shifted my weight as the sound of our unanswered call played through the speakers. "Do you think Harris will pick up?"

"Considering what happened to Purity's troops, she'd be a fool not to," Sol said, but there was a crease of worry between his eyebrows. Sol had been true to his word. As soon as Ken gave the alliance his stamp of approval, Sol placed a call to Harris. Now it was my job to convince her . . . assuming she ever answered.

I shifted my weight back to my other foot.

The speakers clicked. At first I thought it was a pop of static, but then Harris's face appeared on the monitor. Dark circles shaded her eyes and the braids in her hair were looking a bit frizzed, but her pale-blue suit jacket and pressed cream blouse were impeccable.

"I didn't expect to hear from you again," she said, leaning back in her office chair. An Impressionist painting of a boat on the sea filled the wall behind her. "Calling to gloat about Purity's failure?"

"I-told-you-so's are for idiots," said Sol. "I'm calling to discuss what happens next."

She folded her hands. "I take it you have a plan?"

Sol looked at me and stepped to the side.

I took center position in front of the camera. "I do."

Harris was already shaking her head. "You've got a lot of nerve coming to me after you went behind my back to break your friend out of PTF holding in Colorado."

"Luke was my only way of getting in touch with the werewolves. If you want to arrest me later, so be it, but right now we've got more important things to discuss." I turned to indicate Ken. "This is—"

"No." Harris pushed back from the desk and stood, looking down at the camera. "I can't trust you. Whatever far-fetched scheme you've hatched, I'll have no part in it."

She reached for the camera, her hand growing to fill the whole frame, and the screen went blank.

I stared at the dark monitor, mouth agape. "She didn't even let me explain."

Sol tapped a finger against the table. "Harris is a proud woman, but also practical. I was hoping her desire to stop the rifters would override her mistrust." He sighed and crossed his arms. "Guess I was wrong."

"Even if the werewolves and the practitioners you have here are enough to stop the rifters on their own, that doesn't solve the bigger problems." I dragged my hands through my hair. "Once the sorcerers are taken care of, the PTF will come after our troops with everything they've got, and the mortal realm will be left defenseless against the fae."

"Then we're better off letting the sorcerers have their way with the PTF and preparing for the fae," Ken said.

"I agree." Marc crossed his arms. "Without the alliance, my primary concern has to be the safety of my pack. I'll fly back this afternoon."

Ken nodded. "And I'll—"

"Wait." I raised a hand between the two men. "That's it? You're going to throw in the towel and run home with your tails between your legs?"

A low rumble rattled out of Ken's chest.

I flinched, but held my ground. "This is a setback. Not a fatality."

Marc raised an eyebrow. "You think you can salvage the situation?" He gestured to the blank screen. "Your PTF contact won't even listen to you, and you'd need to convince the whole board of directors to make this alliance work."

I looked at Sol.

He frowned. "There are a few other people I could call, but Harris was our best bet."

"Then she's still our contact point," I said.

"But . . ." Marc pointed at the screen.

"I'll get through to her." I set one hand on Marc's shoulder and the other on Ken's. "Please. If I haven't got Harris on board by the end of the day, you can both return to your packs and batten down the hatches. I won't bother you again."

Ken looked me up and down. He glanced at Marc, then returned his gaze to me. "You have until sunset."

I clasped my hands together. "Thank you."

He nodded and walked out the door.

I turned to Marc. "And you?"

"I don't know, Alex. I'm a long way from home. If things go south with the PTF, I risk not being with my pack when the fae come. Even if we do forge the alliance, one extra wolf here won't make much difference."

"One alpha wolf," I said. "One wolf I trust. That makes a big difference to me. I get not wanting to be away from your people, but do you really think Auntie Yu can't handle things for a while? Or Sarah?" I chuckled. Auntie Yu, second-in-command in Marc's pack, was a tiny Asian woman who scared the shit out of me. And Sarah Nazari was a tough-as-nails cop when she was on two legs. Either one could wipe the floor with most fae I'd met. "I'd love to see you tell either of them you don't think they're up to the challenge. I'll wait on the sidelines with an ice pack."

He laughed. "You really don't understand pack hierarchy."

"Maybe not, but I understand taking care of the people you love. What do you think will benefit your pack most? Having you there to hold their hands in the short term, or creating an alliance that will let them return to their lives with the promise of safety?"

"*If,* Alex. There's a very big *if* in there."

"When is there ever not?"

He sighed and stared at the ceiling. "One day, Alex. I'll give you one day." He followed Ken out without looking at me.

"You're getting better at communicating," Sol said. He was standing beside Nicki, watching the show. "But how do you plan to make Harris hear you out?"

I slapped him on the shoulder. "Magic, of course."

As I left the building, I traced the silvery thread of my connection to James. His awareness drifted. He was still asleep.

James.

His thoughts scattered, then coalesced with more focus. *Alex?* Confusion. *Where are you?*

Meet me at Morgan's place on the east edge of the waste.

A rumble vibrated through the bond that I interpreted as irritated agreement.

I shifted my focus back to my surroundings and followed the eastern path away from camp.

I CRUNCHED UP the gravel walkway to the house Morgan claimed and raised my hand to knock, but stopped when I heard voices inside.

"What's the point of delaying?" The man's voice held a slight accent that rolled his L's into R's. It was familiar, but I couldn't quite place it.

"What's the point of retreating before there's any reason?" Morgan countered.

"Bael's intentions are clear enough," said a deeper voice. "We needn't wait until he's through the portal to know he's coming."

"And since when does Dimitri run from Bael?"

"We're not running, just getting out of his way."

"Hiding," Morgan said.

Dimitri was Lord of the Shadow Realm. If the visitors were bringing Morgan orders, I had a pretty good idea who they were.

I pushed the door open without knocking and followed the voices to the living room. Morgan's twin brother, Galen, stood near a red-brick fireplace cold with disuse. His skin was the same color as the unswept ashes, and when he looked at me, his eyes were the same amber as Morgan's. Like his sister, Galen seemed to prefer dark clothes—maybe that was a shadow walker thing.

Beside Galen stood his lover and errand-runner, Enzo. Enzo had skin the color of almond milk, GQ-styled black hair, and tattoos that covered one side of his face and disappeared under the collar of his gray shirt. Lightning danced in his stormy eyes when he turned to face me.

"You both remember Alex," Morgan said with a dismissive wave in my direction.

"What's going on?" I asked.

"Galen's come to ruin my fun."

He rolled his eyes. "Morgan has been ordered home by our lord."

I stammered, my heart in my throat. . . . If Morgan left now, my plans fell apart. I had no other way of reaching my father by noon. No way of sneaking into Harris's office to get a second crack at her.

Morgan raised one finger. "I've been ordered not to engage with Enchantment's invasion. Be specific, brother."

"It boils down to the same thing."

"Home by curfew or I get grounded. Consider your message delivered."

Galen shook his head. "I'm not leaving here without you."

She spread her arms. "Then make yourself at home."

"Why must you be such a pain in my backside?"

"When did you become such a stick in the mud?"

"Since the last time I went gallivanting after an adventure and ended up in a vampire's prison," he shouted.

Morgan and Galen glared at each other. Enzo leaned against a wall, arms crossed. I got the impression these sorts of outbursts were common between the siblings.

Morgan looked away first, but it was Galen who apologized. "I don't want to see you make the same stupid mistakes I did."

"I'm not you."

"But you're just as reckless."

"She just has to avoid Enchantment's army?" I asked. "Because they're not here yet."

Galen looked at me. "Our sources say your lord is preparing to invade. Dimitri has ordered our people to withdraw until further notice."

"My grandfather," I said. "*Not* my lord." I ran my fingers through my hair. "So Morgan can technically stay until Bael makes his move."

"Once the invasion begins, travel may become difficult," Enzo said. "Even for us."

"But not impossible." Morgan turned to me. "Don't worry, I have no intention of running off before I see the outcome of this crazy gambit of yours."

I sagged on my exhale as some of my tension eased.

"I take it you're here about our secret mission?"

I glanced at Galen and Enzo.

Morgan waved at them. "They don't care."

"Not quite," I said. "Although that's still on the schedule today. We have another errand to run first. Can you get into PTF headquarters in Falls Church?"

She frowned. "Never been there. Is it set up with fae defenses like the holding facility we raided?"

Galen raised an eyebrow.

"I don't know."

"Then we'll need some recon." She glanced over her shoulder at Enzo. "Want to take a peek?"

Enzo stared at Morgan for a moment, then looked to Galen, who shrugged. "The sooner she's had her fun, the sooner she comes home."

Morgan grinned at her brother, then turned back to me. "What are we doing at PTF headquarters?"

I took a deep breath. "Kidnapping the regional director of the western United States."

Silence filled the house until the front door creaked open and James poked his head into the living room. He glanced between the fae, taking in Enzo's wide eyes, Galen's look of long-suffering resignation, and Morgan's glee. He stepped fully into the room and rested a hand against my back. "What's going on?"

I looked into his not-quite-James eyes but focused on the familiar comfort of his touch. "We're planning a little field trip, and I need your help."

Chapter 26

"NO IRON IN THE offices," Enzo said. Arcs of bluish light crackled across his skin, and white sparks danced in his storm-cloud eyes for a second before the glamour of his human appearance slid back into place. As a raiju—a lightning elemental—Enzo could travel through electrical wires. Unfortunately, he couldn't take others with him the way the shadow walkers did. He brushed a spark of static off his sleeve. "It's almost like they designed this place to accommodate fae."

"They probably did," said Galen. He was leaning against the beige-brick wall of the office building we stood in the shadow of. "PTF officials have to meet with fae liaisons *somewhere*, and I can't see them sitting on rocks and logs in a reservation with their dry-clean suits and dress shoes."

"Good point," I said. "Did you see Harris?"

"She's in a corner office on the third floor," Enzo said.

"Any convenient shadows?" Morgan asked.

"Not much in the office but a desk, a couple chairs, and a liquor cabinet. So unless you want to come out between Harris's legs, I'd suggest the bathroom across the hall. Lights are off unless it's occupied."

"Then we've got our entrance," Morgan said and held out her hand.

I shook my head. "Not me. Accommodating architecture aside, I'm sure Harris has some kind of security alert in her office if a guest gets out of hand." I turned to James. "You can subdue her fastest."

"There were security cameras too," Enzo said. "One in each office and a bunch in the halls."

"Can you fry them?" I asked.

Enzo huffed. "Are you joking?"

"Right, so you take out the security system with a totally acci-dental-looking power surge, Morgan waits in the bathroom, and James grabs Harris. In and out in no time at all. When the power comes back, it looks like Harris stepped out on her own."

James nodded. "Works for me."

"Right, then." Enzo rubbed his hands together and looked at the unlit streetlight above us. A bluish-white streak seared my vision. A second later there was a crack like thunder in the distance. Then silence—the eerie silence of a power outage, when the ambient hum of the modern world is suddenly gone.

"Guess that's our cue." Morgan grabbed James's wrist and pulled him into the shaded brick wall.

I opened and closed my mouth. I didn't know why I'd expected them to wait for my say-so before acting, but their sudden absence left me floundering. I rubbed my gloved right hand over the back of my left, then switched. I pressed my lips tight and started to pace. I was getting used to being in the thick of things. Sitting on the sidelines had never been easy for me, but now it seemed impossible.

"You look nervous." Galen's gaze followed me, but he remained lounged against the wall.

"I'm not used to being left behind."

"You weren't left," he said. "You stayed because your presence was unnecessary."

I stopped pacing, caught off-guard by the word "unnecessary." I'd fought so hard to get back to my life as a quiet nobody. Now that I'd accepted that would never again be my reality, the idea of being uninvolved in the unfolding of events, even for a moment, left me feeling adrift.

"You made the right call." He smiled up at the streetlamp.

A blaze of lightning flashed from light to sidewalk. For a second, a blue-white serpent seemed to coil on the concrete. Then Enzo was a man again.

"I took out the nearest substation. But they'll be back up in less than fifteen minutes."

"Are we interrupting?"

I spun to find Morgan right behind me. James was holding her hand. An unconscious Harris in her pale-blue suit was slung over his shoulder like a sack of potatoes.

"Wow, that . . . went really smoothly," I said.

Morgan quirked an eyebrow. "You sound disappointed."

I shook my head. "No, I'm just . . ." *not used to being unnecessary.* "Come on. Let's get back to camp."

HARRIS LIFTED HER head with a groan. Her many braids shifted and slid against her back and shoulders. She blinked and jerked against the duct tape we'd used to secure her to a carved wooden chair, then her wide-eyed gaze roamed frantically around the rustic bedroom—the matching log dresser and bed frame, the maroon quilt with deer and other forest creatures depicted in patterned cloth, the heavy drapes that framed the winter forest beyond. Finally, her dark-brown gaze settled on me, standing in front of the room's only door.

"Do you want some water?" I asked.

She looked around the room again. "Where are we?"

I also looked around the room. "I guess you'd call this the rebel camp."

"Where's Solomon?"

"I thought it best we speak first, in private."

She shook her head. "You really don't like being told no."

"I'm going to prove that an alliance between regular humans and paranaturals is not only possible, but necessary."

"And this is how you plan to convince me?" She strained against the duct tape for emphasis. "I refused to release your friend, so you broke him out of prison. I refused to grant you an audience, so you abducted me. What will you do if I refuse to back your alliance? Declare war on humanity?"

"I realize you have no reason to trust me at this point—"

"No. I had no reason to trust you when you called and offered to turn yourself in. Now I have *proof* that you're a selfish brat whose sense of self-importance has gone to her head."

I took a deep breath and looked out the window. The sun was a hazy glow filtered through a gray sky. I crossed my arms and turned back to her. "I can't deny that I color outside the lines more often than in them. But that doesn't mean I'm wrong." I crossed the room, pulled the knife David had given me out of my back pocket, and cut through her bindings.

She tore off the remaining tape from one wrist, then the other. She glared at me the whole time.

"Hear me out. See what we have to offer." I closed the knife and tucked it back in my pocket. "I'll have you back in your office before noon, whatever you decide."

"I'm supposed to take your word on that?"

I frowned and lifted my palms. "At the moment, I have nothing else to give."

She peeled the tape off her ankles. When she was free, she crossed her legs, leaned back and folded her hands in her lap like a queen at court. "So what are you selling today?"

"First, I owe you an apology." I moved to the bed and sat down on the quilted deer.

Harris's gaze darted to the door. She stared for a moment, then shifted her attention back to me.

I exhaled. Was she honestly curious about what I'd say? Or had she realized the door was not her only barrier? Either way, I had my chance. I couldn't waste it.

"When I told you earlier that the fae refused to come to the PTF's aid, I didn't get to tell you the whole story. The sorcerers, while certainly reason enough, are not the only reason I think it's crucial we establish a paranatural alliance."

She frowned, but didn't interrupt.

I took a deep breath. "The fae, or at least the Realm of Enchantment, see the PTF's loss of control over its sorcerers as a sign of weakness. They're going to attack."

Her frown grew deeper. "When?"

No shock, not even surprise. Just weary resignation.

"After the PTF and rifters decimate each other, while the mortal realm's defenses are in disarray."

"So even if we succeed in putting down the sorcerer rebellion, we'll be facing an even greater foe . . . with no way to counter their magic."

"Unless you have the local paranaturals on your side."

"And there it is." She waved a hand in my direction. "The threat and the solution. A nice, tidy package."

I stiffened. "You think I set this up?"

"Why not? You said you had the ear of the fae, that you could negotiate a new treaty . . . and maybe you will. Rights for the fae. Rights for the paranaturals. It's obvious where your loyalties lie."

I shook my head. "That's not . . . Look, I get how you might see me—part fae, part practitioner—as being against humans. But I'm not. I grew up as a human. I hated the fae for the better part of my childhood, and there's a lot about practitioners I still don't understand. I'm not any one thing, and neither is this world. When I tried to deny the new aspects of my personality, all I created was pain and problems. If you don't accept all the races that make up this world, you're going to have the same result."

She crossed her arms. "We tried integrating the sorcerers and look what happened."

"You never treated the sorcerers as equals. You treated them like tools, slaves. That's why they rebelled. Don't make that mistake again.

Practitioners aren't guns to be pointed at your enemies, and werewolves aren't animals to be caged. They're *all* people—humans—different but the same."

She sighed and looked at the ceiling. "Even if you're right, and I'm not sure you are, you're wasting your time. Passing an equal rights act isn't something that can be done overnight. Certainly not by one regional director and a mouthy nobody who admits her loyalties are divided."

"What would it take?"

"Off the top of my head? Dedicated representation from each group and a majority vote by the PTF directors."

"Could you call for a vote?"

"I'm not doing that."

"Because you don't think I'm right?"

"Because I don't think you can convince *them* you're right, and I'm not putting my ass on the line for your half-baked dream of world peace."

"You don't get it, Harris. We're way past the luxury of *dreams*. Peace—or at least a truce—is *necessary* if any of us want to survive what's coming."

She stared at her lap and pressed her fingertips together until they turned pale from the pressure.

I stood up and gestured toward the door. "Let's take a walk."

James was in the hallway, staring out a window at the far end. His desire to be outside would have been obvious even without the impatience leaking through our connection. He straightened as Harris and I stepped out of the room.

"This is James." I took his hand. "I'm sure you recognize him from his wanted bulletin."

"Mr. Abernathy, the boyfriend-slash-business associate," she said. "Recently dodged allegations of drug trafficking, hiring prostitutes, and murder."

He gave her a cold smile. "Nice to meet you."

I considered various ways to introduce Morgan, Galen, and Enzo as we went downstairs, but the three weren't in the main area of the house.

I squeezed James's hand. *Do you know where Morgan is?*

He shook his head.

Hopefully she was just hiding in a shadow somewhere to avoid dealing with Harris.

We left Morgan's house and started toward the center of camp, but as soon as we cleared the building, Harris froze.

Her eyes were wide, her jaw tight. Small bursts of steam puffed from her nose as though she was a dragon about to breathe fire. Her gaze was locked on the bleached trees and whitewashed land behind Morgan's house.

"You're hiding near a waste," she said. "Strange choice for magic users."

"Stranger than you know." I turned back to the path and started walking, hoping she would follow. I couldn't make her trust me, but not treating her like a prisoner seemed like a good first step.

The camp was bustling when we reached the clearing around which the main cluster of buildings was situated. Soldiers ran to and fro hauling bags and boxes. I followed the flow toward the vehicle area. Harris's gaze swept over the people, the buildings, the supplies, everything, while we walked. Two Humvees and three vans were being loaded in the vehicle area, and as expected, Sol was directing. He froze with his arm in the air and his mouth hanging open when he caught sight of us. A man waiting for instructions sagged under the black plastic crate in his arms.

Sol cleared his throat and told him to put it in the second van. Then he walked away from the bustle to join us at the edge of the clearing.

"Everly Harris," he said as he approached. "How did she convince you to come?"

"She didn't." Harris crossed her arms and raised her chin.

Sol raised an eyebrow.

"I sort of . . . kidnapped her." I ground the toe of my boot into the frozen dirt.

Sol's laughter burst like a clap of thunder.

Harris scowled. "You should know better, Solomon. You can't coerce my cooperation. I was trained by the best."

"I remember." Sol smiled. "Top marks. Uncompromising. I might have recruited you for this little enterprise from the beginning, if not for your unwavering faith in the system." He glanced at the soldiers loading the vehicles. "Tell me, how's your faith these days?"

"I still believe the PTF is necessary. That practitioners and . . . whatever other forms of paranaturals are out there are a threat that must be monitored."

"I agree," he said. "But people who register firearms aren't thrown in prison as a matter of course for having the potential to do harm."

"So you believe in Ms. Blackwood's 'can't we all just get along' dream?"

"I believe there is a balance to be struck. Humans will never fully trust beings they cannot control—not even other humans—but trying to oppress those beings is like poking a wasp's nest with a stick. They're going to get stung, every time, just like they're being stung by the sorcerers right now." Sol sighed and swiped a hand over his close-cropped hair, jostling his glasses. "I believe the PTF is necessary too, but not as it is. Something needs to change. Maybe Alex's idea of an alliance is that something. Maybe not. But if we treat new practitioners, and now these werewolves, the same way we always have, we'll end up in the same boat again and again."

Harris pursed her lips. She looked at the men behind Sol, at the trees around us, at the trampled grass in front of her pointy-toed pumps. "How many practitioners do you have?"

"Twenty-three."

"How many were sorcerers?"

"Nearly half."

She shook her head. "I guess I know why you turned down the directorship to remain a handler."

"I needed to know who I was working with, who I could trust."

"And do you?" She pinned him with an intense glare. "Trust them?"

He met her gaze head on. "Every person here."

She snorted and looked away. "Let's see this rebel force you've recruited."

THE TRAINING FIELD was as busy as ever, despite the fact that a third of the troops were already on their way to various "key locations," as Sol called them.

Ken was fighting at one end of the field, trampling the ritual circle we'd used to imbue the—hopefully—demon-killing bullets.

His opponent turned, revealing Bryce's lopsided scar. My heart skipped a beat, then began to race. The last thing I needed while trying to prove the viability of interspecies cooperation was a fight between my vampire liaison and the local werewolf alpha.

Bryce landed a lightning-fast blow on Ken's jaw that sent him stumbling. I took a step forward.

James gripped my arm. *They're only sparring.*

I blinked, and the tunnel vision I'd been experiencing faded. Ken and Bryce weren't the only fighters on the field. Kai and Marc were similarly engaged. The four wolves who'd accompanied Ken were also sparring, though they fought with fangs and claws rather than fists and feet. Gasps, grunts, snarls, and growls punctuated the matches as combatants exchanged blows. The snow that had covered the ground overnight had been trampled into nonexistence.

At the opposite end of the field, eight practitioners juggled fire and lightning. Mira stood beside Garrett, watching the pyrotechnics and offering commentary. Another group of practitioners, including Emma, stood in a smaller group. Luke was demonstrating something on a young man with sepia skin and an impressive beard. He ran his hand back and forth over the stranger's arm, fingers clad in the greenish glow of his magic.

Between the extremes, men and women in black fatigues fired pistols and rifles with deadly accuracy at targets backed to the river. I glanced at Harris, who scanned the field from end to end with a serious expression. She didn't bat an eye at the grappling wolves or the fireballs the practitioners played catch with. What held her attention were the ordinary soldiers in the middle.

Harris would have expected the practitioners and werewolves, maybe even some fae, but had she realized so many humans had joined our cause? And how many of those humans were recruited straight from the PTF?

"This is your army?" she said at last.

"Part of it," Sol said. "Some are overseeing preparations. Some are resting. Some are already in the field."

"And some haven't arrived yet," I added. "Most of the werewolves are still in hiding, waiting to hear if they'll be greeted with handshakes or firing squads if they show up to help."

"David," Sol called.

David, who'd just emptied his magazine into the center of one of the targets on the riverbank, turned.

Sol waved. David tucked his gun into its holster and trotted over. The motion caught the attention of almost everyone else on the field. Garrett barked at the spell-wielding practitioners not to get distracted. Emma, however, grabbed Luke's arm and dragged him away from his lecture, calling over her shoulder for them to keep practicing.

Kai, Bryce, Ken, and Marc similarly broke off from their training to join us.

"Is this your PTF contact?" Emma asked as she pulled Luke to a stop in front of Harris.

"Everly Harris," I said, "meet Emma and Luke. Both practitioners."

"But not sorcerers," Luke quickly added. "I'm a registered healer."

Harris nodded. "The one Alex broke out of the Genoa facility."

Luke cringed.

"You don't intend to fight?"

"I'm a skilled healer, but I'm no soldier. I'll support the troops as best I can from the back lines."

"And you?" Harris shifted her attention to Emma.

"I'll be with Alex," she said without hesitation. "I'm going to be her paladin."

Harris glanced at Sol. "You're maintaining the sorcerer-paladin relationships?"

"Not specifically," he said. "But Alex is a special case. She'll need all the support she can get."

Harris raised an eyebrow. Everyone looked at me.

My cheeks grew warm, tingling in the cool air. I cleared my throat and gestured to Kai. "This is Kai. He's a knight from the Realm of Enchantment."

Harris stiffened. "Do you represent the fae here?"

Kai laughed and shook his head. "Not in the slightest. I'm a friend, here to keep Alex safe."

"And this is Marc and Ken." I indicated each in turn. "They'll be negotiating on behalf of the werewolves."

"You have the authority to do that?" she asked.

The two alphas looked at each other. Then Ken said, "Insofar as it affects our territories."

"What does that mean?"

"It means I speak for the werewolves in this area. The ones who will help you fight the sorcerers."

"And I speak for the wolves of Colorado," Marc said, "who will honor any alliance made here."

"Even after what happened on that video? The execution?"

A tendon twitched in Marc's neck. "My understanding is that O'Connell was acting with Purity and not the PTF when he captured two of my pack. My goal now is to ensure the safety of the remaining members."

Harris pursed her lips. "What about other areas?"

"Once the alliance exists, the leader of each territory will decide if their pack is to join or not," Marc said. "But I believe most will agree if their rights are guaranteed."

"And I take it these two will negotiate on behalf of the practitioners?" Harris waved at Luke and Emma.

"No," I said.

Everyone looked at me again. I wiped my palms on my pants. It really was hard to get used to so much attention. I pointed toward the tree line, where Garrett and Mira were directing the sorcerer training.

"Garrett was trained under the current structure. He understands both the needs and dangers of practitioners better than most. He should speak for the practitioners when we negotiate with the PTF."

I met the eyes of everyone in the group. No one objected.

Sol chuckled. "He isn't going to like it."

"Tough," I said. "He's the most qualified, and we all have to do what we can do."

"And who are you two?" Harris looked David and Bryce up and down.

"David is my protege," Sol said at once. "He's in charge of the human troops here."

"But a firm supporter of equal rights," David cut in with a wink.

Harris focused on Bryce.

"I'm—"

"That's Bryce." I waved him to silence. "He's currently serving as my bodyguard. He won't be participating in the negotiations."

"But I'll observe them with great interest," he added dryly.

Harris studied me. "How many bodyguards do you need?"

"Alex is extremely talented at getting into trouble." James smiled and draped an arm over my shoulders.

The others nodded.

Delivering a sharp elbow to his ribs, I shrugged James's arm off. "Anyway . . . you can see that we already have a working alliance of all interested parties. We need your help to implement it on a larger scale."

"You have a diverse group of dissidents," she corrected. "People unhappy with the current state of things. The PTF directors rose to power under the current system. They're comfortable with the world the way it is. They aren't looking to change it."

"The current system is falling apart. Change is coming at this point no matter what the directors want. The only question is if they'll be a part of shaping that change or not."

She pursed her lips. "Can you prove you're not in cahoots with the sorcerer rebellion?" She waved a hand to encompass the training yard. "You've got defectors right here. People who've betrayed the very institution you're trying to convince." She looked at Sol. "It's no stretch to think you're working both sides of this scam to ensure you get what you want."

Stress lines wrinkled the skin around her eyes and traced her mouth as she stared at me expectantly. I realized she wanted me to have an answer. She wanted to support our call for equality. But she didn't trust me.

Without Harris's cooperation, I'd have nothing with which to convince my father peace was possible. The odds of him breaking off his attack if I couldn't provide another way to free the sorcerers was . . . well, I might have to test those imbued bullets sooner than I'd like.

"Isn't our willingness to fight them enough?"

She shook her head. "Words don't ensure action."

"Do you accept that a fae cannot lie?" Kai asked.

Harris nodded.

"Then I tell you plainly, Alex has had no dealings with the rifters and is doing everything in her power to stop them."

Harris stared at Kai, lips pursed.

I held my breath.

"Okay," she said at last. "I believe you."

I exhaled.

"But the other directors won't be so easy to convince."

Chapter 27

"THE BOARD OF directors is meeting at three o'clock to discuss the possibility of using the remaining sorcerers in our custody against the rifters. That'll be your best chance to convince them of the merits of this"—Harris waved her hand to indicate the various species sur-rounding us—"alliance. As things stand, I don't expect the vote to go in the sorcerers' favor. Most of the board is against the idea of relying on magical help."

Sol nodded. "They think the sorcerers will turn on them and side with Darius."

"Or be corrupted like the reanimated Purity soldiers," she said. "Either way, they become another cog in the rifter army, and another enemy we have to face."

"It's a valid concern," Sol said. "One without an easy solution." He looked at me. "Not as long as Darius is alive."

I looked away. "So we crash the pre-vote discussion and make our case to the board. Where will the meeting take place?"

"A conference room on the fourth floor of the building where you abducted me." She crossed her arms. "I'll talk to a few of the directors I think will vote pro-practitioner, see if I can soften them up for you. With a little luck, I can convince maybe a quarter of the board to back your proposal. The rest will be up to you."

I drummed my fingers against my thigh and looked at Ken. "A fun-damental change on an individual level."

Harris's brow wrinkled.

"The directors might decide the law, but ultimately it's the general population we need to convince." I continued to drum a steady rhythm as I sorted my thoughts. "Are PTF meetings recorded?"

She nodded. "For oversight."

"Is there any way to broadcast the meeting?"

"We sometimes livestream meetings about public policy, but not when we're discussing sensitive information."

"Could we hijack the equipment and stream our discussion?"

"I'm not sure how many people actually tune in to our channel," she said with a grim smile, "but yeah. We can broadcast your speech."

"We've got our own channels," Sol said. "Nicki will make sure the feed gets seen."

"Then that's the play," I said. "Let the world see both sides of the argument and come to their own conclusions. If we can convince the board, great. If not, maybe the trip won't be a total waste."

"You'll need to be careful what you do and say if you've got the whole world watching," Sol cautioned.

"We all will." I nodded to Harris. "Come on. Let's get you back so you can get to work." I brushed James's hand as I moved past him. *I need imbued bullets. Don't let them see you.*

"The rest of you get back to your training," David said behind me. "No matter the outcome of Alex's plan, we've still got a fight on our hands."

James split off as soon as we stepped into the trees. Harris raised an eyebrow, but didn't ask. Just before we came into view of Morgan's house, he joined us again and handed me a clip of demon-killing rounds for my Ruger. I slipped it in my pocket.

I hoped words would be enough to convince my father. If not. . . . *Everything in my power to stop them.*

Morgan was sitting on the porch, tall black boots dangling over the rail. Her dark clothes and washed-out skin made her look like part of the waste, drained of color. All except those amber eyes that watched us approach.

"We're ready for the return trip," I said with a wave.

She glanced at Harris, then at James. "You're good with illusions, right?"

He nodded.

She hopped off the railing and strode toward us. "Then put this lady under so she doesn't remember what's about to happen."

Harris took a step back, her eyes growing wide. "I thought we were trusting each other."

"Morgan's not a member of our alliance," I said. "She's . . . helping with transportation."

"Trade secrets," Morgan said. "You want a ride, you follow my rules."

"You'll be fine," I said. "I promise."

James lifted a hand, which drew Harris's attention. A second later, she was slumped, unconscious, in his arms.

I chewed a corner of my lip. One of the things that distinguished James from other vampires was that he sought consent. Granted, he wasn't planning to feed from Harris, but the way he ignored her concerns made my insides squirm.

We don't have time for hand-holding if you want to make the rendezvous with your father.

I jolted, then cleared my throat and looked at the quiet house. "Are the others coming?"

"I convinced them to leave," Morgan said.

"How?"

"With a promise." She offered her hand. "Are we going, or not?"

I STEPPED INTO the intersection of Seventh and Chesapeake in Baltimore and glanced behind me, scanning the shadows of the concrete piers supporting Highway 895 where James and Morgan were lying low—hopefully far enough away not to violate Dad's "come alone" command while still being useful if this meeting went south. Harris was, presumably, back in her office. We'd revived her in the alley across from the PTF building so she could walk in on her own two feet.

Turning back to the problem at hand, I studied the two enormous warehouses that dominated either side of Seventh Street. Dad had only named the intersection, not where to go once I arrived, and there was no sign of him on the street.

The building on my right was red brick with an accent of corrugated metal painted blue. The windows were boarded over and painted the same rust color as the bricks. Three large bays and a blue access door lined one wall. On the left side of Seventh Street, the second building matched the first in size and construction, though its metal components were au naturel and its door was red. A small office sat to one side of the loading dock. Both properties were large enough to house an army.

I tapped my foot on cracked asphalt and examined the buildings. Would Dad emerge at high noon like a gunslinger at a duel? Or did he expect me to find him?

I looked at the blue and red warehouse doors, and through the large windows of the little office. I shook my head. *Not the office.*

I listened for any hint of what was concealed in the larger buildings, but found only the thrum of distant traffic and an occasional bird call. Sighing, I looked at the flat, gray clouds above me.

"He wouldn't make it obvious," I said to the sky. "What would I notice that no one else would?"

I pulled out my locket and ran my thumb over the stylized "A" engraved on the front. Then I slid my nail into the latch and popped it open. On the left interior were etched the words, *I'll give you the world.* Dad's face stared out from the right side with eyes that mirrored my own. But blue-gray eyes weren't all I'd inherited.

He'd come to me in a dream, one practitioner to another—and practitioners could see more than most.

I shifted my focus, finding that hidden layer beneath reality where the energy we channeled for magic swirled and swelled. Above the red door was a stylized "A" in faintly glowing light. Above the blue door was another "A," but only one matched the script on my locket.

Taking comfort from the thrum in my soul that told me James was with me even when I couldn't see him, I snapped the locket closed and headed for the blue door.

The warehouse was dim inside. Faint illumination filtered from emergency lights along the ceiling. Metal shelves stacked with cardboard boxes made a labyrinth of the vaulted space. The aisles were wide enough to drive a car through, and a row of forklifts stood to one side. My shoes squeaked against the waxed floor as I moved along the outer wall, peeking down intersections.

"Hello?" My call bounced back from the rafters, faint and distorted.

When I was about fifty yards in, a figure stepped out from behind a plastic-wrapped stack of boxes two aisles ahead.

The last time I stood face to face with my father, I'd barely reached his collarbone. When he'd lifted me into the air, I'd giggled and marveled at his strength. The man before me now was thin, frail looking, and I met his gaze as an equal. A black suit hung off his frame as though tailored for a man twice his size. Dark stubble clung to his sunken, sagging cheeks, and deep hollows shaded his eyes. Neither his appearance on TV, nor his visit in my dreams, had prepared me for the truth of seeing him in the flesh.

"You don't look well." The words popped out before I could stop them.

The stranger who was my father blinked, then laughed—a high, throaty sound. "Time takes its toll," he said when he'd recovered. "As does magic, as I'm sure you've learned."

"I'm starting to." I took a step toward him. "I only just found out I'm a practitioner."

He nodded, lips pursed. "Sol kept a lot of secrets. Though his scheming kept you out of the Church's sorcerer program. I suppose I'm grateful for that, even if his motivations were selfish. Tell me." He crossed his arms. "Did he order you to kill me?"

The weight of the gun holstered at my hip felt like a betrayal.

"I don't take orders from Sol, and I don't want anyone to die today."

He nodded and came closer. "If I'd known you were alive after your mother died, I would have come for you. Or at least found some way to contact you."

I choked back the lump in my throat. "Done is done. I'm more interested in how our future relationship is going to go."

He smiled. "As am I. That's why I called you here. I want you with me. I want to get to know the person you've become . . . Be a part of your life again. Be a family."

My heart swelled to bursting as the words I'd wanted to hear since I was a lonely little girl filled the empty warehouse.

"I want that too." My voice came out a cracked whisper.

He stopped a few steps away and held out his hand.

I stared at the invitation, at the slight space between us. I could cross it in a heartbeat.

"Will you end your attack?"

"This is not an attack," he said. "It's a revolution."

"I know the sorcerers have been—"

"No, you don't." He let his arm drop. "No one does. We were shuffled off to a dark corner of nowhere and pronounced dead to the world so no one would ever learn the truth of what was done to us. I volunteered to fight for the freedom of my world. In return, my own freedom was stripped from me. As a soldier, once I tested positive for practitioner abilities, the choice was fight or die. With a gun to your head, which would you choose?"

"You have a different choice now." I extended my own hand, palm up. "We can build a better system . . . together. A system that honors the rights of paranaturals and humans equally."

"You're naive."

"Maybe, but I've got the werewolves and free practitioners on board, as well as a PTF director." I strained my fingers, willing him to take the last step. "You wanted to get the world's attention, and you've done that. There's no need for more violence. Now is the time to show people the better side of who you can be. Come to the negotiations. Help me convince the board that peace is possible."

"But it isn't. Not the way you imagine. The people you're looking to convince have no desire for peace if it means losing power, and they'll never see you as anything but a tool. Even in service, even unto death, you'll never be equal." His fingers curled into fists. "The human troops who fell beside me in the war were buried in Arlington with honors, while the sorcerers who gave their lives were shuffled off without ceremony, thrown away with the rest of the Church's trash."

"Which is why we need to show them we're more than tools to be used and discarded."

"If they can't control you, they'll destroy you. The only way to correct the system . . . is to end it."

"That's the demon in you talking."

"The demon doesn't control me," he said. "We share a common goal. That's why I made this bargain, and why it keeps its distance. Otherwise I would have burned out years ago."

"If overthrowing the Church was always your plan, why wait so long to strike? Why now?"

"I was under too much scrutiny during the war. Then that damn treaty was signed, and I was . . . shelved. The Church has ways of keeping its assets in check." He shifted his weight and his eyes lost focus for a moment. "But with the peace between humans and fae becoming untenable, veterans like myself were brought out to air, giving me the liberty to act."

"Well, your timing's had another effect," I said. "Some of the fae see this unrest in the mortal realm as an invitation to attack."

"Not unexpected." He shrugged. "Once I put the humans in their place and unite the remaining practitioners, we'll be more than a match for the fae. We'll take back our world and seal their portals behind them."

"*I'm* part fae," I said tersely.

"But part human. Halfers like you will be allowed to stay, so long as you remain loyal to your human heritage."

"And if not?"

A small spasm twitched under his right eye. "You would side with the invaders?"

"What is it with people and choosing sides?" I huffed.

He waved my comment away. "Once the portals are closed, and you're free of fae influence, the matter will be moot."

"So you'll fight the humans, and you'll fight the fae." I shook my head. "You've envisioned a very bloody future."

"It's what has to be."

"No, it isn't." I reached into my side pocket, pulled out my sketchbook, and held it out to him. "This is *my* vision of the future. One you can help me build *right now.*"

He took my sketchbook, and for the briefest moment our fingers brushed. An electric spark surged through me. Then he settled back on his heels. As he flipped through pages of drawings imbued with my feelings and intent, the lines around his eyes softened. He glanced up when he reached the final sketch of the monument I wanted to build. His eyes gleamed with emotion, but I couldn't tell which ones.

"You're quite talented," he whispered.

"Thank you."

"And your vision is beautiful." He closed the sketchbook. His expression shut down. "I'm sorry it's not practical. I see now that reaching an agreement at this point is impossible, but we'll have plenty of time to understand one another once the future is secure." He raised his free hand and brought his fingers together with a resounding *snap.*

Chains of teal light sprang from the shadows. I waved my left hand, pulling a surge of energy though my center and focusing it into a compressed wave to knock the links aside. My right hand dropped to the gun at my waist and tugged it free. I flicked off the safety and centered the sights on my father.

He stared down the barrel with calm confidence, stormy eyes unblinking.

I tensed my finger on the trigger.

The living chains swept toward me again.

My hand shook. I could end the sorcerer threat here, now.

My father smiled, though his eyes were sad.

Metal wrapped my ankle and snaked up my waist.

I exhaled. My finger was cramped in place. I couldn't squeeze the trigger.

The magic chains continued to climb, coiling around my extended arm. Then a streak of darkness barreled out of the aisle beside me and tackled me to the ground. My shoulder crunched. The gun went off. Sparks flew from a metal scaffold.

James tore at the chains binding me, which snapped and shattered into blue light that fell around me like snow.

My father *tsked* and took a step toward us.

James wrapped an arm around my waist and dragged me toward the aisle he'd careened out of.

Darius's gray-blue gaze met mine. "See you on the fields of honor."

James's fingers closed around Morgan's wrist, and we fell into that place without temperature or texture that connected all the shadows of the world.

Chapter 28

I RUBBED MY HANDS together, trying to get them to stop shaking, as James and I walked away from Morgan's house. The chains of the rusty swing groaned under her weight.

My heart rate was almost normal when I reached the center of camp.

"Alex." Sol was standing on the wraparound porch where he'd first told me my father was alive. "Come here."

Shit. I was the cliché of a teenager sneaking in after curfew, only to find an overprotective parent waiting to flick on the light.

I took a step toward Sol. James followed. I set my fingers against his wrist. *Go ahead. I'll be there soon.*

James frowned, but continued along our original route while I veered left and climbed the ramp to the porch.

I expected Sol to lead me inside, but he moved to a wooden chair farther up the deck. Beside his seat was a large stump topped with the chess set I'd made for him. He gestured to the empty rocker where I'd eaten lunch my first day in camp. "You owe me a game."

"Now's hardly the time to—"

"Sit. Down."

I opened my mouth to argue, but thought better of it and dropped into the seat with a sigh. Sol knew the time crunch we faced as well as I did. At least the game would give me something to do with my hands while we talked. I spun the board so the organic shapes with the darker finish were nearest me. "I'm black."

The first few moves passed in silence, a quick exchange that resulted in half my pawns being decimated. I took a knight. He took a rook. The armies clashed in the middle of the board, but slowly the line of conflict pressed closer to my side as more powerful pieces converged on the right for a run at my king.

Sol traded his pawn for my knight and looked at me over the top of his glasses. "You were gone a long time."

I glanced up, then back down at the unfolding conflict. I'd kept my mission to see Darius a secret because I didn't want Sol to stop me. That wasn't a concern anymore. And while I was still angry Sol had lied to me about my father being alive in the first place, I could see now why he'd thought it necessary.

I slid a pawn forward, then opened and closed my mouth twice before I finally managed, "I went to see Darius."

Sol moved his castle.

"You don't seem surprised."

He sighed and leaned back in his seat. "I'm not a fool, Alex. I've known you since you were a child. And I knew when you learned your father was alive there was a risk you'd want to see him, maybe even join him . . . though I'd *hoped* you wouldn't be that reckless."

I stared at the board. "I thought I could convince him to join us, to negotiate a peaceful solution." I traced my finger along the edge of my remaining rook. "We're fighting for the same cause."

"Not quite." Sol studied the board. "Don't get drawn into thinking you and your father are the same." He moved a pawn. "You may have the same talents, but your personalities couldn't be more different."

"I took some imbued bullets with me in case I couldn't convince him." I shook my head and continued in a whisper, "I had him in my sights, but . . ."

"I take it he's still a threat?"

I nodded and charged with my knight.

"You're safe. That's all that matters." Sol set his bishop in line with my king. "Check."

I stared at my queen and worried my lip. She could block the path, but was it worth sacrificing her? I chose to retreat my king instead, fleeing to the left side of the board. Better to save my strongest piece for a counterattack. "I shouldn't have risked meeting with him. If James hadn't been there . . ." I sighed. "I should have been more cautious."

"Caution is good." Sol moved a pawn. "But playing it safe will only get you so far. Sometimes it's the risky move that wins the game."

"Or loses it." I moved the king back another step, putting some distance between him and the advancing army. "Sometimes retreat is the best option."

"Sometimes," he said. "But sometimes it's just running away." He slid his second bishop into place. "Checkmate."

I stared at the board, looking for a way out, but all the exits were blocked. I was dead.

"It really is a beautiful set," he said. "Pity you never had much of a head for the game. If you'd sacrificed your queen, you could have had me in four moves."

I continued to stare at the board, frowning.

"When the time comes—and it will—you can't hesitate." Sol stood up and walked to the porch's railing. He set his hands on the weathered wood and looked out at the forest. "You did your best to change his mind. You've seen his resolve. Yours must be equal."

"I don't know if I can do it." I hugged myself. "I couldn't last time."

"Then we're as good as dead, because there isn't another practitioner in this world strong enough to bring Darius down."

I thought of Mira, but I'd given my word to keep her secret. I just hoped she'd lend her full power when the time came. "You're assuming I'll get another chance. We don't know which target he'll attack. The battle might be over by the time I arrive."

He turned his back on the wider world to face me. "He didn't say anything? Give any indication of his plan?" Sol narrowed his eyes. "The Darius I knew loved to gloat."

I reviewed our conversation. "Right before I got away . . . he said he'd see me on the fields of honor."

"Fields of honor?" Sol's gaze became unfocused and he scratched the scruff on his neck. "That doesn't ring any bells." He looked into the rafters. "A metaphor maybe? Or one of the memorials? There are plenty of those in Washington."

I stiffened, jerking the rocker. "Arlington!"

Sol frowned. "A cemetery of soldiers would certainly fit the description, but if we're going to commit our troops, we can't afford to be wrong."

"Earlier in the conversation, he said something about how human troops were buried with honors in Arlington while the sorcerers who died beside them were thrown out with the trash. He sounded really bitter."

"With good reason."

"And he's a necromancer. There've got to be thousands of soldiers buried there that he can raise as an army to attack whatever strategic locations he wants."

"Hundreds of thousands." Sol pursed his lips. "All right. We'll focus our forces around Arlington."

I reset the chessboard. The armies were ready to wage war. "Time to meet the PTF directors."

I STUMBLED INTO a porcelain sink, bruising my hip and losing my grip on Morgan's jacket. James bumped my back. Someone found a light switch, and the bathroom blazed into focus. Nicki, Marc, and Sol were crowded around Garrett's wheelchair, all with pale, drawn expressions.

"This is cozy." Morgan sat on the toilet tank, her feet resting on the closed seat.

I pressed as far as I could into the corner between the sink and the trash can. "Glad we kept this group small."

Kai had pitched a fit when I told him to go with the remaining soldiers heading for Arlington, but having a fae in our group when we addressed the board would needlessly complicate an already delicate situation. Likewise, this was as far as Morgan would come. If all went according to plan, we'd meet them via regular transport outside Arlington Cemetery, along with Ken and his werewolves and David and his troops. Hopefully I'd be bringing a promise of cooperation from the PTF. If our negotiations went south . . . well, Sol had a plan for that, too, but I wasn't eager to test it.

Wishing we still had Enzo to knock out the security cameras, I nodded to Morgan. "See you at Arlington."

"Assuming you don't all get thrown in prison." Morgan flipped the light switch, plunging us back into darkness. By the time my eyes adjusted to the glow filtering under the door, she was gone.

I counted to twenty and prayed that was enough time for Morgan to take out the guards watching the security feeds. If not, we wouldn't get far. "Time for phase two." I squeezed past my companions and opened the door a crack so I could peek into the hallway. "All clear."

Sol went first, pushing Garrett, since the two of them looked more like they belonged in a corporate office than the rest of us. Nicki and Marc waited a moment, then followed. James and I brought up the rear. My limbs were cold and stiff. A black hole opened up in my chest. I tugged my shirt collar in a futile effort to get more air.

Sweat broke out over my clammy skin. What had I been thinking? I'd once thrown up in the middle of a school play when I only had three lines. Now I had to make a speech, and I had that same queasy feeling. There was a reason I'd never gone out for the debate club.

Don't worry. James took my hand. *One way or another, we'll convince them.*

I glanced into those not-quite-James eyes and wondered about his confidence. There was no hesitation in him. The directors would accept our proposal. I tried to ignore the little "or else" that wanted to attach itself to the end of that sentence.

The elevator at the end of the hall dinged. Sol and Garrett climbed in. The rest of us took the stairs. Just one more hallway between us and the conference room.

I peeked out the stairwell. One uniformed PTF agent stood in front of our target door. His gun was holstered. His hands were relaxed. He swayed slightly, as though moving to music only he could hear.

I smiled. Morgan had done her job.

James touched my shoulder, moving me out of the way. He was down the hall and on the guard before the man knew he was under attack. An unpleasant *crack* and a soft *thud*, and the guard was sleeping on the thin gray carpet.

James waved us forward.

The elevator dinged. The doors opened. Sol spared a glance for the man on the floor, but headed straight for the conference room. He took a deep breath, then pushed through the door. James and Marc entered next to secure the room, though we didn't expect any more soldiers until someone sounded an alarm.

I grabbed the unconscious guard's jacket and pulled him into the conference room, which was full of shouting. Several people were standing behind a U-shaped table, but no one had stepped away from their seat. Sol raised his hands and addressed the room in a strong voice that was just shy of yelling.

"Please, take your seats. We mean you no harm."

I slipped the guard's gun out of his holster and checked him for other weapons while Nicki hurried to a laptop set up at a desk on the far side of the room. Marc joined her to encourage the man sitting behind the desk to move over, and Nicki started working.

Marc moved the guard I'd searched into a back corner with the IT guy and told them to sit tight. Meanwhile, the directors shrank back into their seats one by one under the double onslaught of Sol's command and James's glare. All save one.

In the center position, behind a nameplate that read *Chairman*, a hunched man with pale, sagging skin and dark-brown eyes stood with his hands braced on the tabletop. A ring of silver fluff traced the back of his head from ear to ear, contrasting the smooth, speckled-egg dome on top. Purple splotches rose in the old man's cheeks. "How dare you burst in here, Solomon, you traitor."

"Now, now, Tom," Sol said. "Sit down before you give yourself a heart attack."

I glanced at Nicki, who gave a thumbs-up and a big smile. "We're live."

Stepping up beside Sol, I gestured to the cameras around the room—and the little red lights that showed they were recording. "We're streaming this feed live to a number of accounts, and backing it up on our servers. The world is watching, so let's keep this civil."

"Says the terrorist who's taken us hostage."

"Not a terrorist," I said, but my response reminded me uncomfortably of Darius defending his actions. I shook my head. This was *not* the time for self-doubt. "We're here on behalf of the paranatural community to offer you our help in subduing the rogue sorcerers marching on Washington."

"What gives you authority to speak for . . . as you call it . . . the paranatural community?" asked a man with a thick accent whose elaborate, royal-blue robes complemented his rich, dark skin. The card in front of him read *Northern Africa*.

I gestured to Garrett. "This man served as a sorcerer in the Church's army. He's fully aware of all aspects of the current system under which practitioners are kept. He'll be speaking for the practitioners who intend to fight." I motioned to Marc. "This man is an alpha werewolf, the leader of a pack. He'll be speaking on behalf of the werewolves who've agreed to help."

Chatter broke out around the room as the chairman spluttered for a moment. Then he pounded a fist on the table, rattling his name card and drawing everyone's attention. "You are not recognized by this governing body, and therefore have no grounds to address this council."

Harris rose, pushing her chair out with her knees. "I move we hear them out, since the topic they wish to speak on has direct relevance to the main motion we're debating here today."

"Seconded," said a thin man with a walrus mustache that hid his upper lip. The card in front of him read *Canada*.

The chairman glared at Harris. "Did you have a hand in bringing them here?"

"Regardless," said a pale woman with a British accent, "a motion has been made and seconded."

"Very well," grumbled the chairman. "We'll vote with a show of hands. All in favor of hearing these interlopers out?" About half the hands went up. The chairman made tally marks on a sheet of paper.

A cold, sinking feeling filled my gut and rooted my feet to the floor. If the vote went poorly, we could hold our position, force them to listen, but that would undermine our cause not only with the men and women here, but those watching at home.

"Those against?"

Another round of hands went up. I tried to count, but I was having trouble concentrating. The vote was close; that much was clear.

"Any abstentions?" Three hands rose.

The chairman tapped his pen against the paper, glanced at the camera in the corner of the room, and looked back at the paper. He made a sucking sound against his teeth. "The motion is passed. Ms. Blackwood and her companions will be allowed to present their case insofar as their topic coincides with the main motion being put forth today. Namely, whether or not practitioners will be allowed to fight in the conflict with the rogue sorcerers currently threatening Washington D.C." He glared at me. "You have the floor."

Squashing a nervous flutter, I took another step forward so I was standing roughly in the center of the room. "My name is Alex Blackwood. For those of you watching from home, you may recognize me from my recent appearance on the PTF's most wanted list. I'm both a halfer and a practitioner, but I was raised as a human who knew nothing about either. I stand before the PTF board, and all of you watching from home today, not as a paranatural or as a human, but as a citizen of the mortal realm." I spread my arms. "And I ask you to help me save it. Not just from the sorcerers marching on Washington, or the fae knocking at our doors, but from the division that's tearing us apart. The problems we're facing now are a result of the inequity and discrimination of our current system of governing paranaturals."

"This conference room is not your personal soap box," the chairman said in icy tones. "Stay on topic or be done."

"The topic you're discussing is whether or not humans will accept magical assistance from paranaturals. I would say the topic of whether or not the paranaturals who live here will agree to *give* that assistance is of equal concern. And let's not forget that the sorcerers you're fighting are only rebelling because of a lifetime of being treated like slaves. The world deserves to know how you've abused them." I glared at the chairman. "I truly believe that granting equal rights to paranaturals could end this conflict without bloodshed, and I came here today hoping for that outcome."

A buzz of whispers erupted around the room. I raised my hands to calm them. "I realize that's asking for too much, too fast. I'll settle for a temporary truce." I looked around the room. "When you cast your votes today, I ask that you not only allow practitioner participation in this conflict, but also guarantee the safety of every paranatural who chooses to fight the rifters. Because, let's face it, you need all the help you can get."

The chairman waited a moment, then asked, "Are you done?"

I nodded.

"Then I open the floor for discussion."

Several hands shot into the air. Others rose more slowly, as though unsure they really had something to say.

The first person called on was a middle-aged man with a well-trimmed beard. He wore a brown suit. The card in front of him read *Russia*.

"After the failure of Purity's supposed 'super soldiers,' there can be no doubt a strictly human force will be woefully outmatched. I say, if these paranaturals want to take the front lines, we let them." The way he sneered at Marc and Garrett made it clear this man wouldn't lament their deaths.

How many of the people sitting here would see this battle as an opportunity to thin the paranaturals who would otherwise remain in hiding?

The man from Russia sat down. The next man the chairman called stood behind an *Eastern Europe* card.

"Who's to say these paranaturals won't simply join forces with the rogues, as the Purity soldiers did?"

I opened my mouth, intending to explain that the Purity soldiers hadn't voluntarily switched sides but were turned into meat puppets with demon drivers, but Sol grabbed my wrist and whispered, "Not until the chairman asks for your response."

I gritted my teeth, but held my tongue. If I wanted the board to take me seriously, I had to play by their rules.

The man representing half of Europe scowled at me. "Maybe this was their plan all along. Get us in a position where we accept their help, then stab us in the back."

A disturbing number of heads nodded at the man's prediction as he took his seat.

The chairman continued to call on directors one by one like a kindergarten teacher. Each person rose, expressed their opinion, voiced their fears, and asked their questions, then sat back down. The light filtering through the windows turned from yellow to orange as the day wore on. Darius's attack could come as soon as sunset. . . .

I pinched the bridge of my nose and shifted my weight from one sore heel to the other. How long were these people going to argue?

This discussion gets us nowhere. James's thought was carried on strings of frustration that scraped against my nerves. *These people don't understand their own position.* A pregnant silence filled our bond. *Perhaps your father has the right approach after all.*

His thought chilled me. Would the James I'd known for years have considered violence as a reasonable course of action? The James I knew was patient . . . but the memories I'd seen proved he hadn't always relied on words to get his opinion across.

I tried to project calm. *Forcing their hand won't get us what we want. We'd win the battle and lose the war.*

Harris stood again, offering many of the points I'd used to convince her earlier that day. When she sat, the chairman called on an elderly man with wrinkled, leathery skin who stood behind a card that named him the director of South America. He promptly rebutted all of Harris's comments, and so the cycle continued. The director representing the Eastern U.S. jumped on the opposition bandwagon with South America, choking me with panic. Then a French gentleman I could barely understand launched into a speech about the American Civil War.

A man with thinning gray hair representing Central Asia rose next. "I can't believe some of you are even considering what this girl has to say." He waved a hand as though he could make me vanish like a magician's assistant. "The only thing she said that makes any sense is that the current system of dealing with practitioners has failed. But the solution isn't to grant them *more* rights. Trying to work with them, thinking they were different from the fae, is what got us into this mess. I say we put them, and their new werewolf friends, back in their place."

A guttural noise came from James. He sped across the room too fast to be mistaken for a mortal, and half-dragged the Asian man over the table by the collar of his dark-blue suit.

"You think halfers and werewolves are all you share this world with? Your ignorance is nearly as great as your hubris. Humans are like a child prodding a dog with a stick. You think to protect yourselves through intimidation and oppression, but it is only by the patience of the dog that the child is not bitten. If paranaturals wanted to eradicate humans, we would have done so centuries ago. The fact that you are still here is proof enough of our restraint. Meanwhile, you continue to jab your stick at the monsters, thinking yourselves grand and powerful." He lifted the unfortunate director higher, speaking through full fangs as his face lost all traces of color. "It is *you* who must learn your place."

I took a step forward. I'd only seen James lose his cool like that twice before—when his silver-eyed demon took over—but when he turned at my approach, his eyes were the same sky blue they'd been since the morning we remade him.

He released the Asian man, who fell into his seat with a whimper.

"Personally, I think humanity should be left to suffer the consequences of its shortsightedness alone," James said. "But you are not alone. This world belongs as much to the paranaturals as to the humans, and wiser races understand the necessity of that balance. Without the assistance of the paranatural community, humanity will fall—if not to the rifters who've sold their souls to be free of their pitiful servitude, then to the fae forces who will follow in their wake like sharks to blood. Your bickering and grandstanding serves no purpose but to waste precious time we could be using to prepare our defenses."

Murmurs broke out around the room as James withdrew.

"Order." The chairman slapped his palm on the table. "Order." When the room fell silent once more, he focused his glare on me. "This is your idea of offering help? Pointing out how superior you are? Insulting us? Insisting the only way for us to survive is to join forces with you?"

I sighed. "He's not wrong. Unlike the vast network of fae realms, we only have one world, and we all have to share it—humans, halfers, practitioners, werewolves"—I glanced at James—"even the unknowns who haven't dared reveal themselves. If we can't find a way to coexist, the fae won't need to invade. They'll just sit back and watch us destroy ourselves. Then they'll walk in and claim what's left, with no one to stop them."

"A pretty speech, but empty words. You've come to bargain because our necks are exposed by the rifter attack. You claim to be superior beings, but your negotiations boil down to simple extortion."

And there it was. No one liked negotiating with their back against a wall.

I recalled Mira's words on my first morning of training, when she was trying to put me at ease. *We've got the upper hand . . . we should go first.*

I shook my head. "We'll help you defend this world even if you vote against the alliance, because it belongs to us as much as to you. Like it or not, the mortal realm is our home. We'll not abandon it because of your stubborn pride."

"Then why did you come here?"

"To make our, and your, position understood." I gestured to the cameras. "To make sure the world heard both sides of this story. And to request your soldiers don't open fire on us when we show up to fight the rifters. Because make no mistake, we do intend to fight."

Harris raised her hand and stood when the chairman gave her the floor. "Since time is of the essence here, and I believe our discussion has grown circular, I move to vote on whether the PTF will accept magical assistance—from any and all available sources—in the current conflict with the rogue sorcerers."

"Seconded," said the Frenchman.

"Very well," said the chairman. "But let the record show that any acceptance of assistance will not be interpreted as a granting of rights for the future, and will not in any way place the PTF in a position of debt to the volunteers who agree to fight." He tore the top sheet off his notepad to expose a fresh piece of paper and said, "Respond with aye or nay." Then he called the name of the first director. He once again tallied marks as the vote continued around the room. I counted in my head. My chest growing tighter with every negative call out.

The final director stood up, glanced at the nearest camera, and called, "Nay."

My internal organs were a roiling soup that turned to ice and dropped to the soles of my feet. Not including the five who abstained, I'd counted more "nays" than "ayes."

Please let me be wrong.

The chairman tapped his pen on his paper as he had before. When he looked up, his eyes met mine. He smiled. "The nays have it. The motion fails by two."

The cold puddle of my internal organs turned to cement, locking my feet in place as I swayed under the impact of his words. We'd failed.

The chairman rose. "Now, assuming you were being honest about your intentions not to harm anyone here . . ." He lifted one eyebrow, as though waiting for me to dispute the fact. When I remained silent, he turned and pointed to the guard who'd come to his senses at some point during the proceeding and was sitting quietly under Marc's attentive gaze. "You, take these people into custody."

Sol raised his hands in surrender, then nodded to James, whose arms slipped around me like smoke but trapped me like a steel cage. The room blurred as James pulled me off my feet and vaulted the table, scattering board members like bowling pins. Glass shattered. The street came rushing toward me as I exited the building from four stories up.

Chapter 29

THE YELLOW BRICKS of the PTF building glowed gold in the sunset as the structure receded in the rear window of the black SUV that was our getaway car. I clutched the gray fabric of my seat, tensing with every bump as we sped toward Arlington Cemetery.

David half-turned in the driver's seat, but kept his eyes on the road. "Since you came out the window instead of the front door, I'm guessing things didn't go so well."

"You could say that." I sagged in my seat. "The vote was close, though. We almost had them."

"Unfortunately, there is no prize for second place," James said.

"And you!" I smacked James in the arm. "What was that temper tantrum in there? You're supposed to be the patient one."

"Those people were so drunk on their own power they didn't even understand what it was they were voting on. I'd *hoped* showing them their position in—and ignorance of—the wider world would help."

"Well, now the PTF knows about vampires. Maybe not specifically, but the pallor and fangs painted a pretty vivid picture." I huffed and crossed my arms. "That was the one thing Victoria warned me against. Now the council will . . . actually, I don't know. What will the vampire council do?"

"That depends on the PTF's response. Either way, it's for the best. The Council of Sin has grown far too comfortable with hiding."

"Then they're not going to be happy we outed them."

He shrugged.

I scowled. The James I knew, the James I loved, wouldn't have rolled the dice on the future of an entire species. He played it safe. He calculated and considered. He weighed his options and their consequences.

He was afraid. James met my gaze. Then he set his hand over mine, amplifying our connection. *The man you knew was only a part of who I was . . . who I am. He was what remained after fear of returning to the demon I had been took hold, paralyzing me. After . . .* He looked away. *I have no wish to return to the impulsive ways of the demon within me. But neither will I live in denial of who, and what, I am.*

So I hadn't been imagining the changes in him. He really was becoming a different person.

This—he lifted my hand and pressed it to his chest—*is the closest I have ever been to my true self. And I have you to thank for that.*

"Heads up," David called. "We're approaching the rendezvous."

I twitched and jerked my hand away from James as David's words crashed through our silent conversation.

We exited the highway and drove through a residential neighborhood to a small park. A pair of benches on the western side sat under the bare branches of trees that would provide shade in the summer. Emma and Ken sat on one bench while Kai and Morgan shared the other. Bryce stood in the open field, face lifted to the sunset like a man at prayer. Mira stood under a tree a little ways away—close enough to observe, but not near enough to be lumped in with the group.

"Alex!" Emma jumped up when I stepped out of the car. "How did it go?"

I looked from her anxious smile to Ken's stern frown, then I stared at the dry brown grass between my boots. "I'm sorry guys. The PTF didn't agree to even a temporary alliance. Anyone who fights will likely take fire from both sides." I glanced at Ken. "I'll understand if you want to withdraw your support. Your people have to come first."

"They do. Which is why we will still fight the rifters."

I jerked my gaze up to meet his.

"You said earlier that helping the humans was the best way to show werewolves could be trusted as allies." He stood up. "That hasn't changed. If my people can't convince the PTF we're more than dangerous beasts, they'll hunt us no matter where we hide. We have this one chance to change their minds, and I intend to take it."

"I can't guarantee your safety."

He shook his head. "You never could."

"You won't fight alone." David stood near the front of the SUV. "The troops Sol recruited, human and practitioner, were committed to this fight before you ever came up with your crazy idea of a paranatural alliance. We knew going in it might be a suicide run."

"Emma." I turned to her. "You—"

"Will be next to you the whole time, so don't even suggest otherwise."

"As will I." Kai handed me the extra sword he was carrying. "You'll need this."

James squeezed my shoulders and whispered in my ear. "We're all done hiding."

I nodded, too choked up to speak.

Bryce groaned. "Could this get any more sappy?" He turned away from the burning sky as the last rays of sunlight lit the branches overhead.

"I take it you won't be coming," I said.

He rolled his eyes. "Of course I will. I just won't be spouting poetry about it."

"Bryce has to keep you alive until Victoria gets her charms," James said. "He has no say in the matter."

Guilt tightened my chest. Much as I loathed Bryce, I didn't want to be the reason someone else was forced to fight.

He doesn't fight for you, James reminded me. *Let it lie.*

"Fine." I turned to David. "Are the teams in place?"

He nodded. "All except ours."

"And your people?" I asked Ken.

"Standing by in various public spaces around the perimeter." He held up a cell phone. "We'll converge when the rifters are spotted."

"Then we'd best get in position."

I SHIVERED DEEPER into my coat and tucked my gloved hands under my armpits. Puffs of breath steamed my cheeks and faded in a rhythmic pattern of cold and colder as I squinted at the moonlit headstones that covered the fields of Arlington. We huddled in a dense pocket of bare brambles at the edge of a parking lot separated from the cemetery by a short stone wall. Other than the sounds of distant traffic, the night was still and silent—free of the insect noises that would plague this area in warmer weather. My knee bumped a pile of paper to-go cups, and the scent of stale coffee residue mingled with the decaying leaves on which we knelt.

The drinks were long gone, along with the meal and snacks Maggie had sent with Kai to keep our energy and spirits up. The stars twinkled overhead, emboldened by the weak presence of the moon. I stared at those tiny lights and fought the pull of sleep. The adrenaline fueling my escape from the PTF boardroom had worn off, leaving me lethargic as I waited for something, anything, to happen.

Maybe I'd read too much into Darius's comments and gotten the location wrong. Or maybe he'd planted a red herring, intending to lead me off course, and I'd followed it like a lamb to slaughter. Or maybe Arlington was the right place, but the attack wouldn't happen tonight. He'd seemed impatient when I asked for the extra day, but maybe he had a schedule in mind all along and we were simply there too early.

I groaned and shifted my legs to keep the blood flowing.

Emma blew a cloud of steam into her hands. "This place is over six hundred acres, and we're stuck looking in from the edges. How are we going to find him?"

"His attacks so far haven't exactly been low profile," I countered. "We've got all the gates covered, plus James and Morgan patrolling inside. Not to mention the regular park police. If I'm right about his target, we'll know as soon as he makes a move."

"Then maybe you weren't right," Mira said. "Maybe he's at the White House right now, and we're freezing our butts off for nothing."

"He hasn't attacked yet." David lifted his two-way radio. "We would've heard."

"I wish he'd hurry up already," Mira grumbled. "Parts of me have gone numb that I didn't even realize I could feel."

"I never thought I'd be *hoping* for an evil sorcerer attack." Emma hugged her knees tight to her chest. "If it doesn't come soon, I'm gonna need more coffee."

"*Shh.*" Ken lifted a hand, cutting off our banter. "Did you hear that?"

Kai tensed. His hand moved to the hilt of his sword. Bryce, who'd been dozing—or pretending to doze so he didn't have to interact with the rest of us—opened his eyes and sat up.

There was a crackle in the dry air that raised the hairs all over my body. Then a dozen streaks of purple lightning seared the sky. I closed my eyes against the painful flash, but not before I saw all those bolts converge over the cemetery.

Static crackled over David's radio. Then a woman's voice rang out. "This is team three. Target sighted near Fort Myer Gate in the northwest sector. Repeat, target sighted in the northwest sector heading east." The speaker was breathless, as if she was running.

I looked north, where the trees were now silhouetted by flickering burgundy light. Team three was assigned the area adjacent to my group. We were their closest backup.

Mira was the first one over the wall, but I was right behind her. Kai and Bryce kept pace on either side of me while Emma and David ran as fast as their mortal bodies could carry them. Ken was slightly slower in starting, having to both inform his people and shift, but by the time my muscles were warm, the big, black and gray wolf I'd met in the back of Marc's truck had taken the lead, clawed paws tearing the dry turf.

Dodging headstones, I crested the third hill since our mad dash began and stumbled to a stop. I braced my hand against the rough bark of an oak tree, panting in frigid air and blowing out billows of steam. The shallow valley before me was full of grave markers, just like the fields I'd been running through, but these ones weren't in tidy lines. Many were toppled, some were cracked, and the earth that should have been uniform grass looked like a freshly tilled garden strewn with bodies.

Patches of orange light flickered over the scene as tongues of flame licked at fallen trees and splintered stumps. Atop the next hill, twenty or so people stood in a circle. Purple light arced between them and cascaded from their fingers. At the center of that circle stood a single man— the focal point of the magic. The necromancer. My father.

A surge of purple energy pulsed from the group. More graves erupted. Hundreds of figures writhed like an unholy mosh pit. Some stood fully upright. Others were still in the process of breaking free from their interment, sloughing dirt and decomposing flesh. A living darkness seemed to cling to the figures, filling their missing portions like gauze stuffed in a wound. Through it all, veins of purple light tied everything together.

Mira whistled. "That's a lot of lesser demons."

Gunshots rang out on the far side of the field. Team three had engaged the enemy. Fireballs danced through the air as they had on the training grounds at camp, igniting the desiccated clothing of the walking corpses.

Emma reached the top of the hill and dropped to her knees beside me, her mouth hanging open. A moment later, James blurred into existence on my other side, drawn to the action from wherever he'd been on patrol. He scanned the scene as I had done, his lips a grim line. Then he looked at me. Fear washed through our connection. Not fear of the undead, the rifters, or even the necromancer standing at the center of it all, but fear of loss. He took my hand. "Are you sure you're ready for this? In the warehouse—"

"I know." I squeezed his fingers to take the sting out of my response. Looking at the rotting bodies of dead heroes dragged from their rest, it finally struck home just how far beyond redemption my father truly was. Whether it was the demon inside him, or his own twisted frustrations that led us here, he had to be stopped. Giving James's hand one last squeeze, I pulled out my gun. "No more hesitation."

A fleshy hand erupted from the ground a dozen feet away. The smell of decay and chemicals wafted over us.

I glanced at my companions. "Let's clear a path. We end this tonight."

My friends and I charged into the chaos in a rough wedge formation. Ken tore at the nearest zombies with teeth and claws. James and Bryce immobilized some by wrenching off limbs, while Kai spun like a dervish, slicing flesh and sinew. David fired into the crowd until his magazine ran empty, then traded clips with practiced ease and continued firing. Where his bullets connected, corpses fell, and each collapse was punctuated by the wail of a demon in pain. My imbued bullets were working.

I fired into the chest of the first zombie in my path—a skeleton whose dried flesh wrapped its bones like shrink wrap. An indigo glow glared at me from the empty eye sockets as the creature fell. The next zombie in my sights was an elderly man who must have been buried recently since his uniform was still intact and his face whole. His milky-white eyes gave the impression he was blind, and he shuffled forward with a limp. He looked like someone's lost grandpa.

I hesitated, then reminded myself that the man walking toward me was just a demon in a skin suit—whatever he looked like—and the stolen bones of a soldier who'd fought for my country wouldn't want to be a part of this destruction, even in death.

The old man lunged. I squeezed the trigger. A hole appeared in his chest. He opened his mouth and let out a terrible cry as thick smoke poured past his yellowed teeth. Then he crumpled. I didn't hesitate to empty the rest of my magazine into the zombies pressing around me. They weren't terribly fast, but there were enough that if they pulled me down, I'd never get up again.

Emma threw blasts of teal light from her palm, visible only to those with magic. Her shots shredded the decaying flesh of her attackers and blew apart bones, but the zombies only staggered and continued their advance. At the front of our group, Mira grabbed a rotting corpse by the throat. The creature twitched as though being electrocuted. The glow I'd seen in Mira the day she taught me how to channel rift energy seemed to encase her whole body, overlapping it like a suit of black, white, and gold armor. The darkness animating the zombie rose in a smoky stream that poured from the corpse's eyes, mouth, and nose until a twisted, screaming face hovered in the air. The darkness was drawn into the light around Mira and vanished into her marbled aura. The corpse stilled. Mira released it and reached for the next zombie.

Another wave of purplish light pulsed over the field as I reloaded my gun. Hands burst from patches of previously undisturbed soil, followed by heads and bodies as new zombies climbed free. The last corpse I'd dropped twitched at my feet. Darkness twisted through it like snakes, tracing the remaining muscles, coiling around the bones. It gave one massive jerk, then the zombie sat up.

Pressure built inside my chest as I watched my work undone. All around me, the zombies we'd managed to take down were climbing back to their feet or dragging themselves on whatever limbs remained.

I sagged. *So long as there are demons left in the rift, the zombies will never stop coming.*

A zombie that might once have been a young woman grabbed my arm, pulling me sideways. I raised my gun, but Ken slammed into her before I could pull the trigger. He rode my attacker to the ground, jaws snapping. Part of my sleeve tore away in the zombie's grip.

We'd covered half the distance to the rifters on the hill, but the wall of undead continued to advance, blocking our progress. And thanks to that latest pulse of magic, the area behind us was filling in as well.

A silver blade severed the neck of a shambling corpse on my left, spraying me with gore.

"This is great!" Morgan shouted as the head tumbled free. Her blade was bloody and her clothes were torn, but she wore a wide grin and her amber eyes sparkled with excitement.

"Where have you been?" I demanded.

She waved an arm to indicate the path of carnage behind her. "I haven't had this much fun since the dorcha wraith hunt for my eighty-seventh birthday."

I gripped her arm and pointed to the purple glow at the top of the hill. "Can you get me up there?"

She shook her head. "Too much light, not enough shadows. But we'll get there eventually." She whirled away from me and plunged back into the wall of zombies, slashing and stabbing with her sword while using her off hand to call up tendrils of dark mist that wrapped the creatures' ankles and pulled them back to earth.

We fought relentlessly, but we weren't moving forward. The gunshots from team three had grown sparse. Either they were running out of bullets, or. . . . I shook my head. More teams would arrive soon to back us up. But the police and National Guard couldn't be far behind—surely *someone* had noticed the light show in the cemetery—and after my failure with the PTF directors, whoever came would likely have orders to shoot us on sight.

A grip like a vise clamped around my forearm and jagged teeth sank into my flesh. I screamed. The zombie's head tore free of its neck, taking a chunk of me with it. Bryce dropped the severed skull. "Pay attention!"

I pressed the barrel of my gun to a creature trying to claw its way up my leg and squeezed the trigger. Bone shattered. My arm burned where the zombie had bitten me. Blood seeped into the surrounding fabric.

A howl rose in the distance.

Ken disengaged from the zombie he was fighting long enough to let out a long, loud note in response.

Dozens of shapes flowed out of the trees and over the hills to my left. Some came toward us, but most headed for the area where team three was no longer firing.

I redoubled my efforts. When I ran out of bullets a third time, I loaded my last clip, holstered my gun, and drew my sword. The last magazine was for my father.

I sliced and parried alongside my friends, but the zombies swarmed like a shoal of piranhas, limiting our effectiveness and whittling away our stamina.

Werewolves tore through the zombies that had risen in our wake, struggling to Ken's side. With their help, we progressed a little faster. Then a volley of fireballs drew burning arcs across the sky as another team joined the fray. Bodies flew apart as magic missiles exploded like mortar shells in the densely packed horde.

The field became pure chaos as we struggled against the waves of animated corpses crashing over us. Then shouts rose from behind.

I spun in hope of seeing more practitioners. What I found was a line of men and women in green camo uniforms with rifles raised to their shoulders. The National Guard had arrived. My friends and I were trapped between the unrelenting undead and a firing squad.

Chapter 30

THE SOLDIERS marched forward in unison until they were close enough that I could see their expressions—this group could have cleaned up at a poker game. The man in the center of the line had suntanned skin and sandy-blond hair cut short. He pointed his gun directly at me as he approached.

My friends had their hands full holding back the zombies. Their backs were exposed.

I took a step toward the soldiers, thrust my sword tip-first in the ground, and raised my hands, meeting the brown gaze of the central soldier. "Please, we're not your enemy."

The man stopped. The soldiers to either side of him stopped.

"Fire."

The world became smoke and noise. I cringed, blinked, and looked around. A zombie that had slipped past David toppled beside me. Half its face was missing. Bryce stomped on the remaining half, crushing the glassy stare of a young man. All along the perimeter, zombies dropped. Then they got back up and were dropped again as the soldiers continued firing.

The man who'd saved me from another nasty bite stepped forward, gun now pointed at the ground. He tugged my sword free and handed it back, hilt first, then snapped a salute. "Second platoon leader Captain Anthony Reynolds, D.C. National Guard."

I glanced side to side. The human troops weren't advancing. They stayed in their line and fired into the crowd, but only zombies fell. "You aren't going to shoot us?"

"I saw your broadcast, ma'am. The brass can bicker all they want about whether or not we'll work together, but the enemy here is pretty obvious. I don't much care for magic or strangeness, but I'll not fire on anyone who's here to help, human or no." He raised his rifle and fired over my shoulder. The sound was deafening. Another zombie stumbled back. "Now I suggest we get back to it and leave the debates to the bureaucrats."

I returned to the attack, reenergized. My sword felt lighter, my steps bouncier. *A fundamental change on an individual level.* I'd failed to win the PTF vote, but I'd convinced one man we could be trusted. My efforts hadn't been wasted.

Our progress up the hill sped up with the soldiers providing cover fire. Blasts of magic on the far side of the field announced the arrival of our fourth team. I kicked, punched, slashed, and stabbed alongside my friends. Zombies fell and got back up until they'd taken so many hits their bodies simply couldn't hold together. Not even a demon could make a pile of goo and bone shards dance.

Mira led the assault, the point of our wedge, sending out occasional bursts of energy that rippled the ground and toppled zombies like bowling pins, slowing their advance. Her shining aura had grown more . . . solid with each demon she fed from, and the pale streak in her hair spread until only one stripe of brown remained. When I caught sight of her face, her eyes were golden, and a wide smile sat on her lips. Her latest victim fell from her hands, intact but lifeless, its essence absorbed.

Frowning, I glanced back along the trail we'd blazed up the hillside. Dozens of corpses remained on the ground, drained by Mira.

I looked at the top of the hill. The purple glow was still present, but I hadn't seen a pulse for a while. The drained zombies weren't reanimating.

I expanded my tunnel vision of the battle right in front of me to take in the whole field. Clusters of conflict continued where my teams and Reynolds's soldiers engaged the zombies, but the horde itself was thinner. Near the edges, zombies broke away and shuffled into the trees and down the pathways, leaving the battle . . . scattering.

A sickening realization settled over me.

We're wasting time. Focusing on my connection to James, I conveyed my concern, and my idea. *A decisive blow is the only way to be sure.*

Agreed. A rush of cool detachment washed over me as James closed on Bryce. I opened my mouth to tell him to wait, but Bryce's head was twisted backward on his neck before the words made it past my throat.

My stomach lurched. I loathed Bryce, but . . . I hadn't intended . . .

James snagged the chain around Bryce's neck as he fell. The links snapped.

"Kai," James called. He spun toward the knight and tossed the pendant into the air.

Understanding flashed across Kai's face. He swung his sword.

Dropping my weapon, I took three running steps and tackled Mira around the middle, screaming, "Take cover."

As we fell, a wave of earth washed up and over us. A burst of blinding white washed out my vision. Then I was buried alive.

Someone grabbed the back of my jacket and pulled me through a shower of dirt. James lifted until my legs were under me again. Mira's gaze found mine. Her left eye was molten gold. Her right was a warm brown. Half her hair had returned to its natural color, and the ethereal form that had been building around her was gone. She stood, spat out a gob of mud, grabbed the front of my shirt, and planted a kiss on my lips.

"Mmmph." I flailed my hands, not sure what was happening.

Mira released me and I tumbled onto my butt. "Thank you." She looked at the zombies scattered over the hillside like toppled dominoes. "That would have been unpleasant."

James offered me a hand.

I stared at it, hearing again the snap of Bryce's neck. A vampire could survive a broken neck . . . but not the burning nova that followed. "You didn't even hesitate."

"I didn't imagine you'd mourn his loss."

I shook my head. "It's not *him* I mourn."

I let him help me up, but didn't meet his gaze.

Captain Reynolds came over, blinking and wiping his eyes as he stepped over prone bodies. "What did you do?"

"Demons don't like sunlight," I said. "So we gave them some."

The area around us looked as if a bomb had gone off. The zombies had been knocked flat in a radiating circle. But the blast hadn't reached the fringes where zombies were still fleeing, or the far side of the hill where the sounds of combat continued. There was no sign of Bryce.

"You men." Captain Reynolds pointed to his nearest troops then toward the escaping zombies. "Don't let a single creature leave the cemetery. If even one reaches the city, there's no telling how many civilians they might kill."

Ken trotted to my side, lifted his massive head, and howled. The werewolves were stumbling among their unmoving enemies—the ones nearest us whimpered and pawed at their faces. At Ken's call, every furry figure came to attention. There was a series of yips that weren't quite howls and weren't quite barks. Then the unengaged werewolves turned as one and took off after the scattered zombies.

Ken looked at Reynolds, then at me.

"I think he's saying the werewolves will help you control the perimeter," I said.

Ken snorted, then ran off.

"How did you know those things would stay dead this time?" Emma was panting, hands planted on her thighs.

I looked toward the top of the hill, where none of the figures I'd seen earlier were now standing. "Because Darius isn't here." Grabbing my fallen sword, I charged across the field of turned earth, cracked tombstones, and fallen soldiers. My friends followed.

A few zombies crawled free of the piled corpses, shielded from the blast by their companions, but they made no attempt to intercept us. They simply ran. They would fall to Reynolds's soldiers or Ken's wolves. I continued to climb.

The fires were dying down and the purple glow was gone, but the moon provided enough light for me to see.

The figures on the hill had been knocked off their feet. They were moving slowly, gingerly, like alcoholics nursing hangovers. The Purity cowboy who'd burned to a crisp on live TV was sprawled on the ground, as was the man who'd launched the car. The blond rifter woman was also there, along with a dozen people I didn't recognize. My father was not among them.

Sword raised, I approached the bodybuilder super soldier. The blond woman extended her arm, and a ripple of blue energy slammed into me like a baseball bat hitting a home run against my abdomen. I flew off my feet, slammed into the ground, and rolled over, tangling with the cold, dead limbs of the fallen corpses.

I groaned and sat up. My sword was gone, lost among the bodies when I fell. My friends landed around me like debris from an explosion.

Mira, James, Kai, and Morgan were back on their feet in an instant. Emma, David, and Reynolds struggled to rise.

Mira looked at me. "The necromancer isn't there."

"Knights and bishops," I whispered, thinking of the chess game I'd played with Sol. I gripped the sides of my head. "Ugh! How could I be so stupid? I totally misread his play."

"What're you talking about?" Emma held her side as she hobbled over. "This was clearly his target. He must've run away when he thought he was beat."

"*Clearly* is right. This was all too obvious. Everything he's done has been to draw attention. The rifters weren't just sowing chaos. They planned this public pilgrimage to D.C. specifically so people could react—the government, the PTF, the military."

"Why put us on alert?" Reynolds asked.

"Because while we're all scrambling to stop the invasion, he's slipping in the back door to assassinate the king."

Reynolds jerked as though slapped. "He's going after the president?"

I shook my head. "Not necessarily. The king could be anything."

"So how do we figure out where he went?" Emma asked.

David pointed to the hilltop where the rifters were regrouping. "Even if we do, we still have this group to deal with."

Mira slapped me on the back, hard. "Take your friends and find the necromancer. I'll handle the middle management on the hill."

"You can't fight them all by yourself."

"Excuse me?" She cocked a hip and crossed her arms. "Which one of us is the expert here?"

"But—"

"Without the necromancer, those rifters are just rifters. And I've got energy to burn after that zombie buffet." She smiled, and both eyes shone gold like twin suns in the night, though the right was slightly darker. "Trust me. This is what I do."

Mira inhaled. The marbled aura I'd noticed earlier swelled, encasing her body, growing more solid. When her molten gaze centered on me, I got the feeling Mira wasn't in the driver's seat anymore. "Remember, the demon inside your father will be hiding, the same way I withdrew when you told me to take cover. To defeat him, you'll need to draw the demon out. Make him use his magic."

She jumped, and her leap took her all the way to the top of the hill. She landed with a sound like thunder and a shimmering teal arc that knocked the rifters down once more.

I stared at Mira . . . or the demon possessing Mira's body . . . then refocused on my closer companions. "This was the distraction, the obvious threat. So where's the king? What's Darius's ultimate goal?"

I ran through possible targets—various monuments, the White House, the Senate, the Pentagon and the Department of Defense, the naval shipyard, headquarters for pretty much all the major intelligence agencies—I stiffened. "What was the result of the very first move the rifters made?"

James frowned. "By killing the leaders of the Church and escaping Rome, they caused an emergency gathering of all the PTF regional heads."

I nodded. "And they gathered *here*."

Emma gasped. "They're going to eliminate the leaders of the PTF."

I frowned. "Kill the directors and their underlings just step up to fill those positions."

A blast of teal light flashed on the hillside. Chunks of dirt rained down on us. I shielded my head, staring at the corpses around my feet. Then it struck me—the way the Purity soldiers stood up with dazed expressions at the end of the battle in Wilmington and walked off the field with their enemies.

"He's not going to kill them," I said. "He's going to control them—turn them into puppets with demons pulling their strings. And with everyone's attention focused here, who would even notice?"

"So he's heading for PTF headquarters," Emma said. "And he has a head start."

David shook his head. "The directors wouldn't still be at the office."

"Most are staying in a nearby hotel," Reynolds said. "The Marriott at Fairview Park. I'll call it in to get some troops over there." He stepped away and pulled a radio like David's from his belt.

"Are you sure about this?" Kai asked. "If you're wrong about Darius's 'king,' you risk taking us out of reach if he strikes somewhere else. It might be safer to wait until he's actually spotted."

"Playing it safe will only get us so far. As long as we're reacting, he's got control of the board." I set my hand on Kai's shoulder. "Sometimes it's the risky move that wins the game."

But is this a game you really want to win? James's thought rolled over me on a tidal wave of conflicted emotions. "Your father is . . . extreme, but he's working toward the same goal you are—fair treatment for paranaturals—and he's close to getting it. After that fiasco in the boardroom . . ." He shrugged. "If we stay, and let events elsewhere play out as they will, we could have the full support of a very different PTF within the hour. But if we take the high road here, and save those fools, it could mean years of struggle before paranaturals can claim even basic human rights."

I stared at him. "I know you're going through some . . . personal changes right now, but we don't let people get their brains melted just because they don't like us."

He pinned me with his blue gaze. *If you fight your father . . . there's no version of that scenario that ends well for you.*

I bunched my fingers to keep my hands from shaking. Now that I wasn't in a mad frenzy to stay afloat in a sea of zombies, the chill of the night was seeping in again. Though the cold I felt was spreading more from inside than out. I looked at David, Morgan, Kai, and finally Emma.

"You're the most purely para-person here. What do you think?"

She shifted her feet, glanced at the hill, then at me. Her eyes were wide and her gaze skittered among the group. "I think . . . if we don't at least try to help the PTF leadership now, we'll be proving we're as bad as Purity and those others think we are."

I nodded. "I promised to do everything in my power to stop the sorcerers, even if the PTF directors voted against us . . . which they did." I set my hand over the small, hard lump of the locket under my shirt, took a deep breath, and exhaled slowly. "We head for the Marriott."

Chapter 31

THE MARRIOTT AT Fairview Park looked like a modern castle, its facade lit by the warm glow of spotlights. Rounded towers with stepped balconies rose on either side of the main entrance, where a surprising number of guests climbed in and out of taxis despite the late hour.

We stepped out of the shadows of a stand of trees, crossed to a little island where three flagpoles rose out of brown grass, and scanned the people milling beneath the covered entrance. An elderly woman in a fur-lined coat stepped out of a blue car. A gentleman in a suit held the door for her. A young man stood near an empty planter at the edge of the lit area, smoking a cigarette. A pair of women in their thirties walked out of the hotel, hand in hand. They were laughing.

My heart sank further with each innocent face. Had I chosen wrong? Or had the shadow roads gotten us there first?

"Let's check inside." I wove past the bystanders and pulled open the large glass door to the main lobby. Golden chandeliers hung above empty chairs and sofas in the middle of the room. A large, dark-wood counter marked the check-in area, where a middle-aged man argued with a harried-looking clerk. A woman with tousled hair and a vacant expression was pulled toward the elevators by a small boy who seemed to have all his mother's missing energy. Standing near the bank of elevators was a man with his back to us. His hair was dark but graying. His hands were in the pockets of the long, black jacket he wore. I glanced down. His boots were muddy.

It could *be him.*

"Dad," I shouted.

The man didn't move. The mother continued to be dragged along by her son. The clerk glanced in my direction, perhaps searching for some reprieve from the verbal abuse of his customer.

James stepped up beside me. "Darius!"

The man by the elevator flinched, then turned. His gray-blue eyes found James first, but settled on me.

As soon as I was certain, I raised my gun.

Aim. Exhale. Fire.

The shot exploded from the barrel. All the mortal bystanders flinched, clapping hands to ears.

There was a flash of light as the bullet burst apart inches in front of Darius's chest.

He glanced down. "So . . . no more hesitation."

"I won't let you harm the directors."

He sighed. "Let me finish what I've started. Then you and I can live together in a world where people don't have to hide who they truly are."

"I don't know who *you* truly are, but I'm a person who doesn't sacrifice innocent lives for personal gain."

A ribbon of guilt drifted through my connection to James.

Sirens wailed in the distance, growing closer. "We've already told the police your plan. Even if you get to the directors, they'll be useless as puppets. You've lost. Turn yourself in."

"I see you've inherited my stubbornness." His lips turned up, but the smile didn't spread. "So be it."

The smile, such as it was, vanished. The blue drained from his eyes, leaving them hard and cold as iron. He raised both hands. Black tendrils sprang from the floor and wrapped my and Emma's ankles, but the less human among us were faster. Kai's sword flashed. Morgan and James jumped aside.

The space to the left of the sitting area shimmered like a desert heat wave, and six people I recognized from the footage at Wilmington appeared as though a stage curtain had dropped. The nearest rifter—the Middle Eastern man whose face had been ruined—made a sweeping gesture. Kai grunted and flew through the air, slamming into the wall beside the wide-eyed clerk. He fell behind the check-in counter with a crash and a shower of drywall.

The small woman with the dark hair who'd taken on the berserker during that earlier battle planted her feet, raised her fists, and launched herself at James. Red and gold carpet shredded under her feet and a divot lined with crushed marble appeared in the floor as she flew across the open space like a human bullet. She slammed into James's chest and took him crashing through the glass doors of the main entrance.

All that happened in the time it took me to inhale. Then Kai staggered to his feet behind the desk and pulled the fire alarm on the wall.

A piercing shrill filled the hotel.

Holstering my useless gun, I pulled energy in through my left hand as Mira had shown me and sent a stream of fire into the vines holding me in place. Not killing me with his first shot had been a mistake. Darius thought he could sideline me, that I wasn't strong enough to do what had to be done. . . . But I *was* my father's daughter—a powerful practitioner determined to fight for what I believed was right.

The vines sizzled and snapped, filling the air with an acrid scent that stung my sinuses and made my eyes water.

Feet pounded overhead as people rushed about. Voices rose in the hallways. The wide-eyed clerk, the man he'd been arguing with, and the woman cradling her now wailing son all raced for the exit. I pictured the crumpled building in Wilmington. So long as the rifters were present, everyone in the hotel was in danger.

The man who'd launched Kai was running toward the check-in desk, a second man close behind, but Kai had already vaulted the counter, sword in hand.

The remaining three rifters came at Morgan, Emma, and me.

Emma followed my example and seared the vines off her ankles.

A crash behind us announced the return of the cannonball woman. She slammed into two of the advancing men, knocking them over like bowling pins. The third—the man I'd nicknamed Dr. Strange because of his goatee—dodged to the side and darted toward Morgan, who was circling the room toward Darius.

James crunched through the broken glass of the front entrance. He used the back of his wrist to wipe a gash on his cheek. The cut sealed as fast as the blood was cleared. "Leave the small fry to us."

"There are too many lights in here," Morgan bellowed as she dodged behind a wooden pillar to avoid being impaled by a shower of foot-long needles.

"Kai," I yelled, and pointed to a bank of switches on the wall beside the check-in desk.

Kai took a step in that direction, but was slammed to the floor as a shimmering indigo dome dropped over him courtesy of a fair-skinned man with short, bleach-blond hair. Kai's first attacker raised his hands. Two shining scimitars appeared in his grip.

I focused my energy into a solid ball and shot it at the blond. My magic projectile hit him square in the back, sending him sprawling. The indigo dome vanished. Kai rolled to the side. The twin scimitars gouged deep into the marble floor.

Kai sprang up and smacked the switches, plunging the lobby into twilight illuminated only by the exit signs and the strobing flash of the fire alarm.

Darius had used our distraction and was nearly to the stairwell.

Picturing the chains and vines he'd used to trap me, I summoned bands of violet light that snapped out of a pillar and wrapped around his arm. He jerked to a stop, met my gaze, and snapped the restraint like crepe paper.

He shook his head. "You don't want to do this."

"You're right." I spread my stance and raised my hands as though getting ready to spar. "But I've made up my mind."

He sighed, then squared off against me. The others battled in my periphery. Kai engaged the swordsman near the check-in counter. A brown-haired man exchanged blows with James at insane speeds. Morgan flitted through the room like a possessed shadow, landing hits and vanishing before the rifters could retaliate. Emma, now free from her imprisoning vines, stepped up beside me with a nod.

"I got your back." She set her hand on my left shoulder, gripping tight. "Take what you need."

With a grim smile, I started siphoning energy. Emma's presence meant I could draw more power faster. Hopefully it would be enough to stop my father.

"You've got a paladin," Darius said. "How quaint." He spread his arms wide. Tendrils of smoky blue energy swirled around him. "I no longer need such a crutch."

He extended his arms, and the blue smoke became a wall that sped toward me. Furniture splintered. Lamps burst.

I crossed my forearms and funneled all the energy Emma and I were channeling into a shield. Violet light erupted around me, scattering my father's attack like a wave against a rocky shore. I grunted under the impact. Emma's grip tightened. The chandelier above us shattered, raining glass and crystal.

I pulled more energy. A dark haze seeped in around the edges of the room. Taking a deep breath, I pictured lances with needle tips and focused my magic into shape. Then I sent the projectiles flying.

Darius diverted the lances into the wall behind him. They quivered for a moment, then dissipated into purple smoke.

Fire erupted to my left, throwing me off balance.

Darius sent another wave of crackling energy racing toward me. I barely got my hands up before it hit. I stumbled back, but Emma braced me and we managed to keep our feet.

The magic didn't splinter apart this time, but continued to press against me. I planted my feet and leaned into the attack, drawing more power to bolster my shield.

The man who'd been throwing needles at Morgan sailed through the center of the room, slammed into a pillar, and slumped to the floor. His chest appeared to be crushed—bone shards stuck through his blood-soaked shirt. A burst of triumph rippled through my connection to James.

I pushed harder against my shield, shoving the blue light back toward its source.

Across the room, Darius frowned. Wisps of dark purple rose off his skin like steam, and for an instant the shadow of another face fell over his features. "Stop making this harder than it has to be. I don't want to hurt you."

Draw the demon out. Make him use his magic.

I took a deep breath and concentrated my focus, pushing my magic back toward my father.

The door to the stairwell opened. Frazzled-looking people in pajamas and bathrobes filed out in response to the fire alarm, but they stumbled to a stop at the scene in the lobby, bottlenecking the door.

"Keep moving!" James appeared beside the front-row gawkers and shoved them toward the gaping holes that used to be the front doors.

The rifter with the light-brown hair drove his shoulder into James's back. I cringed as echoed pain and surprise slammed through me. The clash of blue and purple light slipped a little closer to my side of the room. Breathing hard, I pulled more energy, pressing back. Emma whimpered.

Morgan launched from the flickering shadow of a burning pillar and tackled James's assailant around the waist. The two fell into a patch of inky black behind a sofa. A second later, Morgan tumbled out of the shadowed elevator alcove . . . alone.

The guests from the stairwell dashed for the visible exit, screaming and shielding their heads as chunks of plaster fell from the ceiling, and my friends and the rifters clashed on either side.

I recognized a few people from the PTF boardroom. The thin man with the impressive mustache who'd seconded hearing me out stumbled on a piece of debris and took a header. The prim woman from England clutched her bathrobe as she ran, curlers bouncing in her hair.

When Harris stepped into the chaos of the lobby, she stopped moving. She didn't seem frozen in fear, as the first people had been. She was scanning the room, taking it all in, assessing like I imagined Sol would in the same situation.

The chairman from the meeting bumped into her back and fell to his butt. The stream of people flowed around them. No one offered to help him up.

Harris was dressed in her clothes from earlier. She reached under the jacket of her suit, pulled a gun from her holster, and leveled it at Darius.

Nine shots split the night. People dove for cover, raking themselves across splintered wood and shattered glass.

The bullets puffed out of existence in clouds of blue smoke before connecting.

Darius looked in her direction.

My purple light slid closer to him.

The shadow features overlying Darius's face grew more distinct. He reached a hand toward Harris. Chains of light sprang from the wall. They coiled around Harris, the chairman, and the director with the walrus mustache, locking them together like a bundle of sticks. Then he closed his hand.

Harris's gun clattered to the floor. Mustache-man screamed. The chairman's eyes bulged and his cheeks turned purple. Even holding my attack at bay, Darius had enough power to kill these people.

"Get ready to jump," I whispered over my shoulder. Gritting my teeth, I planted my feet. My heart was racing. Sweat dripped into my eyes. "One, two . . . three."

I waited until I felt Emma move. Then I kicked off as hard as I could, diving to the side. My magic unraveled as soon as I stopped funneling energy into it. A shock wave tore through the space I'd been. Something that felt like a bowling ball slammed into my ankle and spun me. I hit the floor and rolled to my knees in the smoldering remains of a burnt chair. Hot ash stung my palms.

Darius's magic blasted a hole the size of a pickup truck in the wall behind me. Through it, I could see the first emergency vehicles racing up the road.

Darius's attention swung away from his prisoners when his magic made contact, but I was already casting. The wave I created was sloppy, and not nearly as strong without Emma's support . . . but it was unexpected.

A shimmer of blue light sprang from Darius's fingertips as my magic slammed into him from the side. The force of the impact blew him off his feet and through the drywall Kai had already dented. There was a *clatter* and a *splash*.

Harris and the others dropped to the floor. The chains binding them vanished.

I'd hit Darius hard—as hard as I could—but it wouldn't take him long to recover. I climbed to my feet, gasping when I put weight on the ankle I hadn't moved fast enough to save.

I met the chairman's wide-eyed gaze and pointed to the missing wall and the emergency units beyond. "Run! Now!" I didn't wait to see if he listened.

Cringing with every other step, I limped as fast as I could toward the hole I'd blown my father through.

Chaos swirled around me as I shuffled forward. Kai was dodging indigo orbs near the elevator. The scimitar-wielding man was on the ground . . . in several pieces. Morgan and the flame-wielding rifter were playing a game of whack-a-fae as she darted in and out of shadows and he launched fireballs that ignited carpet, paintings, and the remaining furniture. James had his hands full dodging electrical blasts as he closed in on the woman with glowing fists. The man whose torso had been smashed was getting up, braced against the pillar he'd collided with. The humans inside were scattering and screaming while those outside shouted for hoses and medics and generally tried to make sense of the situation.

Emma lay on her stomach in front of the check-in counter. She was propped on her elbows, breathing heavily. Blood trickled from a gash on her forehead.

I dropped to one knee beside her. "Are you okay?"

She rolled her eyes. "You really want me to answer that?"

"Are you okay enough to keep fighting," I amended.

She nodded and pushed up to her knees. I reached out a hand to steady her.

"Let's get the bastard," she said.

Together, we clambered over the front desk. Drywall dust sifted down from the hole, filling the air and making me cough. Mixed with the dust and smoke was a scent of . . . chlorine.

I scraped my back and caught my foot climbing through the hole. The room on the far side had a vaulted ceiling and glass walls that looked out on a garden area and second pool. Deck chairs were scattered and tipped where Darius must have plowed through them. On the far side of the pool, dripping and gasping, was my father. The dark shadow that had peeked out earlier now encased him, much as Mira's demon energy had encased her. Swirls of blue light coiled in a lazy whirlpool, gathering near his feet.

"Look out!" I tackled Emma as she emerged from the hole in the wall.

Blue light arced over my head. More of the wall burst apart, showering us with debris.

I rose and pulled Emma to her feet. "Give me everything you've got."

She nodded.

I faced Darius across the pool. Emma pressed her palms to my back. Both palms. She wasn't filtering. She was drawing every ounce of energy she could from the room. I opened myself up, drawing both through her and through myself. Lines of pale blue drifted toward us. Now there were two energy sinkholes. The water in the pool surged, caught between opposing currents. Dark smoke, too solid to be from the fire in the other room, swirled above. Eyes flashed in the darkness. The demons had come to watch.

Darius threw another bolt in my direction, but I deflected the blow with my violet light and sent a shot right back. Arcs of power volleyed back and forth, cracking tile and melting plastic as they ricocheted around the room. Emma was panting. Her fingers dug into my shoulders. The demons above dropped closer, but kept clear of the blue tendrils spiraling around us.

Darius sent an arc wide—a clear miss. A second later, a vending machine flew at me from the left. I blasted the machine less than a foot from impact. A piece of sheared metal sliced through my arm. Emma yelped. She sagged and clutched my shirt, but didn't stop the energy transfer.

More of Darius's attacks became indirect. He showered me with chunks of ceiling and threw lounge chairs at me. I blasted the second-story windows, raining glass down on him. He created a tidal wave that I swept aside. I churned the ground beneath his feet as Morgan had done on the zombie hill, but he barely stumbled before smoothing it out.

I used every practitioner trick I'd seen or heard about—everything I could imagine. The air rippled with energy and filled with steam as elemental attacks collided, combined, and burst apart.

As we fought, the demon shadow overlying my father's body grew, became more distinct, until my father was nearly lost within the darkness. The demon's face was long and thin. It didn't look human, or like any animal I'd ever seen. A crest of smoky feathers sprouted between coiling horns and cascaded over its shoulders like a cloak. Deep burgundy tinted the liquid darkness of its eyes.

The demon was exposed, the bond tethering him to my father at its weakest.

Mimicking his earlier attack, I swelled the water in the pool to a tidal wave and sent it crashing over him.

He flicked a wrist and the water turned to steam, but while his attention was on the obvious threat, I pulled the Ruger from its holster, said a silent prayer, and unloaded four bullets into the shadow possessing my father.

Chapter 32

THREE HOLES APPEARED in the demon's chest, just above my father's head. Both man and demon reeled back. The last shot missed.

A high-pitched screech pierced the air. Burgundy light pulsed through the demon like blood through veins.

My father screamed and collapsed to his knees. The same ribbons of light surged through him, twisting through his body. He shook as though having a seizure. His cheeks sank in as I watched, skin pulling tight over bones as the demon took what it needed.

Light filled the demon's wounds, then dimmed like cooling metal.

The demon stopped its wail. My father stopped screaming. Both looked at me with cold hatred.

Even exposed, the demon's tether to my father was too strong. I couldn't kill one while the other survived.

I lowered the gun until my father's face was in the sights, just as it had been in the warehouse. Then I exhaled and emptied the magazine.

The bullets burst against a blue barrier like Fourth of July fireworks.

"So." My father rose. He dusted off his knees. His sunken gaze never left mine. The gray-blue of his eyes had been replaced by cloudy darkness. "You really are my daughter."

I dropped the useless gun and braced my forearms as a bolt of blue lightning slammed into my barrier. I slid into Emma, and we were both knocked off our feet. I skidded over tiles until my back slammed into a wall. I coughed. My ribs screamed.

Emma was gasping and shaking nearby. I took her hand. "Still with me?"

"That sucked." Her face was slick with sweat. Her eyes were glassy. The cut on her forehead was still bleeding. "Any more bright ideas?"

Darius walked around the edge of the pool, coming toward us with a measured gait, wary of retaliation.

I sat with my back against the wall. My bones ached. My muscles felt like jelly. My eyes threatened to close as the oppressive weight of exhaustion pressed down on me.

Matching skills as a practitioner hadn't worked. My trump card had fizzled. I'd failed both as a diplomat and a soldier. I shook my head. "Unless he wants his portrait drawn, my particular talent set isn't—"

I blinked. I stared at Darius, picturing the way the tendrils of light had snaked through his body—the way they writhed and twisted when the demon was injured—just like the demon inside James when I tried to force it to change. Long-term possession required a delicate balance between parasite and host. If I could upset that balance . . . make the host unsuitable. . . . But I'd never tried to imbue something I wasn't touching.

Darius stopped a dozen paces away. He made a quick gesture and inky vines sprang out of the floor and wall, pinning Emma and me in place. "I promised we'd try to save you . . . but you're more troublesome than I imagined."

I remained still—not difficult, as tired as I was.

My father had reached across miles to find me in a dream—a place where the lines between energy and matter blurred—because we were connected by the rift energy we both channeled. If he could cross that kind of distance, what were a few measly feet?

I inhaled, exhaled. I was going to get the demon out of my father even if it killed him. But even working recklessly, it would take time. I needed a distraction—a big one.

I glanced at the ceiling above us, a second-story balcony that overlooked the pool.

This was a terrible idea. . . . It was also the only one I had. I just hoped Emma and I were far enough back.

"Emma?" I stared into her fevered expression and hated myself for the danger I'd put her in—was still putting her in. "One more idea."

She squeezed my fingers, then closed her eyes and let her head droop. Emma's energy flowed into me, bolstering my paltry supply. I opened myself as far as I could. Where once the air had seemed thick with magic, I now felt like a climber on Everest, gasping in the thin air.

I pictured the tiles beneath Darius's feet turning to liquid.

He stumbled and sank up to his knees.

Then I reinforced the ground, trapping him.

As he growled and reached for the floor, I took out the pillars supporting the balcony. Chunks of concrete and panes of glass broke as the ceiling twisted under its uneven weight. A treadmill and two exercise bikes fell through a hole, along with the materials that once supported them.

Forgetting the floor, Darius raised his hands, catching the avalanche on an umbrella of blue energy. His arms buckled, sinking even with his face, which was twisted with strain. He bellowed. The smoky form of the demon solidified around him, lifting the weight of the exercise room I'd dropped on his head.

This was my best . . . my *last* chance.

I continued to pull at the dwindling energy around me, then channeled it all into the rosy glow of my fae magic. My doubts and fears swelled along with the rising magic, but I didn't turn away. All the conflicting emotions of finding my father again only to lose him; of risking the people I loved to save people who'd just as soon see me dead; of being raised up as a savior only to fail at the end; of tainting everything I touched. . . . They all poured into me. My throat closed. Tears brimmed in my eyes and spilled over my cheeks.

I focused on the weight of the locket against my sternum. I imagined the inscription, the picture inside, the memories it represented. Then I found a thin red strand in my soul that echoed with those memories. I thrummed the strand, as I did when I reached out to James. There was no direct response, but there was . . . something. A distant buzz of harmony.

Holding tight to that feeling, I reached out through the energy of the rift.

A place where practitioners can walk if they're strong enough.

For one disorienting moment I was both strapped to the ground by Darius's black tendrils and floating in the air above our heads. Then I found the other end of that strand of memories—a thin red hair buried amid a tangle of black, blue, and a burgundy so dark I could barely distinguish it. As with James, the pulsing strands of the demon infested Darius's whole body, strangling the man beneath. There was no way to disentangle them, but I wasn't trying to disentangle this time. I was going after those demon vines with a machete.

Time seemed to slow as I centered my concentration on tearing loose the burgundy veins spreading poison through my father's body. I homed in on the sliver of bright red that thrummed with an echo of connection to my own soul, diving deeper into my father's core. I had to cut the demon out at the root—had to destroy enough of the tether that their symbiosis collapsed.

I was vaguely aware of more of the balcony collapsing. My father was screaming and thrashing, knocking debris away as best he could to avoid being buried alive. A chunk of cement, followed by a bench press, shattered the tiles inches from my foot.

The collapse was more widespread than I thought it would be, but I couldn't split my focus enough to protect my body.

Stiffening my resolve, I dove deeper, right to the center of my father's core. Memories flashed past as they had with James. I felt the push of being unwelcome, but he didn't have enough energy to force me out.

I walk through dank stone passages beneath the city of Rome. Places once reserved for the dead, now home to those the Church needs but is ashamed to need. The training grounds are full. The flock is ripe for culling. We've waited so long . . . been so patient. But we have enough now. We'll make them pay. We'll make them all pay.

I tore away from the memory and the dark desires filling me.

My boots squelch in black blood. The hillside is covered with bodies, all in shades of gray. Color has washed out of the world. We've been ordered to withdraw. The war is over. But we didn't win. Across the field, fae are picking themselves up and walking away.

"This is all wrong." I grip my sword and stare at the black smears on my knuckles. "We're not done."

"You cannot fight your human masters," says a voice inside my head. "Not alone."

I glance behind me. My paladin presses his hand to a woman's shoulder. Her sleeve ends in blood-soaked tatters where her arm should have been.

I turn away and whisper, "I know what you are."

"And I know what you've sacrificed. Will you let it be in vain?"

I watch the fae vanish into those godforsaken portals that let them plan this ambush, and squeeze my hilt until my fingers go numb. "A treaty is not what I agreed to."

I took a shuddering breath as the scene faded. My heart ached with betrayal.

I tumbled deeper. Scenes of conflict flashed through my mind, too many to focus on—humans and fae clashing on a large scale. Tidal waves that drowned whole cities. Fires that decimated hillsides. Earthquakes that tore down buildings. Corpses, burnt and bleeding. Soldiers calling out in pain. Loss, anger, pride. My father screamed to the sky with rage and triumph, and I screamed with him as the force of his memories washed over me.

I fall to my knees. Dust puffs off the ground where the grass has been worn away by hundreds of booted feet.

"Impossible."

"I'm afraid there can be no mistake," says a woman with a clipboard. She wears

a white lab coat and a pair of rimless glasses.

I cover my face with my hands.

Practitioner. The word festers in my mind. I feel ill, tainted. Boots pound the ground behind me as the soldiers I've trained with for the past three months continue their drills. They will fight the fae. They will save the world from magic, while I . . .

"Will you serve?" asks the woman.

I've seen the men selected before me. Some fought. Some left willingly. None ever returned to the ranks.

No matter what I decide, my life is over.

Despair swelled in my heart like a balloon about to burst.

A piercing cry fills the air, echoing off the sterile white walls of the delivery room. The doctor hands me the baby, swaddled in a blanket with pink and purple polka dots.

"Congratulations. It's a girl."

I'm paralyzed, afraid if I move I might hurt the baby in my arms. I lean in close and whisper, "Hello, Alyssandra. I'm your daddy."

I was in my own body, watching the baby I'd been. The doctor paid me no mind as he wiped his hands and walked out the door.

"Is this an illusion?" This version of my father—younger than I'd ever known him—met my gaze.

"It's a memory," I said.

He looked down at the child in his arms. "This was the happiest moment of my life."

I stepped closer to get another look at my baby self. "My face is all splotchy."

"You were perfect."

I looked away. My mother was asleep in the hospital bed, sweat-slicked hair plastered to her forehead. Her skin was a sickly yellow, but her face showed none of the weary tension I'd always known to be there. "How did we all change so much?"

"We made choices," he said. The baby began to fuss and he bounced it slightly in his arms until it settled down. "We're still making choices."

He sighed and set the baby in a bassinet beside my mother's bed. "I started all this because I wanted to make the world a better place for you. I wanted to ensure a future where you would be safe."

I hugged myself. "I don't feel very safe right now."

He nodded. "It seems my choices led us down a difficult road."

"You could make it up to me," I said. "Help me stop this madness."

"I would if I could, but I can't break my connection with the demon at this point . . . no matter how much I may want to."

"I can." I took a step toward him. "I can change you—take away the part of you that makes you a practitioner."

He frowned. "I've been a practitioner for a long time now, studied all the old texts in the Church's archive, and I've never heard of magic like that."

"It's fae magic."

He pursed his lips. "If you . . . erase the practitioner part of me while I'm channeling magic . . ."

"You'll have a burnout."

He nodded slowly, his gaze unfocused. "You'll still have the demon to deal with." He looked at me. "Necromancers are very hard to kill."

"Will the backlash affect him?"

"It should." He pressed a fist to his mouth and stared at the baby in the bassinet. "Those bullets you shot me with, do you have more?"

"No . . . but I might be able to make one."

"Hit him with that when my magic snaps. He won't be able to draw the energy he needs from me, and the shot should be enough to send him packing before he can reestablish a connection."

I took a deep breath. "If I go through with this . . . you'll probably die."

He smiled down at the baby and stroked a finger over its . . . my . . . splotchy cheek. Then he looked up with tears in his eyes. "No more hesitation."

I nodded.

The memory dissolved around me. I was at the very center of my father's core. The place where everything that made him *him* was anchored. There was the red thread of his connection to me, the burgundy poison of the demon, and the brilliant, electric blue of his practitioner ability.

I wrapped my will around that blue thread . . . and burned it away.

A high-pitched wail filled the air, but this was no baby's cry.

My consciousness snapped back to my physical senses. My father was screaming and writhing. Blue light coated his body like flames. The black vines holding me in place fell to ash.

Emma lifted her head beside me. Her fingers were still linked with mine, feeding me a trickle of power.

Feeling like my arm was moving through molasses, I reached up with my free hand and snapped the chain around my neck. I stared at the engraved "A" on my locket.

The demon shadow thrashed wildly, but it was out of sync with my father's movements. The exercise equipment and remaining ceiling he'd been holding in place began to fall.

"Where energy and matter blend." I pushed a tiny thread of magic into the locket, balanced on the edge between thought and form.

My father's body fell backward, bent at the knees where he was still trapped in the floor.

"You gave me the world," I said. "I'll take it from here."

With a final burst of energy, I propelled the locket like a shot from my Ruger.

The tiny heart sailed through the rain of concrete, glass, and metal, and found its target in the demon's chest.

Burgundy light radiated from the impact like fissures in dry earth. The demon arched. It didn't howl this time. It didn't flail. It vanished in a puff of dark smoke.

"That was anticlimactic," I muttered. But my lips didn't move and the sound came out as a burble lost in the roar of an avalanche. I closed my eyes.

"Alex?"

Somewhere in the depths of my mind, Emma's panic registered, but there was nothing I could do about it. I'd finished my job. It was time to rest.

The crash of falling debris grew muffled.

Emma grunted.

It was getting difficult to breathe.

Then a strong arm wrapped around my waist, and I fell into cold, black nothing.

A WHISPER DRIFTED through my mind. A word. No, a name. A name no one was supposed to know.

I jerked awake. My forehead collided with something solid and I fell back.

"Damn it!"

I opened my eyes again and found Kai kneeling in front of me, rubbing his brow. Morgan was sitting in the shadow of a police car. I rolled my gaze up. My head was supported on James's lap. He smiled down at me.

"How long was I—"

"Not long," he cut in. "Malakai donated enough energy to revive you."

The white noise around me resolved into voices, some quiet, others shouting. There was the rumble of idling engines and a stampede of feet that shook the frozen ground beneath me.

I sat up more slowly and took in the chaos. People were running every which way. Men and women wearing everything from pajamas to evening gowns huddled under blankets on ambulance bumpers. Stretchers were wheeled to and fro. Some were empty. Some held sealed black bags.

I followed the flow of traffic with my eyes and found the hotel on the far side of a blackened garden full of bleached trees. The dead area was marked by a clear line centered around the collapsed remains of the hotel's pool. I covered my mouth with both hands.

We'd created a new waste.

I glanced at James. "My father?"

He shook his head. Guilt bubbled through our connection. "The building was collapsing. There wasn't time to get him out."

I nodded and looked away.

"The rescue crews haven't searched that section yet," he added. "Too unstable."

"What about Emma?"

"Injured and unconscious, but alive. She was taken to a nearby hospital."

"Ms. Blackwood."

I twisted to find the chairman of the PTF board meeting walking toward me. Several other directors flanked him.

I climbed to my feet, braced on either side by James and Kai.

The chairman stopped well out of arm's reach. He glanced at my companions, then met and held my gaze. His Adam's apple bobbed. "It seems I owe you an apology," he said at last. "I assumed your promise of help was a tactical ploy to sway the vote in your favor. But"—he gestured to the disaster behind me—"here we are."

"Are they still fighting at Arlington?" I asked.

Harris stepped even with the chairman and shook her head. "The National Guard, assisted by your werewolf and practitioner friends, managed to dispatch the remaining undead." She shot a sideways glance at the chairman. "We don't know how many rifters escaped in the chaos."

I wanted to ask about Mira, but held my tongue. Hopefully she'd killed the rifters on the hill and gotten clear before the PTF cavalry arrived to see her in full demon mode.

"And my friends?"

"The werewolves fled when the PTF arrived. Luke Miller set up a triage station at Arlington. The non-healer practitioners are . . . holding position." Again she glanced at the chairman, then back to me. "I gather they're waiting on word from you."

I focused on the chairman. "What's that word going to be?"

He cleared his throat and half-turned, as though checking to make sure the other directors were still behind him. "Under the circumstances, we believe another discussion about the possibility of future cooperation with paranatural beings is in order." He straightened and clasped his hands like a soldier at parade rest. "As such, a meeting will be convened first thing tomorrow morning. In the meantime, we ask that you and your friends be our guests in a hotel that we've rented for that purpose."

I raised an eyebrow. "Guests under guard?"

Kai's grip tightened on my arm. Anticipation flowed from James. Both were prepared to fight for my freedom. I had only to ask.

The chairman met my gaze. "Your actions were courageous, but still illegal. I realize we don't have the means to force you to comply . . . but your cooperation in this matter would be an excellent step toward the partnership you spoke of earlier."

"And the PTF gets to save face by pretending they have everything under control," James said.

I squeezed his forearm. The last thing we needed at this moment was another outburst. "I think we could all use some rest." I nodded to the chairman. "We'll take your offered hotel."

Chapter 33

LIGHTS BUZZED overhead—a nearly imperceptible whine just loud enough to be annoying. I shifted, trying to get the feeling back in my butt. The hard plastic chair I'd been sitting in for three hours had all the give of a rock. Lined up along the wall to my right were James, Kai, and Sol. David, Marc, and Garrett were on my left. They all sat ramrod straight with blank expressions.

The rest of our allies were under guard at the hotel the PTF had provided. All except Emma, who Harris told me was still in the hospital. Luke had been allowed to visit, and he'd done what he could, but she hadn't woken up. Hopefully, when she did, it wouldn't be to handcuffs and a prison cell.

I slouched lower and turned a hunk of scorched silver over in my hands. The locket Harris returned to me was fused, my father's image sealed inside. The "A" was gone.

I chewed my lower lip. My father had a pulse when he was pulled from the hotel wreckage. That's all Harris would tell me.

I tapped a slow rhythm on the tan tiles with my boots. Heel-heel-toe-toe, heel-heel-toe—The boardroom door opened.

I slammed my soles flat and straightened to match the posture of the others.

Harris stepped into the hall. "We're ready for you."

Mouth dry, I walked into the room. The directors were arranged as they had been before, with the chairman in the middle and the others seated in a horseshoe shape. The window James and I had smashed through was boarded over, but a cold breeze snuck in around the edges. The cameras around the room each bore a red light that showed they were recording, but I had no idea if we were live.

Every eye focused on me when I entered the room. My companions spread out behind me. When we were all inside, Harris closed the door and returned to her seat behind the *Western United States* name card.

As soon as Harris sat down, the chairman stood up. "Alex Blackwood, you came to us yesterday with a proposal for cooperation between the

PTF and the paranatural beings who live in our world, both known and unknown. We chose not to accept that proposal. However, we have convened today to reassess our position on that vote." He cleared his throat and glanced around the room.

I followed his gaze. Some of the directors were smiling at me. Others looked like they wanted to throw up. More than a few were sporting bandages.

"After careful deliberation, and exhaustive arguments from both sides, the majority of this council has voted to adopt a trial alliance with the paranatural community."

The words hit me like an ocean wave, stealing my breath.

"You, Alex Blackwood, will work in conjunction with Director Harris to oversee a combined PTF organization based in Colorado. This council will reconvene in one year to assess the success of that trial, at which point we will discuss the possibility of widespread adoption." He clasped his hands behind his back. "Any paranatural who fought against the rifters at Arlington or in the conflict at the Marriott last night will be pardoned of any criminal activity resultant from that situation. However, only Colorado will adopt an open policy to paranaturals at this time. Any unregistered paranatural of *any* species apprehended outside that location will be treated in accordance with our current laws. Do you accept these terms?"

Prove we could play nice for a year and they'd *think* about letting us stay. Meanwhile, paranaturals in the rest of the world would be on their own. Hiding. Hunted. And from the expressions around the council room, there were more than a few directors hoping we'd fail.

You expected them all to accept you just because you saved their lives?

I glanced at James. *A little near-death gratitude would be nice.*

He laced his fingers with mine. A fierce pride swelled through me. *Changing even some of the minds in this room was a feat worthy of legend. Take the victory that's offered. With it, you'll have time to convince the rest of them, including the paranaturals you've yet to recruit.*

I squeezed his hand. *And help to do it.*

I looked along the line of my companions. Marc and Garrett nodded their consent, as did Sol and David. Kai only smiled and shrugged, reminding me that the fae would still be an issue no matter what deal was struck here.

"Very well, Mr. Chairman. On behalf of the soon-to-be-official paranatural coalition, I accept your terms."

He nodded. "There are some logistics to work out, but for the time being . . ." He looked at Harris.

She walked around the table and offered her hand. "I look forward to working with you."

I gripped her palm. "Likewise."

After repeating the greeting with each person present, Harris led us back into the hallway, downstairs, and out the front door. When I stepped onto the sidewalk, I stopped and looked back. There was no alarm. No guards shooting at me.

"What's the matter?" Harris asked.

I shook my head and smiled. "Nothing at all."

I took a deep breath of cold, crisp air and stretched my fingertips to the sky. "One crisis averted. Now on to the first official mission of this new and improved Paranatural Task Force." I met Harris's gaze. "Stop the fae invasion."

"Do you know where they're going to strike?"

"Hopefully nowhere, if I can get to Bael first. Does anyone know what happened to Morgan?"

"Haven't seen her since she—" Kai flicked his fingers in a "poof" gesture.

Morgan had faded into the shadows as soon as I surrendered to the PTF. She offered only a grim smile and a little wave. I guess sitting in a guarded hotel room wasn't her idea of fun.

"Then we'll have to travel the old-fashioned way." I looked at Harris. "How fast can you get us to Colorado?"

"We can be there this evening."

"Good. We'll need to be on ground where our new alliance has authority to operate. Kai, can you get in touch with Bael using that glass marble Hortense has?"

"Not across realms."

"Then you'll need to go to Enchantment. Convince Bael to meet me at the entrance of the Colorado reservation just after sunset tonight. Preferably *without* an army."

"I'll do my best." He turned to Harris. "Can you arrange a ride to the Appalachian reservation?"

She nodded.

"James." He was at my elbow when I turned. "It's time to call in my favor from Victoria."

He brushed a finger over the back of my hand. *Are you sure you want to, considering what you promised in return?*

We need to show all the strength we can to have any chance at getting Bael to back down. I'll face the consequences after.

What shall I tell her about Bryce?

I pulled my hand out of reach, suddenly uncomfortable. "He was killed during the battle at Arlington."

He drew back from the intimacy of our connection. "As you wish."

Shifting my weight, I looked around at my friends—my chess pieces. I was getting better at seeing the whole board. Maybe I could win this game after all. "We've got a chance at real peace here. Let's make sure it lasts more than a day."

I STOMPED MY boots to keep feeling in my toes as the sun slipped behind the hills to the west. The cold dry air of Colorado stung my cheeks and the tips of my ears. I stuffed my gloved hands deep in my pockets. The lights of Crestone winked on, one by one, in the valley below as the purple and orange streaks of sunset fell behind the horizon. Headlights flashed on the single road that led from the human town to the gates of the fae reservation.

"Sol should be here." David rubbed his hand over the security emblem on the sleeve of his fresh-pressed PTF uniform. "Or Harris."

"Neither of them know about vampires." I patted him on the shoulder. "And Sol trusts you or he wouldn't have recommended you for chief of security."

"You really think you can convince the fae to back down?"

"I hope so."

"There's still time to call reinforcements from Crestone. If the threat is this one fae lord, an ambush might be our best bet."

I shook my head. "An ambush would just guarantee my negotiations fail."

He pursed his lips and went back to studying the sky.

Marc stood between two big wolves, one white, one gray with a brown undercoat. The darker wolf was police officer Sarah Nazari. I didn't recognize the white wolf. There were a lot of members of Marc's pack I'd never met.

Luke paced at one edge of the gravel clearing. He hadn't been thrilled to get selected for the dubious honor of representing practitioners in this show of force—pointing out that Garrett was the official liaison—but I needed someone with actual magic to face Bael, and Emma was still out for the count.

James sat on a rock to one side of the iron gates, tracking Luke's progress.

Does his pacing bother you?

James jerked. His gaze shot to me. *His heart rate is . . . distracting.*

Headlights swept across our little group. A black luxury sedan with tinted windows parked beside the cars we'd arrived in. The engine cut off, but the doors remained closed.

I glanced up. The last patches of pink faded from the bellies of the clouds. "Showtime."

Two large men stepped out of the car. One had olive skin; the other's was milky white. Both wore suits fit for a funeral. The driver opened the back door, and Victoria emerged. Her pale skin seemed to glow, contrasting her dark hair and an indigo evening gown that fell just short of dragging in the mud. A stole of thick, black fur draped her shoulders. Her emerald gaze drifted over the guard station—temporarily empty at Harris's command—the open iron gates, and us.

"So this is a reservation." She strolled toward us. "I must admit, I've never seen one." She stopped in front of me. "Not as impressive as I'd imagined."

I cleared my throat. "Thank you for coming, Victoria."

"A deal's a deal." She narrowed her eyes. "Though losing Bryce was a surprise."

I continued to meet her deep, green stare.

"But *you're* alive, so perhaps he proved useful." She extended her hand, palm up. "My necklace?"

"It was destroyed when Bryce died . . . that's actually *how* he died."

She pursed her lips. "Then I shall take the one you made for James."

"The deal was five charms to be made and delivered *after* you back us up with Bael. Then an audience with the vampire council to discuss permanent inclusion in the paranatural coalition."

"Yes, I saw your little show." She frowned at James. "You walked rather a fine line there in regards to our secret. I doubt the council will be pleased."

He lifted his chin. "You know as well as I, they cannot stay in the shadows forever."

She looked back and forth between us. "I shall be patient . . . for now. But I expect to be your highest priority once this showdown is over."

She and her guards took a position as far from the werewolves as possible.

The sky faded from blue to indigo to black. The moon rose—a thin sliver that smiled at our discomfort. The temperature continued to drop as stars filled the sky.

Victoria tapped one pointy-toed pump. "You said sunset. Where is he?"

"Technically I told him *after* sunset."

She gave me a blank stare. "So he can make us wait as long as he likes."

"If he's even coming," David added.

"He'll be here," I said.

"Nice to know you have faith in me."

We all spun toward the new voice.

Bael rode out of the trees atop a gaala with silky black fur. The huge beast came to a stop just before crossing the boundary of the reservation. It stamped the ground with one of its six hooves and shook its massive antlers. Steam billowed from its nostrils.

Four smaller gaala emerged behind him, stepping out from between the pines. The first carried Rhoana, Captain of the Palace Guard. Shedraziel sat on another, her cerulean skin glowing in the starlight.

In the back were Kai and a fae I'd never met, but whose green and leather uniform marked him as a Knight of Enchantment.

Bael relaxed his gaala's reins but stayed mounted. He wore a suit of golden armor that seemed to shine like the vanished sunlight. His dark hair was braided tightly down his back, exposing pointed ears and every aspect of his teenage face.

"*This* is the Lord of Enchantment?" David whispered.

"He's older than he looks," I whispered back.

"And he has excellent hearing." Bael narrowed his gaze at David, who had the good sense to bow his head.

"He meant no disrespect," I said. "Your youthful appearance simply caught him off guard. As it did me when we first met."

He pursed his lips, then smiled. "I was surprised to get an invitation to the mortal realm." He inhaled deeply. "It's been a while since I breathed this air."

"We appreciate you agreeing to meet with us."

"I was especially surprised you didn't simply show up at my keep as you so often do. Did you perhaps doubt my word not to detain you?"

"Not at all," I said. "But some of my companions would not have been able to make the trip."

He glanced around the group. "Yes. I see you're keeping company with more than one abomination these days."

"And I see the fae are as conceited as ever," Victoria said.

I held up my hand to cut them off. "I know there are complicated histories between all the races, but we're not here to discuss the past."

"Indeed," Bael said. "I assume you've called this parley to attempt to dissuade me from attacking. Or perhaps to discuss terms of surrender?"

"The first one."

"As I predicted," Shedraziel chimed in. "She wishes only to delay our victory. If what Malakai reported is accurate, the Church-trained sorcerers are no more. We will not get a better opportunity."

"I agree," I said. This brought the fae to attention. "We're never going to get a better opportunity than this . . . to establish a sustainable peace in the mortal realm. I assume Kai also told you that the PTF has granted us one year to prove humans and paranaturals can live and work together?"

Bael nodded.

"As you can see"—I spread my arms—"we've got humans, werewolves, and vampires on board. If you attack now, you'll be facing a united front, not the easy pickings you were expecting."

The white wolf by Marc's side bared its teeth for emphasis.

"It does seem you've scraped together a defense." Bael looked at the werewolves on one side of our little group, then at the vampires on the other. "But you're hardly unified."

"Neither are the fae," I said. "If your quick, decisive strike turns into a drawn-out war, how many lords do you think will support you? And how many will make the same decision you did when I asked for help fighting the rifters? They'll sit back until you're too weak to defend your own throne, then sweep in and take it."

He glared. "You underestimate me."

I licked my lips. I was getting dangerously close to insulting his pride, but I needed him to see the big picture.

Shedraziel lifted her chin. "Enchantment boasts the strongest fae army, led by the greatest general. We need no support from the other realms."

"Really?" I quirked an eyebrow. "You believe Enchantment can stand on its own against both the mortal realm *and* the other fae?"

"Not supporting us and outright attack are two very different things," she said.

I caught Bael's gaze. "Might I have a word in private?" I indicated the forest on the fae side of the border.

"My lord—"

Bael cut Rhoana off with a gesture. "I will walk with my grand-daughter."

Marc cast me an anxious look. Victoria crossed her arms.

Bael dismounted and the two of us walked a little way into the trees. When we could no longer see either group he said, "I'm impressed with the way you've handled this situation. You have true leadership qualities."

"If you respect my ability to lead, then trust the direction I'm taking this realm. If our experiment is a success, that will open the doors for tolerance not just for local paranaturals, but for the fae too. People just need to see that it's possible."

"I've promised my troops conquest and glory. To reverse course now would be . . ." He shook his head. "A lord does not retreat."

"But he can strategize."

He turned to face me.

"A leader must always do what is best for his people and his realm. In this case, the best thing you can do is wait. Give us the same time the PTF did. Your lifespans are infinitely longer than ours. One human year would be only a small delay. Then, if our experiment fails, there will be no unified defense against your invasion. And if we succeed, you'll have more options."

He pressed his lips tight and looked into the pines surrounding us. "There is logic in your argument."

I released a shaky sigh.

"However, there's a factor you've not accounted for."

My muscles tensed. "What factor?"

"Shedraziel," he said. "Now she's free, she will not be content to wait patiently."

"You're her lord. Surely you can restrain her for a year. Put her back in her timeless prison if you can't control her in your keep."

He glared at me. "That was dangerously close to a demand."

I bowed my head. "I apologize. But surely the will of a single courtier should not sway the decision of a lord?"

"Yet here you are, trying to do just that."

"With logic and reason. I want what is best for your people as much as what is best for mine."

"Mine," he repeated. "So you've chosen your side?"

I opened and closed my mouth. Once again I'd failed to realize the importance of a single, simple word before it left my mouth. I sighed. "I have no side. I am neither fae, nor practitioner, nor mere mortal. But because I stand apart, I believe I can see more clearly."

The corner of his mouth lifted. "Well spoken. But you haven't addressed the issue of Shedraziel, and even a delay in my plans may be seen as weakness among the lords. I risk an attack either way."

Bael was balanced on the precipice. I needed to push him over . . . but logic alone wouldn't do it. I took a deep breath. "How might the other lords react when they discover you've deceived them?"

He frowned. "Deception is part of court life. It is expected."

"Even when a relic you claim to have destroyed is sitting on a shelf in your workshop?"

He narrowed his eyes.

"When you first sent Kai to me, it was to retrieve a magic artifact the rest of the fae lords believed you had destroyed—the artifact you used to decimate the dragon homeworld. As I understand it, that box would be reason enough for the other realms to unite against you. Even with the largest army, Enchantment cannot stand alone. And even if it could, you wouldn't have enough troops to *also* attack the mortal realm."

He pursed his lips. "I could kill you now, and protect my secret."

I met his gaze. "And give up your chance for an heir?"

He studied me for several long minutes. Then he grinned. "Well played."

"You'll withdraw?"

"On one condition."

I frowned.

"You will allow me to cast a geas—a binding—that will make it impossible for you to ever speak of that artifact again." His grin turned feral. "I'll not allow myself to be blackmailed twice."

"Like how you made it so Pimm couldn't talk about anything relating to you or your court before you handed her over as a prisoner?"

He nodded.

I pictured Pimm—a nasty piece of work who'd helped Shedraziel kidnap children. After Bael cast his spell, he'd asked her to say my name. She'd screamed and collapsed before the first syllable was out.

"And you promise not to cast anything else on me? No secret tracking spells or anything?"

"Just the geas to enforce your silence about the artifact, nothing more. You have my word."

I lifted my chin. "Very well. My silence in exchange for postponing your invasion for at least one Earth year."

He stepped forward, pulled off his golden gauntlet, and set his fingertips against my forehead.

A rosy ribbon of magic wound into my core, anchoring in the existing strands, connecting pieces that hadn't touched before. The spell took only a moment, but when it was done there was an intricate knot tied at the center of my soul. I reached out with my own magic to inspect it, but when I touched the new strand a jolt of pain seized my muscles and dropped me to my knees.

"To prevent you tampering," Bael said. "An imbuer is uniquely qualified to place, and remove, a geas. One of many talents I still hope to teach you some day."

Breathing hard, I climbed back to my feet. "I look forward to learning."

He motioned toward the reservation gates and our waiting companions. "Shall we?"

Everyone's attention snapped to us as Bael and I stepped out of the forest. Luke looked on the verge of fainting. The vampires and werewolves looked ready to attack. It seemed I wasn't the only one Shedraziel had a talent for unsettling. James, however, was smiling. Being able to sense my emotions meant he already knew Bael had agreed to withdraw.

I gave my team a nod as I returned to my starting spot. David exhaled noisily and closed his eyes. Victoria looked almost disappointed.

Bael swung onto his gaala. "Our business here is concluded."

"The invasion?" Shedraziel demanded.

"Postponed."

"You would back down to this . . ." She spluttered and waved her hand at me. ". . . this *child*?"

Fire flashed in Bael's eyes. Static charged the air, lifting the hairs on my arms. "I back down to *no one*, Shedraziel. Best you remember that."

"Then why?"

"My granddaughter has brought to my attention an . . . opportunity. We do not suffer from the mayfly existence of mortals. We have the benefit of time. If peace with the humans can be attained without the risk of spilling fae blood, I'm willing to let her try. Should her experiment fail . . ." He met my gaze. "My troops will be ready."

He turned his mount toward the heart of the reservation. "Come."

"My lord." Kai scrambled down from the back of his brown-furred gaala and dropped to one knee. "I request to remain. I wish to be a part of the history that unfolds here."

Bael frowned. "You are young yet, and unused to the bright allure of mortals. You've allowed yourself to be swept up in their fervor, but it will not last."

Kai glanced up, then back down. "If you will not assign me to stay, then respectfully and with all due gratitude, I ask to be released from my vow of service."

Bael stared at Kai with a stony expression. "You'll have many centuries to reflect on the choice you make here. Be sure you won't regret it."

"I would rather regret a chance taken than one missed."

Rhoana gasped.

I took a step forward, but James grabbed my wrist.

Don't interfere.

Kai pressed his forehead to the damp ground.

"So be it." Bael raised one hand. "Malakai Bartelby Kairn, I release you from my service. From this moment forth you shall no longer be a Knight of Enchantment or a member of its Court."

I shifted my focus in time to see a glowing strand at Kai's core snap like a cut ribbon. The severed tie burned to nothing. Kai tensed, then sagged. When he looked up, his glamour had dropped. His pale face was drawn and sweaty. The swirling galaxies of his eyes seemed unfocused.

Bael nodded once to Kai, then to me. "I wish you luck." He *clucked* his tongue and retreated into the forest.

The unnamed knight took up the reins of Kai's gaala and led it into the trees.

Rhoana leaned down and whispered something to Kai.

Shedraziel nudged her gaala forward until the beast's warm breath blew into my face.

James slid his grip from my wrist to my hand, anchoring me as I stood my ground. I squeezed his fingers in gratitude.

Shedraziel leaned down until her sea-green gaze met mine. "I will not be denied my conquest."

A low rumble drifted out of Marc's throat, echoed by the wolves on either side.

Kai stepped up beside me. He looked as though he was recovering from the flu, with pale skin and fevered eyes, but he stood tall and his voice was firm. "You are bound by the lord you serve."

She bared her teeth. "And you are adrift, nameless and lordless. The next time I see you, I shall make you my puppet."

Rhoana cleared her throat. Her hand rested on the hilt of her sword.

"The lord has ordered us to withdraw."

Shedraziel made a hissing sound, then yanked the reins and gave her gaala a vicious kick.

Once Shedraziel was past her, Rhoana nodded to us and turned to follow.

When the last hint of movement stilled, I sagged. "I thought she was going to kill me where I stood."

David slapped me on the back. "I can't believe you actually convinced him to back down."

"Neither can I," Victoria said, stepping closer. "What did the two of you discuss in the woods?"

Even thinking about the secret I'd used to blackmail Bael made my throat squeeze closed. I shook my head. "Privileged information, I'm afraid."

Victoria narrowed her eyes. "If you wish to maintain good will between us, I suggest you don't treat me like one of your subordinates."

"Alex doesn't have subordinates." James smiled at me. "She has friends."

"Actually," said David, "she does have subordinates now. Or she will, once she starts her new position with the Colorado PTF."

Ice filled my gut at the thought of being somebody's boss. Lots of somebodies. "That's gonna take some getting used to."

"You'll adapt," Marc said. "We all do."

"Just don't forget what you owe me," Victoria said. "I'll expect delivery within the month." One of her goons raced ahead to open the car door. The other walked behind her, guarding her back as she traversed the frozen ground in her inappropriate footwear.

I bit my lip. I'd had to play my ace to get Bael to back down, so having the vampires there had been overkill. But I'd thought seeing a united front would be enough to sway Bael—and it might have been, if not for the complication of Shedraziel.

I sighed. I really hoped Bael could keep his bloodthirsty general on her leash. The Colorado governor, being a Purist, would no doubt work to undermine our alliance, and Victoria would probably turn the vampires against us once she realized I couldn't deliver the day-walking charms I'd promised. The last thing I needed was Shedraziel's interference while I tried to hold my house of cards together.

A house I wasn't done building. Still, the foundation was coming along.

"Thanks for being here, Marc. It really meant a lot to have the werewolves represented."

He smiled. "Though, like Victoria, I get the feeling our show of solidarity wasn't the deciding factor."

"But that solidarity *will* decide the overall success or failure of this experiment."

He nodded. "Ken has already let me know that several of his pack responded to your call for recruitment. They should arrive next week."

"Will there be any problem mixing members from different packs?"

"Probably, especially once more packs become involved, but we'll figure it out."

I slapped David on the back. "Sounds like the safety and security division is going to have its hands full keeping order."

"Not if the lead recruitment officer does her job well." He shoved me back.

Again the idea of being in charge of people—hiring and firing them, pairing partners, handing out assignments—slammed into me like a cold weight. I was about to give the PTF an identity overhaul. Somehow I had to make not just wolves from different packs but people from different species play nice together.

"That's why you have advisors." James indicated the group. My advisors. My friends.

A werewolf alpha. A spy-turned-soldier. A lordless knight. A day-walking vampire. And a human who was, well . . . whatever I was. Once Emma woke up, we'd have a full circus.

My circus.

"Yeah," I said. "This is gonna go great."

To be continued . . .

About the Author

L. R. BRADEN is the bestselling author of the Magicsmith urban fantasy series. Her work has won the Eric Hoffer Book Award for Sci-Fi/Fantasy, the New Horizon Award for debut authors, and the Imadjinn Award for Best Urban Fantasy. She lives in the foothills of the Colorado Rockies with her wonderful husband, precocious daughter, and psychotic cat.

To connect online, visit lrbraden.com

L. R. Braden

CPSIA information can be obtained
at www.ICGtesting.com
Printed in the USA
BVHW031020120521
607131BV00006B/133